SILVER

Also by Chris Hammer

Fiction:
Scrublands

Non-fiction:
The River: A Journey Through the Murray-Darling Basin
The Coast: A Journey Along Australia's Eastern Shores

CHRIS HAMMER

SILVER

WILDFIRE

Copyright © 2019 Chris Hammer

The right of Chris Hammer to be identified as the Author of
the Work has been asserted by him in accordance with the
Copyright, Designs and Patents Act 1988.

First published in Great Britain in 2020 by
WILDFIRE
an imprint of HEADLINE PUBLISHING GROUP

1

Cataloguing in Publication Data is available from the British Library

Hardback ISBN 978 1 4722 5535 8
Trade paperback ISBN 978 1 4722 5534 1

Map by Aleksander J. Potočnik

Offset in 11.05/15.24 pt Granjon LT Std by Jouve (UK), Milton Keynes

Printed and bound in Great Britain by Clays Ltd, Elcograf S.p.A.

Headline's policy is to use papers that are natural, renewable and recyclable
products and made from wood grown in well-managed forests and other
controlled sources. The logging and manufacturing processes are expected
to conform to the environmental regulations of the country of origin.

HEADLINE PUBLISHING GROUP
An Hachette UK Company
Carmelite House
50 Victoria Embankment
London EC4Y 0DZ

www.headline.co.uk
www.hachette.co.uk

FOR GLENYS AND KEVIN

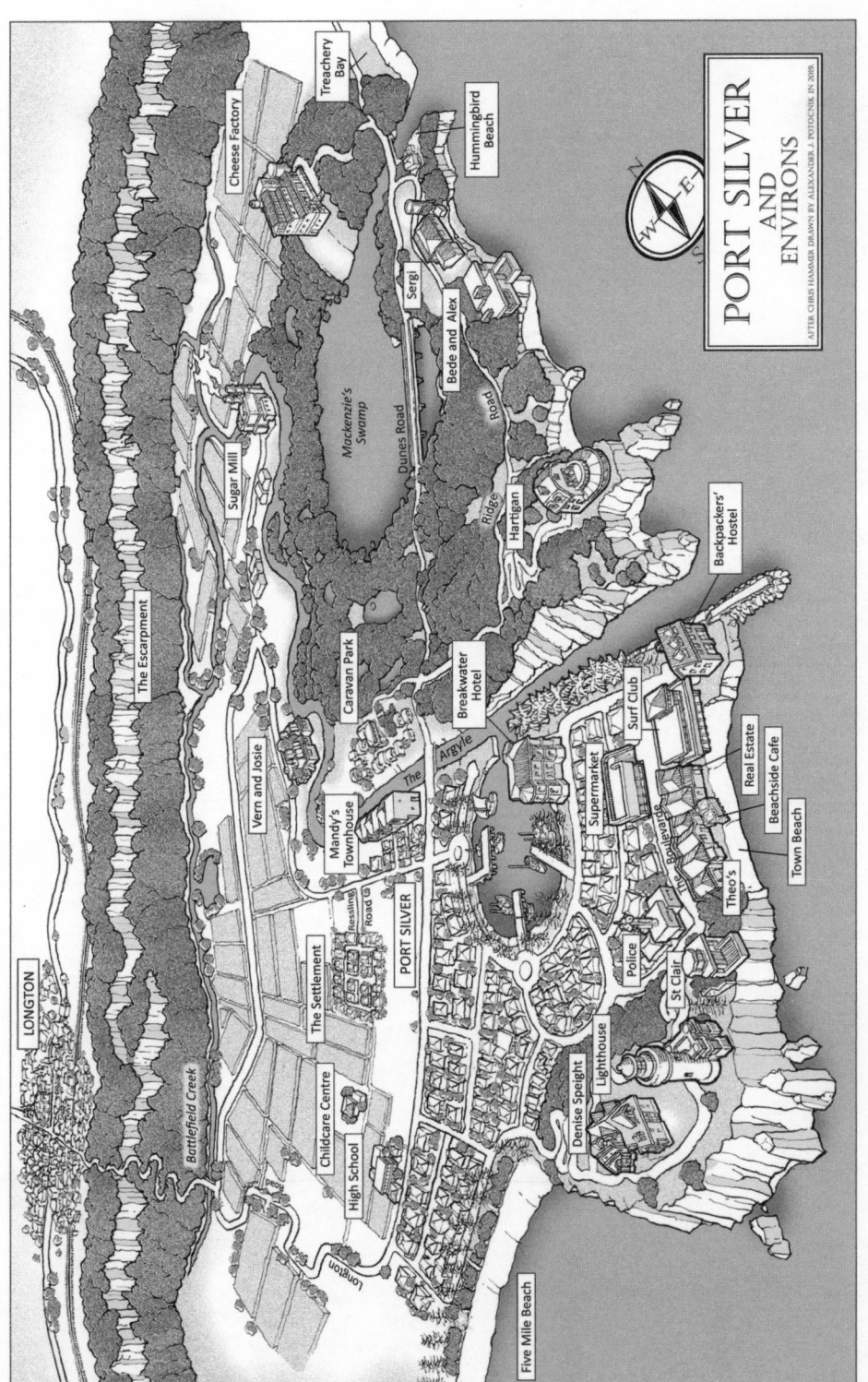

MONDAY

chapter one

THE SUN SLIDES AND GLANCES, FLARING IN HIS EYES. HE CAN'T SEE THE BALL and swings blind, hoping: hoping to connect, hoping he doesn't get out, hoping he doesn't get struck. Hoping he escapes embarrassment, just this once. So he swings, eyes closed, useless to him, as if in prayer. And somehow, by some divine whim, the bat does strike the ball. Through the wooden handle, through its perished rubber grip and unravelling string, he feels the power of the stroke, the ball collected by the very heart of the bat. He feels the spongy tennis ball flattening, compressing, then expanding, sent on its accelerating arc, launched away, as if dictated by heaven. And he feels in that moment of impact, in that instant, perfection. He opens his eyes, releasing the handle and shielding his eyes in time to see the ball, wonder at it, as it goes soaring over the wooden palings, over into the neighbour's yard. A six. Six and out. Dismissed, but in glory, not in shame. No dull thud of ball into garbage bin, no raucous leg before appeal, no taunting laughter greeting a skied catch. A six. Over the fence. A hero's death.

'Fuck me, Martin. What a shot,' says Uncle Vern.

'Language, Vern,' says his mother.

'You hit it, you get it,' says the bowler, the boy from down the street.

But Martin says nothing, does nothing, doesn't move, caught in the moment. The moment he connected. That perfect moment, caught in time.

And then.

The phone rings. 'Mumma, mumma,' calls Enid, or Amber, one or other of the twins, the inseparable, indistinguishable twins. And his mother goes, before she can compliment him on his shot, gift him the praise he deserves. To the phone, to the call that bisects the world, that draws the clearest of lines between before and after.

Thirty-three years later Martin Scarsden drives, driving into memory, driving down towards Port Silver. Part of him is concentrating, intent on the road, navigating the hairpins as he guides the car down the escarpment; part of him is lost in the past, lost in that perfect day, the day when fate flared so brightly and so briefly, the same day it dropped a curtain upon them, like the end of a play. This day the sun is filtered, flickering through the rainforest canopy, strobing. Squinting, he cannot see the ocean, but senses it, knows that should he pull over, if there were space on this narrowest of roads to stop the car, he would be able to see it: the Pacific. It's there, beyond the trees, the great blue expanse. 'Can you see the sea?' his father asks him through the years, just as he asked it each and every time they descended through these hairpin corners. 'See the sea, get home free,' he'd say with a laugh.

Martin never could see it, though; never. But a time had come when he hadn't needed to, he had come to know it was there, beyond the bottom of the escarpment, beyond the dairy farms, the cane fields and the river flats, past the fishing harbour and the holiday shacks and the long white sands. He couldn't see it, but he could feel it.

And so it is on this early autumn day, as he winds the car down through the spotted gums and the cabbage tree ferns, the palm trees and the staghorns and the cedars trailing vines, bell-birds chiming. He can feel it in the air, moist and cool becoming moist and warm as he descends, ears popping, towards the ocean, the tugging dryness of a drought-ravaged inland left the far side of the coastal range. And in the distance, still unseen but already imposing itself: Port Silver. The land of his youth, revisited.

'Vern! Vern!' she cries, voice infused with some unknown emotion. 'Martin! Girls!' He's climbing back over the fence, grey wood splintered and dry to the touch, ball in hand, his glorious dog-chewed trophy, when his mother bursts out through the screen door, laughing and crying at the same time, emotions sweeping her along like an incoming tide. 'We done it. Jesus Christ. We won the bastard!'

Martin looks to his uncle, but sees Vern's own incomprehension at his sister's unprecedented swearing.

'Hilary?' prompts Vern.

'The lottery, Vern. The fucking lottery! Division one!'

Martin leaps from the fence into a yard unfamiliar, ball forgotten, bat abandoned. The lottery. They've won the lottery. *The fucking lottery*. Vern hugs one or other of Martin's sisters, she hugs him back, happy and uncomprehending, then they are dancing, all five of them: his mother, the twins, himself and Uncle Vern, dancing on the Victor-mowed wicket as the boy from down the road returns scampering back down the road, wide-eyed and open-mouthed, carrying the news before him like a southerly: the Scarsdens have won division one. *The fucking lottery.*

The escarpment joins the plain, the rainforest ends and the dairy farms begin; PORT SILVER 30 KILOMETRES states the sign. Martin Scarsden returns wholly to the present. Port Silver, its ghosts sheltering from the iridescent sun, but awaiting him nevertheless. Port Silver. For pity's sake, why had Mandy chosen this town of all towns, his home town, to restart their lives? He crosses the old bridge over Battlefield Creek, the stream flowing along the base of the range, the boundary between the natural world of the escarpment and the imposed geometry of the dairy farms and cane fields. He's about to shift into a higher gear in preparation for the faster roads of the flatlands when he sees her: the hitchhiker.

Her legs flash in the subtropical sun beneath denim cut-offs. There's a tank top, a bare midriff, her thumb casually extended. A foreigner then, if she's using her thumb. Her hair is out, and so is her smile, broadening as he pulls onto the shoulder: a gravel clearing at the juncture between the hills and the plain, near the turn-off to the sugar mill. Even before he stops, he sees her companion, his hair dark and long, sitting with their packs, back from the road, out of the sun, out of sight of approaching motorists. Martin smiles; he understands the deception, takes no offence.

'Port Silver?' asks the young woman.

'Sure.' It's not as if the road goes anywhere else.

Martin uses his key to open the boot, the internal release of his old Toyota Corolla long broken. The man hefts the backpacks effortlessly, drops them into the cavity, closes the lid. Martin can see his arms, tattoos on sculpted flesh, the musculature of youth, wrapped in the smell of tobacco and insouciance. The young woman climbs in beside Martin; the man gets into the back seat, shoving Martin's meagre possessions to one side. She smells nice, some sort of herbal perfume. Her companion removes his sunglasses and offers a grateful smile. 'Thanks, man. Good of you.' He reaches over the seat, gives Martin a powerful handshake. 'Royce. Royce McAlister.'

'Topaz,' says the girl, replacing her companion's hand with her own. 'And you are?' She leaves her hand in his for a flirtatious moment.

'Martin,' he replies, grinning.

He starts the car, guides it back onto the road, childhood memories banished.

'You live in Port Silver?' asks Topaz.

'No. Not for a long time.'

'We're after work.' Her accent is American. 'Heard there's plenty up here this time of year.'

'Maybe,' says Martin. 'Holiday peak is over, kids back at school, but you might get lucky.'

'What about fruit picking?' It's Royce, leaning forward, his accent unmistakably Australian, broad and unpretentious. 'Greenhouses?'

'For sure,' says Martin. 'But it's harder work than waiting at a cafe or catering for tourists.'

'I need it for my visa,' says Topaz. 'I work for three months outside the cities, I get another year in Oz. We took the overnight train up to Longton. Word in Sydney is there's plenty of work up this way.'

'Possibly. I wouldn't know,' says Martin. Back when he was a child the greenhouses up the river were full of migrants, itinerant labourers gaining their first foothold in their new country. Nowadays foreign backpackers are supposedly the workforce of choice.

Topaz talks on, her enthusiasm infectious, recounting some of their adventures: how she met Royce in Goa, how he followed her to Bali, then Lombok, how they fell for each other and came to Australia together. Royce is chiming in, interjecting with observant quips and laughter. It's like a performance, a two-hander, with Martin the audience; he's grateful for the distraction. Royce has put his sunglasses back on. They sit askew, one arm missing, but he shows no sign of being bothered by the deformity, as if all sunglasses should be made this way. 'We just go with the flow, man,' he says, summarising the moral of their story. It's all Martin can do to keep his eyes on the road as he steals glances at the pair of them, Royce in the back seat with his square jaw, open smile and defiant sunnies, Topaz next to him in the front, seatbelt carving a valley between her breasts. She seems aware of his attention, appears to welcome it. And soon Martin is talking as well, the car propelled towards Port Silver on a road canefield straight, advising them on the best beaches and surf breaks, fishing spots and swimming holes. Then Port Silver is upon them: a new high school, a car lot, a budget motel, a clump of fast-food franchises. Squat palm trees line the road. Changed yet familiar after twenty-three years. The hitchhikers say he can drop them anywhere, but he insists on taking them to a place they've heard of near Town Beach, a backpacker hostel. Sure enough, there it is, a two-storey weatherboard, painted an eye-catching blue. SPERM COVE BACK-PACKERS says the sign, adorned with a smiling whale, one eye winking, one flipper forming a thumbs-up. He parks next to it, overlooking the beach, and helps Royce retrieve their packs. He's almost sorry to leave them.

Alone in the car once again, he doesn't start the engine straight away. He can feel the warm breeze on his face, the touch of it unchanged in two decades, warm and moist and gentle, so different from the parched gusts of the interior, or the gritty second-hand air of Sydney. Below him, on the beach, more backpackers loll in the sun, chatting in groups or playing soccer. He feels a pang of envy: he'd never gone with the flow, lived for the day, romanced a pretty girl in the islands of Indonesia. There had been no gap year, no floating through Asia, no great Australian road trip. Adolescence was something to be endured; why extend it? It was straight to uni and, before he had even finished his degree, straight into the newspaper. His travelling had been different: sweating over laptops in war zones instead of smoking reefers in Bali; interviewing self-important men in suits instead of serving eccentric locals in an English pub; sleeping with affection-starved strangers instead of falling in love. Maybe now it will be different, living here with Mandalay and her son Liam; now he has this chance to start life over. Not going with the flow, but his big chance, an opportunity to catch up with life and embrace it before it heads over the horizon and leaves him stranded for good. He decides the hitchhikers have done him a favour. He turns from the beach, starts the engine. Port Silver isn't about the past, he tells himself, it's about the future. About making a future, shaping it. And the future looks bright and welcoming. Mandy is here, waiting for him, the single mum he met and fell for out on the edge of nowhere. Surely that has its own romance, as good as Goa or Lombok.

He feels a surge of optimism and longing; for a fleeting moment, as he puts the car into gear, the world seems to be spinning back towards equilibrium. He can't wait to see her, to begin this new life.

—

There is blood everywhere. He pushes the door open and there is blood everywhere. The door is ajar, keys in the lock, so he pushes it open, a greeting forming on his lips, and there is blood everywhere. He has located the townhouse, parked the car, found the door. The door is ajar. Now there is blood. Everywhere. Splattered on the hallway wall, a scarlet handprint like a child's stencil, red drips on the cream-tiled floor as if left by a careless painter. He can smell it, its metallic odour engulfing him, penetrating his pores. And amid the blood, a body. Lifeless legs protrude from an archway off the passage, legs dressed in beige chinos, brown shoes with translucent rubber soles, the colour of dull amber. Men's shoes. The body, torso unseen, is lying face down. And blood is still flowing out, advancing, pooling on the tiles. Everywhere. The sight stops Martin in his stride, mouth still open, her name on his lips, unuttered, horror invading his mind, flooding in through his eyes. He feels confusion, then panic.

'Mandy!' he yells. 'Mandy?!'

He stops. Listens. Nothing. The pool of blood, glistening, still silently expanding. Is the person alive?

'Mandy!' he calls again, voice edged with fear. Is she in here? Is she close? Is she hurt?

He inches forward. Now he can see the full body, legs stretching from the passage, the torso in the living room, a scarlet circle between the man's shoulder blades, like a target painted on his linen shirt with a gaping bullseye, flesh parted and blood-filled. On the floor, the pooling flow is so very red against the cream tiles. Martin needs to get past it, past the body and its glistening moat. He backs up, runs, leaps the enamel pool where it has spread across the passage and reached the wall, landing beyond it at the bottom of some stairs. The man is unmoving. Martin can't see the face, but the body is thickset with dark hair, first signs of grey at the temples, well groomed, the patch of blood sticking his white linen shirt to the wound in his back.

A killer. There's a killer. Is the attacker still here? 'Mandy!' his voice flares again.

His mind starts working, thoughts emerging from beneath the panic, the adrenaline and the shock. He squats at the edge of the blood, convincing himself to become perfectly still. He watches, listens, but he can detect no sign of life. He reaches out, supporting himself with one hand on the doorjamb, below another red handprint, using the other hand to feel for a pulse in the man's neck, detecting nothing. The flesh is warm, giving; the man has only just died. There is blood on Martin's hand.

There is something in the man's left hand, held firm in his dead fingers. A postcard; it looks like a postcard, blood pooling around its edges. Martin leans close, stretched above the body, still supporting himself with one arm on the doorjamb. The card is obscured by the dead man's hand and his creeping blood, but it looks religious, a depiction of Christ or a saint, with a golden halo.

A sound. And it's now that he sees her, through the archway, sitting motionless on a couch in the living room, hands bloodied, staring at the dead man. It's as if she can't see Martin kneeling there, just the body next to him. Her hair is different, reddish brown instead of blonde, but that's not what draws his eyes. *Hands bloodied.* A trail, drops of blood spattered on the tiles, link her to the body.

'Mandy?' There is blood on her clothes as well. His voice is urgent, but there's no response. 'Mandalay!'

She looks at him, dazed. She shakes her head ever so slightly, perhaps a gesture of disbelief, perhaps a sign that he shouldn't be here.

Martin thinks of her ten-month-old son, his heart pounding out his concern. 'Mandy, where's Liam? Where is he?'

But she can only shake her head. He's not sure what the gesture signifies.

Martin pulls out his phone, half expecting there to be no signal, not in this alternative reality. But the signal is strong. Five bars. He dials triple zero, asks for the ambulance. And then for police.

He's lost Mandy's attention; she's staring at the body once more. The dead man is sprawled through the archway, but the blood has not yet extended all the way across the entrance to the lounge room. And yet Martin doesn't move, he doesn't go to her. Instead he returns to his phone, finds the number of a Melbourne law firm, Wright, Douglas and Fenning. Mandy's solicitor: Winifred Barbicombe. She's going to need Winifred more than she needs him.

chapter two

THERE IS SOMETHING REPTILIAN ABOUT THE POLICE SERGEANT, SOMETHING predatory. His eyes are hooded, his lips thin, his skin scarred by acne. There is a greyness to his complexion that doesn't belong in a beach town. He stares at Martin for a full minute, until Martin can no longer hold his gaze and looks away towards the constable standing by the video camera next to the interview room door. She looks as uncomfortable as Martin feels, shifting her weight from one leg to the other, staring resolutely at the camera's screen, as the silence endures. Only once eye contact is broken does the policeman deign to speak, his voice flat. 'Interview conducted by Sergeant Johnson Pear with Martin Michael Scarsden. Port Silver police station. Two-ten pm, the fourth of March.' Martin waits, but the policeman pauses again, his eyes unreadable. The tally light on the video camera flicks on and off every five seconds or so.

'All right, Mr Scarsden. In your own words. Please recount how you came to be at the residence of Mandalay Blonde today.'

Martin clears his throat, feeling uncomfortable, as if he stands accused of something, even as he reminds himself he is blameless. 'Last night I stayed in Glen Innes. I drove there yesterday from Sydney, up the New England Highway. I stayed in a pub called the Great Central Hotel. You can check. They'll have records. I continued this morning, arrived in Port Silver at about eleven o'clock.'

'And you went straight to the townhouse of Mandalay Blonde at fifteen Riverside Place?'

'No, not straight away.' Martin recounts picking up the two hitch-hikers, Topaz and Royce, dropping them at the backpacker hostel.

The policeman writes this information down. He has a brand-new notebook, a big one. 'Surnames?'

Martin thinks. 'Royce told me his. McAlister, I think. Not sure about the girl.'

'Never mind. We'll find them. They'll be able to corroborate your movements. Makes our job easier.' If he's pleased his eyes don't show it; they appear devoid of emotion. 'Can you say at precisely what time you dropped the couple at the hostel?'

Martin shakes his head. 'Not precisely. As I said, it was round eleven.'

The policeman looks unconvinced and Martin feels himself squirming under his gaze. The tally light on the video camera winks like a metronome. God knows how he'd be feeling if he'd actually done anything wrong.

'Mr Scarsden, we'll be accessing data from mobile phone towers that will give us a more accurate account of your movements, especially between Glen Innes and Port Silver. Is there any reason why we shouldn't gain access to that information?'

'No. Please do.'

The policeman stares for a long ten seconds and then writes again in his notebook, taking his time. He appears to be framing his next question when the door behind him bursts open and a young man pushes into the room, breathing hard. His hair is a mass of unkempt black wool, his stubble so dense it looks woven, his eyes black. He's wearing board shorts and sandals, chest hair erupting from beneath an erratically buttoned Hawaiian shirt.

Sergeant Pear doesn't turn immediately. Instead he waits a moment, sighs, and then swivels in his chair.

'Nick Poulos,' pants the man. 'I'm Nick Poulos.'

'I know who you are, son. What are you doing here?' asks Pear.

'I've been appointed as Mr Scarsden's lawyer.'

'Is that right?' The policeman swivels back to Martin. 'Can you confirm that?'

'No. But I'd certainly like a lawyer.'

Pear remains impassive. 'Interview adjourned at two-sixteen pm.' The constable turns the camera off. 'Okay, you two sort out your relationship. I'll give you five minutes and then we're back on.'

'Thanks, mate,' says Poulos with a huge grin, seemingly unaffected by the policeman's frostiness. Sergeant Pear and the constable leave, and Poulos turns to Martin, his arms wide as if he's about to hug him. 'Martin Scarsden. Can you believe it? Martin fucking Scarsden. Country's most famous journalist. My client!'

Martin blinks, silenced momentarily by the young man's eagerness. 'Are you sure you're a lawyer?' he asks, assessing the man's casual clothes, his apparent lack of years. 'Tell me you're on your day off.'

'Yeah. I was on my day off. So what? Now I'm here.'

'Who appointed you?'

'Melbourne firm. Wright, Douglas and Fenning. Rang me out of the blue. Asked me to come straight away. Top dollar.' The lawyer's eyes are wide; he's still panting, like a puppy.

Martin understands: Mandy's solicitors have appointed the solicitor, repaying Martin for alerting them of Mandy's plight. 'Why you, Nick? Why call you?'

Poulos laughs, pulling out a chair, sitting down, as if Martin has already agreed to hire him. 'Not much choice. There's one big firm here, Drake and Associates, and me. A few more up in Longton.'

'So why didn't they hire Drake?'

'They did. Drake are representing Mandalay Blonde, at least until their own people get here.'

Martin grimaces. Mandy's solicitors may be helping him out, but they're keeping his counsel discrete from her own, just in case his interests and hers don't align. Just in case they need to throw him under a bus. He looks at the lawyer, who shows no sign of settling down. 'Nick, you're not high, are you?'

'Shit no. Don't drink, don't do drugs. Can't handle that shit. Spazzes me out.'

'You do a lot of criminal law?'

'Shitloads. I'm up before the magistrate most weeks.'

'This isn't exactly one for the magistrate.'

'You're telling me. Murder. How good is that?' Poulos rubs his hands together, oblivious to the look on Martin's face. 'The Supreme Court. Shit, man, that's the big time.'

Martin is still wondering how to respond when Pear returns.

'You two sorted then?' he asks. For the first time Martin detects some emotion seeping through the officer's taciturn hostility: amusement.

'Yes,' says Martin. 'Mr Poulos is my lawyer. For now.'

'Glad to hear it. Let's get going then.'

They resume their former positions—Martin sitting across the interview table from Pear, with the constable operating the video camera—except now Nick Poulos is sitting by Martin's side. The interview recommences, Pear an image of stillness at the centre of Martin's vision, Poulos in constant motion at its periphery. It doesn't take Martin long to recount what happened: finding the door ajar, keys in the lock, the body on the floor, the blood spreading. He tells Pear of seeing Mandy, apparently in shock, how he rang the ambulance.

'Did you see anyone enter the townhouse or leave it?' asks Pear.

'No. No one.'

'And you heard nothing? No struggle, no cry for help, nothing?'

'Nothing. It must have all finished before I arrived.'

'Yet your impression is that the attack must have only just taken place?'

'Yes. The pool of blood, it was still spreading. And when I felt for a pulse, the victim's neck felt like he could have still been alive. It was warm and pliable. Just no pulse.'

Pear engages in another of his ponderous pauses before resuming. 'And the victim . . . did you recognise him?'

'No. He was face down. Who was he?'

'Local real estate agent. Jasper Speight.'

'Jasper?' exclaims Nick Poulos. 'Fuck me.'

But Pear isn't distracted. His eyes are boring into Martin, whose own eyes have grown wide, even as dread begins to churn within him.

'You knew him?' demands the policeman.

Martin is unable to answer immediately; something feels profoundly wrong, as if the world has shifted in its orbit. 'Yes. We went to school together. We were friends,' he manages to say. 'Good friends.'

'Is that right? Here? In Port Silver?'

'Yes. I grew up here.' A tremor runs through his hands. He holds them together to keep them still.

The policeman writes in his notebook; apparently Martin's connection to Port Silver is news to him. 'And when was the last time you saw the victim, before this morning?'

'Twenty-three years ago. As soon as I finished high school, I left town.'

'And never came back?'

'No.'

'Not ever?'

'No.'

'And no other contact with Jasper Speight in the interim? Letters, emails, phone calls?'

'No. None that I remember.'

Pear thinks that one through. 'So why come back now?'

'I'm moving back here. With my partner, Mandalay Blonde. She moved up recently.'

'When?'

'Three weeks, maybe a month. I'd have to check.'

'So why are you only just arriving?'

'I've been holed up in Sydney, writing a book.'

'No shit!' exclaims Nick Poulos. 'About all those murders out west? Can't wait.'

Martin stares at his lawyer, incredulous, while Pear simply shakes his head. 'Mr Poulos, this is a police interview. You can get Mr Scarsden's autograph when we're finished.'

'Yes. Righto. Sorry, mate,' says Poulos, although his contrition doesn't extend to keeping still; he continues to fidget by Martin's side.

Pear returns his attention to Martin. 'Was this morning the first time you visited Mandalay Blonde's townhouse? The only time?'

'That's right.'

'And apart from the hallway, you didn't enter any other part of the house?'

'That's right.'

'And at no point did you touch the weapon?'

'There was no weapon. Not that I saw.'

'What wounds did the victim have?'

Martin needs only to close his eyes; the scene comes immediately: technicolour gore, the air flooded with the stench of blood; the body on the floor, blood still leaking.

'It looked like he'd been stabbed in the back, right in the centre. There was a circle of blood around a wound. You could see where the shirt had been sliced, the cut itself. But not so much blood. All that blood spreading on the floor, he must have been stabbed, or cut open, in his front, but I couldn't see those injuries, just the one in his back.'

'Did you touch the body?'

'Yes. I touched his neck, searching for a pulse, but that's all. That's when I got some blood on my hand.'

'There was blood on his neck?'

'I don't know. But that's the only part of him I recall touching. And I did get blood on my hand.' Pear squints, his gaze unwavering, as if Martin's words hold great significance. Martin continues, 'He was holding something. It looked like a postcard, some sort of religious image.'

'Did you touch it?'

'No. What was it?'

Pear shakes his head, as if in sorrow. 'I can't tell you that.' Another pause. 'And you didn't go to Mandalay Blonde? You didn't try to comfort your girlfriend?'

'No.'

'Why not?'

Martin doesn't answer immediately; he doesn't know the answer. 'I can't say. I guess I was in shock. We needed help. We were out of our depth.'

'Mr Scarsden, did you kill Jasper Speight?'

'Steady on,' interjects Nick Poulos.

'It's okay,' says Martin. 'Let's have it on the record. I most certainly did not kill Jasper Speight or harm him in any way. He was dead when I arrived.'

'Very good,' says Pear, although there is nothing in his tone to suggest Martin's response is good, bad or indifferent. He asks several more questions, mainly about Mandy's appearance and her attitude, then brings the official interview to an end. The constable turns the camera off, extracts its memory card and takes it with her as she leaves the room.

Pear remains seated, waiting until his subordinate has closed the door behind her before he speaks again, voice more matter-of-fact than menacing. 'This is a murder inquiry. Homicide will be arriving from Sydney any time now, so they'll be taking over. They wanted your recollections on the record as soon as possible. We'll need to detain you until they get here.' He turns to Poulos. 'You understand that isn't my call?'

'My client is cooperating fully. He rang the police. You don't need to detain him,' says the young lawyer. 'He didn't witness the murder.'

Pear addresses Martin, not Nick Poulos. 'I'll be talking to homicide. It's their call. We'll get on to tracking your phone and I'll get down to the backpackers to confirm your alibi. The forensic team from Sydney are also flying in, although some of their equipment is coming by road. We may need to hold you overnight.'

'Not good enough,' says Poulos, almost cheerfully. 'Unless you intend charging him, he needs to be out of here by—' he checks his watch for effect '—let's say six-thirty. Okay?'

The policeman regards the lawyer for a moment. Martin thinks he's starting to detect subtle changes in Pear's face; is that contempt penetrating the mask? 'That's right, son. We can only hold him for four hours. Plus any time it reasonably takes to conduct forensic procedures. Which may mean until tomorrow. As I say, it's homicide's call. They'll be here soon enough; you can argue the toss with them.'

Pear stands, but before he moves to the door he speaks again, this time addressing Martin. 'Know this. Your lawyer here seems to view those murders down in the Riverina as something of a lark. I'm sure you don't. As a police officer, I'm grateful for the assistance you gave in bringing a murderer to justice. But one policeman lost his life and another will be going to prison. Do not

expect me to be doing you any favours.' Pear gives him a withering glare, extends it to Nick Poulos, then heads towards the door.

'What about Mandy?' Martin asks, almost too late. 'How is she?'

'Sorry,' says Pear over his shoulder, sounding anything but, 'not my call.'

—

It's a new cell, fresh and sterile, scrubbed clean of graffiti and misery, smelling of disinfectant, not piss. It boasts a solid metal door with a small hatch at eye level, giving him a sense of privacy even as a video camera, peering down from high in one corner, insists he has none at all. Martin remembers the old cells, reeking of shit and vomit, the marinated aftermath of lives gone wrong. No cameras back then, but no pretence at privacy either: one wall nothing but steel bars fronting the corridor beyond. He'd been locked up a few times, for teenage drunkenness and tomfoolery, put away for the night for his own good by old Sergeant Mackie, dispenser of arbitrary justice. No magistrate's court for him, no habeas corpus, just Martin and Jasper and sometimes Scotty, detained at Mackie's pleasure, released with a flea in the ear and a boot up the arse.

What was it they had done? That night with Scotty? Drunk too much grog, that much was a given. Goon bags and shoplifted Bundy. And dope? Probably. Jasper liked dope. It starts coming back.

They're in the supermarket car park, up on its flat roof, sitting out of sight below its ramparts, drinking and talking and laughing. It's night time. They're maybe sixteen, the bodies of men and the minds of children. Drunken children. The shopping trolleys are just sitting there, waiting to tempt them. Jasper starts it, climbing into one, demanding to be pushed.

In his cell, Martin closes his eyes, hears the sound of the trolley rattling over the gaps in the concrete, clanking like a train, feels the vibrations in his hands.

They take turns pushing each other, narrowly missing light poles, crashing into kerbs. Martin sent flying, banging his knee and scraping his elbow, inspiring unmitigated laughter. The three of them on the ground, laughing, holding their stomachs, tears in their eyes, captive to the moment. It doesn't hurt; not his knee, not his bloodied elbow. How drunk is he?

Now Jasper wants to race, challenges them, but it's not possible, not with just the three of them. And then the inevitable idea. It doesn't matter who suggests it; it's immediately embraced: a race down the ramp from the roof. So they line up their wire-framed chariots, climb in, count down and push off, accelerating quickly, screaming with exhilaration, careening out of control, all three of them crashing, only Scotty still screaming, his arm broken and his tooth missing. Jasper and Martin ploughing headlong into a parked car—the mayor's car—thrown out of the trolleys by the impact, lucky not to be more seriously hurt.

Martin smiles at the memory and wonders at it. Were they really that reckless? That wild? He hasn't thought of it for years, but then he hasn't thought about anything to do with Port Silver for years. Deliberately so. And now Jasper is dead. Twenty-five years since the supermarket and dead on arrival, Martin's arrival. Jasper, with his mop of dark hair and twinkling blue eyes, always up for a laugh, ready with a quip, riding his luck. Chatting up the girls with his cheesy lines, just for the fun of it, surprised when they flirted back. Jasper. Stabbed to death, emptied of blood, with no more luck to ride.

Scotty ends up in hospital, Jasper and Martin in the slammer. And then Jasper is going, his mother Denise rushing in to collect him, grounding him for a month. Jasper winks at Martin as he leaves, giving him a conspiratorial smirk, uninjured and still drunk. And now Martin is alone, the pain returning first to his elbow and then to his knee, before spreading to his head, imposing a regime of suffering. He tries lying down, but his head begins to spin. He sits up, fighting back the urge to vomit. No one is coming to collect him, to ground him; only Mackie will discipline him. But he's not scared, not intimidated—it isn't the first time. On some other night he'll be the one at home and his father will be in here sleeping off a big one, their roles reversed.

Martin opens his eyes, trawls his memory; when did he resolve to stop drinking, promising himself that he would never become his father? One night in the cells, drunk and miserable, or one morning waking with a heavy head, a dry mouth and a rebellious stomach? Old Mackie appearing with breakfast, bacon and eggs floating in a pool of grease, before sending him on his way, telling him that he never wants to see him again. Maybe the message had eventually got through? No, Martin knows when it was. That night out in the Settlement, the night his father died. He stands up, paces, putting the memories away, back where they belong. It shouldn't be too long until he's released; he can leave them in here.

There's the sound of movement outside the cell. Martin peers through the hatch. The curve of her neck, a flash of her hair, no longer blonde.

'Mandy!' he calls.

She pauses, looks back, trying to locate his voice. She's holding her boy, Liam, asleep in her arms. She manages a wan smile, eyes burdened. A timid wave, gaze slightly off centre, looking at the wrong door. Then she's gone, escorted away by the same constable who had operated the video camera.

Martin sits down on the cell bed. There's a thin mattress and nothing else. No pillow, no blanket. She smiled, he's sure she smiled. And Liam is safe. A wave of emotion hits him: relief, longing, a compulsion to protect her and her boy. He feels it roll over him, unsure of his emotional footing. At the age of forty-one he's still getting used to this, these surges of emotion, this undertow of affection. Once, not so long ago, he'd been in control, sailing a placid sea, oblivious to the currents and tides pulsing beneath. Now, closer to the shore, the waves can catch him unawares. He looks at the painted wall, breathes deeply, letting the emotion ebb.

The police will soon clear him, but they'll need to investigate Mandy. An image comes to him of her sitting on the couch, quietly going into shock, hands bloodied. What would the police make of that? They'll ask if she sliced Speight open then finished him with one violent blow, plunging a blade into his heart. Martin knows it can't be true; in the Riverina, she'd held a knife to a killer's throat, a man about to slaughter her defenceless child. She hadn't killed then, under the most extreme provocation, so he can't believe she would kill now, not even in self-defence. Not the final blow, the fatal blow. Not when the victim was already so seriously wounded. Not when he'd turned his back.

But if Mandy wasn't the killer, who was? Martin realises she mustn't know. If she had witnessed the murder, if she had seen the killer, she would have told the police by now and Martin wouldn't still be in custody. So she must have arrived after the fact, only shortly before Martin. Maybe she had heard something and come downstairs to find Jasper dead, just before Martin arrived.

And yet he hadn't gone to her; he'd left her sitting bewildered and lost; he'd stayed in the hallway, awaiting the police. She'd needed him but he hadn't moved. What had immobilised him? Another image comes to him: Jasper Speight with his blood pooling about him. No longer a body, but Jasper. Martin trembles involuntarily and fights the urge to be sick, no longer the dispassionate and impervious foreign correspondent.

———

Sergeant Mackie and the old police station may be long gone, but the breakfast remains unchanged. The same eggs, the same fatty bacon, the same layer of grease. This time around Martin declines; he's not hungover and he's not broke. A second police constable, a young bloke yet to shed the last of his puppy fat, seems to take it personally. 'That's good food, mate. You know that? Plenty would be grateful for it.'

'You eat it then. All yours.'

'I will at that,' says the constable defiantly, taking the plate back. The puppy fat will linger a while yet.

'Hello, Martin. Not hungry?' It's Detective Inspector Morris Montifore, replacing the constable in the doorway. Only six weeks have passed since Martin helped the homicide detective solve a set of brutal murders in the state's parched interior, more than a thousand kilometres from Port Silver. And now here he is again, an unexpected encore. He can't be much older than Martin, but he looks fatigued, the creases on his forehead permanent, as if he's witnessed too much. Perhaps he has.

'Morris. Fancy seeing you here.'

'I was thinking the same thing.' The homicide detective's eyes are alert. Alert and amused.

'I have a lawyer, you know,' says Martin. 'I want him here if you're going to interview me.'

Montifore smiles. 'No need. You're free to go. Sorry you were kept overnight, but we needed to tick all the boxes. This is just a courtesy call.'

'You have the killer?'

'Not yet.'

'But your forensic team, they've put me in the clear?'

Montifore shakes his head. 'This is a police matter. A murder investigation. I don't want you muddying the waters, you understand? That's the courtesy part of the call: don't get involved, leave it to us. Okay?'

'What about Mandy? Is she free to go as well?'

'She's already out. Let her go last night. Better lawyers, I guess.'

Martin doesn't bite. 'Her boy. Is he okay?'

Montifore grows serious. 'He is. Now come on, I'll walk you to the desk and get you signed out. But I'll need to talk to you again. And to her.'

TUESDAY

chapter three

THE FIRST THING MARTIN DOES, BEFORE LACING HIS SHOES AND THREADING HIS belt, before leaving the overbright foyer of the police station, is to ring Mandy. She answers on the third ring.

'Martin,' she shouts. He can hear traffic noise; she's on speaker. 'Are you out?'

'Yes,' he says loudly. 'Where are you?'

'Driving up to Longton. I'm picking up Winifred from the airport.'

Airport? He wasn't aware there was one. It must be a general aviation airport, Mandy's solicitor chartering a plane to fly in from Melbourne. 'Good. Are you okay?'

The pause is so long that he thinks the connection has dropped out. 'Will you be there when I get back?' she asks.

'Of course I will,' he says.

'Good. See you then.' And she hangs up.

He looks at his phone, unsettled by the abruptness of the call. She must still be recovering from the shock of Jasper's bloody demise. Winifred is on her way, Montifore wants to interview them, Mandy remains a suspect. No wonder she was terse: it's not over.

He walks into a town transforming, not so much a teenager blooming into adulthood as a middle-aged woman who's undergone cosmetic surgery. The town of his youth is being nipped and tucked, its face lifted, its skin botoxed, its patchy exterior exfoliated; tarted up for the tourists and the retirees, the sea changers and the telecommuters. He sees it in the promised security of the new two-storey police station, concrete and brick, defended by scrubbed steel bollards, capped by satellite dishes, with an underground car park protected by steel gates. He sees it in the streetscape, in its flowerboxes, speed humps and pedestrian crossings, in the seasonal banners hanging from streetlights. He sees it in the main thoroughfare, The Boulevarde. The street has slimmed down, making room for the footpaths to expand, footpaths paved with herringbone bricks, wide enough to host outdoor cafes with chalkboard menus and umbrellas emblazoned with Italian coffee brands. The last time he was here, the footpaths were narrow strips of bitumen dotted with discarded gum, cigarette butts and dog turds.

He looks across the road, a time traveller fresh from his Tardis. The old fish-and-chip shop, Theo's, is still there, a remnant, with fading Coke signs and a hand-painted declaration that fish is a health food. It's where he, Jasper and Scotty once savoured caramel milkshakes in aluminium containers and potato scallops in butcher-paper wrappers. But the op shop next door has gone, replaced by a swimwear boutique, a Chinese massage centre next to it. Once, vacant blocks had dotted The Boulevarde like missing teeth, providing easy access to the beach on one side and nearby houses and holiday rentals on the other. But now The Boulevarde is growing more orthodontically correct, the vacant lots fewer and farther between, commerce spreading, the beach receding from sight and easy access.

A black Range Rover with personalised plates eases past, halting long enough to allow a skinny woman to emerge. She's dressed in a sarong and a spray tan, her over-large sunglasses flashed with gold. She clip-clops on cork wedges over to unlock the boutique.

Martin walks across the street. An old man meanders past, unhurried by responsibility, unburdened by employment, dressed in ironed shorts, a creaseless polo shirt and deck shoes, his Panama hat blemish-free. He ignores one of his contemporaries, unshaven and bleary-eyed, slumped on a sheet of cardboard, talking passionately to himself, a bottle in a brown paper bag on one side, a small dog on the other, a hat upturned in front of him with a layer of coins thinner than his cushion. A peloton of middle-aged men rolls into view, lycra-clad and chatty, pulling into a bakery, carbon-fibre bikes slotted into council-built racks. They take a table next to a group of roadworkers, dressed in hi-vis and wolfing down egg-and-bacon rolls in silent unison. A glassy-eyed hippie shuffles, dreadlocks and dirty clothes, sandals scuffing.

For a moment Martin sees the two towns superimposed: the tough working-class community of his youth and the gentrified retirement village it is becoming. Some fairy godmother has visited in his absence, sprinkling the silver pixie dust of family trusts, self-managed super funds and negative gearing, but sprinkling it unevenly. Struggle town hasn't gone altogether, but it's in retreat, pushed inland, away from the water, away from The Boulevarde, banished west of the Longton Road, where the sea breeze blows less frequently and DOCS is never far away. He knows exactly where it will still be found: lurking in the Settlement, stalking the fibro-lined roads of his youth and loitering around the smaller farms. He looks along The Boulevarde and wonders if the tide of prosperity that has washed through Australia's capitals for so long has deposited any lasting wealth with the battlers of Port Silver.

Martin attempts to order a coffee at the counter of the Che Bay Cafe but is informed it's table service only and instructed to take a seat. Only then does the graceful young waitress approach, wearing an apron advocating revolution and brandishing a smartphone instead of an order pad. She seems disappointed when he shows no interest in selecting a blend from the coffee menu or hearing the benefits of fair trade organics. He orders a generic flat white and some sourdough raisin toast.

He tries calling Mandy again, but the call goes straight to voice-mail. Either she's out of range or on another call. He searches the net for a number for Nick Poulos. The phone interrupts, asking him if he wants to join Port Silver's free wi-fi. The town has free wi-fi. Of course it does. He accepts the conditions without reading them, but the connection times out. Instead, he uses his 4G connection to find the number for the lawyer.

'Nick? It's Martin Scarsden. Where are you?'

'Getting the kids ready for school. You out?'

'Yes. Can we meet?'

'Of course. Top priority. How about the surf club at eleven?'

Martin looks at his watch. It's not yet nine. 'You can't make it any earlier?'

'Ten-thirty?'

'Okay. Don't let me inconvenience you.' He hangs up. The sooner he can ditch the training-wheels solicitor, the better.

His coffee arrives and he starts scanning news sites on his phone, but can find no mention of murder in Port Silver: not on Fairfax, News, the ABC or any of the other mainstream sites. The cops must be keeping it under their hats for now. Was that why they'd kept him locked up all night? To keep it out of the media for another day? Or maybe, this far from the capitals, it just doesn't rate a mention. A dead local in a seaside town; how can that compare to Sydney celebrities, Melbourne house prices or the latest reality television program? He recalls there used to be a local paper that covered the whole district, based up in Longton, the regional centre on the highway above the escarpment. He finds a website, the *Longton Observer*, days out of date, and then the reason why: the once daily paper is now a bi-weekly, published Wednesdays and Saturdays. It's Tuesday. Maybe the editor, some bloke called Paulo, is working up a screamer on Jasper Speight's murder for tomorrow's front page. Maybe.

Martin checks his emails, but there's nothing, just spam advertising wine, frequent flyer points and hotel bookings. He drains his coffee, pays and leaves, walking further down The Boulevarde. A couple of schoolgirls skip out of a sushi shop, almost bumping into him, giggling as they go. They're wearing straw hats and green-and-white-checked cotton dresses, and they carry matching green backpacks emblazoned with the school badge and motto of Longton Grammar: *Service and Success*. They pile into the back of a waiting SUV. A private school in Longton. The world is indeed changing. He watches the car, a gleaming Hyundai, pull out into the traffic. It's only as he turns back to the street that he sees her:

Denise Speight, unlocking her real estate business just ten metres away. Jasper's mother.

He takes a few steps towards her, uncertain. 'Mrs Speight?' he queries, reverting to the formalities of childhood.

She turns, sees him, her eyes bloodshot and sleep deprived. 'Martin? Is that you? Martin Scarsden?'

He nods. 'Yes. It's me.'

Her hand goes to her mouth and a tremor runs through her. 'Good God. Martin.'

He closes the gap between them, unsure what to do, what to say. She takes his hand, gripping it with force. 'He's dead, Martin. Do you know? Jasper is dead?'

'Yes. I know.'

'I had to go to Longton. The hospital. To identify him.' And she shudders again, tears welling. 'It was him.'

An elderly couple walks pass, frowning with concern.

'Let's go inside,' says Martin. 'Talk there.'

'Yes,' says Denise Speight. 'Yes. Let's do that.' She releases his hand, opens the door. Inside she turns on the lights, a hum followed by clicks as the strip lighting sparks to life. An array of FOR SALE posters covers the plate glass of the shopfront, filtering the light from the street and providing a degree of privacy. There's a vacant receptionist's counter with two glassed-in offices behind it. More FOR SALE and FOR RENT flyers cover the walls.

'Mrs Speight, sorry, but what are you doing here? Today? At work?'

'What else can I do? I can't bear to stay at home. I couldn't sleep.'

Martin remembers her as fierce and sharp-tongued, disapproving of Scotty and himself, but now she seems lost, small and vulnerable. She's dressed for her job: dark slacks, low heels, white blouse. Her grey hair is cut short. On any other day she would exude professionalism, but not on this day. On this day her clothes can't prop her up; she looks like a collapsed bag.

'Is there someone who you can be with?' asks Martin. 'Relatives? Friends?'

She shakes her head.

He persists. 'You should take some time off. Someone else can look after the business for you.'

'No. It was just Jasper and me. He was taking over altogether at the end of this year.' She looks around the office, silent and empty, and stifles a sob. 'It was all for Jasper.' Another tremor. She's barely holding herself together. The space seems full of her son, so recently gone.

'Come on,' says Martin gently. 'Let's go somewhere else. Have a coffee. Have a talk.'

'No. The police will be here soon. To search Jasper's office. That's his, that one there.'

The door to her son's office is closed. Martin feels an urge to look inside, but there's no way he's about to leave his fingerprints on the doorhandle, or any evidence he's been in there. He walks across and peers through the glass. He can see a desk, papers spread across it. There's a pen there as well, its cap off next to it, ready to write the next sentence. A cup of coffee, half empty, a skin of milk on its surface. A coat hangs on a hatstand. Two vacant chairs face the desk.

'It's like he's coming back any minute, isn't it?' Denise has moved to his side.

'Yes, it is,' he whispers.

'Come on,' she says. 'Come into my office. Let's talk there.' Her voice is a little more even, as if she's overcome some internal obstacle.

Inside her office she takes her chair; Martin sits on the other side of the desk in one of the chairs provided for customers, like he's interested in renting a house instead of mourning a much-loved son. Behind her are framed photos. Her son. Children. A fading shot of a black-haired man.

Denise looks at Martin, eyes red. 'The police say you found him,' she says.

Martin nods, uncertain. Outside she'd asked him if he knew Jasper was dead, now she's saying she knows he found her son, demonstrating her disorientation. 'Yes. That's right. I found him.'

'What happened, Martin? Who killed him?'

'I don't know. I don't think the police know either. Not yet. I only saw a single blow, in the back. It would have struck his heart. Jasper wouldn't have known what hit him. He would have died instantly. Almost instantly.'

Denise looks at him imploringly. 'He didn't suffer?'

'No. I don't think so.'

'That's kind of you, Martin. Kind of you to say that. But I know it's not true. The police say he was stabbed in the stomach and chest first, that he was trying to get away. His hands were cut.'

Martin doesn't know what to say, so he says nothing.

'They think he may have known his assailant.' Denise is looking into some imagined distance, talking to herself as much as to Martin, before bringing her focus back to him. 'They said they were questioning your girlfriend. Interrogating her. Mandalay

Blonde. From down there, from all the death and mayhem in that country town.'

'They've released her,' says Martin calmly. 'There's no evidence she was involved.'

'But she was there?'

'I think so. In the house. But I don't know if she witnessed the attack.'

'So she didn't hear anything? Didn't see anything?'

'I don't know,' says Martin. 'I haven't spoken to her yet.'

'They said they were questioning you, as well.'

'That's right. I'm doing everything I can to help.'

That seems to satisfy her. She settles back into her chair, intensity draining out of her, grief flowing back in.

'Can I ask you something, Mrs Speight?'

She smiles at that, feigning amusement. 'I think you can call me Denise, Martin. You're not a schoolboy anymore.'

'Thanks. Denise. Was Jasper religious?'

'Not that I know of. Why do you ask?'

'It was difficult to see, but when I found him, he was holding a postcard or a photograph. It looked like a religious image, of Christ or maybe a saint.'

Denise smiles weakly, as if a fond memory has presented itself. 'One of his postcards. He had thousands of them. He collected them. It was his hobby.'

'Religious postcards?'

'No. All sorts of things. Places, mainly. You started it.'

'Sorry?'

'You sent him one, when you first got to Sydney. You and Scott. You remember?'

Martin blinks. He has no memory of ever writing to Jasper.

'He always spoke of travelling. He followed all your reports from round the world. And he collected postcards. But, in the end, he never really saw much of the world. Never went overseas. Not like you.'

Martin wonders if he hears bitterness in the mother's voice; lets it go. 'Do you know why Jasper was visiting Mandy at her townhouse?'

Denise smiles again, a hybrid expression: mouth upturned but eyes sad. 'No. We've been renting her the place for almost a month now, but there was no reason I know of for him to go there. Although he always had an eye for a pretty girl.' She shrugs. 'But I think he wanted to see you.'

'Me? Why?'

'My word, Martin, you have no idea how proud he was of you. He always read the paper, was always showing me your stories. The foreign pages and, more recently, those front pages from out west. Always told anyone who'd listen what great mates you two had been.'

Martin feels a surge of guilt, of remorse. Now it's his turn to feel emotion catching in his throat. 'I wish I could have seen him again. I was looking forward to it.'

'He heard you were moving back. He thought you could help him. As a journalist.'

'What do you mean?'

She leans forward, intelligence sparking, grief set aside for another moment. 'This town has changed, Martin. Every year, every month, there's some new building. Money washing north from Sydney and Melbourne, developers coming south from Brisbane and the Gold Coast, meeting here. Just ask down on The Boulevarde: we're the new Byron Bay, the new Noosa. Some of them want us to be the new Gold Coast, like that's a good thing.'

'Sounds like a good place to be a real estate agent,' interposes Martin, regretting his words as soon as they are out of his mouth. 'Sorry. I didn't mean to imply anything.'

'That's okay. You're right. We've done very well. Jasper's kids won't go without.'

'Kids? He was married?' asks Martin. He looks again at the framed photos: Jasper's kids.

'*Was* is the operative word. Divorced seven or eight years ago. All his own fault. Couldn't keep his hands to himself.' It's a frank assessment from the dead man's mother.

'Where is his ex? And the kids?'

'Susan? New Zealand. I contacted her last night. She may come back for the funeral. She may not. More interested in how it affects her alimony, if I know her.' There's an edge to the statement; she closes her eyes, as if admonishing herself. 'I can't say I blame her; kids are expensive.'

Martin considers this before speaking again. 'You've lost me. You were telling me the town is booming. You've made good money. But what's that got to do with Jasper and why he wanted to see me?'

Denise frowns, as if she too has lost track of the conversation's thread, or as if what she is about to say pains her. 'We're real estate agents, not property developers. The big money is in developing. We benefit, to be sure, but that doesn't mean we have to like everything the developers do. Jasper used to be very ambitious, very money hungry, but after his wife walked out on him, he got depressed, started to reassess himself. Medication, support groups, spiritual retreats. He came through it okay, got his old spark back, but he was less of a larrikin, more considerate. I wouldn't describe him as a greenie—far from it—but he's helped the campaign against a new development planned for up on Crystal Lagoon.'

'Crystal Lagoon? Never heard of it. Where is it?'

'Mackenzie's Swamp. It's been rebranded.'

Martin laughs, shakes his head. 'You're kidding. It's full of bull sharks. No one in their right mind would develop that.'

'The sharks have gone. After the cheese factory closed.'

'The cheese factory?'

'You'd be surprised.'

The cheese factory. He can't picture it, can't ever remember going there, and yet he knows where it is, out on Dunes Road, well north of the town. He has some tendril of memory, a feeling his father may have once worked at the factory, but when he tries to pin the memory down, he can't be sure if the recollection is real or imagined. 'Why was Jasper opposed to a development? What was he protecting?'

Denise stands, walks around her desk. On one wall two maps are pinned up: one setting out the streets of Port Silver with individual block numbers, colour-coded for zoning, the other a larger-scale depiction of the surrounding district. She goes to the district map, black and white with contour lines in green. Martin joins her.

'We're here in town,' says Denise, pointing. 'The bridge takes you north across the Argyle onto Dunes Road. The road is raised, a causeway through the swamplands. The lagoon is mostly off to the left, the cheese factory up on its northern bank.'

Martin examines the map, reacquainting himself with the landscape of his youth. Dunes Road is dead straight, running north for twenty kilometres from the Argyle River. The land on both sides is low-lying—Mackenzie's Swamp—with water at its centre: the rebranded Crystal Lagoon. 'Flood prone,' Martin says.

'Yes. Can't be built on.'

Martin continues to examine the map. The land east of the road, beyond the lagoon, rises sharply, up to a hundred metres or more above sea level, culminating in cliffs running north–south along the coast. Someone has marked out private holdings with a pencil, with clifftop houses drawn as small squares. His eyes return to the road, following it north, up to another, smaller bridge. This is where the lagoon opens to the sea. 'The lake. It's tidal?'

'Yes. Every now and then the mouth will silt up, but then a big storm will come through and open it up again. And there's the site of the old cheese factory, there. It's on the only bit of high ground west of the road.'

The green contours on the map confirm the real estate agent's assertion. Again, someone has drawn the boundaries of the private holding surrounding the factory in pencil. The land beyond it looks dead flat, as if the separation between land and water is debatable. 'What about all this, these wetlands? Is this Crown land?'

'Nature reserve. There's been a native title claim on it for years, but who knows when that might be resolved.'

'What's there? Anything?'

'No. Not west of the road. Just the old cheese factory site; the rest is mangroves, mudflats and sea water. Full of mosquitoes, ticks and leeches. It may be Crystal Lagoon some day, but right now it's still a swamp. But good fishing, so they tell me, and prawns when they're running.'

'So why was Jasper opposed to developing it?'

'He liked the idea of leaving something unspoilt, some green space on the other side of the river. For future generations.' At the thought of her son, of his hopes, the momentary distraction of real estate falls away and her face again turns down.

'What's planned for it? Is there a firm proposal?'

Denise sighs. 'A marina. On the south bank where the estuary meets the lagoon, just west of the bridge. But Jasper thought it would kill off the mangroves and ruin the environment.'

Martin considers the plan. He knows there is money in marinas, but the development strikes him as wildly unlikely. 'It's a long way from town to park a boat. Is there housing planned as well?'

'Not at the marina itself. Too low-lying, too flood prone. There's a development planned for the east side of the road, here at Hummingbird Beach on private land.' Denise points out the site on the map. Martin can see a north-facing beach close to where the tidal lake joins the sea. The beach is backed by higher ground, the green contour lines declaring it flood proof. Denise continues: 'It's prime real estate. The beach is sheltered and catches the winter sun. Beautiful. There's a big outfit, some multinational, that wants to build a high-end resort there. For tourists, but maybe with strata titles for the wealthy, with a walkway under the bridge to the marina. Stage three would be a golf course around the rest of the lagoon, with a clubhouse above the flood line, where the old factory is now. Jasper didn't have any issues with the resort at Hummingbird Beach; he thought it was a good idea. He just wanted the lagoon and the land west of the road left alone.'

'What about you?' asks Martin. 'What do you think?'

Denise shrugs. 'I don't think it's doing anyone any good just sitting there. I'd like to see it developed, provided the local Gooris don't get shafted, that they get a bit of money and some employment. That would be win-win.'

Martin looks at the map. He can see the attraction for the developers, and he can see why environmentalists would want to protect the tidal lake and the surrounding land. 'What's the company that's pushing all this development?'

'Two companies. The one that wants to buy Hummingbird Beach is a big French outfit. Jasper has been representing them. The marina and the golf course is a local developer, Tyson St Clair, trying to piggyback on their investment.'

Martin blinks. Denise Speight is attempting to sound matter-of-fact, but there is something in her inflection, something akin to distaste. 'You don't approve?'

'The man won't be satisfied until he owns the whole town.' This time, the bitterness in her voice is more evident.

Martin takes a moment to assimilate this. 'So Jasper was representing the French, trying to win approval for their development at Hummingbird Beach, while at the same time opposing Tyson St Clair's proposed marina and golf course?'

'Yes. That's right.'

'Surely that must have led to some tension?'

'I wouldn't know.'

'You two didn't discuss it?'

'No. He knew I don't approve of St Clair. We didn't talk about it.'

Martin makes a mental note to check out the property developer. 'So Jasper wanted to enlist my help to get the story out to a national audience? That's understandable. But no one is going to kill him for that. Was there something else he wanted to tell me? Something more sensitive?'

Denise Speight smiles, another weak approximation. 'I don't know, Martin. If there was, he didn't tell me.'

'I see.'

The smile vanishes as quickly as it appeared. 'Will you investigate it? Why he died? For me? For him? He always loved your investigations.'

Martin sees the pleading in her eyes, hears the quaver in her voice. 'Yes, of course,' he says. 'I want to know as well.' Denise offers up her frail smile once again, this time touched with gratitude. Martin continues: 'You say you don't know if he had any information that could have got him killed. Is there anyone else who might, perhaps someone he could have confided in? About the development, for example, or his relationship with St Clair?'

Her smile flickers like a torch with a flat battery. 'You could try your uncle. Vern.'

Vern.

———

Vern and he are walking away from the Settlement along Ressling Road, through the cane fields, the sunshine setting the world aglow. They're laughing and they're chatting, embraced by the warm winds of fate, towards a town where suddenly the light looks cleaner and the air smells better. His mother has taken Vern's car, put the twins in the back, driving off to find Martin's father and tell him the life-changing news, to tell him to down tools, to say goodbye to shift work. To tell him of the lottery and division one and their new beginning. No other winners, no one else to share it with. Just them. Half a million dollars. A fortune.

They walk towards the main road, Vern and he, the surface baking black in the sun, the bitumen searing through the thin soles of his thongs. 'Tell me again, Vern. Tell me what we're going to get.'

'Fish and chips, matey, but not flake, not this time. We'll get Tassie scallops, real scallops and Victorian lobster, we'll get prawns from the Gulf as big as bananas, and wild barramundi from the Territory. We'll have the biggest feed you ever saw.'

'Calamari rings, Vern. Can we get calamari rings?'

Vern laughs. 'Sure, mate, as many as you like.'

'And Coke, Vern. Big bottles. Icy cold.'

'And champagne, matey. The best we can find. French.'

'Will I like it, Vern? Champagne?'

'Maybe not yet, but you'll have to get used to it now.' And Vern laughs, his spirits bubbling, and Martin likes the sound of it, of drinking champagne.

He likes the thought of other things as well: a new bike with proper gears, a real cricket bat, maybe even a surfboard. The family can buy a new television, a big rear-projection one. Vern is thinking bigger, saying they can stop renting, move out of their fibro house, move out of the Settlement and get a place down by Five Mile Beach where the girls can have a bedroom each. He says they could even get a new car—not a new second-hand car, but one straight off the showroom floor from up in Longton, a car that's never been driven by anyone else before.

'What about you, Uncle Vern? What will you buy?'

'Me? Nothing, matey. It's your money. Your mum won it. It's for her; for you guys.'

'But what about you?'

And Vern just laughs. 'Mate, I don't need anything. I got no wife, I got no kids. I'm happy the way I am.'

And Martin holds his hand as they cross Longton Road and he loves his uncle all the more, and quietly plots to surprise him with a new fishing rod with a gold-plated reel that glints like magic in the sun.

chapter four

BACK ON THE STREET OUTSIDE SPEIGHT'S REAL ESTATE, MARTIN'S PHONE SAYS it's nine thirty-five. Another hour before he meets with Nick Poulos. He rings Mandy, but again the call goes through to voicemail. He's considering his next move when he sees Morris Montifore approaching along the footpath. 'Morning, Martin. Trust you're not putting your nose in where it's not wanted.' The policeman's tone is teasing, but Martin is feeling drained by his meeting with Denise Speight and burdened by memories of the murder scene. He's not up to banter.

'Just find his killer, Morris. Let me know if I can help.'

Montifore picks up on the seriousness of his tone. 'Of course. Sorry. Take care of yourself.' From the other side of the street, carrying a tray with three takeaway coffees, comes Montifore's sidekick, Ivan Lucic. He acknowledges Martin with a grunt before following his boss into the real estate office.

A little way along The Boulevarde, Martin finds a covered arcade leading through to the beach. He passes a second-hand bookstore, a noodle bar, two empty shopfronts with Speight Real Estate FOR LEASE signs and a surf shop, and walks out onto a footpath threading its way between Norfolk Island pines above the dunes. He walks along it, then descends some concrete stairs onto the beach proper.

Someone has raked the sand. Who rakes a beach? The local council, no doubt, with some sort of tractor. But why? Why groom a beach? An old man passes, stooped over a metal detector, the skin on his back like brown leather. A memory comes to Martin of himself as a teenager, mowing the lawns of local pensioners for pocket money. Magpies would follow in his wake, searching for worms, pecking surgically at the new-mown grass. The beach-comber reminds him of the magpies. As Martin watches, he stoops, picks something up, examines it and drops it into a dillybag strung over his shoulder. Martin had forgotten all about the lawn mowing.

The man is not alone; the beach is already filling up with the glistening limbs and polished insouciance of backpackers, some dozing on their towels, some smoking, some on their phones posting envy-inspiring images to relatives still gripped by northern winters. No one seems to be talking, as if last night's partying has emptied them of words. Out on the point below the lighthouse a gaggle of surfers float about, hoping the gentle swell might conspire to push up a rideable wave. The sky is clear and the sun is growing potent. The calendar has officially ticked over into autumn, but summer lingers here on the subtropical north coast of New South Wales. Only the quality of the light, the angle of the sun, suggests summer is ebbing. In his youth, on a Tuesday morning, on a working day, the beach would have been all but empty; just Jasper and Scotty and him, wagging school and smoking cigarettes among the dunes. No longer.

He looks again to the south. The lighthouse is the same: unchanging and judgemental, dominating the skyline atop the headland, glowing white against the blue clarity of the sky. Sprinkled below the lighthouse, Martin can see the trophy homes of the wealthy: cashed-up retirees and sea changers from Sydney and Melbourne, the holiday escapes of company directors and bankers, locals made good. Nobb Hill, they'd called it as kids. It had always been Port Silver's premier address: brick houses in a fibro town. Now the brick is vanishing, replaced by steel and concrete, stone and stained wood, floor-to-ceiling double-glazing and decks cantilevered out high above the hoi polloi, providing views of sunrises, passing whales and the long golden arc of Town Beach to the north and Five Mile Beach to the south. Martin wonders if that's where Jasper Speight ended up, on Nobb Hill, among the success stories of Port Silver. Martin wouldn't be surprised; whatever Denise Speight might say about developers getting the lion's share, real estate would generate a pretty penny in the town Port Silver is becoming.

'Martin!'

He turns. It's the hitchhikers, Topaz and Royce, approaching along the beach. Royce is wearing board shorts, his bare stomach washboard flat, a beach bag over his shoulder, his one-armed sunglasses at a rakish angle. But it's Topaz who seizes Martin's attention. She's almost naked, her bikini no bigger than the mermaid tattooed to one side of her navel. He doesn't quite know where to look and, as if sensing it, she sways her hips a degree or two more as she comes to a halt, her shoulders back, breasts thrust forward unapologetically.

'Hey, what happened?' asks Royce. 'The filth came looking for us, checking us out. Wanted to know if you gave us a lift or not.'

'What did you tell them?'

Royce shrugs. 'The truth, of course. You picked us up, you dropped us off. The time of day, how you seemed. What happened?'

'I stumbled across a murder scene a few minutes after I dropped you at the hostel.'

'You shitting me? Murder? Here?' Royce looks around at the serenity of the beach. 'How heavy is that?'

'Yeah. Thanks though. You ended up providing my alibi.'

'Is that right? You were a suspect?' asks Royce, sounding awestruck, as if Martin has emerged from a true-crime podcast.

'Not for long, thanks to you two.'

'Super,' says Topaz. 'You can spring for dinner some time.' Her expression is playful, confident.

'Sure,' says Martin.

'Great. See you,' she says and saunters past. Royce smiles, raises an eyebrow above his lopsided sunnies and follows. Martin can't help but turn and watch them go. Topaz's buttocks bounce provocatively as she walks. *You are pathetic*, he reprimands himself.

The Port Silver Surf Life Saving Club still occupies the same prime location overlooking Town Beach, but the volunteer-built shed of Martin's youth is gone, its cinder-block simplicity replaced by a gleaming two-storey imposition emerging from the dunes like an airport terminal. A steel-form deck stretches its entire forty-metre length, extending out across the white sands; it's already well patronised despite the early hour. Walking towards it along the beach, Martin can see that the lower floor, in the shade of the deck, is devoted to the club's founding purpose: open roller doors reveal old-fashioned surf boats, rope reels, surf skis: the traditional equipment of competitive surf lifesaving. Down on the beach, the equipment is more up-to-date: a jet ski gleams on a trailer behind a quad bike, ready for action. A small observation tower looks out over the red-and-yellow flags. Lifesavers in bulging red speedos preen at its base, casually flexing their muscles and checking out passing backpackers. When had they started patrolling the beach on weekdays? Are they still volunteers?

There's no access to the deck from the beach, so Martin enters from the footpath above the dunes, the doors facing back towards The Boulevarde. The foyer is lined with honour boards, gilt writing on darkening wood, and trophy cabinets, silverware blackening in the sea air, relics from the old clubhouse, looking like museum pieces. Black-and-white photos of smiling men in outdated swim-wear fade slowly in their lacquered frames, shoulder to shoulder with grainy reminders of more recent decades, men with large moustaches, hairy chests and tiny swimmers, red-and-gold caps ageing to less certain colours.

There's a counter with the usual pads for casual visitors to sign themselves in. Instead, Martin spots a young woman reading from a device as she walks, hair tied back, dressed for an office not the beach, exuding competence. 'Excuse me,' he says. 'Membership?'

'You want to join?'

'If I can.'

'You local? You should be local.'

'Yeah. Just moving here.'

She frowns.

'Moving back, actually. Grew up here.'

Her face brightens. 'Well, no worries then.'

'How much?'

'Twenty bucks for a year, fifty for three. Twenty per cent discount on all food and drink.'

Martin smiles. 'Hard to argue with that.'

'Three years then?'

'Sure. The pokies must be doing well.'

'Yeah, miserable things.'

Through the foyer, the club is one large space, its glass doors concertinaed open to allow unfettered access to the deck, the sea breeze wafting through, the atmosphere prosperous and casual. There's an area partitioned off for the pokies up the far end, but that's it; the rest of the room is divided into zones defined only by the occasional rubber plant and variations in the furniture: tall round tables circled by stools in front of the bar, tables and chairs for dining and coffee close by the bistro, lounge chairs facing a huge screen at the opposite end of the building to the pokies. There's cricket on the TV, a meaningless game in Doha that no one is watching. The back of the building, towards the foyer, is fronted by a long bar and the serving counters of the bistro and a cafe. Most of the patrons are out on the deck; inside, the club is all but empty.

Martin looks at his watch. It's not yet ten o'clock, still more than half an hour before Nick Poulos arrives—if he's on time. Martin checks his phone. No message from his lawyer, nothing more from Mandy. He calls her, but the phone again goes straight to voicemail. No doubt she's already deep in conversation with her lawyer even as he waits for his. Or maybe she's with Liam—as good a reason as any to ignore a phone call. He goes to the cafe counter and orders another coffee. This time it's cash up front and no quibbling over blends. It costs half as much and tastes just as ordinary. He takes it out onto the deck and finds a vacant table. Overlapping sections of sailcloth extend above the deck, held taut by steel cables, providing shade and colour: blues and whites and yellows. He looks out across the raked sand and sculpted bodies, up to Nobb Hill and the lighthouse and, below them, the flat-sea surfers. It might get hot later on, but here in the shade, with a slight breeze wafting off the ocean, the day seems perfect. If only Jasper Speight were here to share it with him, with a cold beer and decades of news.

His phone vibrates on the glass tabletop: a text message. *Change of plan. Meet at drakes. Noon. Level 3, 18 the boulevarde. Nick.* Martin shakes his head with irritation, but replies with a thumbs-up emoji and then saves the lawyer's number into his contacts. Another two hours. He should find somewhere to have a shower and change clothes; after a night in the cell he fears he's starting to smell, an intrusion on Port Silver's postcard perfection. He can fetch his car, still parked outside Mandy's townhouse with his luggage on the back seat. He can swim at the beach, shower in the change sheds. He's finishing his coffee, plan decided, when he sees him over the rim of his cup. Vern.

His uncle is a couple of tables away, staring at him. He's not alone, he's facing two other men, their backs to Martin, but it's his nephew who has commandeered his attention. Their eyes lock. Martin can't think; this hadn't occurred to him. Not like this.

Vern stands, walks over. 'Martin.'

Martin stands. 'Vern.'

'You're back.'

'I'm back.'

And then, creeping across his uncle's face like the dawn across the sea, the smile comes, small at first but growing until his lips crack open and his teeth shine forth, a smile full of happiness and welcome. 'Martin. My boy. Welcome back, welcome back!' And Vern steps forward, wrapping his arms around Martin, hugging him tightly. Martin can feel the strength of his uncle's arms, the power of his chest and the depth of his feelings. He hugs him back: Vern, his one living relative.

The embrace ends. Martin can see his uncle's companions have stopped talking, have turned to witness the scene. Vern turns to them, his voice joyful. 'It's Martin. My nephew. The journalist. My sister's boy. He's back.' Now he's grinning madly at Martin, slapping him on the back. His hair is flecked with grey but still thick, there are wrinkles at the corners of his eyes but his face is youthful, the skin at his throat is beginning to loosen but his blue eyes are clear and sparkling. Martin is forty-one, his uncle must be in his mid-fifties.

'Vern,' says Martin. 'I'm sorry.'

'Sorry? Sorry for what?'

'You know for what. For everything.'

'Piffle. Forget about it.' Martin can't quite believe it. Vern has every right to resent him, yet there is nothing to see in his uncle's face except joy. 'How long you back for?'

Martin smiles then. 'For a while. Maybe for good.'

'For good? Holy shit. For good?'

Martin laughs. 'Maybe.'

'I don't believe it. Hard enough keeping you in the country, let alone Hicksville, New South Wales.'

'Hicksville seems to be doing all right,' Martin offers.

'It's a girl, isn't it? Has to be.' Vern is grinning. 'Don't tell me; it's that blonde from the papers, isn't it? That looker from down in the bush? Drop-dead gorgeous.'

Martin can't help himself; he grins back.

'It is? Ha, I knew it! You lucky bastard!'

Martin can feel himself starting to blush, the hardened foreign correspondent reverting to teenagerdom. He speaks, trying to sound in control. 'Her name is Mandalay. Or Mandy. Mandy Blonde.'

'Well, fuck me rudderless,' exclaims Vern, clapping his nephew on the shoulder. 'I like this Mandalay Blonde, luring you back here. When am I going to meet her? I need to buy her a drink.'

'Soon. Soon, I hope.'

'Good. But let me buy you a drink now. Let's celebrate the return of the portable.'

'Prodigal, Vern.' Martin laughs. 'It's prodigal.'

But Vern has stopped smiling. 'Shit. Sorry, Martin. I forgot, you don't drink.'

'No. It's okay. I do a bit nowadays. Picked it up again after I finished uni, when I became a journo. But maybe not at ten in the morning.'

Vern turns to his friends, mutters a few words, then collects his coffee and the remains of a toasted sandwich. They sit at Martin's table.

'This has made my day, Martin. Fuck, it's made my year. I'm so glad to see you.'

'Me too, Vern. I'm glad to see you. I'm sorry I've been such a self-centred arsehole. You deserve better.'

'Don't know what you're talking about.'

But of course he does. And Martin knows it too. It was Vern, aged twenty-one, who had become the emotional bedrock for an eight-year-old Martin. It was Vern—who had left school officially at fifteen, unofficially at twelve, who could barely read or write—who had eventually housed him and supported him and insisted he finish his last two years of school. And it was Vern, full of love and pride, who had sent money as Martin worked his way through university. Vern, whom Martin had then cut adrift. The gun reporter, self-obsessed and determined to put Port Silver and its grief behind him, determined to build his career, who had hardly thanked his uncle, receiving birthday cards and Christmas cards but rarely responding, embarrassed by their ill-formed letters and childish spelling. Later, after university, when he was financially independent, the cards still came. After a time, they came addressed care of the *Sydney Morning Herald* because Vern no longer knew his home address. And yet still they came. At one point, wanting to forget, wanting to leave Port Silver permanently behind him, Martin had sent a cheque, a repayment, some restitution for all his uncle had done for him. Vern never cashed it, but the cards had stopped. Martin looks into Vern's eyes, those kind blue eyes, and wonders how he could ever have been so relentlessly thoughtless.

'Truly, Vern: I'm sorry.'

'Matey, don't worry about it. You're back now, back in the fold.'

'Did you hear about Jasper Speight?'

'No. What?'

'He's dead.' His words wash the smile from his uncle's face. 'I'm sorry, Vern.'

'Dead? You serious?'

'I found him yesterday. Stabbed to death.' Martin can't keep the emotion from his voice; one moment he's like a blushing teenager, the next like a broken child, voice wavering. Until a year ago he'd been a correspondent, wearing his profession like a carapace, proud and remote and emotionless, but no longer. Something had happened in the Middle East, something more down in the drought-stricken Riverina. He's changed, the shield has been stripped away. And this is no section editor he's addressing, it's his uncle; he's not briefing a news conference, he's looking into the eyes of the man who raised him. Who believed in him. Who rescued him. He sees the distress in his uncle's eyes and feels the moisture in his own. He realises, even as he shudders, that the years of distancing and denial have been futile: there are things you can't escape.

Vern is shaking his head. 'Jasper, hey? So that was him, the man killed yesterday in Riverside Place?'

'Yes,' says Martin, and he struggles to keep even the single syllable free from quivering.

'That's awful,' says Vern. 'No one deserves that.'

'Can I ask you about him, Vern? About Jasper?'

'Yeah, sure. Why?'

'I want to find out who killed him.'

Some light returns to Vern's eyes. 'Do you? Good lad. A *Herald* investigation.' And then the shadows are back as he remembers what they are discussing. 'Well, anything I can do to help, just ask.'

'Thanks.'

But before he can posit a question, Vern interjects. 'Listen, Martin, I'm sorry, but those blokes I'm with—it's business. I got to get back to them. But tell you what: you come to dinner tonight, you and your girl, okay?'

'Yeah. Maybe. I'm not sure she'll be up to it. I haven't seen her yet.'

'Well, you come. We can talk. Here.' Vern has a business card out. Martin watches as his uncle laboriously writes his home address on the back, pen gripped in his fist like a child. He hands it to Martin, beaming as if proud of his penmanship. 'Ring if you can't make it, but don't leave it too late. I'll fire up the barbie. We'll have a feed, talk about Jasper, about old times.'

Vern stands and so does Martin. His uncle looks him over once more, as if reassuring himself his nephew is real. 'Martin Scarsden, hey? Back in Port Silver. How good is that?' And he pulls Martin into another quick bear hug before releasing him. 'Got to go, matey. See you tonight.'

As he moves back to his friends, Martin looks at the business card. *Vern Jones—Fishing charters & whale watching.* And on the back, the address, letters askew, spelling approximate.

chapter five

THE SEA IS STILL THE SEA, THE BEACH IS STILL THE BEACH. NO MATTER THE changes sweeping The Boulevarde, no matter the new money whitewashing old miseries, no matter the ringing changes in his own life, the water is still the water: embracing, disinterested, constant. He skips through the foaming ankle-high wavelets past the stamping toddlers, past the backpackers skimming a ball to each other in the shallows, past the kids on their first foam boards, wading deeper, pushing through larger waves, feeling the water surge around him. He pushes further, diving under a clear green wall as it rises before him, eyes open, touches the bottom with his hand as the wave licks his feet. Surfacing he puts in some freestyle strokes, his shoulders welcoming the well-remembered sensation, swimming further out, beyond the breaking waves. Out the back.

He swings upright, treading water, his feet no longer able to touch the bottom, feeling the gentle pull and push of the sea, the ocean's mighty breath. He inhales deeply, dives down, eyes open, through the sun-straddled translucence. Down he goes, into colder water, touches the sandy bottom again with satisfaction, rises again, not kicking but letting his buoyancy float him back to the surface, towards the spearing shafts of gold. The water feels so good, so honest, washing away the residue of the police cell, lifting the lingering taint of death, scrubbing the recent past from his pores.

Treading water again, breathing harder, he looks around him. The sea is open, not threatening. Memories come to him, swirl around: wild surf in a storm-brewed sea, caught in a rip, swimming out of it sideways, out beyond the waves, only to be dumped by a huge breaker on the way back in, the air knocked from his lungs, the struggle to breathe. Another memory: kissing a girl in the dunes only to have her laugh at him and walk away; loitering with Scotty and Jasper, smoking cigarettes and drinking, flicking butts with practised nonchalance, mocking the conformity of the clubbies and their silly caps.

The water flows over him, cooling and calming. Fifteen metres away, parallel to the beach, an elderly man is swimming towards him, arms moving methodically, in no hurry. Martin watches him as he passes, wonders if he's swimming back and forth in the zone defined by the red-and-yellow flags, or if he cares nothing for the lifesavers and their attempts to regulate the sea. The way he's swimming, slowly and effortlessly, he might be an old clubbie himself, a life member, a veteran of Port Silver.

Martin dives again, down into the deepening green, feeling again the mild swell and benevolent currents. The water holds him, forgives him and releases him to surface again. The sun and the sea, the land and the wind. And for the first time since Mandy revealed her plans to move here to the cauldron of his youth, for the first time since he finished his true-crime book, refocused and left Sydney, for the first time since he descended the escarpment, he feels that maybe it's not such a bad thing, returning here. The past is immutable, but it's distant, controllable; the future is yet to be determined, to be shaped by the present, to be fashioned by Mandy and himself. The sea is still the sea, but the town is evolving. Maybe, just maybe, it's all going to work out.

In the change sheds, above the beach, between the lifesavers and the backpacker hostel, across the burning sand and scorching concrete, Martin stands under the stream of water, eyes closed beneath the shower. Vern. Maybe his return to Port Silver is fated, giving him a chance to make amends, to reconnect with his uncle even as he comes to terms with his own past.

A memory emerges. He's returning home to Vern's from somewhere, school maybe. He finds his uncle at the kitchen table, tears in his eyes. Before him, a form, an application for some sort of boating licence. Martin sees him there, the frustration on his face, the anger and shame in his eyes. Martin silently completes the form, quickly, no words spoken, pointing to the space awaiting Vern's childlike signature. Leaving the kitchen again, feeling bewildered and embarrassed by his uncle's incapacity, unable to understand how a man so quick-witted and capable could be so slow to learn.

———

A receptionist, her hair as straight and perfect as a nylon wig, her pencil skirt as sharp as a nib, her perfume polite in the air-conditioned coolness, leads Martin through the offices of Drake and Associates to a conference room of smoked-glass walls, black leather swivel chairs and a table of seamless black wood. The table is so polished, so flawless, that Martin initially mistakes it for stone or resin. It supports, at its precise centre, a white ceramic vase containing fresh-cut lilies. A large television, screen dark, hangs behind the head of the table from sandstone bricks, the only wall that isn't glass. There's a sideboard with a silver water jug and glasses at the other end of the room, a room as free of dust as any computer-maker's clean room, leaving only the smell of lilies, leather and money. The offices of Drake and Associates, occupying the entire top floor, the third floor, wouldn't be out of place in a Manhattan skyscraper.

A man of about sixty enters the room. He has thick grey hair and the smooth skin of self-satisfaction. His suit is well cut, his cufflinks catch the light, his teeth are perfectly aligned. 'Harrold Drake, Martin. Welcome.' They shake hands and the receptionist, hovering by the door, asks Martin what blend of espresso he'd care for. Martin says he wouldn't mind a cup of tea.

'Take a seat, Martin,' says Harrold Drake. 'The others won't be a moment.'

Martin is about to comply when he hears Mandy's voice. 'Is he here yet? Martin?'

And she's through the door and into his arms, squeezing him tight, head on his shoulder, before pulling back a little so she can look him in the eye. He can see the love there, the relief. She kisses him, not for long but with passion. 'Am I ever glad to see you,' she says, but her words are a mere subtitle, it's her face that fills his screen, cinematic perfection. For a moment his heart pumps out emotions, not blood: longing, caring, love. He realises anew how precious this woman is to him, how she has broken down his defences, thrown a lifeline into the dark sea of his solitude.

'And I'm so glad to be here—for you,' he says, surprising himself with his unfiltered sincerity. And then to lighten the mood: 'I like the hair.'

'Thanks.'

'Where's Liam?'

'I dropped him at child care on the way up to collect Winifred.'

'Let's get to it then,' says a voice, all business.

Martin looks beyond Mandy to see Winifred Barbicombe. The solicitor is much as Martin remembers: posture erect, an understated suit of silk and fine wool, half-moon glasses hanging from a thin gold chain. She must be late sixties at least, but there's no evidence age has impaired her in any way. Her voice is resonant and her eyes alert. 'I'm glad you're here, Martin. Where is your lawyer?'

'Here,' says Nick Poulos, bustling into the room ahead of the receptionist. 'Am I late?' He's wearing a blue linen suit over a white linen shirt, both crumpled, conveying casual professionalism. His brown elastic-sided boots are polished and he's shaved, the five o'clock mat reduced to a dark promise. Martin wonders if this is how he presents himself before the magistrates court. Probably.

'Thanks, Harry,' says Winifred. 'We'll take it from here.'

Harrold Drake looks momentarily nonplussed at being dismissed from his own conference room, but recovers quickly enough. 'Right you are. Call the girl if you need anything.' And he departs—glowering at Nick, as if the young lawyer is trespassing—closing the door behind him.

Winifred moves to take the chair at the head of the table, then thinks better of it. Instead she arranges them on either side of the table: Martin next to herself and opposite Mandy; Nick next to Mandy and opposite Winifred. Martin appreciates the pattern: it's not one team against the other.

'Here's what we know,' says Winifred, not bothering with niceties or introductory comments. 'Late yesterday morning, an unknown assailant or assailants stabbed a local man, a real estate agent named Jasper Speight, to death. The murder occurred in the hallway of a townhouse that Mandalay is renting from Speight's company. It's near here in Riverside Place. Mandy was in the upstairs bathroom at the time. She heard a commotion and went to investigate. She got downstairs in time to find Speight dying on her floor. There was no sign of the assailant or assailants—he, she or they had fled. Mandy tried to save Speight, but there was nothing she could do. He died shortly afterwards. Moments later Martin arrived and found Speight dead. Mandy was in the lounge room, going into shock. Martin called the police and emergency workers. And us.'

Winifred looks around the table. Nicks nods, Mandy nods, Martin nods.

'Here's what else I have gleaned from the police in return for our full cooperation. The murder weapon is almost certainly a knife, very sharp, possibly a filleting knife with a thin blade about twenty centimetres long. The police have requested we keep this information strictly to ourselves; they don't want it made public as yet.'

Again, she scans the table; again, the nods of concurrence.

'The townhouse comes fully furnished. The owner has already confirmed the inventory is intact; the killer must have brought the murder weapon with them. This is important. If the killer brought the knife to the scene, it suggests the stabbing may have been premeditated, not opportunistic. And if the police intend pursuing Mandy for this crime, then they would have to demonstrate where she obtained the knife and, more importantly, how she disposed of it afterwards. To date, it has not been found. They have also found some physical evidence suggesting the assailant fled out the back door of the townhouse and along the river, possibly after being disturbed by Mandy. Again, this is information the police don't want made public. They aren't saying as much, but I believe that at this stage Mandy is not the prime suspect.'

Martin looks at his partner, sees the relief on her face. He gives her a reassuring smile.

Winifred continues: 'It appears the dead man, Jasper Speight, put up a fight. He was seriously wounded, sliced open across the chest and abdomen, and received cuts to his hands. He may have been trying to flee when he was stabbed through the back. It's likely that blow killed him, although he was probably mortally wounded already.'

Winifred, pauses, letting the significance of the information rest there, like a piece of physical evidence to be examined. Martin and Mandy are staring at the table, captured again by the horror of the death scene.

It's Nick who speaks next. 'The knife—you say it was a filleting knife. Like one used by fishermen?'

'Just so,' answers Winifred. 'Ten a penny in a town like this.'

'The knife is gone, but what about other physical evidence?' asks Nick. 'Did they find fingerprints?'

'Lots of them, but they're not confident they'll be of any use. They think the killer was wearing gloves. Again, this suggests premeditation. And again, it helps absolve Mandy. If she was wearing gloves, where are they now? Alternatively, if she wiped the handle clean with a cloth, where is the cloth now? Where is the knife? Martin's testimony is critical here. He arrived so soon after Jasper Speight's death that Mandy had no time to dispose of those things.'

Martin is leaning back in his chair, feeling the tension ebbing away. 'So the police know we had nothing to do with it. We're in the clear.' He looks to Mandy, who smiles.

But there's silence from the lawyers. Winifred takes a deep breath before speaking. 'The unknown assailant is definitely the leading theory, the one they are compelled to pour resources into for now, but we shouldn't relax. There are other scenarios: that the killer is known to Mandy, or to the both of you, that you are accomplices or are protecting them for some reason. Or that there is no unknown killer; that the two of you acted in concert, Mandy luring Speight to her apartment and Martin killing him, then disposing of the gloves and the knife, fabricating the evidence of the assailant fleeing out the back, and only then calling the emergency services.'

'That's ridiculous,' says Martin, incredulous. 'The ambos were there in no time. They'll testify that Speight had only just died.'

'Yes. They have a station here in town. They've already been interviewed.'

'There's another possibility,' says Nick quietly. 'Another scenario.' All eyes are on him, but his head is down, looking at the table in front of him. 'What if the assailant didn't follow Jasper into the townhouse? What if it was the other way around? He saw the assailant entering the townhouse and followed them inside, challenged them, and he or she then attacked him.'

Martin and Winifred turn to Mandy, her eyes wide with the implication. 'Someone was coming to harm me?' she asks.

'Was your door open?' asks Winifred. 'Could someone else have gained entry before Jasper?'

Mandy shakes her head. 'No. I'm sure it was locked.'

'There were keys in the door when I arrived,' says Martin.

'Then Jasper let himself in,' says Winifred, looking directly at Mandy, emphatic in her reassurance. 'He was the target, not you.'

'I guess,' says Mandy, sounding unsure.

'He let himself in and the attacker followed him,' says Martin, the sequence of events suddenly clear to him. 'I spoke with Denise Speight this morning, Jasper's mother. She said the police believe Jasper was attacked, tried to fend off the knife, then tried to run. The killer was behind him, in the hallway, and Jasper was trying to run into the house. The position of his body confirms it.' He looks around the table, sees only agreement.

'There is one other thing.' Winifred addresses the group as a whole. 'The police already know, so should you. Mandy?'

Martin looks across at her. She's biting her lip. He's familiar with the gesture; it indicates she's unsettled about something.

'I heard the noise and started downstairs. I was cautious. Then I saw Jasper, laid out on the floor, just where you found him. But he wasn't dead, not yet. I went down, tried to help. That's how I got the blood on my hands. But there was nothing I could do. He was kind of . . .' She stops, trembles, skewered by a shard of memory. 'He was kind of . . . gurgling. Trying to breathe, to speak. There were bubbles, red bubbles. Like he was drowning. I couldn't understand him. He started to go into spasms, coughing blood. Only one word made sense: *Martin*.' She lifts her eyes, looks at him. 'I'm sorry.'

'So he was coming to see me?'

Mandy nods. 'He was holding something in his hand. I tried to take it from him, but he was gripping it tight, trying to speak. That's when he said your name.'

'I saw it too,' says Martin. 'A religious image. Christ or one of the saints. It was probably a postcard. His mother told me he had thousands of them. A collector.' He looks at Winifred. 'Did the police mention it?'

Winifred shakes her head, her face filled with concern, her voice low. 'No. Mandy?'

'Yes, they asked me about it, but I don't recall it as well as Martin.'

There's silence. The police have told Winifred about the knife, about the wounds sustained by Jasper Speight, but not about whatever it was the dead man was holding.

'How did Jasper know I was arriving yesterday?'

'I told him,' says Mandy. 'Last week. I said that you were finishing the book and would be up here on Sunday or yesterday.'

'If you only arrived in Port Silver yesterday, how did the victim know you?' asks Winifred.

'He was my friend,' says Martin. 'We grew up together. We were best mates at high school.'

'You grew up here?' asks Winifred, half a question, half a statement.

'Yes.'

Winifred turns to Mandy. 'You knew this?'

Mandy's face is troubled. 'Yes. Jasper told me. He was looking forward to having you back. He said how good it would be to have such a kick-arse journo living in the town.'

Winifred and Nick exchange a glance, but they can all feel it, the link with Martin. Winifred turns to him. 'Just to be clear: when Mandy told you she was moving to Port Silver, you didn't tell her you grew up here?'

Martin spreads his hands, a conciliatory gesture, accepting fault. 'I thought I did, yes.'

Mandy frowns, shakes her head. 'Martin said he knew Port Silver well. That's all I remember.'

The two lawyers again make eye contact, but neither pursues the matter.

Instead, Nick addresses Mandy. 'How did you come to know Jasper? And were you expecting him?'

'He was the real estate agent; he rented me the townhouse,' says Mandy. 'And I was expecting him sooner or later. He was meant to be dropping the keys to my house.'

'What house?' asks Nick.

'I've inherited a house. It's why I decided to move up here.' She's frowning again, frowning at Martin. He wonders if this is something she's told him already, when he wasn't listening, when he was obsessed with writing his book. She gives him a scornful look and continues, talking to Nick. 'I'm the beneficiary of a big estate, that's how come Winifred is my lawyer. I inherited a lot of property down in the Riverina around a town called Riversend, but also a house up here. It belonged to my paternal grandmother, Siobhan Snouch. It was her family home.'

'Your grandmother?' asks Martin.

'Yes. My father Harley's mother. She died years ago and her estate passed to her husband Eric, and now to me. Winifred and

Harrold Drake have been clearing up titles and paying back taxes and old rates and getting a survey done. I was hoping to take possession this week. So maybe Jasper was coming with the keys.'

'I don't think so,' says Martin. 'I spoke to Jasper Speight's mother, Denise. I'm sure she would have mentioned that.'

'Yes,' says Winifred. 'The survey is almost finalised, but not yet.'

There's silence as four minds struggle to process their understanding of the crime. Martin wonders about Mandy's inheritance. It's why she chose Port Silver; she owns a house here. He remembers all too well her telling him she was moving here; maybe he was too shocked to hear the reason why. He shakes his head. It's not good: for a couple anticipating a future together, they're not communicating very well. Or, rather, he's not listening very well. Then again, while he'd been pumping out his book in Surry Hills, he hadn't been communicating with anyone, apart from his editor.

'Where's the house?' he asks.

'Across the river, on the point, looking out to sea.'

'Siobhan Hartigan?' asks Nick.

'Shit a brick,' says Martin.

———

She's waiting for him, sitting in the shade of a Norfolk Island pine at a picnic table above the beach, staring at the waves, thoughts elsewhere. He's bought fish and chips for himself and sushi for her. For a moment, transfixed by the glittering waves, she's unaware of his presence. The sun is out, the day is hot, the sea gleaming. He pauses, watches her. She's like a vision made real, sun playing off her newly auburn hair. She turns, alerted somehow, smiling as he approaches; he feels the earth returning to its correct axis, the horror of the murder beginning to fade under the clarity of sunlight. She smiles as he lays out the food, gasping with joy at the sushi, telling him she's still relishing fresh fish after the years in the bush.

As they eat she points at schoolkids in a surfing class, her laughter like sea spray, as they try to stand, then tumble into the gentle sea. He points out an overweight man, shirt off, stomach and breasts like jelly, as he shuffles along the waterline with all the movements of jogging but the velocity of a slow walk. Martin says that's him in a few years' time; Mandy says it might be him now. Her eyes glint, taking pleasure in the small talk, the inconsequential exchanges of regular life. He compliments her on her hair colour; she says she didn't want people to recognise her as the woman in the papers. He says it looks wonderful; she says she did it herself. He tells her she is a wealthy woman, she can afford a hairdresser. She invites him to fuck off.

They sit in silence for a moment after that, comfortable in each other's company, while they eat. The fish and chips are hot, greasy and salty, tasting of heaven. Fish and chips; his mother's Friday night treat. Despite everything, he'd never grown tired of them. As a young boy, he'd imagined a life of wealth, luxury and leisure, far from the struggles of the Settlement: he'd live on Nobb Hill, drive a flash car and eat fish and chips morning, noon and night. He smiles to himself: maybe he'll get there yet.

A steady stream of beachgoers passes by—backpackers, tourists and retirees—their feet squeaking in the powder-fine sand, the raked neatness of the morning lost, the natural patterns restored, peaks and troughs, echoing the rippled surface of the sea. The people settle here and there, obeying an unspoken pattern, not too close to their neighbours. The young are bare-chested and loose-limbed, bikini-clad and sunscreen-sheened; the old wear broad hats and broader sunglasses, skin wrinkling like fruit drying in the sun. There are few kids, surfing lesson aside; it's a school day. The breeze is light and the early afternoon sun hot, and Martin is grateful for the shade of the tree. He wonders about the strangers aligned before them like dot points in a presentation. They look so relaxed, caught in the perfection of the day. Are their lives really that simple: food, sleep, the beach, filled with the minor decisions of everyday life? Or is that merely the smooth surface and, like Mandy and himself, they're troubled by deeper currents? Surely no one has a trouble-free life; everyone experiences their own dramas, of love and hope, of desperation and despair. Yet it's difficult to believe any of these sunbathers have endured anything to rival the travails he and Mandy have already experienced in a year only just entering its third month.

Down by the water's edge, two mothers play with their preschoolers, building a sandcastle, their chattering voices carried on the breeze between the crunch of the waves.

'Where's Liam's child care?' Martin asks.

'Out next to the high school on the road to Longton.'

'That's handy.'

'Yes. It's only been open for a few weeks. Perfect timing. The manager is a single mum. Lexie. Lives out the back. She's taken a real shine to Liam and is happy to babysit out of hours, on weekends, whatever. She's a godsend.'

'Isn't he young for child care?'

Mandy smiles. 'No, not really. He's ten months. It's good for him. Normality. Some start when they're a few weeks old.' Then she bites her lip, concern in her eyes. 'He'll be okay, won't he, Martin?'

He wipes grease from his hand. 'Of course. Why wouldn't he be?'

Her concern remains, the light leaving her face. 'I can't shake it, Jasper lying on the floor like that. Choking on his own blood, spitting and bubbling and fighting for breath. For life. I shut my eyes and I'm right there, the sounds and the smells. I open my eyes and I look out at this, this paradise.' She gestures at the beach. 'I see this and I can imagine a future here, but when I close my eyes, that's all I see, the past. It's always there, waiting for us.' She breathes, a long exhalation.

'Mandy, it only happened yesterday. Give yourself time. The police will find the killer and it will fade into the past. The future will still be here, waiting for us. Waiting for us to make it. To make it with Liam.'

She nods, as if accepting his wisdom, but her brow remains creased and her eyes sad. 'Why didn't you tell me that you grew up here?'

Martin sighs. 'I don't know. I should have. I guess I didn't want to spoil it; you were so excited.'

'Spoil it? How?'

He looks away, unable to match her gaze for a moment. He swallows. The truth; now is the time to start. He returns his gaze to her face, looks her in the eye. 'It wasn't a good childhood. My parents died. My sisters died. I was the only one left.' He tries to say it matter-of-factly, as if such things are commonplace, but he knows he fails, knows his voice betrays him, knows she detects the suppressed emotion beneath his words.

'Oh, Martin.' She reaches out, squeezes his hand, but he can no longer hold her gaze. Instead he's looking, unseeing, out at the sea, fighting to control a groundswell of emotion. Finally, he turns towards her. 'Port Silver was okay,' he reassures her. 'It really was. Before it all turned to shit. Being a kid here, it was good. I'd forgotten that.'

She doesn't respond immediately; when she does, her voice is low and sympathetic. 'Is that why you didn't come straight away? Why you stayed in Sydney to write your book?'

He shrugs, feigning nonchalance. 'Maybe. I don't know. I just thought it would be simpler to get it out of the way. Finish with Riversend, put it behind us, then start anew up here.'

She says nothing as she studies his face. He's unsure what she's thinking. He changes the subject, tilting the conversation back towards the future. 'So it's the house, Hartigan's—that's why you chose Port Silver?'

She smiles. 'Yeah, the house. I needed to get away from Riversend, away from the drought, away from the past. Make a clean break. I always wanted to live by the sea. I thought about Sydney—Bondi or Manly or Balmoral—but not with Liam, not the city. I considered somewhere like Bermagui or Tassie. And then Winifred told me I'd inherited the house up here. It sounded perfect. It *is* perfect, will be perfect. I've already had a look at the outside. You should see it: an old weatherboard up on the cliff with a view that goes forever. And I've enrolled in uni, distance edu-cation at Southern Cross. There are campuses at Lismore and Coffs Harbour; I just need to show up for a few weeks a year, the rest I can do from here. Fix up the house, raise Liam, study literature. Eat fish.' And she smiles again, a little of the previous lightness returning, dimples and mischief. 'And you. If you're up for it.'

'Of course I am,' he says, holding her hand. The demons of his youth are not her demons; his past is not their present.

But now her smile fades, swept away like a squall crossing a beach. 'You think it can be? Perfect? Jasper Speight dying in my hallway, like some sort of omen. A warning.' She fixes her eyes on Martin, her gaze intense. 'Do you believe in fate?'

Martin grins. 'We've had this conversation before.'

'Really?'

'When we first met. In the bookstore in Riversend.'

'You have a good memory.'

'It was unforgettable. You were unforgettable.'

She beams at that, dimples prominent. 'Smooth,' she says, before growing serious again. 'You've changed, Martin Scarsden.'

'I hope so.'

'What was your answer?'

'To what?'

'Fate?'

'No. We make our own.'

'What about karma?'

Martin looks down at the sand, at the sunbakers, the separate trajectories of their lives coalescing together at this precise moment, on this day, on this beach. 'Don't know. Maybe.' He knows that just a few months ago he would have ridiculed the idea. Now he doesn't elaborate. Maybe he has changed.

'If someone wanted to kill Jasper, why do it at my place?' asks Mandy.

'Mandy, it's not an omen. The house, the uni. The coast, Liam. You're right: Port Silver is perfect.'

'The past is always with us, the ghost in the room.'

Now it's his turn to frown, unsettled by her tone. 'You think?'

'I do.' Thoughts ripple across her face. 'We are barricades, bulkheads sheltering the next generation, keeping the past from hurting them. Protecting them, protecting Liam. It's all back there, the crimes of his father and his grandfather. It's the same with you, whatever happened to you here. We have to live with that, move with it, move past it. But Liam, he is born afresh, untainted. Innocent. That's why I want to be here, that's what I want from Port Silver. I want him to grow up here like any other child, free from what went before.' She turns to him. 'And I want you here as well. It's our chance, Martin.'

'And fate?'

'Fuck fate.' Again, there is a smile, but one built on defiance, not amusement.

'Fuck fate,' he echoes, holding her hand.

The sea looks so smooth, so benign. He's seen it on other days, boiling and deadly, foam from one end of the beach to the other, boats locked down in the harbour for days on end in the aftermath of northern cyclones and east coast lows. And now, to the south, on the horizon past the lighthouse and the surfers, Martin can see a front of clouds. A southerly change is on its way, carrying memories with it, isobars of regret. He's said enough; he'll tell her more, but not yet. They need to recover from the shock of Jasper Speight's murder first.

'Tell me about the house then,' she says, as if reading his thoughts. 'You and Nick Poulos seemed to know all about it.'

Martin grimaces. He knows he needs to tell her of his past here. The house is a good enough place to start.

'When we were kids, no one lived there. Siobhan Hartigan must have moved to Riversend before we were even born, so it was sitting up there on the headland, deserted. Slowly going to ruin. Maybe they used it as a holiday house, I don't know, but we always thought it was empty. Among us kids, it had a legendary status. We thought it was haunted.'

'Haunted? That's something.' She smiles. 'Did you ever go there?'

'Only the once.'

chapter six

THEY COME TO THE HOUSE BY WAY OF THE RIVER, THE THREE BOYS: MARTIN AND Jasper and Scotty. By accident. The three of them, aged twelve, on the cusp of puberty, the tectonic shift to adolescence approaching, the girls and the drinking and the delinquency, the febrile hormones, the fractured families and fragile identities. But for now they are still boys, floating, innocent of the future, adrift in Scotty's canoe. Carefree and careless on the Argyle, down past the caravan park and under the bridge. After days of storm, the sun is hot and the breeze mild, even as the tide turns, beginning to assist the river's flow to the sea instead of impeding it. They laugh and point as first the port and then the town drift by. Jasper stands, drops his pants, moons Port Silver. The canoe rocks dangerously as the boys squeal, laughing at his audacity.

Then, as the town begins to recede, it's time to turn back. But the flow of the swollen river, reinforced by the accelerating tide and the pent-up pressure of rain-fed tributaries, is against them. They paddle hard against the current, but the retreating riverbanks tell the story: they are going backwards, out towards the mouth of the river, the treacherous sandbar and the sea.

'No good,' says Scotty, already breathing heavily at the head of the canoe. 'We can't fight it.'

'It's like a rip,' says Jasper, seated in the middle. 'We need to go sideways, get to shore. Or go with it, out the mouth. Head across outside, come back into the beach.'

'Fuck that—let's get to shore,' says Martin, the mood suddenly urgent.

There is no question which shore to try for: the river is pushing them away from the town and the populated southern shore, towards the less hospitable northern bank; this far down the river the flatlands near the caravan park are gone and the bank is steep and covered in a tangle of vegetation. They turn the canoe sideways to the flow, feeling it push them seawards, feeling its pressure, understanding it could so easily flip them. 'Row!' shouts Scotty, and they row, following his lead, pushing hard with silent intent. The bow is pointing at the bank, but the current is taking them further and further sideways, so that the trees shift past, from right to left, as if the canoe is mounted on a conveyor belt. Martin fears they won't make it; the tide is accelerating as the river narrows one last time, the bank passing faster and faster. On the right bank, the town is almost spent, the breakwater beginning. He's about to call it quits, to call on his mates to turn the bow towards the sea before they hit the surf side on and capsize. And now they can see it, hear it: the sandbar, foaming white and roaring its appetite. Their eyes widen with fear and, for just a moment, they stop rowing, shirtfronted by fate. But just as they think that all hope is gone, they sweep past a small headland, a large rock, and the river widens again. The current that has held them so tightly relaxes its grip. Desperately, they recommence their rowing, pushing hard across the current, Martin and Jasper matching Scotty's rhythm. There is no talking, no shouting, just concentrated effort and aching muscles.

The waves breaking over the bar are close, just fifty metres away, clearly visible. They can hear the power in the surf's roar, feel the sea mist on their faces. The swell is high, provoked by days of storm, the rain-fed river smashing into it. The bar, dangerous on the best of days, is a foaming, roaring beast. This is their last chance. Either they make the shore or they enter the maelstrom. How has this happened so quickly? They're well past the rock now, and even as the current eases the shoreline recedes, revealing a small beach, still inside the bar but facing towards the sea. A secret beach, its promise of sanctuary tantalisingly close even as it too begins to recede. And then. And then, the current is easing its grip, releasing them as they pass completely out of the river's flow. 'Keep going!' yells Jasper above the roar of the approaching surf, but his tone has lost its desperation. For the water by the beach is calm, beyond the river's authority and protected by the bar from the angry sea, a small patch of tranquillity. The canoe is once again under their control. Their momentum alone carries them the last few metres. The bow scrapes onto the sand; Martin feels relief, tension washing out of him, joy flowing in.

They're all breathing hard, muscles distraught. They're silent for a moment, each one captive to his own thoughts. But the adrenaline is still pumping and first one then the others succumb to laughter; it breaks over them like a wave, sweeping the mood upwards. Martin lies back in the canoe, ribs hurting, hysterical and short of breath, tears running from his eyes, overcome by the euphoria of salvation.

Eventually they drag the canoe up the beach, much further than necessary, right up above the high-tide mark to the bottom of the cliff. They sink to the sand, sitting in a row, looking out across the still bay to the bar and the open sea. The surf is surging and wild, snow white and churning, growling like a thousand hungry mouths. None of them say anything, but they're all thinking the same: their flimsy craft would never have survived the passage.

'We'll need to wait for the tide to turn,' says Scotty.

'Three or four hours, at least,' says Martin.

'Longer,' says Scotty. 'The tide will still be running out for three or four hours. We'll need it coming in strong just to give us a chance against the flow of the river. It's been raining, there's heaps of water coming down.'

Jasper and Martin exchange glances. Scotty is right. But it's already five o'clock. It might be midnight before the conditions on the river are ideal. And until then they're marooned, with the river and the surf in front and, behind the beach, a precipice covered in rainforest.

Martin points to the surf, kept back from the beach by the bar and the river's flow. 'If the swell gets any bigger, the waves will be over the bar. If it's too dark, we won't see them coming.'

'Should we brave the bar?' asks Jasper. He sees the incredulity on his friends' faces. 'Just asking,' he says.

'Maybe we can wave down a fishing boat?' suggests Scotty.

'Too late for that—the fleet's in by lunchtime,' says Martin. His uncle Vern is a fisherman; he knows their routine. 'Maybe someone else will see us, coming back from a day's fishing.' They consider the ferocity of the bar; no recreational fisher would be crazy enough to brave the churn, not with the tide running against them.

'My old man is going to kill me,' says Scotty. 'It's his canoe.'

'I'm hot,' Jasper declares. 'I'm going for a swim.'

'Careful of the current,' says Scotty. 'Don't go too far.'

'Yeah. Whatever.' Jasper strips off his t-shirt, steps out of his thongs and plunges into the water. 'Come on, you soft cocks!' he yells, treading water just off the beach.

'We should build a fire,' says Scotty. 'Ration our water.' Martin smiles; his two friends can be so different sometimes.

Martin collects their bags from the canoe. Scotty has a plastic canteen half full of water and a small packet of biscuits. Jasper has half a bottle of Coke. Martin has three smokes, stolen from his father. Scotty surveys the collection. 'That won't last long. We could be getting pretty thirsty.'

'Beats drowning,' says Martin, finally able to enunciate the boys' fear.

Martin and Scotty collect firewood: driftwood from the beach and kindling from the dense bush behind it. They pile it next to a rock circle left by previous visitors, an old campfire above the tideline. Jasper finishes his swim, sunbakes on the beach for a while, then joins them. 'How you going to get it started? Got any matches?'

Martin smiles, revealing his disposable lighter.

They get the fire going, more for something to do than to stay warm. It's summer; it won't be dark for a couple more hours. They smoke the cigarettes, each of them trying not to cough, each of them trying to look tougher than they feel. Jasper tries making smoke signals, holding his shirt above the fire, but soon succumbs to coughing and boredom.

'If they're looking for us, someone might see the smoke,' says Martin.

'No one will start looking until we're not home for dinner,' says Scotty.

'Oh shit,' says Jasper. 'Look.' He's pointing south. There are thunderheads on the horizon, still distant but full of menace. 'They weren't there half an hour ago.'

'That's all we need,' says Scotty.

'What do we do?' asks Jasper.

'Build the fire up big as we can,' says Martin.

'No, find shelter,' says Scotty. 'Maybe there's an overhang some-where. Shift the fire there before it rains.'

Scotty heads towards the far end of the beach, looking for shelter under the headland, while Jasper does the same at the river end, down by the rocky outcrop. So it's Martin, searching for shelter at the edge of the rainforest, who finds the stairs cut into the rock, overgrown and splotched with moss, but unmistakable. He calls the others.

'Where do they go?' asks Jasper.

'Up to the headland proper,' says Martin. 'If we can climb them, there's tracks up there. We can walk out. Get to the road before it's dark.'

'The Hartigan house,' says Scotty. 'That's what's up there. On the headland.'

Martin and Jasper look at each other, momentarily hesitant.

'Let's go then,' says Jasper. 'Before the rain. Before it gets dark.'
Before we get trapped up there, thinks Martin.

⁓

Martin's tale is interrupted by Mandy braking sharply to avoid an elderly woman blithely crossing The Boulevarde on her motorised scooter, orange flag oscillating merrily above her. They're driving through town, heading to collect Liam from child care. Mandy has declared the townhouse bad karma and wants to pick her son up early so the three of them can search for somewhere else to stay. Martin can't say he blames her.

'We only need something for a week or two,' declares Mandy, 'and then we can move into the house.'

'Is it habitable?'

'It will be.'

Mandy gets them through the traffic, driving past the entrance to the harbour, then negotiating a couple of roundabouts. They turn onto the Longton Road and head south past a nest of fast-food outlets. The childcare centre is attached to the high school, a recent development. When Martin was at high school, it required a daily bus trip, slow and precarious, up the escarpment to Longton High; another reason why so few local students finished year twelve.

'I like your story about the old house,' says Mandy. 'I assume you got up the stairs and sheltered there from the storm. Good karma.'

'Yes,' mumbles Martin. 'Good karma.'

Their progress is slowed almost to walking pace by a tractor towing some sort of oversized farm machinery. To his right, through the intermittent palm trees, Martin can see the fibro shells of the Settlement, the baking streets of his youth, separated from the town proper by the main road and a buffer of cane fields, part of Port Silver and yet quarantined, as if poverty and bad luck are contagious. Who knows? Maybe they are. Surrounding the houses lie the fields and, on the horizon, the long green rise of the escarpment. Straight ahead, to the south, the clouds are still building, the billowing folds of an electrical storm, topped by a telltale anvil.

'Hey, Martin,' says Mandy, frowning, 'how come Nick Poulos knew about the house? I thought he was a recent arrival.'

Martin sighs. 'Well, there's a bit more to the story.'

Climbing the stairs is easier said than done. From the beach to the top of the headland, it's maybe sixty metres, straight up. When the stairs were well maintained, half a century ago, the ascent would have taken a few minutes. But now the path has fallen into disrepair. The first few metres up from the back of the beach are relatively easy, the steps carved into the sandstone. The years have covered them with moss and the boys struggle to push through branches from overhanging trees and shrubs, but the steps themselves have weathered well. Not so the path above them. The once-clear trail switching back and forth across the slope is overgrown and ill-defined. For a few metres it is deceptively easy to follow, both sides lined with rocks, but then it vanishes, consumed by the bush, only to reappear as little more than a suggestion. The friends scramble through ferns and undergrowth, losing and regaining the trail, unable to distinguish it from myriad wallaby paths. The sky is lost to them, consumed by the canopy. They have no idea how close the storm has come. Anywhere else they might grow confused, even become lost, but here the sheer fall of the land and the constant sound of the surf keep them orientated. Slowly, ever so slowly, they make progress. A few metres more, where the incline turns close to vertical, more boulders than bush, they discover the remnants of wooden stairs, with handrails and risers, bolted to the rock face. But rust has eaten at the bolts and rot at the wood, so that what remains of the structure is peeling away and threatening to collapse.

'We're on the right path, then,' says Jasper optimistically.

'Let's go around,' says Martin. 'Keep zigzagging. As long as we're going up, we'll get there. We're sure to find the trail again.'

'Righto,' says Jasper. 'Lead the way.'

'Me?' says Martin.

'Yeah. You're the one with shoes.'

Martin looks at his friends' feet. Like him, Scotty is wearing sandshoes, but Jasper has bare feet, muddy and flashed with red. He's carrying his thongs, useless in the steep and slippery terrain. 'You okay?' Martin asks.

'Sure,' says Jasper. 'Shoes are overrated.'

Martin pushes on, thrusting aside ferns, stepping over fallen logs, exploring hesitantly, unable to see the ground, extending one foot at a time before entrusting his weight to his new foothold. Once he almost falls, heart in his mouth, and is only just getting his breath when his feet do slide out from under him. Desperately he grabs at plants, claws at a tree trunk, anything to stop him plummeting. He scrapes both knees, cuts one of his hands, but comes to a halt, a termite mound arresting his fall. Tiny white ants, blind and translucent, swarm. In the silence that crowds out the sound of the surf, a roo goes crashing through the undergrowth, close but unseen. Martin wraps a hand round the exposed root of a Pandanus tree and pulls himself upright before moving back up the incline on all fours, warning his mates to take care.

Now a fresh urgency overtakes them. As they climb higher and the sound of the waves recedes, a new sound imposes itself: approaching thunder. The sun vanishes, and the bush loses its dappled clarity to an ominous shade. The air grows still, the gentle breeze dies, the day holds its breath. Martin's ears pop; he's about to say something when a lightning strike creases white across the sky, penetrating the canopy like an X-ray, followed almost immediately by a rolling peal of thunder, moving around and past them, so that they feel its resonance in their guts and the very ground seems to tremble at its power. As if shaken loose by the force of the lightning strike, large raindrops start to fall, spattering here and there noisily. The storm is almost upon them.

'Let's go,' says Martin. 'Hurry.' And he forgets about looking for stairs and seeking out the old trail; instead he heads straight up, pushing with his feet, grabbing with his hands, careless of scratches and loose footholds. Up he goes, as best he can, hearing the others following. Five metres up, then ten, a few more and he bursts out onto a better-defined path, even as the incline becomes shallower. 'This way!' he urges. 'The track! The track!' He waits as first Scotty then Jasper emerge from the bush to join him. Jasper's left foot is coated with blood. 'You okay?'

'Never better.'

And the wind hits, roaring up through the bush, swinging the trees wildly, shaking through the undergrowth. And with it comes the rain, no longer individual drops, no longer constrained by the canopy, but a sheet of water, slicing in sideways, cold and stinging and malicious. Another lightning strike, blinding in its intensity, arcs across the sky, leaving an afterglow inside Martin's eyelids, the thunder closing in immediately, booming like the voice of God. The boys no longer need to speak; they run as if the devil himself is chasing them. They burst out of the bush and there it is, the old house: Hartigan's.

Do they hesitate? Perhaps for a moment they do. And as if sensing their hesitation, the storm increases its fury. Another shrieking bolt of lightning, another bowel-shaking peal of thunder. The rain turns to hail, hurting as it comes cutting through the air, painful as it strikes thin shirts and bare arms and grazed legs. They run, hesitation banished, up to the house and onto the verandah. But the weather is coming in almost horizontally, the awning provides no shelter, the old house seeming to sway and voice its own complaint. They follow the verandah around to the leeward side, the northern side, and only there do they find shelter from the wind and rain and hail, only there do they find a place still dry, a place quiet enough for them to speak. Around them the old house is moaning, as if protesting at the storm's violence, or their presence, as the hail shrieks and hammers at its steel roof.

'This is good,' says Jasper. 'We're safe.'

'This is bad,' says Scotty. 'My mum and dad, our families, they're going to think we're out in this. They'll think we've drowned.'

'And when they find out we haven't, they'll be too relieved to worry about anything else, like the canoe or going too far down-stream, or sheltering here,' says Jasper.

They sit for a moment then, just looking out into the grey wall of the storm. Even the closest of the trees, just twenty metres away, are hard to discern through the tempest. Martin shivers; they're safe, but they're cold and soaked through.

'Jeez, I wish we hadn't smoked those durries,' says Jasper.

Martin turns to speak, but his words are halted by the sight of Jasper's foot, still oozing blood from a deep gash. 'Shit. Give us a look.'

'It's nothing,' says Jasper, his defiance undermined by an involuntary tremor. Martin takes his friend's foot, sees the blood coming through the mud between his toes. Water is teeming off the verandah's awning. 'C'mon,' says Martin, 'let's get it clean.' Jasper stands, hobbles to the edge of the verandah, holds his foot out under the flow, wincing as the water strikes his wound. Martin rubs at it, cleans away the dirt, revealing a cut, deep and jagged, sliced into the sole of the foot, still pumping blood.

'Shit,' says Martin again.

Jasper pivots, twisting his foot around so he can examine the injury. 'Seen worse.'

Scotty has joined them. 'Might need stitches.'

'You reckon?' asks Jasper.

'Maybe. But we need to put some pressure on it, hold it up, see if we can stop the bleeding.'

'Where'd you learn that?'

'Scouts.'

'Of course.'

Jasper shivers again; the storm is unrelenting. They all know where this is leading. They need to get into the house. Staying out in the storm is ridiculous. Even without Jasper's cut, they're all soaked to the skin, all freezing. And night is coming.

They try the French doors at the end of the verandah, where it wraps around the eastern end of the house, but they're locked. Martin braves the rain, circumnavigates the house, but the other doors, the two facing the access road and the forest, are also locked. He returns, dripping and colder still.

'Here,' says Scotty. He's found a broken window, a piece of plywood nailed to the frame. It's rattling in the wind; the nails are loose. 'Let's get this off.' He slips his fingers behind it, starts working it free. Moments later he pries it off, revealing a sash window, its upper pane broken. 'Bingo.' He reaches through, careful not to cut himself, and releases the catch. He and Martin place their hands under the frame, working the window loose, until they can raise the lower pane. 'Well done,' says Scotty.

Inside, it's dry and dark and somehow still, even as the house moves and groans about them. They're in a large room, a lounge, windows curving on three sides. Martin and Scotty pull at the curtains, fragile with age and heavy with dust, one drape ripping as Scotty tugs it along its rail. The light inside the room increases marginally, as does the noise of the storm. Martin tries a light switch; there's no surprise when it doesn't work.

Scotty wrestles a two-seater couch over into the light of the window. 'Here, Jasper. Sit here. Foot up.' Jasper hops over to the couch, does what he's told, lying sideways, propping his red-streaked foot up on an armrest. Martin and Scotty look at each other. The foot is still bleeding. They need bandages. Around them, the house is talking, murmurs and pops, squeals and shrieks beneath the drumming of the rain. A squall hits, and more lightning, flaring through windows, shutters and curtains, filling the room with light. They brace for the thunder, and it comes pounding through, shaking the house, rattling windows and picture frames. There are two doors, one at each end of the windowless wall, leading back into the main part of the house. Between them is a large fireplace.

Martin tries the left door, Scotty behind him. It opens into a long corridor running along the south side of the house, windows shuttered. Martin peers through the gloom, inches forward. There is one door off to the right, then another, then stairs ascending to the second floor. The passage ends at the front door. 'Let's go back,' he whispers.

Returning to the lounge, they give Jasper the thumbs-up, then try the other door. It leads into a dining room, windows on the right. But it's the dining table that demands their attention, solid wood, covered with dust, dead flies and mouse shit, plates and cutlery and empty bottles, discarded napkins and bones, the remains of a feast. At some time, weeks or months or years ago, someone has come in here and hosted a banquet, leaving the remains of their meal behind. 'Someone left in a hurry,' gulps Scotty, eyes wide.

There are two doors, both shut: one to the left, which must connect with the corridor; one straight ahead. They creep forward past the table with trepidation, making for the far door, not the one to the corridor. On one side the storm is raging, on the other side the abandoned feast. Martin shivers, telling himself it's the cold. They reach the door, but something is wrong; something is thumping in the room beyond, audible above the storm. Martin and Scotty exchange a fear-laden glance. Scotty signals silently: he wants to do rock, papers, scissors. For fuck's sake. Martin reluctantly nods. One, two, three. Martin has paper, Scotty has scissors. Martin grips the doorhandle as Scotty edges back towards the lounge.

Ever so slowly, Martin eases the door open. It leads into a kitchen. An empty kitchen. He quickly identifies the source of the thumping: a loose shutter, banging in the wind. He sighs, releasing his pent-up breath, turns back to Scotty, signalling him forward. The boys enter a generously sized room with a table and four chairs beneath a window. The benches are covered with dirty dishes and discarded food packaging.

'It's different,' says Scotty.

'What do you mean?'

'It smells.'

He's right. There's the smell of rotting food, of spoilt meat, permeating the room. Martin looks at the banging shutter; the sash window is open a couple of inches. There is air flowing into the room, but the smell endures. Water drips into a sink full of unwashed dishes and festering remains. Someone has been here far more recently than the dining-room feasters.

'Let's get out of here,' says Scotty.

'No, we can't move Jasper,' says Martin. 'Find a container and fill it with water. I'll look for bandages.'

Scotty moves reluctantly towards the sink. Martin checks a cupboard, retrieves a blue plastic jug, its bottom coated with dust and the powdery remains of moths. 'Here,' he says, and tosses the jug to Scotty, deliberately casual. Scotty panics, flails, and only just catches it. Martin smiles. He searches drawers next to the cupboard, full of placemats and kitchen implements. The third drawer down holds what he needs: dishcloths. The top one has a thin layer of dust and mould, accumulated even inside the drawer, but those underneath are clean and neatly folded. He grabs a handful, waits for Scotty to finish scrubbing out the jug and filling it. The boys nod at each other and return quickly the way they came, through the dining room and into the lounge.

Jasper is still in the chair by the French doors. He's holding his foot up, looking at it with an anguished expression. Relief sweeps his face as he sees his friends. Martin thinks there are tears in Jasper's eyes but neither he nor Scotty say anything.

'Here, let me,' says Scotty, kneeling beside Jasper. 'We did it in scouts.'

It's dry in the house and sheltered from the wind, but Martin's starting to shake with the cold. He walks to the fireplace. A wire fireguard has been cast aside. There are some dry branches, cut or broken, in a pile to one side of the hearth. If he can find some kindling, he can get a fire going. He searches the room, looking for a newspaper or magazine, finding neither. He's tossing up whether to venture further into the house again when he sees a bookshelf under the windows on the north side of the room. Books. The lower shelf has a set of *World Book* encyclopaedias and, wedged in beside them, a dozen or so comics. Martin pulls them out: the Phantom. No way is he burning them. He takes them over to where Scotty is cleaning out Jasper's wound. 'Here, check it out,' he says, handing the comics to Jasper, who takes them with a grin.

Back at the bookcase, Martin ponders which encyclopaedia to sacrifice. He selects the slimmest volume: U–V. No one will miss U–V. He returns to the fireplace and, before ripping out any pages, he starts using the book to clear a hollow in the ashes.

'Holy shit,' he says, turning to the others. 'Scotty, come here.'

'In a minute, I'm almost done. What is it?'

'The fireplace. It's still warm.'

Silence falls upon them with an ominous weight. Jasper is staring at him in disbelief; Scotty's eyes turn upwards, looking at the ceiling, the floor above.

'Good,' says Jasper, adopting an approximation of confidence. 'They can help us.'

Martin thinks of the dining room, the abandoned feast, the foul and fetid kitchen. His guts are telling him there is nothing good about it.

Scotty ties off Jasper's foot, now a bulging swaddling of tea towels, and walks over, kneels and holds his palm above the ashes, confirming Martin's discovery. 'We need to get out of here,' he whispers. All they can hear is the hostility of the storm, wailing outside.

Martin is about to suggest Scotty stay with Jasper while he runs for help, when the door from the hallway bursts open. There's a man, grey hair wild and eyes wilder, a sneer revealing yellow and broken teeth, a curse on his lips. And in his hand, upright with its blade forward, an axe.

For a moment, a microsecond that stretches forever, they're frozen there, a confrontation held motionless by its own enormity, its implicit horror. Scotty is the first to move, springing to his feet, shoving past Martin, heading towards the dining-room door. Martin glances at Jasper, who's on his feet, moving towards the French doors. 'Stop!' bellows the axe man. 'Stop!'

Martin doesn't stop, he flees, following Scotty through the dining room and into the kitchen. Scotty is madly twisting the knob on the outside door, but it's locked. 'Shit,' says Martin. He slams the door to the dining room shut, wedging a chair up under the knob like he's seen in the movies. He jerks the kitchen table over, so its leg is wedged in behind the chair. 'The window,' he says. 'Out the window!'

Scotty looks at the window, comprehending, is about to say something when the axe head comes through the door. In an instant the boys are at the window, yanking it up and open. Scotty dives through and Martin does the same, landing on the rain-sodden ground, water sheeting off the roof on top of him. He looks back through the window, sees the doorknob explode off the door to the dining room, bashed free by the axe.

'Come on!' says Scotty. 'Run!'

'What about Jasper?'

'He's got a fucking axe!'

'Stop. I won't hurt you.' It's the man, his head thrust through the window just a metre away, but his words are belied by the axe in his hand. Scotty is off, disappearing into the storm. But Martin backs away slowly, lingering. The man is too large, too old. He can't easily come through the window after them. Martin looks him in the eye, sees the madness there, full of desperation and murderous intent but also something else, something pleading, imploring Martin to understand. 'Don't go,' the man says. 'I'm not dangerous.' Martin wants to run, knows he has to run, but realises the longer he stays, the longer he keeps the maniac's attention, the better chance Jasper has of getting the French doors open and hobbling away. Unless he's already dead.

'Who are you?' Martin shouts. 'What are you doing here?'

'No one. Just sheltering. Like you.' His words struggle to be calm, reassuring, and they almost manage it. Martin hesitates. And then the man's head disappears. Almost too late, Martin realises: the other door, at the end of the corridor. The front door. He bolts, sprinting into the blinding rain. He finds himself on a driveway, a bush track. Glancing behind him, he sees the man come striding out through the front door. He takes a few paces into the rain. To Martin, he looks like he's limping. Martin realises he's safe, that the man can't possibly catch him. The man turns, still wielding his axe, and retreats inside the house. Martin starts jogging down the driveway and into the rainforest, strangely safe and hospitable despite the pelting rain and gathering gloom, yelling Scotty's name.

Mandy pulls the car over, bringing it to a stop on the shoulder, hazard lights flashing. This new storm has broken upon them just short of the high school, the rain thundering off the roof, flooding the windscreen, wipers unable to cope, the reduced visibility making it too dangerous to drive. Her eyes are wide with delight and wonder, the rain still a novelty after the years of hinterland drought, not fazed in the slightest by Martin's childhood escape. 'Fuck I love this,' she says.

Martin smiles. He knows this weather: sudden storms with pounding rain lasting a few minutes before sweeping off, while a kilometre or two away they won't catch a drop. Such a different sort of storm from the front that had assaulted the younger Martin and his friends at Hartigan's.

'What happened?' she asks. 'Jasper obviously got away.'

'No, he didn't, as it turned out. I finally caught up with Scotty. Found him crying by himself. He thought Jasper and I were both dead. By the time we got down the track onto a bigger road and then out onto Dunes Road, it was dark. We were almost at the bridge back into town when the local copper, Sergeant Mackie, found us. They were out looking for us.'

'What happened?'

'We told Mackie about the guy with the axe. He dropped us at the station, picked up a local bloke. They took guns, and headed up to Hartigan's. They found Jasper in the lounge room where we left him. But with a fire going, foot properly bandaged, eating baked beans and toast. The old man had fixed him up, then left.'

Mandy smiles with relief. 'That's a wonderful story. The man was harmless, the house saved you. Good karma.'

Martin is tempted to leave it there, let her hold on to that thought, but his eyes betray him.

'What? What is it?'

'The man. He wasn't harmless. He was a fugitive. Wanted in Victoria for murder and worse.'

Her face grows still as she considers this new portent. 'And he was living there? In my house?'

Martin knows what he needs to say. 'It *is* good karma, Mandy. Of course it is. The house did save us. No one got hurt. And at the same time, it gave up a killer who'd evaded the police for months. Mackie was no dill; he wasn't fooled by baked beans and a fire. He tracked him down, arrested him. Karma doesn't get any better than that.'

Mandy looks out at the rain, her expression unsure. 'I guess,' she says.

The cloudburst eases then stops abruptly. The sun breaks through, the horizon returns. To their right, cane fields stretch to the escarpment, glowing an almost iridescent green, ripe and harvest ready.

'Look,' says Martin. A rainbow has appeared off to their left, low in the sky but well defined against the grey wall of the passing front. Mandy raises her eyebrows, as if conceding the point. She starts the car, concentrates on driving, brow furrowed.

Martin regards the rainbow, at the sun-laden swathe of the cane fields. He doesn't tell her of the reward, twenty thousand dollars, split between the three boys, of how Scotty got a chemistry set and a tennis racquet, and Jasper got a trail bike and a bank book. And Martin got nothing. And he doesn't tell Mandy of the police station: Scotty's parents waiting there, beside themselves with worry, crying with elation at being reunited with their son, canoe forgiven and forgotten, and Denise Speight, glaring daggers at Martin, then praying quietly to herself as Mackie and his deputy set off to discover Jasper's fate. And he doesn't tell her how, when Mackie dropped him home close to midnight, his father had woken from a drunken stupor in front of the television. 'Martin? Thought you were in bed.'

chapter seven

THE HIGH SCHOOL HAS BEEN CARVED OUT OF CANE FIELDS AT THE EDGE OF TOWN, on the road to Longton. It consists of rectangular buildings on a rectangular block of land, as if sourced from Ikea and put together with an oversized allen key. Squares of primary colours try and fail to add vibrancy. A fence of black steel bars, modestly spiked, either to keep intruders out or students in, marks the boundary between school and fields. The cane matches the height of the fence and presses against it on three sides, the greenery moving in the wind as if on the march, challenging the inflexibility of the barrier and the permanence of the school. Martin wonders about snakes. The fence wouldn't keep them out. Are there still snakes lurking among the sugary stalks, or have they been exterminated, suiciding en masse, gorging on cane toads? There's no shortage of the feral amphibians revelling on the school oval after the rain, leaping about in their own ugly ballet. A few lie flattened into the asphalt of the drive, having pirouetted too far from centre stage. Mandy squashes a couple more as she drives into the school, oblivious to their fate, a local already. When Martin was a kid they hadn't reached this far south; dogs, cats and snakes had roamed in safety. There was confidence the cooler winters of New South Wales would keep them in check. Now, climate change could see them reach Sydney eventually. Toads in the harbour, carp in the Murray. What next? Crocs in the Brisbane River?

The most impressive thing about the school is its sign—DOUG ANTHONY HIGH SCHOOL it shouts from its mounting on an imposing stone wall, chaperoned by a larger steel sign declaring the school's construction was funded by the federal government. The benefits of living in a marginal seat. Martin wonders why the school was built: to meet increasing demand or simply as an electoral bribe? Maybe both.

The school is too new for shade; the drive and the fence are lined by saplings no more than a metre tall, black watering tubes extended like the demanding beaks of baby birds. The dated cars of staff and students bake in the car park, distinguished only by their insignia: P-plates and marijuana-leaf silhouettes versus *Baby on Board* and Broncos stickers. Everyone is inside, attending to the last lessons of the day. Apart from the cavorting toads and the swaying cane, there is no movement. Mandy proceeds through the car park before turning back out through the fence and off the asphalt onto a track surfaced with packed bluestone gravel, a straight line between ranks of cane. A hundred metres and the greenery bows aside, opening at the childcare centre. It's the original farmhouse, its sheltering trees tall and cool, the building low and settled into the landscape, weatherboard walls freshly painted and a new Colorbond fence ringing the property, snake and toad proof. A golf club rests beside the entry gate, a nine iron, an open invitation to parents and guests.

Mandy parks in the shade of a line of poplars. She cuts the engine, but before she gets out of the car, she takes his hand, speaking softly, bringing him back from his musings, her face serious. 'You know all about my parents. I was conceived when my father raped my mother. She's dead, he's a fugitive. It doesn't get worse than that.' She pauses. 'Look at me.'

Martin realises he's been looking straight ahead, staring unseeing at the childcare centre. He turns, sees her concern.

She continues. 'It hurts, Martin. It hurts knowing what happened to my mum, how diminished her life became. But I can't change it. If there is shame there, it's not my shame; if there is guilt there, it's not my guilt. I'm dealing with it. For me. For Liam. For us. You get that? For us.'

Martin nods. He knows what she's saying, can feel her waiting for his response. If he wants to sustain a relationship with this woman, he needs to let her in, to tell her of his own past. But first he needs to confront it himself. No, not confront it. That's not the right mindset. That makes it sound like a struggle, something he's fighting against. He needs to accept it. He draws a deep breath, breaks eye contact, stares back at the childcare centre. 'My mother and my sisters died when I was eight. A car accident. My father died when I was sixteen.'

He can sense Mandy looking at him, her eyes trying to penetrate his silence, to see what lies beneath. 'Are they buried here?'

'I guess so.'

'You don't know?'

He turns back to her. 'Yes. They're buried here. They must be.' He swallows; she waits. 'I've never visited their graves.' Mandy says nothing. 'It was too raw,' says Martin.

'You didn't go to the funerals?'

'No.'

'Is that why you didn't tell me you were from here? I told you I was coming to live in Port Silver and you glossed over it. It's still that painful?'

'Not really. I'd just blocked it out. Like you said, I put it behind me, looked to the future.'

More silence. Mandy nods, as if making up her mind. 'So you had a shitty childhood. I get it. So did I. But ignoring it is not an option. I know, I tried that. It didn't work. It will haunt you; it will damage us.'

'I know,' he says, chastened. 'You're right.'

'Good. I don't want bits of you; I want all of you. Don't blow it.'

He looks at her. Nods.

But she isn't finished. 'I can't tell you how much I was looking forward to you getting here. Moving into the house. Starting life completely afresh. The only thing I want from the past is Liam, nothing else. But if it comes looking for me, I'm ready. I'm going to stare it down. It doesn't own me, not anymore. I'm not going to let it dictate who I am, and you can't let it dictate who you are.'

'So, I'm not the past? I don't belong down there in Riversend?'

She smiles, a smile of wonder and longing. 'No, Martin. You're not from the past. You're the present. And I'm hoping you might be the future.'

She squeezes his hand and gets out of the car, leaves him watching her as she heads into the childcare centre. He marvels at her, at her strength and her resilience. She's the one police are investigating for murder; she's the one who witnessed Jasper Speight's horrific death just the day before. He's the one who should be supporting her, not the other way around. He needs to lift his game. He may no longer be the bullet-proof foreign correspondent of yesteryear, but that doesn't mean he has to be pathetic.

Martin arrives home, back from somewhere forgotten, from hanging with Jasper and Scotty, or from walking by himself, or from reading by the river. From somewhere not home. How old is he? Eleven, maybe twelve. Still a boy. It's a warm night but starting to rain; it's time to be indoors and out of the elements. With any luck, his father will still be out, boozing it up at the surf club and feeding the pokies. Or maybe Sergeant Mackie has locked him up for the night. If he is home, Martin hopes Ron Scarsden is so drunk that he's already passed out on his vinyl recliner, belt undone, singlet smeared with food and grog and drool, television blaring inanities. That's the hope: that he doesn't have to engage with the father who no longer seems interested in engaging with him. Not a violent man, not a cruel man, just absent. And perpetually drunk. So yes, maybe Martin is twelve, drifting towards adolescence.

But this evening it's worse, far worse. His father is drunk—of course he's drunk—but he's not asleep. Far from it. Martin hears it as soon as he enters: the high-pitched tittering, the porcine grunting, the slap, slap, slap of flesh on flesh. His father, at it with Hester from down the road. She's bent over the dining-room table, his father chugging away behind her like a steam engine low on coal. Slap, slap, slap. Martin stares, overwhelmed by the ugliness, wondering if luck will gift his father a coronary, pondering if this is the origin of the word 'slapper'. Slap, slap, slap. Hester looks up at him, grinning lasciviously, left tit flopping about, cheeks blurred by rouge. His father, too intent on shoving it in and out to notice him at first, then turning, gasping for air with none to spare to evict him. Martin turns, leaves. The rain is cold but it's clean. Cold and clean.

In Mandy's car outside the childcare centre, as the sun works to expunge the effects of the cloudburst, Martin shivers and he squirms, dozing in the heat. But the dam is broken, it's coming back to him. The past, like a canefield serpent, awaiting its time, awaiting its chance.

It's later the same night, Hester gone, his father comatose in bed, the lounge room to himself: the giant rear-projection television, last of the lottery spoils, beaming in pictures from Berlin. Martin sits and watches, entranced. The wall is coming down, the hated wall. Men are taking to its graffitied concrete with sledgehammers, with cold chisels, with their bare hands, and all around them people are singing and yelling, crying and laughing. Young men with bad haircuts sit straddling the wall, passing a bottle between them, offering peace signs and grinning at the camera. A wide shot: a surge of people pushing through a gap in the concrete, sweeping through this breach in history, shoving their way into Martin's consciousness. And amid the ebbing, swirling, yelling crowd stands a man, calm and unruffled, addressing the camera with clinical precision, his diction perfect, his blue shirt wrinkle-free, standing above the tumult and speaking with the gravitas of prophecy, putting it all in perspective, an island of logic in a heaving sea of emotion. 'This is, without doubt, history. History in the making,' states the foreign correspondent, and Martin knows it to be true.

——

Denise Speight's real estate agency is shut. A handwritten note taped inside the glass door tells the story: *Closed until further notice. Death in the family. Funeral arrangements—Longton Observer.* She's accepted Martin's advice after all and taken time off.

'Now what?' says Mandy, rocking Liam on her hip.

'Hotel?' replies Martin.

'Really? Can't we do better than that? I want somewhere private, with a kitchen and a bathroom and a laundry. I can't look after a baby in a hotel room. And I don't want to be out in public, with people pointing and talking.'

'The townhouse?'

'No. I told you: I'm not staying there. I can't.'

'I'll try Airbnb. And Vern. He'll know of somewhere.'

'Vern? Who's Vern?'

'My uncle.'

She looks at him, disbelieving. 'Your uncle? You have an uncle here?'

'Yeah. Mum's brother. I ran into him earlier today. By chance.'

Mandy shakes her head with annoyance. 'Right. And you were going to tell me that when, exactly?'

Martin examines his feet. 'He invited us to dinner. At his place.'

'What? When?'

'Tonight.'

'Oh, for fuck's sake, Martin. No.' Her irritation is all too evident. 'I'm a murder suspect, unless you've forgotten. Your old schoolmate bled out in front of me yesterday morning, his blood all over me. I spent half the night in a police cell. I have a ten-month-old baby to care for. I'm not going out, eating nice food and drinking wine with your relatives. I'm just not.' There's an edge to her voice, almost hysterical. Martin realises she must have had very little sleep, the long day and the pressure of police scrutiny catching up with her. Liam is quiet, staring at his mother, as if sensing her mood.

Martin knows himself to be a dick. 'Listen, take Liam and grab a coffee or have something to eat. I'll find somewhere to stay, okay? I'll call you.'

———

They meet at the townhouse, sitting at the end of its cul-de-sac, backing onto the river. Martin has booked a self-contained cabin at the caravan park on the opposite bank of the Argyle. Nothing flash, but on the phone it sounded big and private. First, Mandy needs to collect her clothes and all the equipment required to care for a twenty-first century baby. From outside, the townhouse looks nondescript, another unremarkable piece of urban architecture, all sharp angles and soft tones. Or it would, if it wasn't for the police tape strung across the gate, the sinister-looking van parked outside, and two officers in blue plastic overalls with FORENSIC SERVICES emblazoned across their backs. The police are in the process of packing up. A middle-aged technician asks Mandy and Martin to wait while he phones for approval. 'It's okay. We've finished; you can come through if you really want to,' he says. 'But why don't you come back tomorrow? The cleaners will have been through by then. It's still pretty confronting in there.'

Mandy is determined. 'No. My baby. I need his stuff.'

The man nods, then leads them around to the back of the property, through some banana trees by the river, along a path carved out by joggers and dog walkers above the retaining wall, and in via the small backyard. Small flags, yellow and numbered, trail out from the door, stuck into the lawn at regular intervals.

'Footprints?' Martin asks.

'Yeah. Possibly the assailant. Whoever it was, he was running.'

'He?'

The forensics man is about to answer, then thinks better of it. 'Sorry. You'll have to ask the investigating officers that.'

'Of course,' says Martin amiably, as he regards the flags. For the most part he can't see the footprints they're indicating, but by the sliding glass door from the house, in the soil where the grass meets concrete, there is a clear impression. Martin crouches by the flag. To his inexpert eye the mark appears as if it's been left by the sole of an ordinary shoe, the sort that might be worn by an office worker.

'Can I photograph it?' asks Martin.

'No. Better not,' says the forensics officer. 'Not with our marker there.' Then he smiles. 'But we'll be gone soon enough.'

Martin stares at the footprint. It's only partial, but it gives him hope: the more physical evidence, the sooner Mandy will be cleared.

Inside the building, patches of fine dust have spread across every surface like fungal spores: black powder on the white laminated benchtops, pink powder on the brass doorhandles. Fingerprint dust. Otherwise, the kitchen and dining room look unremarkable, the mess of everyday life. The forensics officer leads them into the lounge. Liam's playpen is there, but that's not what draws their attention: dominating the archway through to the passage, a large rust-coloured pool of caked blood lies like a challenge. It stops them, and they stare at it. It's not flat and smooth, not the way Martin would have imagined it; it must have started to congeal before they removed Jasper Speight, and there is the vague outline of the victim's body. Martin stares; Mandy gags.

Their guide leaves them and they carry cardboard boxes in from the garage. In the kitchen, Mandy loads equipment, what she needs for Liam: steamers and blenders and sterilisers, bottles and teats and plastic kitchenware. Upstairs she loads clothes, nappies, blankets. Martin helps, cautiously navigating his way clear of the blood at the bottom of the stairs. He dismantles Liam's cot and a changing table and a high chair and the playpen. He's never realised how much paraphernalia a small child requires.

The townhouse is tidier than he remembers Mandy's house in the country. Maybe she cleaned in preparation for his arrival; maybe she was yet to fully unpack and move in. The sink in the upstairs bathroom is spattered with brown liquid; for a moment he thinks it's more blood, then realises it must be from dyeing her hair. He's still fighting an uncooperative bolt in the changing table when the forensic team leader reappears. 'We're off,' he says. 'All yours. Cleaners will be through later today or in the morning.' Martin sees him out, then stalks through the apartment, photographing everything with his phone. In the yard, he takes every possible angle of the footprint, lying his car keys next to it for scale.

———

The caravan park sits on the Argyle River on the opposite bank from the town and to the west of the bridge, where the Longton Road becomes Dunes Road. But Martin figures it doesn't matter which side of the river you're on, the closer to sea level, the closer to the breadline: there are no retaining walls on the north bank. He's driving his ancient Corolla; Mandy and Liam follow in her new Subaru. He leads the way through the entrance, a rusting scaffold of triangulated metal supporting a faded sign, paint peeling: RIVERSIDE CARAVAN PARK. A plywood cut-out of a dolphin hangs from its nose, the bolt supporting its tail having broken off. Sooner or later, either the dolphin or the whole archway will come down, perhaps in the next big storm. Martin hopes they'll be long gone by then, cocooned in their new home on the cliff, Hartigan's. Through the entrance, the drive is lined by rocks and swans cut from old tyres, all painted white. And there are signs: CHILDREN AT PLAY and 10 KPH and ALL VISITORS MUST REPORT TO RECEPTION and CAMP ONLY IN ALLOCATED SITES and many, many more, a veritable forest of instructions and prohibitions. Martin wonders if there is some unwritten law: the lower the price, the higher the signage.

The driveway splits. Yet another sign indicates the fork to the right is for PERMANENT RESIDENTS, while the path to the left is for TOURISTS—SHORT STAY. Sitting between the forks like a tollbooth is a two-storey house on stilts. It appears to favour short-stay customers; it's leaning precariously in that direction. Martin pulls up next to it, beside a large red stop sign and an arrow: RECEPTION. Mandy stops behind him. The office is up some stairs, on the lower level.

A middle-aged woman is sitting outside reception smoking a pipe. She's wearing shorts and work boots, making no attempt to hide her prosthetic leg, a modern construction of gleaming metal and hi-tech composites. A blue heeler curls around her feet, blue smoke around her face. The dog raises its head, sniffs the breeze and returns to sleep, unimpressed, as Martin climbs from his car. 'Afternoon.'

'Afternoon,' says the woman.

'I rang earlier. About a cabin? Martin Scarsden,' he says, standing at the bottom of the stairs.

The woman regards the two cars, packed with luggage and equipment. 'No problem. You want to take a look first?'

'Sure. Is it by the river?'

'Not likely. Over there, behind the trees. River views, though.'

'Right,' says Martin. For some reason he's been imagining a balcony overlooking the water.

'Floods,' says the woman, sounding as if it should be obvious. 'The only things by the river are campsites and self-drive spots. Cabins and ablutions on higher ground. Permanent residents higher again. Not high enough, mind you. We're all screwed when the big one comes.'

'I see,' says Martin. 'I'm surprised the council lets you stay.'

That elicits a laugh from the woman, a throaty, tobacco-laden guffaw. 'Ha. The council needs us. It's like a retirement village, all the old coots who can't afford anything better, plus the single mums and the invalid pensioners. And over here we're out of the way. It's either here or the Settlement, but who wants to live there?' The woman glances at Mandy's car, the new Subaru. 'Don't worry. They're a good mob, they won't disturb you. But keep yer valuables locked up, just in case.'

chapter eight

VERN'S HOUSE IS A SPRAWLING AFFAIR, THE ORIGINAL WEATHERBOARD COTTAGE having thrown out extensions over the years like a tree trunk sprouting branches, an organic budding of fibro, wood and weatherboard, so that the original building is hard to distinguish, all but engulfed by the additions. The roofline is covered with oddly angled solar panels, television aerials, satellite dishes, water heaters, chimneys of brick and steel, and what looks like foliage. Emphasising the building's eccentricity, different parts of it are painted distinct hues, as if colour-coded by date of construction. It sits above a curve in the river on a five-hectare block, a rare peninsula of higher ground a few kilometres west of the bridge, out past the brick veneer and fibro rentals of the Settlement, beyond the town's hospitality workers, manual labourers and fruit pickers, the invalid pensioners, the unemployed and the single mums, and miles from the high-tide mark of interstate money, out where the tourists never venture. The sun is low in the sky as Martin eases his car along the drive, passing citrus, avocado and banana trees, pulling up between a dark green hatchback, a battered and dusty Toyota truck, a HiAce van, and a red-and-black trail bike with L-plates and panniers. To the west, the last rays of sunlight bounce from the gleaming plastic shells of greenhouses spread patchwork across the plain.

The front door is opened by a barefoot boy of about twelve wearing a bedraggled Nike t-shirt and a surly expression, his hair a bird's-nest bouffant. 'Yeah? Watcha want?' he challenges.

Before Martin can answer, Vern appears sporting a tattered apron and a broad grin. He ruffles the boy's hair affectionately. 'Come in, come in. Welcome!' Vern shakes Martin's hand with enthusiasm.

There is no entry hall; the front door opens directly into a living room. It's a small room made smaller by kids and clutter. Young children run here and there, playing some sort of hide-and-seek; one minion seizes onto Martin as a potential hiding place before deciding there is better cover to be found elsewhere. Older children, a bunch of three now joined by the tousle-haired boy, are sitting in front of a whopping great flat-screen television, ensnared by a video game. There's a swell of noise: machine guns and myriad explosions from the TV mixing with the squeals and laughter of the younger children and the sound of the Rolling Stones throbbing out from somewhere deeper in the house. Semi-sorted washing is piled on chairs, a motley collection that would do any charity stall proud, and toys lie discarded on the floor. On one wall, a new air conditioner is working hard.

It's not what Martin had been expecting; he didn't know his uncle had kids. Another little tacker of about three latches on to Martin's left leg, insisting he be swung along. 'Piggyback,' demands the boy's marginally older sister.

'Jeez, Vern. Are they all yours?'

'Nah, only half-a-dozen or so. I lose count.' He beams with pride.

A woman appears. There's nothing reticent about her; she moves straight to Martin, engulfs him in a hug. 'Welcome, Martin,' she says, before releasing him. Martin sees her smile, broad and welcoming, and the warmth in her soft brown eyes. 'I'm Josie.' Only when she steps back does he notice the suggestions of her Indigenous heritage: the broad nose and darker complexion. She's younger than Vern, maybe around the same age as Martin. She's carrying a little weight but carrying it well; she seems fit and vital, wearing the khaki shirt and shorts of a ranger. 'It's so good to meet you at last,' she says. 'I feel like I already know you. Vern is always showing me your articles.'

'Right.' Martin feels awkward, glancing at his uncle.

'Pity about the wedding, but you can't be in two places at once,' Josie continues, bending down to prise the child from his leg.

Wedding? Christ.

'Home brew?' asks Vern, holding up a longneck lacking a label. 'Or we've got some soft stuff, if the kids haven't drunk it all.'

'Home brew sounds good, thanks.'

'So you do drink nowadays?'

'Yeah, now and then.'

A fight breaks out in front of the television; two teenage boys disputing possession of the video-game controller.

Neither Vern nor Josie makes any attempt to arbitrate; Vern merely raises his eyebrows and rolls his eyes. 'C'mon. Let's get out of here.' He leads Martin down a passageway, Josie following, with the two smallest children trailing behind. The lino-lined floor is soft and giving, unpainted plasterboard walls are covered in childish scrawls, finger painting and butcher-paper art. Martin glimpses cluttered bedrooms and bunk beds through open doors. There's a smell of incense and dust and humanity. The corridor dog-legs to the right and back again and, through a recycled window, he can see why: the house has spread out and around a large macadamia tree, now dominating a small courtyard.

'Catch you in a mo,' says Josie, peeling off into a large kitchen, followed by the two infants. The room looks like a more recent addition, bright and airy, self-built but with appliances of stainless steel gleaming in the light from wide windows, skylights and a bank of LED bulbs. There's a stockpot on a stovetop, gently steaming; Martin catches the odour of soup.

Vern and Martin emerge onto an expansive deck—still under construction at its far end—extending along the back of the house. In the fading light Martin can see the decking nearest the door has seasoned to a pale grey, the wood darker out towards the new work. 'Our second eldest, Josie's girl Lucy May,' says Vern by way of explanation. 'Knocking it up between jobs.' The deck may still be incomplete, but it's already in use: there's a huge gas barbecue sheltering against the kitchen wall, lurking beneath a spotless black plastic cover, and a long table, enough to sit a dozen people comfortably. It's been cobbled together from two well-weathered predecessors, their ends sawn off at a shallow angle, the complementary sections joined together to make a larger whole. An assortment of chairs ring it, scavenged from who knows where, no two the same. Sitting by the table is an ancient esky full of ice. Vern extracts a longneck of home brew, cracks it with an opener tethered by string to the icebox. 'Here you go. See what you reckon.'

The bottle is cold in Martin's hand. He raises it to his lips, takes a tentative sip, is relieved to find the beer light and clean, not the over-hopped brew he anticipated. 'Bloody good,' he says, and the two men clink their bottles, raise them to their lips and take a simultaneous draught.

Vern leads Martin down off the deck via jury-rigged stairs to a well-used barbecue, made from cinder blocks built into a wall of river stones and concrete. A fire is already burning brightly, yet Vern busies himself building it higher, fetching wood from a nearby lean-to of corrugated iron, splitting it on a stump with effortless axe swings, and feeding it to the flames.

Martin's eyes follow the smoke up into the sky, scanning the wide dome, from the residual glow of the sunset to the darkening of its eastern edge. It's a warm night, clear and still; the sporadic wind of the day has subsided altogether, sighing to a rest, work done, relaxing into the subtropical evening. To the west, the sky is still aglow, pinks and oranges, mauves and yellows, a lingering pattern cast onto a smattering of clouds above the black solidity of the escarpment. Beneath the hills the sunset reappears, reflecting in the flat expanse of the river, a ribbon of light running towards the house, diverting around the bend below Vern's allotment before flowing on to Port Silver and the ocean. The elevated position of the house makes the sky seem even larger, the eastern horizon appearing somehow to be lower than the house. A shower of sparks crackles, floating skywards, flickering within the column of smoke.

'What a spot,' says Martin. 'How long you been here?'

'Getting close to twenty years. Just a cottage when I got it. Not so long after you left.'

'Safe from flooding?'

'Should be. River hasn't ever got this high, not in whitefella history. Doesn't mean it won't happen, but it will take something biblical.'

'At least you can get insurance then,' says Martin.

'Fucked if I know. Never checked. If we get flooded, or it burns down, I'll just rebuild it. Lucy May is an apprentice carpenter. She can do it. After she finishes the deck.'

Martin smiles. He's glad to see children haven't stripped Vern of his laidback, roll-with-the-punches attitude. When Martin was a kid, everyone else had seemed to be wound so tight: his mum and dad, his teachers, Bruce and Scotty's parents. Not Vern; he'd always been Mr Cruise. Martin wonders how much of it was genuine, how much compensation for his uncle's lack of literacy. Mostly genuine, he concludes. He raises his bottle, takes another long slug of his beer. It tastes somehow appropriate, mixing with the warm air, the smell of wood smoke, the flow of the river. Off to the north-west, up where the Argyle curves towards the escarpment, he can see the lights of the sugar mill starting to take effect, chimney puffing like a contemplative smoker, adding a residual sweetness to the air. The peace of the evening, accentuated by the seemingly distant noise of kids and rock music drifting from the house, seems to leach into him. Above him, bats are flying silently across the sky, moving out for another night in search of fruit.

'You seem happy here, Vern.'

'Oh, I am, I am. Count my blessings every day.'

'How'd you meet Josie?'

'Fishing.'

'Fishing?'

'Yeah. Not professionally, not out at sea. I went looking for a stream up on the escarpment. It was a stinker of a day, thought it might be cooler up there. Found a waterfall, forgot about fishing, went swimming instead. She found me there. Stole my clothes.' Vern's eyes shine in the flickering light of the fire, his smile broad. 'She already had Lucy May, I already had Levi. We teamed up and had four more. Plus a couple of strays we've picked up along the way. Almost got our own cricket team.'

'So what do you do for a crust, if you don't mind me asking? Your card said fishing charters.'

'That's right. The government pretty much closed the fishery down, bought out most of the licences, including my two. Ninety per cent of the coastline is marine reserve now. There're just a couple of diehards with limited licences, servicing local restaurants, and that's about it. Plus recreational fishers. I'm able to sell a bit on the side, but it's the tourists who pay the bills.'

'That's tough. You must miss it.'

'Nah, not really. It happened just at the right time. Gave me the money to pay off this place. Got us out from under; the fish stocks were collapsing and the banks were circling. I sold the big boat, kept the little one for charters and whale watching. It's good in summer and okay in spring and autumn. Levi gives me a hand; he's a good kid. In between times and in winter I do odd jobs around the place, handyman stuff, or help out the local tradies if they need an extra set of hands. Still have my carpenter's tools, the ones Lucy May hasn't knocked off. Josie's full-time. She's an Indigenous ranger, the real breadwinner. So, I do a lot with the kids. Life's pretty full. You have kids?'

'No. Yes. Kind of. My partner has a baby boy. Now I'm here, I guess I'll be getting more involved.'

'Good for you.'

'Any tips?'

'Love 'em, look after 'em, support 'em. Set 'em straight when they need it. But don't think you can change them. They're who they always were. Simple as that.'

Martin nods, wondering if Mandy could ever be so relaxed with Liam. If he could. 'Mandy sends her apologies, by the way. She wants to meet you, but she's still in shock.'

'From finding Jasper?'

'Uh-huh.'

'What about you?'

'I'm okay. I've seen it before.'

'Seen what before?'

'Death.'

Vern takes a slug of beer, considers his words. 'Reckon it must be different though, when it's a friend.'

'Maybe. I guess.'

The men pause. Vern pokes at the fire. The sky is darkening, the first stars appearing and, below them, the lights of Port Silver.

'Well, you were never much of a talker,' says Vern, breaking the silence. 'But if you need someone to confide in, if you don't want to trouble your woman, I'm always here.'

'Okay. Thanks, Vern. That's good of you.'

'Seriously. And look after her, Martin. A good woman is hard to find.'

'Is that right?'

'Sure as shit it's right. Josie practically saved my life. Well, made it, anyway. Can't imagine being without her. She even taught me to read and write a bit.'

Martin nods. He can't imagine life without words. Was this why he had been so quick to distance Vern? One of the reasons?

'I got dyslexia and a few other things happening. Makes it hard. But she helped me.'

'That's great, Vern. It can't have been easy.'

'It wasn't. Some of those analysis pieces you write, when you're on your high horse, I still can't follow them. I get Josie to read 'em out loud for me.'

'My articles?'

'Sure. It was how she taught me. Figured it would be easier if it was something I was interested in.'

Martin doesn't know what to say; he says nothing, glad the night is growing darker so his uncle can't see the emotion on his face.

'But the main thing she taught me wasn't words or numbers. The main thing was that I wasn't dumb. Until then, I thought I was stupid. Now I don't. That's some gift she gave me.'

'You were never dumb, Vern.' It's true: Martin had never thought his uncle unintelligent. But, unlike Josie, he'd never done anything to help him overcome his disability. Nor to bolster his self-esteem.

'That's why you want to look after this Mandy. If you catch a good one, don't let her get away.'

They fall back into silence, Vern busying himself with the fire, Martin looking on, thinking about Mandy, alone at the caravan park with Liam. Vern is right: he should be with her. But he can hardly walk out on his uncle now. Instead he wonders what he should do while he's here: whether or not to question his uncle or to give it a break, surrender to the seductive warmth of the evening and the hypnotic cast of the fire. It's been a long day after a restless night in the police cell. He can feel the fatigue settling upon him as the beer starts to flow out through his veins. He shakes his head, trying to clear his thoughts, regain his purpose.

His uncle drains the last of his beer. 'You ready for another?'

Martin's bottle is almost empty. 'Yeah, sure. Let me get them.'

Returning from the esky, he hands a bottle to his uncle. 'Vern, I saw Denise Speight this morning.'

'Poor woman. How's she holding up?'

'Not good, I'm afraid.'

'I'd better take her some fish, see what else we can do.'

Martin smiles at the image, Vern arriving at Denise's home with condolences and mullet. 'Denise said that Jasper was opposed to some development at Mackenzie's Swamp. A marina and a golf course.'

'That's right. But you don't think that's what got him killed, do you?'

'I don't know. Maybe. Denise reckons he was keen for me to write a story about the development proposals. She said you were working with him.'

'Loosely. Josie's people have a native title claim on the lagoon and surrounding land. We're trying to put a caveat on any development until the claim is settled.'

'A caveat? You have a lawyer then?'

'Yeah. Young hotshot in town. Greek guy.'

'Nick Poulos?'

'You know him?'

'We've met. He's a hotshot, is he?'

'If he's working pro bono he is.'

There it is again; Vern's laconic turn of phrase. 'What do you reckon your chances of stopping it are?'

Vern sucks on his beer. 'Not sure. But the marina and golf course won't go ahead unless the resort at Hummingbird Beach does. Denise tell you about that?'

'Yep.'

'Without the resort, the marina would be a white elephant. Same with the golf course.'

'So what's stopping the resort? Is there a native title claim there as well?'

'No. It's all private property on that side of the road, freehold, but as far as I know the owner isn't inclined to sell.'

'Who's the owner?'

Vern stops poking at the fire, turns to regard him. Martin feels as if his uncle is looking for something in his face, some recognition, before he answers. 'Local woman. Jennifer Hayes. Known to everyone as Jay Jay. You remember her?'

'No. Name rings a bell, though. Wasn't she a champion surfer or something?'

'That's her. Back when you were a kid. She returned to town a few years ago, inherited the land when her folks died. Another clapped-out dairy farm. She's set herself up in business, so she can pay the rates and make a living. Shacks on the beach for backpackers, surf lessons for foreigners, yoga sessions for middle-aged women.'

'And she's making enough to get by?'

'She is now, ever since she got herself a swami. You must have heard all about that.'

'A swami? Like a guru? Really?' Martin laughs. 'Why would I know about that?'

'Swami Hawananda. It was all over the news a month or so back.'

'The news? Are you serious?'

'Sure. Imported him from India. Four-five-seven visa.'

'Don't tell me: the *Longton Observer* didn't approve.'

Vern shakes his head, laughing. 'No, not the local rag. The national news. I can't believe you don't know about it. A big soapie star, Garth McGrath, left his wife and moved up here to become one of Hawananda's devotees. There were all sorts of stories about orgies and drugs and parties. The local coppers were giving them grief, even raided the place. The photographers were in boats off the beach, flying drones over it, the whole shit show.'

A memory seizes Martin: a news report on the old television in his motel room down in the Riverina, people dancing in a circle, semi-naked, like some latter-day Woodstock. That was Port Silver? 'So what happened?'

'Nothing. It was just media bullshit. Cops didn't find any drugs, just a couple of backpackers with pot. And sex isn't illegal. It was still the holidays and I was busy with charters, but Jasper and Nick helped Jay Jay out. Jasper thought it might have been some effort to discredit her, get the council to close down her business, force her to sell.'

'Really? Could that happen?'

'Not without any evidence of serious misconduct. Half the council are greenies, so she's not without support. And it's all blown over. When the cops found nothing, the media lost interest. You can only run so many pictures of a soap star with his old fella swingin' in the breeze.'

'Is the swami still there?'

'As far as I know. I reckon they could be hard to come by.'

'So Jay Jay Hayes—she's definitely not selling?'

'That's what Jasper reckoned. Said she's been having the time of her life and making enough money to get by while she's doing it.'

'And there's no urgency to contest the plans for the marina and the golf course?'

'Not that I can see.'

'Why would anyone kill Jasper, if the development isn't going ahead?'

'Fucked if I know. Probably not connected.'

Martin takes another slug of home brew, reluctant to let go of the possibility that Jasper was killed because of his opposition to the development of Mackenzie's, no matter how tenuous the theory is beginning to look. Another memory leaps into Martin's consciousness: how he had all too readily leapt to conclusions out west, got things so badly wrong that he lost his job. He needs to learn his lesson: no more going off half-cocked, no more letting his imagination carry him into dangerous waters. 'Denise thought Jasper might have something for me. Some information. Any idea what it might have been?'

'No. Not a clue.'

'Apparently he collected postcards.'

'Is that right?' says Vern, sounding nonplussed. 'You think someone killed him over a postcard?'

Martin can't help laughing. 'No. Of course not.'

A young man comes down off the deck. He's a good fifteen centimetres taller than Martin and Vern, with rippling muscles and tattooed biceps and the colouring of an Islander. He walks straight up to Martin, his voice assertive. 'So you're the great Martin Scarsden then? Heard all about you.'

'Not sure about great, but that's me.'

'I'm Levi. Your cousin.'

'Right,' says Martin, holding out his hand, trying not to wince as it's crushed by the young man's handshake. And all the while his mind is racing: Vern's children are his cousins. Of course they are; why has it required Levi to point out the obvious? Cousins. He smiles at the thought. 'It's bloody great to meet you, Levi. I never knew I had so much family.'

'Yeah, bloody Vern,' his cousin says with mocking good humour. 'Who knows how many more he's sired about the place? They reckon half the Settlement are his.'

Vern does nothing but laugh; it seems to Martin that Levi has outgrown the range of a parental reprimand.

'I'd better get back inside and lend a hand. Mum wants to know how long before you need the meat?'

'Any time,' says Vern. 'The fire is just about there.'

'Big lad,' says Martin, watching Levi spring up the stairs to the deck in two strides.

'And only seventeen. Hope like hell he's finished growing. Food bill is killing us.'

The flames are subdued, the fire burning down to coals, a glowing bed of red and black in the darkening night. Vern rakes them out evenly and is placing a grill above the embers when, right on cue, Levi and a teenage girl with an Asian face—maybe the carpenter, Lucy May—appear carrying plates of meat, fish and sausages. Martin makes himself useful, cutting up a string of sausages and spiking them with a fork while Vern cooks, filling up the grill in stages, depending on cooking times. Levi and his sister sit up on the deck, talking quietly to each other.

'Righto!' Vern yells to his kids. 'Five minutes!'

Lucy May returns inside to alert the others. Levi comes down to help out. Levi and Martin hold the platters; Vern stacks them high. Josie and Lucy May emerge from the house, accompanied by a squadron of kids who immediately start setting the table and lighting kerosene and gas lamps, citronella candles and mossie coils. Salads appear, piles of white bread, glasses, jugs of water, four-litre containers of tomato sauce, a stockpot of steaming minestrone. There is something practised about it, every child knowing their job; the apparent chaos of the front room replaced by coordination. A row of multi-coloured party lights strung along the roof flicker to life, and suddenly the night is full of sound and light, people and laughter. Martin counts ten kids, ranging from the two infants to a couple of boys aged about fifteen and Lucy May and Levi. Martin is positioned at the head of the table, the seat of honour, Josie on one side and Vern on the other. No one touches the platters of food; the children's eyes are all on Josie and Vern. For a moment Martin thinks they're waiting for someone to say grace. 'Righto,' says Vern instead. 'Leave some for Martin; he's family.' And as if a starting gun has been fired the kids bog in, but not in an ill-disciplined way: the older kids help serve the younger ones, passing platters of food to each other. Martin watches as Vern and Josie pile food onto his plate; soon he needs to call a halt, before they give him too much.

Later, after the meal is over and the kids have cleared the table and returned inside under the supervision of Lucy May and Levi, the three adults sit beneath the stars, embraced by the warmth of the air. Josie leans over the table, concentrating on rolling a joint, and soon the air is thick with the rich smell of marijuana smoke, sparking memories in Martin of teenage transgressions. There is something comforting in the smell, something familiar, the way the smoke curls in the humid air. Josie passes the joint to him and he accepts it, more from politeness than desire. His eyelids are already growing heavy, the food and the drink combining with the fatigue of the day to nudge him towards sleep. He takes a couple of cursory tokes, listening to it crackle, and passes it on to Vern.

Martin's eyes ease shut and he feels the night wrap its soporific tentacles around him. He can hear music coming from inside, blending with the sounds of the night: frogs croaking, dogs barking somewhere down amid the greenhouses, a sporadic crackle from the dying fire, a fish jumping in the river.

He comes awake with a start; Vern's hand on his shoulder. 'C'mon, soldier, let's get you home.'

Martin struggles to his feet, full awareness taking its time. Josie has gone. 'Shit, how long was I asleep?'

'Not long. A few minutes. Let's go. I'll take you back.'

'You can drive?'

'Not a car. Not with the coppers about. We'll go by river. Levi can take us.'

'Right.'

'You're welcome to stay, Martin, but I was thinking your girl might be getting worried.'

That wakes Martin up properly. Mandy. He checks his phone, sees it's only ten o'clock. It feels more like midnight. He sends her a quick text: *Leaving now. Back soon.*

Levi leads them down to the river. He has a lantern, its shape old-fashioned, its LED bulb casting a wide pool of light. The path is well worn and easy to follow. At the river there is a small inlet, a tinnie lying low on the sandy mud, tied to a casuarina tree. The tide must be out. They haul the boat into the water, Levi holding it steady while his father and Martin climb aboard. Levi wades out with the tinnie, then nimbly boards. He tilts the motor into the water, fires the engine with a couple of effortless yanks on the starter cord. The engine catches and settles into a gentle putter.

Out on the black-ink water, the moon is rising in the east, bats circle and Martin sees a fish plop, radiating concentric circles of reflected light. The glow of Port Silver comes closer, the stars glimmer from above. The Milky Way is mirrored in the surface, breaking apart as the bow waves wash out. For a long moment, Martin feels a sense of profound peace, of belonging. Perhaps Port Silver will prove to be a sanctuary after all, providing a space for him and Mandy to heal, to raise Liam, to build a life together. Vern, Josie. Cousins. Family.

At the caravan park, there is a wharf hovering in the darkness under a solitary light. A steel ladder drops into the darkness. Levi manoeuvres the tinnie in beside it with practised ease, standing to grip the ladder, holding the boat steady so Martin can clamber up the slippery rungs. Before he does, he addresses his uncle. 'I'm sorry, Vern. Sorry for not staying in touch. It's unforgiveable.'

'Don't trouble yourself. I was there, remember? I knew how much you were hurting.'

'You knew?'

'Of course.'

There is more to say, much more. But there will be plenty more time to say it. Martin climbs up the ladder out of the darkness and into the small circle of light.

WEDNESDAY

chapter nine

LIAM IS HAPPY IN HIS BOOSTER SEAT; THE SAME CAN'T BE SAID FOR THOSE IN front. Mandy is driving Martin to collect his car from Vern's. Martin's remorseful, Mandy's resentful; he wants to apologise, she turns up the radio news. He sighs. She had said he could go to dinner at his uncle's, but he now realises it was a mistake to take her words at face value. He returned to the cabin late, drunk and stinking of dope. Then found himself sleeping in a bunk bed in a lesser room. Only now, as he's getting out of the car, does she speak. 'I'm meeting Winifred in town. I'll call you if we need you.' If. And he's left standing in the driveway, watching her go. She doesn't look back. Lesson learnt.

He knocks on the door of the ramshackle house, but except for a cacophony of dogs, there's no one home. The cars have gone, the truck, the van and the hatchback; only the trail bike remains. He's about to get into his car to leave when he hears the whine of a power saw. He circumnavigates the house, past discarded trikes, a vegetable garden and a chook yard, to find Lucy May out the back, working on the deck. She's wearing headphones over a baseball cap, dark hair tied in a ponytail, safety glasses over her eyes. In her sensory cocoon, she doesn't notice him at first. Martin looks on for a long moment, bewitched by her competence, by her ease and assurance. A memory comes to him of his father, his father before the accident, working out in the back shed, those hands of his, his magical scarred and roughened hands, hands that could make or fix anything. Martin recalls something else as he watches. Something from when he was very young: how he believed his father's hands operated somehow separately from the man himself, fixing and mending, creating, repairing lawn mowers and washing machines and television aerials and making chairs and tables and chicken coops, dismantling car engines with the assurance of a heart surgeon. Ron Scarsden's hands had a life of their own. Martin looks at his own hands, soft white-collar hands. They have no independent life; they belong resolutely to him. He's happy enough with that; there was a time when they had felt foreign to him. He decides the days he longed for hands like his father's, magical hands, are long gone.

'Hello there.' It's Lucy May, becoming aware of him at last, removing her headphones and glasses. She looks very young, her unblemished face at odds with her obvious skill.

'G'day,' says Martin. 'Vern and Josie gone?'

'Yeah. Chaos over for another morning. Kids at school, parents at work.' She wipes her brow; the morning is still cool, but the physical work has drawn perspiration. 'Anything urgent?'

'No. I left my car here last night. Just came to pick it up.'

'Goodo. You got a minute? I could do with a hand.'

'Sure.'

'Thanks. It's easier with two.'

It's almost as if she's been expecting him, conjured him up with her own pair of magic hands. She has just cut two joists to length, the last two supporting cross members for the far end of the deck. He helps her lift them into place one at a time, then he holds them steady while she taps them into perfect alignment with a rubber mallet before fixing them with a couple of angled nails, deftly struck. Martin admires her, this slight young girl, the disguised power in her slim arms.

'You've had a bit of practice. Vern teach you?'

She smiles. 'Ever since I was a little kid. More like I caught it from him.'

'How old are you now?'

'Almost seventeen.'

'And an apprentice?'

'Yeah. TAFE day today. Just getting a bit done before heading up to Longton.' She checks her watch. 'I'd better get a move on. Thanks for the help.'

'No problem. Say hi to Vern and Josie for me.'

Driving back towards town, he thinks of his uncle and his wife, feeling a sense of wonder at their mixed family, how they're making it work. And clearly it does, through the pandemonium and competing needs, Vern's laconic calm and Josie's warm competence. He considers if he and Mandy will ever be able to relax into that same calm assurance, that go-with-the-flow confidence. He's not optimistic; they both seem too wired, too on edge. Or maybe that's the death of Jasper Speight, the unsolved crime, standing like an obstacle between them and their future. All the more reason for him to do what he can to help the police find the killer.

He's almost back to town when he sees the sign for Ressling Road. By the time he brakes, he's past it and needs to double back. But there it is. Ressling Road, running off through the cane fields into memory. There's another sign under it, white letters on blue: WASTE MANAGEMENT DEPOT. He takes the turn, passing another sign: NO THROUGH ROAD. The surface is a mosaic, patches of bitumen upon patches of bitumen, so that none of the original is left exposed, with new potholes demanding yet more patching. He only has to travel half a kilometre and the cane fields end. And there it is: the Settlement, four blocks, as straight and rectangular as any suburban grid, but dropped in the middle of nowhere, out of sight and out of mind, the streets not even worthy of names, just A, B and C avenues in one direction and First, Second and Third streets in the other. He reaches the first houses and stops the car, knowing without opening his door that little has changed. Here the air will be hotter, drier and dustier, removed from the town, exiled from the sea breeze. He knows it all too well, can taste it on his tongue, the acrid tang of poverty, the flies wafting in from the tip. There is a house directly in front of him, as neat as a pin, lawn mown and watered, roses in the garden, a birdbath, with an ancient Holden in the drive, the car polished to a gleam despite blotches of bog and corrosion. And next door, a house where the screen door is hanging from its hinges, a yard of bare earth and dead grass half a metre high, with an abandoned fridge and half a motorbike rusting by the porch. And on the roof, a satellite dish, and in the drive, a brand-new Jeep, dusty and mud-spattered. The inhabitants will be different from his youth, but their stories look the same. He can't see any people; there is no one on the streets, only dogs, the descendants of the mongrels and bitsers that roamed the neighbourhood when he was a kid, wandering aimlessly, noses to the ground. He knows these streets too well, could walk to his old home blindfolded, to 13 C Street. But he doesn't. He turns the car around and heads back the way he came.

By the time he gets to the main road, he's decided on a course of action: to concentrate on the here and now, to secure the future before venturing too far into the past. He wants to see Hummingbird Beach, the heart of the development plans for the north shore of the Argyle. He drives past the fast-food outlets, a petrol station and a low-slung motel, crossing the bridge above the Argyle, the river glittering in the morning light. Beyond the bridge the speed limit increases and Martin accelerates. Dunes Road carves a straight line through tea-tree scrub, the land low and flat, the verges sandy, the salt-laden wind whipping in through his open window. To his right, he can see the scrub rising from the brackish water, proper trees emerging as the slope climbs higher towards the coastal cliffs; to his left, through the veil of vegetation, he catches glimpses of water and mudflats. They may call it Crystal Lagoon, but with the tide out it still smells like Mackenzie's Swamp.

Suddenly he's crossing a smaller bridge, the one above the inlet to the swamp. He's come too far, missing the turn to Hummingbird Beach. Another hundred metres and the road begins to deteriorate rapidly from a wide and well-maintained blacktop to a winding track with a single strip of potholed and patched tarmac running along its middle. He pulls up, recalling Denise Speight's map: the road keeps going, winding through the dunes, linking remote beach access to the east and a scattering of dairy farms and cane fields to the west before petering out altogether. A road to nowhere. He edges the car around, begins to return the way he has come, but just as he's approaching the good road, an SUV comes hurtling across the bridge towards him before braking sharply, its garish markings catching his attention as it turns left: a Channel Ten news car, its windows tinted, heading through a set of open gates. A news crew. Here. Why?

Martin follows, journalistic curiosity firing. There's not a television station for hundreds of kilometres. Has Channel Ten discovered something newsworthy? He slows as he reaches the gates. The cyclone wire fence bears a large sign, the original message still visible under a thin coat of paint: MACKENZIE'S CHEESE AND PICKLES. The rest of the original sign is obscured by new lettering, official and red: PRIVATE PROPERTY—KEEP OUT and TRESPASSERS PROSECUTED, and beneath it another sign: 24-HOUR SURVEILLANCE—OMNIVU SECURITY. But the gate is open. He drives through it. One of his old editor's maxims comes to him: forgiveness is easier to obtain than permission.

He knows almost nothing about the former factory. Only that it closed down some years ago and that a local property developer called Tyson St Clair has plans for a golf clubhouse; plans opposed by Vern and Josie. And by Jasper Speight. Another memory comes, another recollection of before: the kitchen table, twins in their dual-seater high chair, his father drinking beer, in an expansive mood. His mother serving dinner. Not sausages, not stew, but meat, pinkish grey and unbelievably tender, like a revelation to his child's tongue. 'Pulled a couple of shifts at the cheese factory,' says his dad, laughing, although his mother shares none of his father's glee and none of Martin's delight.

Martin frowns, feeling put out, not by the memory itself, but by its spontaneous surfacing after so many years.

The factory drive is wide, built for milk trucks and refrigerated vans, its asphalt surface potholed and starting to fall into disrepair. It rises gradually through tall trees, circling a wooded hillock. Martin is trying to remember Denise Speight's map, to visualise his location, when he emerges from the trees and brings his car to a standstill. The factory is laid out before him at an angle, not the low-rise brick and corrugated-iron functionality he's anticipated, but something altogether grander, more poetic: a building of cement-rendered permanence and frosted windows, like a still from Studio Ghibli. It has three levels, each floor smaller than the one below, rimmed between floors by a skirting of red corrugated-iron. The top level is long and thin, completely glassed in along the sides, an extended, two-sided skylight sitting under a gabled roof of the same red roofing, rising at the same pitch as the lower skirting. The building is older than he'd imagined, 1920s, possibly older. The whitewashed render has taken on the multiple hues of neglect. And growing up the front wall and curling around the sides are vines and ivy and climbing plants, some boasting large red blooms, the rainforest reclaiming the building.

There are three loading docks facing him, their doors of painted green wood, patinaed with age, swing doors, not the roller doors of the modern era. Parked in front of the loading docks are the television SUV, a large van and a four-wheel drive. On the far side, beyond the vehicles, he can see the lagoon glinting, framed by a row of fat palm trees and a jetty. He eases the Corolla down the slope and parks by the other vehicles. He's just getting out when two people emerge from the side of the building not ten metres away, a man and a woman dressed in white boiler suits and wearing industrial dust masks. They both appear to be carrying metal detectors, like cordless vacuum cleaners except with large circular bases. They stop, surprised.

'Morning,' Martin says cheerfully. 'How's it going?'

The two people don't move.

'Saw the gate was open. Thought I might have a look about.' He's reached them now.

The man turns to the woman. 'Get Mike,' he says to her, and she goes back inside the building. The man faces Martin again. 'Just a moment,' he says, voice neutral.

'Sure,' says Martin, maintaining his lightness of tone, arms spread in a gesture of openness. He notices the man has protective covers over his shoes, like repurposed shower caps. 'What are you up to? I thought this place was mothballed.'

The man just looks at Martin, not responding. Martin is considering some other gambit when a huge man, a Maori or an Islander, emerges from the shed, followed by the woman. This man is dressed in black—black jeans, black sunglasses, a black t-shirt with a single word—SECURITY—in white. He has the same shower-cap protectors stretching over his black boots. One arm boasts a tribal collar tattoo circling a mighty bicep; he looks like he could play for the All Blacks. He walks right up to Martin, right into his personal space, stopping with his face mere centimetres above Martin's. The man is sweating and Martin can smell him, the scent of testosterone and aggression. He must be a good two metres tall. 'What . . . the fuck . . . do you want?' he asks, voice slow with menace, each word enunciated, stretched for effect. Martin takes a step back but the man simply steps forward, this time jabbing his finger ever so softly into Martin's chest. 'Who . . . the fuck . . . are you?'

Martin shrugs, hands wide, as if he has nothing to hide. 'Sorry. I just wanted to take a look. It's no big deal. I'll leave.' But his conciliatory tone has no impact.

'I'm . . . going . . . to break . . . your fucking . . . arms,' whispers the giant.

Martin feels a surge of real fear; the man is serious.

Then, out from the cheese factory, out from the recent past, steps a familiar face, a smiling face: Doug Thunkleton, television newsman. 'Martin?'

'Doug?'

'You know this arsehole?' the enforcer asks Doug, his speech no longer disjointed.

'Yeah. He's a colleague.'

'He's working with you?'

'No, not exactly. But there's no need to heavy him.'

'You sure?'

'Yes,' says Doug. 'Never, ever heavy a journo. Don't they teach you guys anything?'

The security man looks again at Martin, as if examining vermin. 'Well, I'll leave you love birds alone then.' He turns to the couple with the metal detectors. 'C'mon, you two. The camera crew are ready.' The three head into the cheese factory.

'Your director?' asks Martin.

'Yeah, thinks he's Ingmar bloody Bergman.' Doug laughs. 'No, he's just security. Chock-full of steroids. Like an unexploded bomb. Try not to get in his way.'

'Lucky you.'

'What are you doing here, Martin?'

'I saw your car. I was curious.'

'I mean in Port Silver. I thought you lost your job?'

'I did, thanks to you.'

That has Thunkleton squirming. He'd done a hatchet job on Martin down in the Riverina. He apologised later, claimed he'd been put up to it by a malevolent producer, but that didn't get Martin his job back.

'I'm not working, Doug. I've moved up here with Mandalay Blonde. Remember her?'

'How could I forget,' says Doug. 'You guys are still together?'

'We're working on it.'

'Half your luck. She's hot.'

'What brings you here, Doug?'

Thunkleton frowns. 'Sure you're not working on something?'

'No. Just editing the book on Riversend.'

'True crime,' says Thunkleton.

'Yeah. That's what the publisher calls it.'

'No, not that—this. True crime. It's why I'm here. A cold case. They want a news special, maybe a full-blown doco if I can stand it up. And a podcast. It's all the go, you know. Podcasts, cold cases, true crime. Punters love it.'

'Right,' says Martin, looking at the factory. 'I thought you were daily news?'

'I'm on probation. They weren't entirely happy with my reporting down in Riversend.' He shrugs, looks off to one side. 'I reckon if I don't come up with something before my contract ends, I might be for the high jump as well.'

Martin feels no sympathy. 'So what's the crime?'

'You really don't know?'

Martin shrugs. 'No.'

'Oh, mate. It's a cracker.' Doug has his enthusiasm back, just like that.

'You going to keep me guessing?'

Doug looks at him, perhaps calculating if Martin remains an active competitor. He must conclude that he's not. 'C'mon. Let's get out of this sun, find some shade.'

There are trees nearby, across the car park, yet Doug leads him along the side of the building. As the land slopes towards the lagoon, supporting pillars of concrete and brick reach down from the building above. In among them there are tanks, vast vats of rusting iron, the underbelly of the beautiful structure. There are sluices and boilers and pressure valves, all silent now, left to decay. Nothing moves; it is dark and silent. There are pipes leading into the water.

The building ends and he looks out across the lagoon. It's quite a sight this morning, sun shimmering on the water, the surface as blue as the sky. Two pelicans float at ease; only birdsong punctuates the silence. The shoreline is rimmed by mangroves everywhere except here, where the land plunges steeply into the water. A few saplings are establishing themselves, not yet tall enough to block the view. There's a concrete path with weed-filled cracks leading to a short jetty. It could be an eco-tourist getaway, some unspoiled idyll: the clear water, the mangroves and tea-trees, casuarinas and palms. It's easy to see why St Clair wants to get his hands on it: the perfect location for his clubhouse. Martin regards the cheese factory, tall and impressive from his low viewpoint, its windows overlooking the lagoon, more like a Belle Époque hotel than an industrial relic.

'Pretty, isn't it?' says Thunkleton. 'Don't come at sunset, though—the mossies are bloody murder.'

'Why are you showing me this, Doug?'

Doug turns towards the lake, his voice suddenly mellifluous and half an octave lower, full of portent. 'It looks like paradise now, but not so long ago, this was the location of one of the country's most baffling crimes—a crime that remains unsolved to this day.' Doug pauses for effect, unaware of Martin's astonishment, before continuing his recitation. 'Now, for the first time, Channel Ten can reveal vital new clues that may at last bring closure . . . and justice.'

'Doug, could you speak normally?'

But Doug is on a roll. 'It was here, on a balmy Friday evening in November just over five years ago, that respected local busi-nessman Amory Ashton wished his employees a good weekend, locked the doors of his award-winning factory, and came here, to this jetty, to throw in a line and savour a well-earned beer. It was the last time anyone would see him, alive or dead.' Doug turns to Martin, his voice returning to its normal conversational tone. 'We've shot a shitload of interviews. His workers saw him heading down here with his fishing gear. Then nothing. We're shooting the shit out of this place in case they demolish it.'

'How do you know he didn't just do a runner?'

Doug turns back to the lagoon, his voice toggling into broad-cast mode once again. 'The following Monday, Amory Ashton's staff arrived at work to find the buildings locked and no sign of their employer. But Ashton was always the first to arrive, always the last to leave, and his staff immediately suspected something had gone wrong. Terribly wrong.' Doug turns to Martin, voice returning to normal. 'The interviews are spot on. All of them say what a fucking martinet he was. Wouldn't trust anyone else to run the show.'

'So what makes you think there was a crime?'

Doug swivels: eyes again on the lagoon, voice again dripping gravitas. 'The alert was raised and that same day, seven kilometres north of here, Amory Ashton's late-model Mercedes was found—burnt out—on a deserted beach along Treachery Bay.' Martin marvels at how much significance the television man can load into those words. *Burnt out* and *deserted* and *Treachery*. 'There was no trace of Ashton. Not then, not since. But here on this jetty, here in this piece of paradise, the question lingers: what happened to Amory Ashton?' Doug switches back from broadcaster to human being. 'I'm thinking of calling it *Paradise Lost*. What do you think?'

Martin eyes the pipes leading from the vats into the water. A couple of cane toads are fornicating at the water's edge. 'Doug, it was a factory.'

'Yeah, right.' The newsman frowns. 'But what do you reckon? Cracker yarn, right?'

'Absolutely. So what are the vital new facts you've uncovered?'

Doug looks at him contemptuously. 'Mate. You'll have to watch the show.'

Martin laughs. 'Fair enough.'

The two men walk back the way they've come. The camera crew has emerged from the interior and is waiting for them. It's a different team from the one Doug had down in the Riverina. They must share the love around. 'You want to get this shot or not?' the cameraman asks Doug. 'It stinks like high heaven in there.'

'Sure. Right with you,' says Doug, before turning to Martin. 'Mate, I'd appreciate it if you didn't mention this to anyone for a while. Any of the colleagues.'

'Of course,' Martin agrees. 'But one question: what's with the muscle? He was about to rip my head off before you intervened.'

'Yeah, sorry about that. He's not ours. Why would we need security for a job like this? Belongs to the owner.'

'Who's the owner?'

'Local bigwig. Tightarse something-or-other.'

'Who?'

'Tyson St Clair.'

'He's the owner, is he?'

'Apparently. Lucky break. A big fan of mine, so he says. He was a mate of Ashton's. Wants to know what happened. Now all I've got to do is stand it up.'

Martin looks again at the old building. Metal detectors. What were they looking for, Ashton's fishing gear? 'You say it might be demolished?'

'Maybe. Not doing much good as it is.'

Martin shakes the television reporter's hand and wishes him luck. He knows he should hate him for what he did in the Riverina, should despise his tabloid sensibilities, but he can't but help feel sorry for him. Stuck in a decaying cheese factory, trying to resuscitate his faltering career, trying to raise the dead. So full of bravado, so completely clueless.

chapter ten

MARTIN DRIVES OUT FROM THE CHEESE FACTORY, ACROSS THE ESTUARY, AND stops, pulling off the side of the road just beyond the bridge. There is no human sound, just the wind in the trees, bird call and the distant rumbling of surf. He walks back onto the concrete span; the bridge and its road a long hard scar upon the softness of the world. He looks down to where the water is flowing, easing into the swamp as the tide comes in. The channel is shallow, sandy-bottomed, the water clear. A skate hovers effortlessly, riding the current as an eagle might a thermal. Small fish, guppies, swim in formation. This is no river, nothing like the Argyle, just a coastal inlet, flowing in and out as the swamp breathes with the tides, similar to hundreds of others scattered along the coastline at the end of every second or third beach. The flow is deep enough for a kayak or a canoe, enough for a tinnie with an outboard when the tide is high, but unnavigable for a boat with a keel. A marina would be ambitious: the channel would require constant dredging, the bridge would need to be rebuilt to allow passage for sailing boats and their masts. It would cost a lot.

Inland, the inlet sweeps away out of sight behind mangroves; the land looks low and swampy apart from the sharp rise of trees obscuring the cheese factory. The marina would need to be raised on piles, above the sand and mud. More money. The factory site would be ideal for a clubhouse, but the golf course itself would require a considerable effort to build and maintain. He recalls a story he once did, reporting on land grabs and Ponzi schemes in Indonesia: mega hotels and golf resorts for the rich, peasants evicted without compensation. He'd learnt that golf course design is first and foremost about water and drainage. But how is it possible to drain land lying at sea level? Any links built around the swamp would need massive earthworks: bulldozers and dredges, retaining walls and canals, even before considering rising sea levels. The amount of money required would be staggering. As he stands on the bridge, the landscape makes real in his mind what the maps in Denise Speight's office suggested: there is no way the marina and golf course could ever be viable without a wealthy clientele, captive and close at hand. Denise and Vern are right: developments west of the road cannot go ahead without the resort on Hummingbird Beach to feed them customers.

And yet Doug had intimated that the demolition of the cheese factory may be imminent. Had something changed, something that made the development possible?

He walks to the other side of the bridge and looks to the east, towards the sea. The land starts rising almost immediately on the south side of the inlet, climbing to a small headland a couple of hundred metres away. Hummingbird Beach itself must lie beyond the outcrop, its north-facing crescent curling towards another headland and beyond that, out past the point, the ocean. From his viewpoint, he can see the mouth of the estuary, roughly opposite the first headland, where the northern shore ends in a spit of sand, a glimpse of the surf breaking beyond it.

Back behind the Toyota's wheel, Martin finds the turn-off just a few hundred metres south of the bridge. The dirt road heads through a wall of tea-trees, climbs a few metres and then levels off. A little way further he comes to a fork in the road. The left-hand track is flanked by two signs. One proclaims in deep blue lettering: HUMMINGBIRD BEACH—CABINS—CAMPSITES—SURFING LESSONS—YOGA. On the other, smaller sign, DIVINE MEDITATION FOUNDATION is written in orange-brown lettering, accompanied by a circular symbol in the same rusty hue. Between the two roads there's an old-fashioned signpost, once white but its paint now motley and peeling, with patches of grey wood and green-grey lichen. HUMMINGBIRD BEACH says a finger of wood pointing to the left-hand track. To the right, the top finger points to RIDGE ROAD and below it others point towards SERGI, CROMWELL and HARTIGAN. Cromwell looks recent, the rest are badly faded. Hartigan. That's interesting. The road must run up through the bush and back towards town, giving access to the properties sitting up along the clifftops. He was unaware there was a second access road to Mandy's house; he makes a mental note to investigate it further. But for now Hummingbird Beach is the priority; he takes the left-hand fork. He reaches a cattle grid and his tyres vibrate as he drives over it, a relic of the old dairy farm.

The road instantly deteriorates into a poorly maintained track, cratered with potholes and puddles, winding here and there, zigzagging through low-lying trees. It climbs a ridge, the trees becoming more substantial, before dropping down the other side, erosion eating at its surface. As he nurses the car down the slope, the forest opens up and Martin catches his first glimpse of the beach through the bush, gold and turquoise flaring from its waves. *Can you see the sea?* The voice comes from nowhere, memory bubbling to the surface. *See the sea and get home free.* He clamps down on the memory. It doesn't belong here; he's never been to Hummingbird Beach.

There's a car park, fallen branches dragged into place to give it a crude boundary. He leaves the Toyota among a disparate assortment of vehicles: a well-kept campervan with a screen door, a kombi from the hippie dreamtime, a can-do four-wheel drive, a rental van adorned with cartoonish breasts and crude slogans, a new BMW convertible, its black cloth roof covered in bird shit, a small hire car with a cracked windscreen and a missing hubcap.

The bush smells clean, like it's just rained. Underfoot, the carpet of leaves is moist and slippery. A kookaburra laughs somewhere in the ridge behind him. He walks down the hill towards the allure of the beach, past a large cinder-block building, maybe the old dairy. Today it smells of soap and water, probably the shower block and laundry. There are a couple of newish cabins scattered among the trees and, towards the centre of the site, the old farmhouse, weatherboard modesty boasting a newish deck overlooking the beach, with a separate cluster of cabins on the far side of it. Below the house, between it and the ledge above the beach, a large swathe of green grass spreads the breadth of

the site, scattered with tents: camouflage green, navy blue, search-
and-rescue orange. A small mob of bush kangaroos graze off
towards the trees: nature's lawn mowers; hard dark pellets of roo
shit dot the grass: nature's fertilisers.

Closer to the beach, where the land has fully flattened out,
there is a covered shelter with tables and barbecues, open on all
sides but protected by a pitched corrugated-iron roof. A group of
twenty-somethings, three men and a woman, dressed in sarongs
and beach wear, are sitting at a table, playing cards and drinking beer. One of the young men, sporting impressive dreadlocks
and a less-convincing beard, offers a friendly wave. Martin waves
back, keeps moving. He wants to check the lay of the land before
engaging in conversation.

The grass ends where the ground falls away a couple of metres
to the beach itself. The waves seize his attention once again, curling
crystal, tumbling parabolas, refracting the sunlight in flickering
greens and translucent golds. The waves are mild and unhurried—
metronomic—the beach protected from the main ocean swell by
a headland and rock shelf at its seaward end. There is the rolling
echo of gentle thunder as a wave breaks upon the sands and then
silence until the sound repeats itself. The breaking waves accen-
tuate the silence; the silence accentuates the sound of breaking
waves: an aural yin and yang. Beyond the waves, the water flattens,
but further north, beyond the sand spit that marks the estuary's
northern bank, the waves are fierce and free, pounding the shore.
The untamed beaches of Treachery Bay, up where Amory Ashton's
car was found. They run for many kilometres, unfettered by headlands, wide and wild, raked by unpredictable currents and shifting

rips, frequented by intrepid fishermen, bushwalkers heading north
to the national park and the occasional nudist.

The sight of that pristine nature, its proximity, makes this
beach, this place, cosseted in its bushland amphitheatre, sheltered
from the open ocean, all the more magical. Hummingbird's north-
facing beach would catch the winter sun, the ridge behind it would
protect it from southerly squalls. At this latitude you could swim
all year round. Little wonder the backpackers want to stay here;
little wonder the developers want to take it from them.

There is a young couple out in a kayak, splashing awkwardly
beyond the tumbling waves, joyous at their own ineptitude, a youth
with blond curls and his dark-haired girlfriend. A middle-aged
pair lie naked on the beach reading books.

Now, in the intermittent silence between breaking waves, Martin
can hear chanting. He turns back towards the bush, searching
out the origins of the sound, and spies a group of about a dozen
people sitting in a circle above the eastern end of the beach, legs
crossed and eyes closed, chanting gently. Martin walks towards
them. A large man, bare-chested, brown-skinned and belly proud,
is leading the mantra, an elaborate henna-coloured bindi adorning
his forehead. So this is the notorious Swami Hawananda, insti-
gator of orgies. From this distance he looks harmless enough.
Yet as Martin nears the group, the man turns his head and his
eyes flicker open, looking directly at Martin as if he has sensed
his approach. Martin stops, disconcerted. The chant continues.
The guru sits totally motionless, gaze fixed on Martin. His face
is without expression, yet somehow serene. He regards Martin for
a moment longer, then closes his eyes again and turns his head,
resumes chanting. Martin feels himself dismissed, judged to be

insignificant. There was nothing threatening or reproachful in the guru's gaze, yet Martin now feels like he's trespassing. The holy man has seen straight through him, recognised his inadequacies and catalogued his flaws. Martin turns back, pausing to gather himself before edging down off the ledge and onto the beach. He walks across to the naked couple, grateful they're lying face down.

'Excuse me,' he says. 'I'm looking for Jay Jay Hayes. Any idea where I might find her?'

'Probably out surfing,' says the woman. 'Off the point. Either that or you could try the office. Or the kitchen.'

'Not with the guru?' asks Martin.

'The swami?' asks the man. 'Probably not.'

'Oh, look,' says the woman, 'there she is.'

Martin looks to where she's pointing: on the flat shelf of rocks below the eastern headland he can see a woman coming their way carrying a surfboard, her black wetsuit silhouetted against the shimmering sea.

'Thanks,' says Martin and walks towards the surfer.

She waves as she sees him approaching, but as he gets closer, she stops, standing still, staring at him as he reaches her.

'Hello,' he says.

'Who are you?' she asks, voice uncertain.

'My name's Martin Scarsden.'

'Scarsden?' she says, doubt in her voice. 'The journalist?' The sun is bouncing from the curling waves behind her; it's hard to read her expression against the glare.

He remembers what Vern told him the previous night, about the media descending on the beach, filling the airwaves with sensation and the tabloids with prurience. 'I'm not here as a reporter,' he states quickly. 'I don't care about your ceremonies. Or whatever they are. Or your celebrity guests. Or your swami.'

This doesn't appear to placate her. 'What then? Why are you here?'

'I just want to ask you some questions.'

Martin can't be sure, but she looks disconcerted, shifting weight from one leg and then back again. 'What about?'

'About plans to develop this place.'

She shakes her head, as if confused. 'Plans? What plans?'

Now Martin feels confused. Surely she knows about the development proposal. How could she not? 'I was told that you'd been approached by a big corporation wanting to buy you out and develop a high-end resort.'

Jay Jay Hayes stares at him, blinks, and blinks again. Then her shoulders relax and she smiles. 'Oh yes. That. Of course. No problem. Give me fifteen minutes. I'll have a shower, meet you at the office.' He watches her as she passes him, progressing along the beach towards the naked couple, board under one arm. She must be at least ten years older than him—she was a champion surfer when he was still a kid—but she still moves with the nonchalant grace of a practised athlete; clad in its wetsuit, her body could belong to a woman half her age.

The office is easy enough to find, fronting onto the deck in the old farmhouse. The door is locked, so he waits outside. He checks his phone, but there's no reception; the beach is isolated from the world, beyond the digital province of Port Silver.

A king parrot—breast scarlet, wings green—lands on the railing, joined almost immediately by his less florid mate. They edge sideways along the railing, cocking their heads one way then the other, tame and looking for food. He photographs them with his phone, capturing the intricacies of their feathers. They exchange a few musical chirps; he feels as if he can almost discern the meaning. Then they fly off, in search of more likely benefactors.

Martin steps off the deck, looking up the hill away from the beach, towards the car park. The land behind rises steadily. It takes little imagination to see the topography through the eyes of a property developer. The natural rise of the land is perfectly suited to low-rise buildings in tiers up the hill, all overlooking the beach, all with the magical view up the coast, all protected from flood by the elevation. The amphitheatre is private and secluded, a hippie haven ripe for exploitation. He can see the development clearly, but for the life of him he can't see the connection to Jasper Speight's death. Perhaps the land is worth killing for, but what did his old friend know, what had he learnt, that could have incited murder? Martin stares out across the perfect scenery and sees no answers.

He hears the door behind him open, causing a small bell to ring. Jay Jay Hayes is waiting for him when he enters, seated behind a desk. Her sandy hair, thick, blonde and streaked with grey, is wet and swept back above her tanned forehead. There is age creeping into this face, in its sun-etched crevices and the folding skin of her neck, yet her eyes are blue and crystalline as if a little of the sea has seeped into them. She's wearing a singlet, her bare shoulders sculpted by years of paddling out through the surf. The shower seems to have washed away her concerns; there is none of the initial tension he sensed on the beach. 'Martin, it's nice to meet you.' She stands, reaches across the desk, smiles warmly, shakes his hand. 'Take a seat. You're most welcome here.'

Martin sits.

'So how can I help you?' she asks.

'I'm trying to help a friend of mine, Mandalay Blonde.'

'The woman in the papers, right? From your stories out west.'

'That's right.'

'I've met her. She seems nice.' And she smiles, eyes teasing. 'And she's your *friend*, is she?'

Martin, embarrassed by his poor choice of words, finds himself smiling shyly. 'She's my partner. I want to do whatever I can to help her.'

'Jasper Speight,' says Jay Jay, her voice even.

'Yes. He was killed in her townhouse. The police are obliged to consider her a suspect.'

'And you don't?'

'No, I don't.'

Jay Jay is no longer smiling; her mention of Jasper has brought a frown to her face. 'Poor Jasper. I liked him.'

'You knew him well?'

'Well enough. He spent quite a bit of time out here.'

'I was told he approached you about selling your land.'

'He did. And if I ever was interested in selling, I would have sold through Jasper.'

'Why?'

She gestures with one hand, as if explaining the obvious. 'He was a good guy. A bit troubled, but decent enough.' Now she takes a deep breath, comes to some sort of decision. 'About a year ago he tipped me off that the council was coming after me. He warned me to get the septic tanks in order, to check the quality of the drinking water, the cleanliness in the communal kitchen. Sure enough, a week or two later the health inspectors came through, including a bloke up from Sydney. In all likelihood, they would have closed me down if Jasper hadn't warned me. A few months later, he told me the council wanted to up my rates. The advance warning gave me time to get the Green councillors on side, find out what the caravan park was paying and the backpacker hostel in town.'

'And now?'

'I have to pay more, but not nearly as much as they'd been planning to slug me. Less than the caravan park, more than the backpackers.'

'More? But that place is smack in the middle of Port Silver, right on Town Beach.'

'Yeah, but it's owned by Tyson St Clair, and he has clout on council. The council reckons the hostel's footprint is much smaller, just one building. The caravan park and this place here have a lot more land.'

Martin considers what she has told him. 'Would it be fair to say that without Jasper's help you'd be struggling to hang on to the place?'

She shrugs. 'That's a hard one. At the very least, he saved me money and hassle. Gave me some breathing space.'

'And Swami Hawananda? All the stories about drug use? Why hasn't that shut you down?'

Jay Jay looks irritated. 'Because it's bullshit. When the police raided us, they found nothing.'

'You think they were put up to it?'

'I don't know. With all the media sensationalism, maybe they felt compelled to act.'

'Health inspectors, a rates hike, a police raid. Sounds like an orchestrated attempt at intimidation.'

Jay Jay smiles. 'And yet, here I am.'

'So why keep on the swami? Are you a follower?'

She laughs at the suggestion. 'I wouldn't say that. But he's a good money spinner. He has his side of the site, what happens there is on his head—but like I said, the police have found nothing.'

'What do you mean his side of the site? I didn't see any divisions.'

'No. Everyone shares the kitchen, the showers, the beach. But this house is like a boundary. The cabins on the east side are reserved for him and his followers. He takes in twelve at a time for a fortnight's retreat.'

'How much does he charge?'

'Five hundred bucks each, something like that. They pay me for the site, they pay him for his course.' She smiles. 'He's harmless enough. A little eccentric but he's kind and humble. I'm fond of him. People come here and meditate, eat vegan food and cleanse themselves. Stay for a fortnight, have a party at the end, leave happy. It helps pay the bills. It's a win-win.'

'So there are no drug parties and orgies?'

She sighs. 'His whole program is all about meditation and reflection and cleansing. It's quite ascetic, almost spartan. But on the last night, there's a ceremony, a celebration, to mark the end of the program and re-entering the world. There'll be one this Friday. He makes up this ceremonial drink—a potion, if you like—and doles it out in a gold cup from an old wooden bowl. I don't know exactly what's in it, but as far as I know it's just alcohol, fruit juices and spices.'

'No ecstasy?' asks Martin.

'Not from him,' she says earnestly. 'People drink, smoke dope, no doubt some take other things. There's often naked dancing. It's great fodder for the papers, but not illegal.'

And good publicity, thinks Martin, but he keeps the observation to himself. 'And what about Jasper? You said he was here a lot; did he do the course?'

Jay Jay laughs. 'He did. Not sure how cleansed he got, but he seemed to enjoy it.' The smile on her face eases. 'Don't be too cynical, Martin. I think he was looking for something, and what the swami offers seemed to help.'

'Was he religious?'

'Jasper? Not that I was aware of. Not in any formal way.'

'When he died, he was holding a postcard. Of Christ or a saint. Did he ever mention anything like that?'

Jay Jay frowns. 'No. Not at all.'

Martin is unsure where the conversation is heading, so he returns to the factual. 'Did Jasper do anything else to help you?'

'Yeah, he did. He said if I wanted to reduce my rates, get them much lower, I could place a conservation covenant on part of my land.'

'A conservation covenant? What's that?'

'It's a state government program. You place a legal covenant on part of your land, preserving it as a nature reserve in perpetuity. Even if you sell, the covenant holds, binding the new owner. In return, you don't pay rates on that part of the land.'

'That could stop this proposed development in one go.'

But Jay Jay shakes her head. 'Can't see why it would. The part they want to develop is the land surrounding the beach here. I'm not planning to place a covenant on any of that. But if it reduces my costs, it makes it easier for me to stay on the place.'

'I see. And the other land, the part slated for the reserve, is that valuable in any other way?'

'No, not really. The trees are worth something, of course, but logging is banned in this shire nowadays. So no. There's some land up along the clifftop that would be valuable, but I'd keep it out of any covenant.'

'And you're not considering selling?'

'No. I'm not.'

Martin considers this. If Hummingbird Beach isn't in play, then the marina and golf course aren't either. And yet Doug Thunkleton seemed to think the demolition of the cheese factory might happen anytime. 'Did a man named Tyson St Clair ever approach you about selling?'

'Sure. He and Jasper were representing the French company that wants to build one of their Longitudes chain of exclusive resorts. St Clair's the one who wants to develop the swamp.'

Tyson St Clair. Denise had mentioned his plans for the marina and golf course, but she'd given the impression it was only Jasper representing the French. Doug Thunkleton said St Clair already owned the cheese factory. 'There's something I don't understand. If Jasper wanted you to sell, why did he warn you of rate increases and health inspectors, the very things that might have pushed you towards a sale?'

Jay Jay shrugs. 'He was a nice guy. Maybe he had different priorities.'

Maybe, thinks Martin, recalling what she had said a few moments before: that if she sold, it would be through Jasper. He had helped her all right, but was it genuine, or was it simply a strategy to curry favour? 'So was he competing with Tyson St Clair for the sale, or were they on the same team?'

Another shrug. 'I wouldn't know. I told them both I was staying put. So it's kind of academic.'

'What can you tell me about Tyson St Clair? He's a local developer, right?'

'The biggest. I thought you might remember him.'

'No. Why would I?'

'He was a friend of your dad's.'

'He was?' Martin can't recall ever hearing the name. 'Did you know my dad?'

'Everyone knew your dad,' she says flatly.

He's not sure how to respond to that. Instead he asks where he might find St Clair.

'Nobb Hill. Drive up towards the lighthouse. His is the only house on the ocean side of the road. I hear he prefers to work from home.'

He's thinking of what else he needs to ask when a couple of backpackers enter. The young woman is wearing a flimsy white sarong made from loosely woven cheesecloth, leaving little to the imagination, while her boyfriend's attire requires no imagination at all; he is completely naked except for a pair of sandals. Jay Jay looks him in the eye, unimpressed by his swaggering manhood.

'Could you wait a moment, please?' she says.

'No. Sorry. We locked our room. Keys inside.' His accent is from Central Europe.

'Okay. I'll be there in a moment.'

'The gas cooker. It is on. Inside this cabin.'

'Right,' says Jay Jay, sighing with exasperation. 'I'll be right back,' she says to Martin. She takes some keys and leads the couple out. In her absence, Martin looks about the room. The desk, some ancient filing cabinets, a bookcase full of dog-eared paperbacks, a rack of tourist pamphlets. To one side are shelves of food: cans of tomatoes, packets of pasta, cartons of long-life milk. Blocks of chocolate. There's a fridge. Martin opens it: milk and beer, cheese and margarine. Martin wonders if Jay Jay has a liquor licence; he suspects not. On the wall, there's a map of the district, some ancient surf posters, a scroll with the Desiderata printed against the backdrop of the ocean at sunset. *Go placidly amid the noise and the haste, and remember what peace there may be in silence* . . .

Martin cringes and moves on. There are some framed photos, taken around the site, including one of a surfer cutting back into a wave with poise and power. Martin looks more closely. It's a woman: Jay Jay Hayes. Martin looks again at the old posters; surely the bikini-clad woman exploding out of a curling tube, blonde hair streaming, is also Jay Jay: the champion in her prime.

He's moving towards the poster when he sees a cardboard box on the floor behind the desk. It contains large envelopes. They're mostly white, professionally branded, too big for a filing cabinet. He crouches, takes a closer look. Scans: X-rays, MRI, PET, ultrasounds. More than a dozen of them, all addressed to Jennifer J. Hayes.

The door bangs. 'You right there?' It's Jay Jay, back from helping the Europeans.

'Sorry,' says Martin. 'I was just looking around.'

'So I see.' Jay Jay appears seriously irritated. 'I think you should leave.'

'Look, I'm sorry,' says Martin, but he's halted by Jay Jay.

She's smiling, even though her voice isn't. 'Just go, Martin. No harm done. But go.'

———

Martin is driving back into town, accelerating along the straight road, pondering property developers and hippie havens, when he sees it: the cross off beyond the verge. He checks his mirrors: there is no traffic, the road is empty, man-made symmetry imposed on nature. He negotiates a three-point turn, drives back, manages a U-turn and pulls over. The cross is made of wood, painted white, in need of a new coat, sitting slightly askew below the level of the road. Martin looks about him; this is where it happened. Such an unremarkable place, nothing special to it. Beyond the cross, the land dips down and the still water of the lagoon begins. There: that must be where the car entered the water. He'd always imagined it had happened on the other side of the road, the western side, where most of the water lies. He hadn't realised the road sat on a kind of causeway, that the water was on both sides. Beyond the fatal site, across the water to the south-east, the land rises towards the cliffs, mangroves giving way to tea-trees and casuarinas and then to gums and palms and the myriad expressions of the rainforest. In the distance, the white lighthouse of Port Silver shines in the morning light. He's alone, just him, the wind and the cross. There is a plaque attached to a rock at its base. *In loving memory—Hilary, Enid and Amber.* The words freeze him; in the heat of late morning, he's motionless. His mother, his sisters. There is a posy of plastic flowers, recently placed, their colours yet to be bled by the sun. Vern. Vern must have built the cross, left the flowers. Martin considers the date. The anniversary of the accident was only a few weeks ago. Thirty-three years and a handful of weeks. How could he have forgotten it? Had he ever remembered it? Was it just something else he had blocked out, refused to remember? Was it always that painful? He doesn't remember it like that, doesn't remember it weighing upon him. He'd played with Scotty and Jasper, had fun, grown into a teenager even as his father deteriorated. Had it really been too painful to honour the dead? He had just turned eight when his mother and sisters died; he didn't leave Port Silver for another ten years. And yet he's never been here before, never in all that time, and never in the decades since. Had it been that easy, had he been that ruthless: shutting it out, compartmentalising his mind? And his heart?

He finds himself down on one knee, reaching out, touching the plaque, trying to connect. With what? His dead mother, his barely remembered sisters? Himself? A memory comes to him. He and Vern waiting in the empty house, happiness and anticipation seeping away, replaced by concern and a growing sense of dread, the fish and chips grown cold and soggy, the condensation on the champagne evaporating in the summer air, the expensive French bottle as unmoving as the Port Silver lighthouse. Martin remembers now: he had offered up a prayer to that bottle, the Veuve Clicquot, with its orange label and its promise of a new life, that talisman of hope with its foreign words and liquid joy. He had prayed that all was okay, that the car had broken down, that one of the twins was car sick and vomiting, that the celebrations would soon begin. But the champagne god had brought no joy, no deliverance. The phone had rung, Vern had answered, his voice low and sombre, and the rift in Martin's life was made real forever.

A van drives past, the one from Hummingbird Beach with its crude montage of tits and misogyny, shattering his contemplation and bringing him back to the present. He looks about as if seeing the scene with new eyes. What was his mother doing out here in the swamplands, so far from town, on a road leading nowhere? In the distance all he can see is the lighthouse.

chapter eleven

THE LIGHTHOUSE DRAWS HIM TO IT: ALONG DUNES ROAD THROUGH THE MANGROVES, across the bridge over the Argyle, past the port and along The Boulevard, through the town and up the slope of Nobb Hill, past the trophy homes towards the shining white tower itself. And as Martin ascends the hill, the affluence rising with him, the lighthouse is whispering. It's whispering money, that it's all connected to money and land, the alluring mixture that captivates every coastal town on Australia's east coast, from Sydney's harbourside to Port Silver's Nobb Hill, from Byron Bay to Noosa, from Bermagui to Port Douglas. It whispers the allure of paradise framed by triple-glazed windows and tempered by reverse-cycle air-conditioning, where tropical humidity is tamed by chlorinated plunge pools. Money and land and greed, it whispers, the silver in Port Silver. And it whispers death. Jasper's death, the death of a real estate man, a trader in land and money and aspiration.

That's what killed him, it whispers: somehow, by the hand of someone, he was killed because of it. Silver. If only Martin can discover the vein, follow it to its source.

A walled compound appears to Martin's left, disrupting his thoughts, disrupting the view out to sea. This must be Tyson St Clair's house, but stopping is prohibited on the coiling road. Martin passes the enclosure, parking instead at the foot of the now silent lighthouse. A squall hits from nowhere, five minutes of peppering rain, the Corolla rocked by staccato wind gusts. And then the shower passes and the sun returns. From this height the sea is a moving two-tone quilt of sun and shade, blue on bluer, as the wind skittles clouds northwards. He walks back down the slope, towards the town. There are houses to his left: architecturally designed, built to impress. To the right the land falls away, revealing the expanse of the sea, the expanding horizon, until he reaches Tyson St Clair's walled compound. The residence is hidden from view, the only house not flaunting itself, the only house confident enough to seclude itself. There's a two-metre wall and a profusion of trees, only the roofline and a single turret visible from the street.

He walks towards it. Some Italian tourists are taking selfies, boisterous and laughing. Beyond them, Martin sees someone exit the compound, a young woman. It looks like the hitchhiker, Topaz, something in the swing of her hips, the swish of her hair, but she doesn't see him as she turns down the hill towards The Boulevarde. He's sure it is her. But before he can follow the Italians have him, demanding he photograph them, the lighthouse again bathed in sunlight and glowing white behind them as they laugh and talk. By the time they let him go, in a flurry of *grazie* and *ciao*, Topaz is nowhere to be seen.

There is a gate in the wall and an intercom: a button, a speaker, a camera lens. Martin pushes the button once.

'Yes?' comes the disembodied voice of a man.

Martin looks directly into the camera. 'Hello. My name is Martin Scarsden. I was hoping to talk to Tyson St Clair.'

There is no response. Martin is about to repeat himself when he hears the click of the gate lock disengaging. 'Come in,' the voice says.

Through the gate there is a short path, then, as the ground falls down and away, a steel bridge, suspended by taut cables, extending to the house, the building perched somehow on the very side of the hill. There are ferns, shrubs, trees, vines. Red flowers, purple. Parrots. It's cool and damp in this hollow between hill and house, a softer, more muted world than the glare and concrete beyond the wall. Martin gets to the door. The same voice greets him through another intercom. 'Come in, Martin. I will be right with you.' Another click. Martin pushes the heavy door and it eases open.

Inside, the entrance hall is quiet, seemingly deserted, lined in exotic woods. It's dark, with a lone spotlight picking out a Brett Whiteley painting. Martin stops, unable to resist. He's never seen a million-dollar painting hanging like this, up close and unpro-tected. It's beautiful, black lines flowing with assurance, the radiant blue of the harbour, the arch of the bridge, the sinuous curves of a nude. He hears an echo of the whisper: this is the beauty that silver can buy. He walks through the foyer, drawn to the light, into a large living area. Through open doors he can see the deck and, beyond it, nothing but sky. He is considering venturing further, out into the blue, when a voice interrupts.

'Martin, sorry. I wasn't expecting visitors.'

Before him is a small and wiry man dressed in board shorts and a Hawaiian shirt, his feet bare. The clothes are casual but look brand-new, as if they're straight off the rack, and somehow expensive. The man himself looks to be in his mid-sixties, tanned, fit and exuding energy, remaining hair trimmed close and brushed forward, like a Roman emperor's. He advances, flashing a smile, teeth radiant, extending his hand. 'Tyson St Clair.'

Martin shakes hands; St Clair's grip is like a nutcracker. 'Martin Scarsden.'

'Yes. The famous journalist. Back in Port Silver. What can I do for you?' The man is at ease; this is his domain and he is its king.

'Jasper Speight. You heard what happened?'

A shrug. 'Who hasn't?'

'I'm trying to find out what led to his death.'

St Clair stops smiling, stops moving. 'I see. And you think I can help?'

'I'm not sure. Can I ask you some questions?'

St Clair examines Martin, as if assessing him, before relaxing into a smile. 'Of course, if you think it might be of use. You want something to drink? A beer? Something stronger? Something weaker?'

Martin frowns. His rumbling stomach tells him it's past lunchtime; he'd prefer food to drink. 'Are you having something?'

'Me? No. Don't drink before sunset, rarely after it. Too much to do.' He smiles again and Martin sees something unnatural in this smile, the lips curling as if snarling, canines exposed. Martin wonders if he's had some sort of surgery, something to tighten his skin.

'Just some water then, thanks,' says Martin.

'No problem. Come on.' St Clair walks off through a doorway into a designer kitchen. Martin is impressed: not by its massive size, or by the marble benchtops, the stainless-steel appliances and the glowing copper range hoods; it's the view down across the town that takes his breath away.

'You have an amazing house,' observes Martin.

'Not bad, is it?' says St Clair, grinning his snarly pleasure. He extracts a large bottle of Italian mineral water from a huge fridge that contains nothing but bottles and hands one to Martin before cracking his own screwcap open and taking a slug. 'Cheers,' he says, raising his bottle and taking another swig.

Martin opens his own bottle and drinks. It's cold, frugally carbonated and almost sweet on his tongue.

'Get it from an importer in Brisbane,' says St Clair.

'It's very nice.' Martin pretends to examine the label.

'So, Martin—Jasper Speight. How can I help?'

'He was murdered.'

'So I understand. In the townhouse of your beautiful girlfriend Mandalay Blonde, right?'

'You've met her?'

'Not as yet. But I hear she's quite something.' And St Clair smiles his predator's grin. Martin wonders if he only smiles when he's pleased with himself. 'So you're trying to find out who killed him? Is that why you're here?'

Martin nods. 'Yes. Or at least to exonerate Mandy. The police will clear her in the end, but there's a danger they'll put her through all sorts of grief before then.'

'I see. I'm not sure how I can assist you, but I'll do what I can.' He pauses, as if to gauge Martin's response as he continues. 'Do you remember me?'

'No.'

'I knew your father.'

'So I'm told.'

'I didn't always live on Nobb Hill. Time was, I lived down the road from you in the Settlement, B Street, worked with your dad. Odd jobs. I had a different name.' He holds up his left hand. For the first time Martin notices the entire little finger and the ring finger down to the first knuckle are missing. 'The cheese factory. Your dad was there. Staunched the bleeding, drove me to the hospital at Longton.'

'I see,' says Martin, unsure how to react. 'Tyson St Clair is not your real name?'

'It is now. Writers have noms de plume, generals have noms de guerre, I needed a nom de development.'

'What was your name?'

'John Pyles.'

The name means nothing to Martin, but an image comes to him: a small boy with an awkward name getting bullied in the school yard. 'Fake it until you make it,' he observes.

St Clair grins, gestures around him. 'It's a long time since I had to fake it.' Then he grows serious. 'I remember where I came from. So of course I will do what I can. But I'm helping you as a person, the son of an old friend, a man concerned about the fate of his girlfriend. I'm not helping you as a journalist. Anything I tell you is not for the newspapers. Understood?'

'Absolutely. I'm not chasing a story here. I'm trying to help Mandy.'

'So you've left journalism behind?'

'I think it might have left me behind.'

Another lupine grin. 'Good. As long as we understand each other. Now, I'm curious. Ask away.'

'You knew Jasper well?'

'Well enough.'

'You did business with him? Through him?'

'Sure. From time to time.'

'What about socially?'

'Not really. I'd see him now and then. Port Silver is a pretty small place. But he wasn't a close friend or anything. He's from your generation, not mine.'

'Can you think of anyone who might want to harm him? Did he have any enemies?'

'No. Not that I can think of.' A pause. 'Although . . .'

'Although?'

'Look, I don't want to speak ill of the dead, but he had a reputation as a bit of a lady's man. I have no idea if that's right or not, but that was the rumour when his wife left him. And I hear he was into those orgies they have out at Hummingbird Beach.'

'Is that what happens out there?'

'So the newspapers say.'

Touché. 'So what are you suggesting?'

'Maybe it was a jealous husband. Or a spurned lover.'

Martin thinks of the murder scene: a crime of passion does seem more likely than a calculated killing. 'Any names you can think of?'

'Me? No. I wouldn't know where to start. I guess I could ask about, if you like.'

'Would you? I'd be most grateful.'

There's a pause. Martin knows the police will be pursuing the same idea, the same motive. Except they're likely to include Mandy among the list of potential suspects.

'Anything else?' asks St Clair.

'There is something. I'm told you and Jasper were representing a French firm that has plans to develop Hummingbird Beach, but he was opposed to your plans to develop Mackenzie's Swamp.'

'That's a fair summary.'

'So you were working together, the two of you?'

'After a fashion.'

Martin remembers what Jay Jay told him, about Jasper warning her of health inspectors and rates increases. Had St Clair been behind those? 'Sounds problematic,' he says.

'How so?'

'You want to develop the swamp, he's opposed to it, yet the two of you were meant to be working together on Hummingbird Beach.'

St Clair shakes his head, as if Martin is missing something. 'No. Business is business. Jasper knew full well that the French proposal could be a game changer for this town.' Then he flashes his predatory smile as if coming to a satisfactory solution. 'You got a few minutes, Martin? There's something I want to show you.'

'Sure. Of course.'

St Clair leads him out of the kitchen and through the living room, passing the doors to the deck, to an alcove where a set of spiral stairs leads upwards. They climb, St Clair first.

Upstairs is a single room, a large study, an octagonal turret with windows on six sides, flooded with light and panoramic views: the lighthouse is to the south, so massive Martin feels as if he could touch it; the blue vastness and curving horizon of the ocean to the east; the town laid out to the north and, beyond it, the river, Mackenzie's Swamp, the wide golden sands of Treachery Bay stretching unspoilt for miles. The Argyle snakes off to the west, towards the cane fields, the sugar mill, the escarpment.

St Clair gives Martin time to soak it in before speaking. 'Quite something, isn't it?'

'You can say that again.'

'It's the real reason I built the house. To put this on top of it.'

'I was told you preferred to work from home. I can see why.'

'Very perceptive.'

Martin tears his eyes from the view, looks around the interior of the room. There's a large desk, a purpose-built octagon at the room's centre. To the west, where the stairs emerge, the two sides of the octagon are panelled wood. Opposite, looking east, the windows are full length, floor to ceiling, but to the north and south the windows only stretch from waist height to the roof. Below them are in-built counters, a metre deep, with drawers underneath. On both the counters, the one facing the lighthouse and the one facing the town, are large models.

'Here, look at this,' says St Clair, walking towards the counter below the lighthouse window. 'This is what you want to see.'

It's a model of Hummingbird Beach, the estuary and Mackenzie's Swamp—not as they are now, but how they might be, rendered in painstaking detail. In Tyson St Clair's vision the water is blue, the golf course is green and the buildings are white. There are standalone bungalows, townhouses and apartments in tiers up the hillside. The car park has gone, banished to the other side of the ridge, with only model golf buggies to be seen in the development itself. There's a new bridge, an elegant span arching between twin towers of spiderweb steel, high above the estuary. The marina is there, serviced discreetly from Dunes Road but with access from the resort by buggy. Martin inspects the bridge more closely: there are lanes for the buggies on the western side of the bridge leading across to the golf club. The clubhouse is two storeys with a wide patio: even in miniature it dominates the lagoon, offering stunning views. The swamp itself has become a well-defined lake, lined by stone retaining walls, the golf course running around the north and west sides, with mangroves allowed to stay in patches on the eastern side, screening the course from the main road.

Martin nods. 'Impressive.'

'Isn't it?' says Tyson St Clair, unable to keep the pride from his voice. 'Stage one is the development at Hummingbird Beach. Stage two is the bridge and the marina, stage three the golf course. And here, let me show you.' St Clair moves to the model, lifting away a huge stretch of scrub between the river and the western boundary of the golf course where the Argyle swings north. He moves it to his desk, opens a wide drawer beneath the model. 'Give me a hand,' he says, and Martin complies. The two men lift the new section into place, like an oversized jigsaw. Now the land between the golf course and the curving river is populated with white cardboard houses sitting on large blocks, each with its own jetty, linked by a single road running back towards Dunes Road to the south of the lagoon. 'Stage four. River views and sunsets on one side, golf course on the other, resort down the way. Retirement heaven. An exclusive gated community.' He pauses to admire his handiwork, the logic of his vision. 'This—all of this: it will be the making of Port Silver.'

Martin examines the model, understands its logic, considers just how much money would be required, how much more might be gained. 'You have the finance for this?'

'I can get it.'

'What about the caravan park?'

St Clair shrugs. 'It can stay. Here. That's it here. But at some point the land will become too valuable and council will sell it.' He points to an outline on the model. The access road to the gated community runs behind it.

'What about flooding? I thought this whole area was vulnerable.'

'Correct. We'll need considerable earthworks and retaining walls. It won't be cheap. But go to the Gold Coast some time, up on Broadwater; they've done amazing things up there. Entire islands developed for housing.'

'I thought there were rules, council rules. You can't build unless you're several metres above sea level.'

'True. We'd need to flood-proof it.'

'Expensive?'

'My word.'

Martin studies the model again. Set out like this, it seems tangible. 'Why are you showing me this?'

'So you understand what's at stake.'

Martin frowns. 'What's at stake? What do you mean?'

'Here. Come around this side.' St Clair leads the way to the opposite window, and another model; the window looks out across the town, the scale model replicates the view. 'There it is, Martin: Port Silver.'

'And?'

'And it's a great town. My town. Your town. But let's be honest: it's a failure. It's never reached its potential and there's a good chance it never will.'

'I'm not sure I follow.'

'Listen. For as long as I remember, we've all been saying that we're the next big thing: the next Byron, the next Noosa, the next Gold Coast. And in the past, I've been the booster-in-chief. We've got the beach, we've got the picturesque boat harbour, we've got desperate politicians hoping to buy votes with new high schools and police stations, ambulance posts and swimming pools. But it's not enough.'

'Why not?'

'The wealthy buy weekenders, but they don't live in them. The backpackers come, the fruit pickers come, the retirees come. But the money doesn't.'

'What money?'

'The big money.' St Clair points back the other way, at the lighthouse, stalks towards it, full of contained energy. 'Look at it, will you? That's the largest lighthouse south of Byron. They built it in the late 1890s, back when they envisaged this place as a port of significance, shipping out cedar from the forests, oil from the whaling station, dairy from the farms, sugar from the cane fields, meat from the abattoir. That lighthouse was the beginning, the beacon of our prosperity. But two things have always stopped us: that treacherous fucking sandbar at the mouth of the Argyle, and that death-trap donkey track up the escarpment. The harbour could never support anything much bigger than a trawler. It's deep enough and sheltered enough, but the sandbar won't allow it. We've done all sorts of geological surveys, oceanographic surveys. There's a huge reef there, solid rock, the sandbar shifts around on top of it. You can't dredge it; you'd need a fucking atom bomb to shift it. So the port never developed—just the opposite. As the boats got bigger, the trade got smaller. The railway reached Longton and kept going, the branch line down the escarpment was never built because there was no port to connect to and the incline is too steep to justify the costs. The timber from the forests got logged out, the whaling station closed, the fishing fleet was repossessed and the cheese factory shut down. And any day now the sugar mill will close; it's already losing money. There aren't enough cane farms down here, no economies of scale. And once it shuts, all the sugar farms are fucked. The dairy farmers can still pool together and get tankers of milk up the escarpment, but there's no way known that you could get cane trucks up there. Not in the volume needed.' St Clair lets out a long emphatic sigh. 'You starting to get the picture now?'

But Martin shakes his head. 'I don't know. It seems more prosperous than when I was a kid.'

St Clair calms down a bit. 'Sure. We've still got the horticulture up along the river. We've got the backpackers. And we attract a lot of sea changers, people retiring here. So yes, there's money. But a lot of it's still government money, marginal seat money. Scrape the surface and there's still plenty of poverty. Not enough jobs. We get the invalid pensioners and the supporting mothers and the druggies and the poor cunts with mental health issues. They can't afford to live in Sydney or Brisbane or Byron; soon they won't be able to afford Coffs and Tweed Heads, so they'll come here. Plus the local Gooris, doing it tough like they've always done it tough. The Settlement's not big enough anymore, the poor have spilt over into the caravan park.'

Martin gestures towards the scale model of Hummingbird Beach and Crystal Lagoon. 'And that's the answer? That and a gated community?' He can't keep the scepticism from his voice.

'Tourism is the answer. Tourism and high-value retirees. And telecommuters. The high school and the swimming pool are terrific, but the real change is going to be broadband. This is a marginal seat: we're going to be better connected than a Macquarie Street lobbyist. I'm going to put a free wi-fi hotspot on top of the lighthouse.' He turns, sneering at the monument. 'Might as well put it to some use.'

'And you really think developing north of the Argyle can overcome a century and a half of stagnation?'

'I do, I do. You see, our mistake was chasing growth. For decades I believed we needed to grow, to get bigger, like all those other boom towns. But I was wrong. Our future isn't in getting bigger, our future is in becoming exclusive.' St Clair works the last word around his tongue, as if it is something to be savoured. 'The escarpment and the sandbar won't be barriers to development; they'll be protection against overdevelopment. I've stopped lobbying to have the road realigned, stopped pushing to have the breakwaters extended. Instead I've started donating to the Greens, pushing for a population limit. I want to get McDonald's chucked out, like in Byron. We want to be small and exclusive, clean and green.'

'I'm not sure draining Mackenzie's Swamp is exactly clean and green, is it? And have the blackfellas taken up golf?'

St Clair laughs, taking no offence at all. 'No, but I want them to be able to. They'll come around. So will the greenies.'

'How so?'

A canny expression comes across the developer's face. 'You been up there? Hummingbird Beach? The lagoon?'

'Just this morning, as a matter of fact.'

'And beyond that, did you go any further?'

'No. Why would I?'

'My point exactly. Nobody does. The beaches up there are too wild, the land behind them too sandy and full of salt. The dairy farms, those that are still there, don't start until a couple of kilometres inland. A few cane fields, but I just told you what's going to happen to them. It's shit country. The government has made most of it a nature reserve because they don't know what else to do with it.'

'What are you proposing?'

'In the next few months, the premier will be here. She'll be announcing a new national park running up the coast, joining with the one further north. There'll be jobs for Indigenous rangers as part of the deal.'

'A trade-off for the swamp?'

'That's what I'm working towards. But I'm trusting you with this: nothing in the papers.'

'No. Of course not.' Martin can't imagine the *Herald* getting too excited over a minor park on the north coast, even if he were still working for the newspaper. 'And the state government is involved with those negotiations?'

'Yep. But don't expect me to say too much more on that. I have confidences to keep.'

'So a national park. A buffer for the Hummingbird Beach development. A guarantee of privacy and exclusivity and unspoilt views.'

'Now you've got it. Luxury and exclusivity on the edge of wilderness, with Port Silver a twenty-minute drive away for amenities and labour. Perfect. Hummingbird Beach is the grain of sand, north of the river is the pearl, and Port Silver is the oyster, growing fat and succulent.' And St Clair bares his fangs in what Martin presumes is his idea of a winning smile.

Martin walks back around the windows, looking again at the scale model of the proposed development. 'I'm told you plan to demolish the old cheese factory.'

This time St Clair doesn't just grin, he laughs. 'Not me. I don't own it.'

'Really? Wasn't that your security guy I met out there this morning?'

'You have been busy.'

'What's he doing out there?' Martin persists.

'Just giving a helping hand to a hardworking journo.'

'Yes, Doug Thunkleton. He seems to think you own it.'

St Clair shakes his head. 'I don't know what gave him that idea. Amory Ashton owns it.'

'I thought he was dead.'

'That's what we all think. But there's no body. And until he's pronounced legally dead, he still owns it.'

'So if Doug Thunkleton finds something, finds a body, that helps you?'

'It does.'

'You were the one who tipped off Doug, right?'

'That's right.'

'And who owns it if Ashton is declared dead?'

'It doesn't matter. I stand more chance of buying it from them than from a dead man.'

Martin frowns. 'Why the metal detectors?'

'Didn't Thunkleton tell you?'

'No.'

St Clair displays his incisors. 'Ashton was a surly old bastard, possibly because of his shit diet. Red meat, red wine and blue cheese. Chronic arthritis. Riddled with it.'

'I don't get it.'

'He had new hips, new knees. Titanium. If he's buried out there, the metal detectors are set for it. Nothing else will give the same signature.' St Clair raises his eyebrows, apparently finding the idea entertaining. He turns, looks out to sea for several seconds, then back to Martin. It's a strange gesture, as if he's put Martin on hold while considering more important things. Now his face is serious. 'The cheese factory has nothing to do with Jasper. Trust me. It's not connected.'

'How can you be so sure?'

'Jasper was opposed to the development, that's common knowledge, so he wasn't in the loop, he didn't know where I was up to.'

'So if it's not relevant, why show me all this?'

'The Settlement.'

'What?'

'You can still see it from here, you know—the Settlement. In summer, there's a kind of haze hangs over it, as if you can see the disadvantage. Welfare cases. Druggos and alcos and refos. Gooris isolated from their own land. It's where you come from, Martin, where the Scarsdens come from. And it's where I come from. I want to change it.'

'By building a gated community? And a golf course?'

'That's right. Real jobs. Real money with real futures.'

'Really?'

'Really. And, Martin, one way or another, it's going to happen.'

But Martin is shaking his head. 'Not if Jay Jay Hayes doesn't sell her land. And as I understand it, she's not selling. And without Hummingbird Beach, everything else collapses.'

'She'll sell.'

'How can you be so sure?' Martin can't help but think of the box of scans behind Jay Jay Hayes's desk, the X-rays and MRIs and so on. Does St Clair know something?

'Human nature. All that money sitting there, tempting her. She'll sell.'

'So the French are still interested?'

'Too right. They left a million dollars on the table. A spotter's fee, if Jasper and I could convince Jay Jay to sell.'

That sets Martin thinking. Jasper had been protective towards Jay Jay Hayes, warning her of impending health inspections and rate rises. Had he been competing with St Clair, or colluding with him? 'Why are you telling me this?'

'I want you to work for me.'

'What?' Martin starts to laugh, thinking St Clair is joking, but is brought to a halt by the expression on the developer's face. 'Work for you? Doing what?'

'Making this happen.' The developer encompasses the model with a sweeping gesture. 'You said it yourself, journalism is leaving you behind. You need a job.'

'What job?'

'Communications. Public relations. Government liaison. There's no one this side of Brisbane with your portfolio of skills. Media experience and connections, knowledge of how the real world works.'

Martin says nothing, but a worm in his brain is telling him St Clair is right. If he stays in Port Silver with Mandy, what is he going to do? Go work for the *Longton Observer*? Scrape around looking for more true crime to turn into books? 'What are you offering?'

'Plenty, Martin. Plenty. But don't do it for that. Don't do it for the money. Help me put an end to the Settlement once and for all.'

Scotty never came to the Settlement. Jasper never came back after his dad died and his mum moved them. They didn't want to come and Martin didn't want to invite them. Not once he realised the stigma attached to the place, of being branded a 'settler'. Not in those years when he and his father descended into squalor, when the lawn turned to weeds and the house stank so much they left the windows open all year round. He learnt to hate his house, but not his neighbourhood. The Settlement was home, the only one he'd known—at least in those years before his mum and sisters died, and again in those final two years when Vern had moved in and they fixed up the house. There were good people there, people with good hearts and shit luck.

Scotty never came to his house and Jasper never came to his house and no one else ever came to his house. Except for Maz. One day Maz came. They were fifteen. He was keen on her and, as he realised too late, she was keen on him. She'd kissed him one night, down above the beach in the dunes, her mouth sweet with Bundy and Coke and sour with menthol cigarettes. He'd never said anything and she'd never said anything, but after that they'd had this thing, this unspoken knowledge that sooner or later they'd get together, become an item. And then she had come to the Settlement, come to his house, uninvited. She must have walked all the way from Five Mile Beach, through the town and out Ressling Road. He was inside, in his bedroom. He saw her through his window, dressed in her best jeans, a kind of floral top, pretty and demure. Her hair shone in the sun; she was wearing make-up. She was just standing at the gate, not moving, just staring. Then she checked the house number and tried opening the gate, the gate that was rusted shut and that he only ever stepped over. And then she stopped, looked once more at the house and turned away.

That was when he started cleaning the place up, when Vern helped him get the mower going, replacing the spark plug, sharpening the blades, scrubbing out the carburettor and changing the oil. He mowed the weeds, then started mowing for those neighbours who were too elderly or too infirm to do it for themselves, for money when they could pay and for nothing when they couldn't. He'd always been outwardly presentable, showering every morning, his school uniform and his street clothes washed if tattered; now he started cleaning the house, one step at a time, his own bedroom the beachhead. He washed his sheets, and when that didn't work he soaked them for days, and when that didn't work he threw them out and bought some new ones with his mower money. He vacuumed and dusted and chucked away clothes that were too small for him, some of them dating from before he was eight. From his beachhead, he advanced on the kitchen. It shouldn't have been so bad; they never cooked. But there were things rotted to nothing in the oven, things rotting more slowly in the fridge, unholy smells emanating from the S-bend in the sink. One weekend it got too much. He scrubbed all through the day and all through the night and into the dawn, pushed on by a manic zeal. And at the end, he felt a sense of achievement, a sense of pride. And then his father threw up in the bathroom. And someone stole his mower.

He used to see Maz often enough after that, it was impossible to avoid her: on the bus to school in Longton, in every second class, sometimes hanging on The Boulevarde outside Theo's and smoking cigarettes in the dunes. She was always polite, never said anything mean, never called him a settler. But there was no longer an understanding. And in her eyes he could sometimes glimpse that most damning of emotions: pity.

On The Boulevarde, Martin stops for lunch. The old supermarket has been converted to a hardware store, but the roof's still a car park. He eases the Toyota up the ramp. It seems so much shorter, the incline so much shallower, than the night they raced their shopping trolleys. It's baking hot on the concrete expanse, sucking in the sun and bouncing it back, heat and glare and not a skerrick of shade, the cloudburst that passed over Nobb Hill as he visited St Clair long gone. It's not the best place to leave a car. Martin winds his windows down, leaves them wide open. If anyone wants to steal the rust bucket, they're welcome to it.

The day has exhausted him; he needs to eat, to gather his thoughts. Confronted by a choice of cafes, his mind again turns to the delicacy of his youth: fish and chips. Two days in a row? Why not? But instead of the new place next to the sushi shop, he remembers his old haunt, Theo's.

Inside, the store remains much the same as he remembers it, lino peeling from the floor, booths with laminate tables, heavy glass sugar dispensers with silver tubes. Two fans hang from the roof, circling slowly. The fridges, emblazoned with Coke livery, have been updated and the bakelite ashtrays have gone, but fading posters in cheap frames still line the walls with dead people: Elvis, Bogie and Lauren, Marilyn, James, Clark, Errol, Judy. Some time in the past quarter of a century, John, Paul, George and Ringo have been added to the pantheon. Not the hippie Beatles, but the mop tops, smiling at the camera, the print in black and white like the others. The pantheon cafe.

At the same counter, the same order: two pieces of fish with chips. The teenager behind the counter doesn't even tell him the price, she just shoves an EFTPOS machine at him. Dyed hair, piercings, tats and attitude. A Port Silver punk.

'Cash?' queries Martin.

'Whatever.'

Martin hands over thirty dollars and receives a handful of small change in retaliation. The surly face looks at him, challenging. Martin can't be bothered, and starts slotting the coins into an empty charity tin one by one. Just as he's inserting the last of the shrapnel, a man bustles out from the back of the store, wiping his hands on his apron. Martin recognises him instantly: not Theo Tomakis but his son, George, who has somehow grown into a facsimile of his father. George, a schoolyard contemporary, once a soccer star, lithe and handsome, with a jawline sharp enough to shave butter. But the jawline has long gone, together with the waistline and the hairline. A grand moustache has sprouted by way of compensation, but there is no doubting who it is. 'George,' he says.

George looks at him, is about to say something, frowns as a mote of recognition floats before him, then smiles. He points his finger. 'Martin Scarsden. Hotshot reporter.'

'George.'

They shake hands, grin at each other. Martin isn't sure why; they were classmates, not friends. George was one of those that had bailed before the end of year ten, off to chase the dream of professional football. Martin hasn't seen him since, but for some reason he's glad to see him now. And then he has it; the fish-and-chip man is a fellow settler, a fellow survivor. 'I heard you were coming back,' says George. 'Jasper Speight told me.'

'You still saw Jasper?'

'Sure. Used to come in most weeks. Fish and chips and a chocolate milk.'

Martin smiles. 'Some things never change.'

'I guess you heard, though?' asks George, face suddenly solemn.

'Yeah, I heard.'

'Mate. This town. We never had anything like that before. Fights and brawls and domestics, sure; the Settlement was no circus. But murder? Sheesh.'

'You're not still out there then? The Settlement?'

'Me? Shit no. Mum and Dad stayed out there for a long time, even after they could afford to move, but not me. Couldn't wait to get out.'

'How are your mum and dad?'

'Dad's dead. Years ago. Heart attack. Only exercise he ever got was playing poker and smoking cigarettes. Mum's with us now. We converted the garage for her.'

'Nobb Hill?'

George laughs, a real laugh, from the belly. 'Jeez no. But nice. Double-brick. Air-conditioned. Right on Five Mile Beach—you can see the waves from upstairs. Gets the breeze, kids can play on the sand. Real nice.'

'Sounds beaut. Did you see much of Jasper?'

'Nah. Just when he'd come in for his fish and chips. Never talked much, sometimes about what you'd written in the paper, where you'd been. And asking when we were going to sell.'

'You own the shop?'

George laughs again, even more warmly. 'Don't tell anyone, but Mum owns half The Boulevarde.'

Now it's Martin who laughs, thinking of the modest old woman, reluctant to leave the Settlement, living out her days in a converted garage. 'So you could live on Nobb Hill if you wanted? I was only joking.'

'She could, yeah. But she's old, she hates climbing up and down steps. And she doesn't want to be up there with the others.'

'The others?' asks Martin. 'Big city lawyers and cashed-up retirees is what I heard.'

'Yeah, tossers. And the locals are worse. Always talking about house prices, how much they're worth, trying to get to the top of the pile. Mate, it's like *Game of Thrones* up there. Mum can't stand it.'

The teenage shop assistant, feigning impossible levels of boredom, starts to pull the stainless-steel basket from the deep fryer, but George intervenes, doing it himself, hanging the basket over the fryer to drain, then does the same with the chips, knocking the basket a few times to release excess oil.

'Won't taste as good as it used to,' says George.

'How do you mean?'

'Used to fry it up with beef lard. Huge white blocks of it. It's all canola oil now. Healthier, they reckon, but bugger-all taste.'

Martin thanks George and takes his food down to the beach. The lard may be gone, but so too is the butcher-paper wrapping. Instead the food is in an open box, inserted into a white paper bag to let the steam out, to retain the crispness. And whatever George says, it tastes just as good. It's like the beach: you can rake it, but it's still the same beach. He bites into the fish, batter hot and crisp, salty. His mouth fills with taste, his mind with memory. Still the same fish and chips, better than the new place.

And as he eats, he's back in the Settlement again, eating fish and chips on the couch, concentrating on the television, trying to ignore his father on his easy chair, wolfing down his burger, dripping grease, leaking condiments. And on the television, the news, the foreign correspondents, with their aloof objectivity, their unerring certainty, possessed of all the facts.

Near the end, it's often like this: his father becoming more immobile, less likely to be at the lifesavers pouring money into the pokies or spraying it around the TAB, more likely to be home, drunk and semi-comatose in his recliner, throwing cash at Martin instead, demanding takeaway. The two eat without conversation, with only the television news and his father's mastication filling the silence. Martin learns the names of the correspondents, tracking their exploits, ingesting the evolving state of the world: the Soviet Union fragments, Nelson Mandela is released, Yugoslavia disintegrates into a mosaic of blood and atrocity.

And sitting above the television, his talisman, miraculously unopened, the bottle of French champagne, its orange label like a rallying flag, the promise of a better life to come, assuring him that one day he too will travel the world and wear a wrinkle-free blue shirt with epaulets, like James Bond, except with a typewriter instead of a gun, a microphone instead of a silencer, a flute instead of a martini glass. He will quaff champagne from bottles with orange labels, toasting his elevation above the sordid banalities and emotional quicksand of Port Silver.

His phone chirps, pulling him back to the present, to his half-eaten lunch. It's a text. Mandy. *Beachside cafe, please come now.*

chapter twelve

THE BEACHSIDE CAFE IS NOT BEACHSIDE, IT'S ON THE BOULEVARDE, ALBEIT ON the eastern side of the street. The only view of the surf, as Martin later discovers, is through the window above the urinal in the men's toilet. It's an undecided establishment: lacking the pretension of its neighbour, the Che Bay Cafe, but certainly more ambitious than Theo's. Its interior is seaside casual: polished concrete floor, wooden tables and old fishing nets strung from the roof. It has a chalkboard menu: order and pay at the counter.

Mandy is waiting for him with an apologetic smile. Winifred Barbicombe is here, but with no smiles to spare. Liam is asleep in his stroller, not in child care after all. As soon as Martin enters, he knows something isn't right.

'What is it?' he asks, taking the seat left vacant for him. 'What's happened?'

'Nothing too serious,' says Mandy.

Martin looks to the elderly lawyer. Winifred doesn't speak.

Mandy sighs. 'The police are getting desperate, chasing shadows, that's all.'

'That's when they're the most dangerous,' he replies, winning a nod from Winifred and a scowl from his partner.

'Nick Poulos rang me from the lifesavers club,' says Winifred, voice sombre. 'He says the police have been down there asking about Mandalay and Jasper Speight. It looks like they're trying to build a motive for Mandalay to kill Jasper.'

Martin stares at Mandy, his voice a whisper. 'What happened? Why there?'

'Jasper and I had a tiff at the club a few weeks ago. Some do-gooder must have told the police.'

'A tiff?' echoes Martin, the word as unwelcome as a second cousin. The only tiff he's ever heard of is a lovers' tiff. Everything else is a fight or an argument or a disagreement or a blue. 'What happened?'

'We were having dinner. I thought he was a nice guy. He was renting me the townhouse, helping with the paperwork on Hartigan's. He'd already told me he knew you, that you were school friends, that he loved reading your articles. I wanted to make friends, connect with the community. He seemed very sincere, telling me about the need to preserve some of the local environment. And then he put his hand on my leg. I asked him to remove it and he did. And then he put it back, tried moving it higher. So I stood up and poured a jug of beer over his head.'

'Right,' says Martin, supressing a smile.

'And gave him a free character reference.'

'Go on,' says Winifred.

Mandy shrugs. 'I told him to fuck off. That's all. I didn't threaten to kill him or anything like that.'

'Everyone in the club saw it. Heard it. You humiliated him,' says Winifred.

'He deserved it. What did you want me to do?'

Martin feels a sense of betrayal, his old friend making a move on Mandy, yet that's not what he says. 'You didn't overreact?'

She looks at him with astonishment, the heat in her voice replaced by ice. 'Fuck you.'

Too late he remembers this morning, her simmering displeasure at his evening at Vern and Josie's. He back-pedals. 'I'm not saying you were wrong. But you know . . .' He trails off and she fixes him with a stare that could extinguish Chernobyl.

'What? I know what? That he was going to end up dead on my floor?'

Winifred intercedes, like a rugby referee heading off a brawl, addressing Martin. 'What about you? Have you discovered anything useful?' The tone of her voice suggests she isn't expecting much; she just wants to move the conversation on.

'Yeah, maybe I have.' And he recounts his morning while Mandy bores holes in his head with her eyes: the cheese factory, Hummingbird Beach and his encounter with Tyson St Clair.

The mention of Doug Thunkleton horrifies Mandy, after his on-air prosecution of them in Riversend. 'That arsewipe? In Port Silver? He's not looking for me, is he?'

Martin reassures her he isn't.

Winifred is intrigued by the plans for the north shore of the Argyle. 'So you think Jasper Speight's death may be linked in some way to these development plans?'

'It's possible. There's no evidence, but these projects, the money involved must run into the hundreds of millions of dollars. That's a lot of motive.'

'It is,' Winifred responds, steepling her hands as she ponders his information. 'Can you keep on that, Martin? See what else you can find out?'

'Sure. Have you spoken to Montifore?'

'Only briefly. Why?'

'The photo in Jasper's hand. Did they tell you what it is?'

'Yes, you were right. It's a postcard—of a Greek Orthodox saint.'

'What was written on it?'

'Nothing. It was blank.'

Martin frowns. A blank postcard, held in his friend's death grip. Why? 'Who was the saint?'

'St Myron of Crete. It was printed on the back, in Greek and English.'

'Who?'

'Myron the Wonderworker. You ever heard of him?'

'No.'

'I googled him. A third- or fourth-century orthodox saint. Bishop of Crete,' Winifred says. 'Any ideas why Jasper had it with him? Why he might have wanted to show it to you?'

'None whatsoever. His mother said he collected postcards but wasn't religious. It's a mystery.'

'Fuck,' says Mandy softly, interrupting them.

Ivan Lucic is standing at the door. The sergeant approaches, speaks to Mandy, his voice almost gentle. 'Come on. Let's go.'

Winifred stands, preparing to leave with her client. 'Martin, tell Nick what's happened, keep him up to speed, okay?'

'Sure.'

'Good. And keep going with your inquiries.' She turns to Mandy, who's still seated, looking distraught. 'Come now, Mandalay. The innocent have nothing to fear.'

But Mandy doesn't stand, not yet. Instead she turns to Martin. He can see the distress in her eyes. 'Liam. Can you look after him?'

'Of course.'

She hands him her car keys, tells him where she's parked the Subaru, says that all of Liam's necessities are in a sports bag. 'He'll be hungry when he wakes. There's a bottle made up in the stroller and a container of mashed vegies. And I bought a backpack for you two, a baby carrier, so you can take him for a walk. It's in the back of the car if you want to try.'

She's trembling as she stands. Winifred and Lucic and Martin remain still as she bends and gently kisses the forehead of her sleeping son. She straightens, eyes moist. 'Take care of him, Martin. Please take care of him.'

And then they file out, the lawyer, the policeman and the suspect, the eyes of the cafe following them, the gossipmongers flexing their tongues, leaving Martin alone at the table, Liam oblivious in his slumber.

⁓

Liam wakes as soon as Martin takes him from the stroller, emitting a piercing cry of need. Martin feels a moment of panic, of rampant inadequacy, before slipping the boy the bottle, instantly pacifying him. He breathes a sigh of relief. But what happens when the bottle is gone? He lowers the now-pliable child into the baby carrier and straps him into place. Then he carefully lifts it, manoeuvring Liam around until the boy sits squarely on his back, the carrier low so Martin's hips can take the weight, tightening the waist strap first, then adjusting the shoulder straps. Satisfied, he crouches awkwardly, keeping his back erect so he doesn't tip Liam forward, and fetches the sports bag from the back of the car: bottles, nappies, wipes. There is so much stuff.

Walking down The Boulevarde, he can hear the boy snuffling in his ear, chugging on his formula, happy with this new adventure, with the height and the sense of movement. Clever Mandy, she must have known her boy would like it. Martin likes it too; so much better than a stroller. Passing women beam at him, projecting approval. Liam chortles, Martin smiles; Liam gurgles, Martin makes stupid little noises over his shoulder. But when Liam drops his bottle the howl of dismay drills directly into Martin's left ear, penetrating his skull. He squats to fetch the bottle, but a young mother, holding her own child by the hand, gets to it first. She returns it to Liam and smiles indulgently at both of them. 'There you go.'

Martin heads for the beach, figuring the boy might like the waves and the seagulls. But first he calls back into Theo's, asking the truculent teenager to fetch George Tomakis.

'Martin. Back so soon? And who's this fellow?'

'Liam. My partner's son.'

'Looks like trouble to me,' says George, smiling broadly. 'What can I do for you?'

'The Greek community here in Port Silver. Is it very large?'

'Nah, five or six families. Hardly qualifies as a community.'

'Anyone from Crete?'

'Crete? Don't think so. A couple of Cypriots up in Longton, that's about it. Why?'

'You ever heard of St Myron the Wonderworker?'

George laughs. 'Nah. Sounds like the name of a band. St Myron and the Wonderworkers.'

'Thanks, George.'

At a picnic table above the dunes, under the shade of a Norfolk Island pine, Martin gently lowers the backpack. Liam, teat of the bottle still in his mouth, examines Martin quizzically. Martin props the carrier on the ground and balances it with one hand, Liam's chubby legs swinging free. With difficulty, Martin removes his own shoes. Inside the sports bag, Martin finds a hat for the boy and sunscreen. Mandy has thought of everything. Liam laughs and squirms as Martin spreads the cream on his face, as if it is some sort of tickle game. Martin finds himself talking to the boy, laughing and playing along.

Then, while Liam is still occupied with his bottle, Martin rings Nick Poulos. The lawyer answers promptly enough. 'Martin?'

'Nick. The police have hauled Mandy in for more questioning.'

'Really? The altercation with Jasper at the lifesavers?'

'I'd say so. Can we meet?'

'Of course, but I'm not sure when. The inspectors are in town. I could be some time.'

'Inspectors?'

'Fishery inspectors. They're checking catches. I'm at the harbour.'

'Doing what? Kerb crawling for clients?'

'Wharf crawling. It's a living.'

'Terrific. You and the seagulls. But listen, there's a couple of things you might be able to help with. Do you know how I can contact Jasper Speight's former wife? Susan, I think her name is.'

'Not off the top of my head, but I can find out. What's the second thing?'

'Have you ever heard of a saint called Myron the Wonderworker, from Crete?'

Martin's ear fills with laughter. 'Not ever. You've got the wrong Greek. I don't know any of that Orthodox shit.'

'Just asking. I'm on Town Beach. I'll walk around and see you soon.' Martin ends the call.

He hoists Liam onto his back once more, but before leaving the shade of the trees, he googles the Greek saint. The internet informs him that Myron was born around 250 AD and could indeed work wonders: whipping up barrels of wine and walking on water like a poor man's Jesus. Martin ponders what the distinction might be between a wonderworker and a miracle worker. He reads that the saint's day falls in August, and considers if that holds any significance, but can't think of what. Elsewhere he finds a curious report stating that just a few years ago the saint appeared in the dreams of local parishioners requesting to be taken from his grave, so the congregation disinterred his relics and put them on display inside a glass case.

Martin reads the article again, then looks out across the white sands of Australia, at the hedonistic beachgoers, and wonders what possible relevance a third- or fourth-century Greek holy man could have to Jasper Speight's death.

The beach is well populated, the temperature approaching its early afternoon peak. People are spread across the sand: the young and the carefree, the old and the careworn. As a kid this was his unacknowledged sanctuary, taken for granted. The beach. He looks at it now, sees it as the European backpackers must, values it anew.

He walks towards the waves, giving Liam—riding high—a better view. A sea eagle comes gliding into sight, wings rigid, riding the thermals above the beach.

Martin points. 'Bird, Liam. Bird.'

Liam makes some guttural approximation and whacks him in the back of the head with his plastic bottle. Having finished his formula, the child has found another use for it. *Clop*. He hits Martin again, this time laughing with glee as he does so.

'Liam. For fuck's sake.'

Clop. Laughter.

Martin swings his arms up and behind him, trying to reach the boy, to catch hold of his arms, but the position of the baby carrier is such that Martin can't reach far enough back. Liam squeals with delight at this new development in his game. *Clop. Clop. Clop.* A blow for each hand, another for Martin's head.

A small group of backpackers in their board shorts and bikinis have stopped marking out a volleyball court in the sand and are pointing, laughing at the show. A grinning young woman advances, holding her phone out before her, recording the scene, fodder for social media. *Clop. Clop.* More squeals of laughter from Liam. Martin, realising he's about to go viral, swings his back to the amateur cinematographer and starts unbuckling the carrier.

'No, no,' protests the young documentarian. 'Is very funny. Again.'

But Martin lowers the carrier to the sand, sitting it upright, kneeling next to it and steadying it with his hand to prevent it toppling. Liam's eyes are alive with mischief. He's holding the bottle by its teat, swinging it back and forth, giving Martin's arm a whack for good measure. Martin smiles. Unlike the hits to the head, this is neither irritating nor painful, so he plays along, making wild faces as Liam whacks him once more.

'He is so cute!' exclaims the bikini girl, reaching them. 'So adorable!' She is no longer filming. Martin takes the bottle from Liam and the boy looks unsure, uncertain if this is a continuation of the game. Martin releases the boy's straps, eases him out, lifting him up for a cuddle. 'Can I hold him?' asks the girl.

Martin is about to decline when he hears raised voices, the air suddenly blue with profanities, the calm shattered. He and the girl turn. Across the sands advance two young men, pushing and jostling and swearing. One of them is Royce, his sunnies still precariously in place. The fight is escalating, the pushing replaced with punches, the four-letter words exclamations rather than insults. The sunnies go flying. Royce's opponent, just as big and just as muscly, with a surfer's mop of blond hair, is smiling viciously, goading Royce. There's more contact, the sound of skin on skin, knuckle on bone, surprisingly loud.

'Hold the boy!' Martin instructs the girl, handing Liam to her. 'Stop it! Stop it!' he shouts, moving forward. They lurch towards him, suddenly he is very close; he can hear their breathing, smell their sweat. 'Stop it!' he shouts, waving his arms. But all he does is distract Royce, who begins to pivot, realises his mistake too late and cops a left hook. He staggers, knees flexing involuntarily. 'No!' yells Martin, unable to move any quicker in the sand, protestations in vain: the follow-up right catches Royce square in the face with a sickening sound of flesh squelching and bones cracking; a spray of blood flies out, red across the golden sand, spattering against Martin's shin. Royce's knees give way altogether and he falls, unconscious before he hits the ground with dull certainty.

'No!' says Martin again, unable to believe what he has seen, unable to believe it cannot be undone. 'What the fuck?' he demands of the aggressor, who is standing victorious, legs wide and eyes wild, like a gladiator. 'You can't do that.'

'Can't I?' says the man, stepping forward.

Martin doesn't even get to answer, to consider the wisdom of answering, to raise his hands. There's a flash of movement, the sound of another sickening blow, and searing pain. And a blood-red fog descending, pulling him down with it. Before he passes out he hears the scream of the bikini girl, the sound of the surf and his head hitting the sand.

—

Darkness, confusion, light. The taste of fish and chips. His father, laughing, his father, young and fit and laughing. They're running, running on a beach. No, it's Martin who's running, around in circles, a toddler, very young, chasing seagulls, the birds waddling away, not threatened enough to take flight. And his mother. His mother is here, smiling indulgently, laughing at Martin and his father playing. On the beach. In the sun. And the sun, the sun is so warm.

The first thing he hears as consciousness returns is Liam crying. Liam! He opens his eyes, the right eye first, his left slower to respond. There is pain high on his face. He closes his eyes again and seeks out the pain with his fingers. He pushes on his left eyelid, but it feels fine. Tentatively he runs his finger around his eye socket, down the ridge of his nose. All okay, nothing broken. He runs his finger up his left jaw, up his cheek. Here it is, the epicentre. He's been punched right at the top of his jaw, almost in the temple. He clenches his teeth, pushes harder with the tip of his finger. The pain comes, but nothing extreme; bruising rather than a fracture, he concludes. He opens his eyes again. The sun ignites pain behind them, echoing at the back of his head. Has he hit his head on falling?

'Easy, mate. Take it easy. Just lie there. No sudden movements, okay?' Martin can't see who is talking, but the voice sounds sensible and measured. He tries lifting his head, swoons and decides to heed the voice's advice. But he again hears Liam's cry and rolls over so he might see. Kneeling over him is a young man, one of the volley-ballers, holding a wet towel. He places it lightly on Martin's face. It feels good. Above him he can see the bikini girl, holding Liam. The baby is reaching out, trying to get to her tits. 'No,' she says, slapping his hands away gently but firmly. Martin laughs despite himself. 'You have a naughty boy, mister,' she says, grinning broadly.

Martin tries sitting, managing to push himself up with the help of the young man. 'How long was I out?'

'Not long. A minute tops.'

Martin looks around, exciting the pain near the back of his head. A larger group has already gathered nearby, circling the prone body of Royce. 'Is he all right?'

The young man shrugs. 'Alive. Breathing, but still unconscious. The ambos are coming. And the police.'

But it's the surf lifesavers who get there first, three of them sprinting across the sand. Two head straight to Royce, but one kneels beside Martin.

'You okay, mate?' he asks. 'What happened?'

'Bloke king-hit me.'

'You remember that? You remember what happened before that?'

'Yes. All of it.'

'Good. What's your name?'

Martin tells him; that and today's date and the name of the prime minister.

'That's good, mate. Excellent. You lose consciousness?'

'For a minute or so, I'm told.'

'Right,' says the lifesaver. 'You've got concussion then.'

'How can you be sure?'

'Because that's the definition: you lose consciousness, you have concussion. You need to go to hospital.'

'You're joking. I was only out for a minute.'

'You need to be monitored for at least four hours, in case there's more permanent damage.' He can see the scepticism in Martin's eyes. 'I'm serious.' The lifesaver looks like he's about sixteen, with an acne-sprayed face and a bum-fluff moustache, but his voice carries the authority of his training. Martin's own hostile environment courses are telling him the same thing: any neurological damage should manifest itself within the next few hours, and hospital is the place to be if it does.

'Royce! Royce!'

Martin hears the call, turns to see Topaz running across the sand from the direction of the backpacker hostel.

'Royce!' She pushes through the circle of onlookers, kneels beside the lifesavers attending to her boyfriend. They've rolled him over into the recovery position, placed a damp towel on his brow, but he's still unconscious.

Martin's head is starting to feel clearer even as the pain in his jaw increases. He again explores the damage, reassuring himself nothing is broken.

'Here,' says the bikini girl. She hands him her phone, the camera activated in selfie mode. He thanks her, uses it mirror-like to examine his face as best he can in the glare of the day. He can see where the punch has caught him flush on the top of his jaw, the bruise already starting to migrate towards his eye. He's going to have one hell of a shiner. But he's lucky: if he'd been hit in the eye socket, there could have been permanent damage.

'Who was that arsehole who hit me?' he asks.

'The hostel guy,' answers the young volleyballer.

'Hostel guy?'

'From the backpacker hostel. Over there.'

Martin looks over to where the Sperm Cove Backpackers sits, bright blue in the sun, dominating a section of beach. He can hear a siren: an ambulance. That's quick. And he can see Sergeant Johnson Pear wading towards them, the puppy-fat constable a few paces behind, the men awkward on the sand in their service-issue boots. Pear moves first to the circle surrounding the still-unconscious Royce. Then someone points across to Martin, and Pear moves over to him. 'Scarsden. You okay?'

'I've been assaulted.'

'So I see. Can you remember what happened?'

'Absolutely. This aggro young shit knocked out that man there and then did the same to me. Punched me in the face.'

'Why?'

'No idea. They were already fighting. I was trying to intervene, to stop them, and I got smashed in the face for my troubles.'

'Right. So that man there and the other one, the one who hit you, they were fighting?'

'Yes. That's right.'

'And you don't know why?'

'No. I was here, looking after the baby, talking with this young woman, when I heard them. It must have started somewhere else, maybe at the hostel, I don't know. But they were shouting and then they were throwing punches.'

'Did you recognise the man who hit you?'

'No, but these people did.'

'Yes,' says the young man, and the girl nods her agreement. 'His name is Harry. He works at the hostel over there.'

Pear nods, the grimace on his face revealing he knows exactly who they are talking about. 'Harry Drake,' he says aloud, and then under his breath, 'Harry the Lad.'

'Drake?' asks Martin. 'As in Harrold Drake?'

'Junior,' says Pear, sounding unimpressed. 'It's a small world.'

'You'll arrest him?'

'Too fucking right I will,' says Pear, looking none too happy about it. 'You have witnesses?'

'Half the beach.'

'Good.'

Pear has his notebook out now and starts taking the names and contact details of the volleyballers. Martin gets up, moving first to kneeling then tentatively standing, but it's fine: he no longer feels faint. The woman hands Liam to him. The boy's eyes are wide, staring past Martin, fascinated by the ambulance as it pulls up in the car park next to the hostel, sirens giving one last wail before falling silent. Two paramedics emerge, gather backpacks from the rear of the ambulance and make their way calmly down onto the beach. Pear has moved on and is now speaking to Topaz, jotting details in his notepad.

Royce is starting to groan and come around as the ambulance officers reach him. They exchange quick words with the lifesavers then take over, talking quietly to Royce, shining a torch into his eyes, requesting he move his arms and legs and squeeze their fingers. They move apart from the crowd and discuss the situation quietly between the two of them. One of them walks over to Martin. 'You the bloke he was fighting?'

'No. An innocent bystander.'

'Good. Don't want a couple of brawlers in the same ambulance. You lost consciousness though, right?'

'For less than a minute.'

'Doesn't matter.' The ambulance officer runs him through a quick series of tests, familiar to Martin from his hostile environment training. 'Okay. No sign of damage. But we need to take the other bloke to hospital; he needs monitoring. You want a lift?'

'You think it's really necessary?'

'It's up to you.'

Martin thinks of sitting in hospital for hours, waiting on the clock. He's about to decline when a thought crosses his mind. 'Do they do scans there?' Martin touches his finger up next to his eye. 'At Longton? Soft-tissue?'

'For your eye? No, mate. Only X-rays and ultrasounds, that's about it.'

'No MRIs or PETS?'

'Are you kidding? Sydney or Brisbane for that. But you don't need a scan, you need an ophthalmologist. They shine a light in through your pupil, check it out that way. Why? Your vision blurry?'

'No, it's fine. I was just wondering.'

The ambulance officer frowns. 'If you say so. You want a lift or not?'

Martin thinks of Liam, trapped with him in the interminable boredom of an emergency waiting room. 'Thanks anyway, but no. I've done the training, I know what to look for. Blurry vision, nausea, loss of motor skills, confusion.'

'Okay. Your call, mate. But don't hesitate, right?'

Martin nods and the ambulance officer returns to Royce, now conscious and talking. The paramedics help him to his feet and over to the ambulance, Topaz hovering by his side. The crowd watches them go, but once Royce is loaded into the back and the van departs, the circle of people melts away, back to their leisure. The volleyballers give Martin a wave and resume their preparations.

Martin is about to ease Liam back into the baby carrier, tucking the empty bottle into a mesh pocket on its side, when he smells the necessity of a nappy change. Just what he needs; his headache throbs. Mandy has warned him of this eventuality, has given him a demonstration. Brilliant: changing the nappies of another man's baby. As soon as the thought comes, he rejects it, repelled by the idea. He loves Mandy and this is part of the package. And he can't help loving Liam: the boy is so alive and wide-eyed. It's not his fault he's not yet toilet trained. Martin looks about, deciding that sand and nappies may not mix. Instead he walks up to a patch of grass by the hostel car park.

He's just finishing the operation—Liam thinks it's a familiar game, fortunately—when Johnson Pear emerges from the back-packers. Alone. Pear sees Martin, grimaces, shakes his head and walks away. Martin's hackles rise. Why hasn't the policeman arrested Harry Drake? Martin is just about to call out when Harry the Lad himself emerges from the blue brightness of the hostel, sees Martin, walks over.

'You all right, mate?' he asks, as if Martin has just stubbed his toe or something.

'No. I'm not.'

Harry smiles, like they're enjoying a joke. 'Mate, I'm sorry. I thought you were with him, pitching in to double up on me.'

'Is that what you told Pear?'

'Exactly. Self-defence.'

'And he bought that?'

'If he's smart, he will,' says Harry, words full of swagger.

'What about Royce? The bloke you almost killed?'

'Killed? Bullshit. He'll be fine.' More swagger. 'He wouldn't be sitting up in the back of that ambulance if I was serious.'

'What did you tell Pear about him?'

'The truth. He threw the first punch, in front of three or four witnesses.' Harry's smile broadens; he's impressed by his own advocacy. Martin doesn't believe him; when the men first burst upon them on the beach they were shouting and pushing, not fighting. But he's not about to contest the issue; the man is inflated with bare-chested bravado. At his side, attached to a belt looping through his jeans, there's a sheathed knife, a multipurpose tool and a key chain. A real Chuck Norris.

'You're Martin Scarsden, aren't you?' says Harry the Lad. 'I heard about you, read some of your stuff. You're moving here.'

'So what?'

'Well, it's a small town. We don't want to be enemies. That guy, he's no gap-year student or a foreign backpacker. He's a drifter, a low-life. A sponge. I know 'em by sight. He'll be gone soon, we'll still be here. I'm sorry I hit you. Let me make it up to you.'

'How?'

'Don't know. I'll think of something.'

He holds out his hand. Martin reluctantly shakes it. He doesn't like doing it, but in his time he's shaken the hands of far worse than Harry the Lad: ethnic cleansers, mafia spivs, Russian oligarchs and pornographers. And more politicians than he cares to count. A source is a source, he decides. Liam farts, as if in contempt.

chapter thirteen

It's Topaz, emerging from the hostel. She is weighed down by two packs: the one on her back and the one in her arms.

'Moving out?' asks Martin.

'Can't stay. Not after that.'

She drops one backpack onto the sand, then shimmies her way out of the other. She stretches, arching her back as if to release the tension, thrusting out her breasts. 'What a mess,' she says, gyrating. Liam, looking on from his perch in the backpack, lets out an appreciative chortle. 'Nice kid,' Topaz says. 'Yours?'

'My partner's.'

'Lucky partner.' She offers a coquettish smile. 'Hope she likes the black eye. It does look kinda sexy.'

'Right.' He lifts a tentative finger to his swollen cheek; it's really starting to hurt. He wonders how far the bruise is spreading.

'Thanks for trying to help, though,' Topaz offers.

Martin doesn't respond; the way he remembers it, he didn't help so much as distract Royce at precisely the wrong moment, giving Harry the Lad the opportunity to deck him. 'Where will you stay?'

'No idea. First stop is the hospital. Is it walking distance?'

'It's in Longton.'

'Longton? Are you serious? Up that goddamn hill?'

'Yep.'

She looks around, considering her options. 'You couldn't look after our packs, could you? While I hitch up and see him? Keep them somewhere safe?'

The last thing Martin wants is to be burdened with the packs. 'No. I've got enough on my hands with the boy. Sorry.'

'Do you know of anywhere else to stay? Any other hostels here or in Longton?'

Martin doesn't know, but it seems unlikely. Longton is a highway town, not on the backpacker trail; all the fruit picking and horticulture is down on the Argyle River flats. He thinks of the caravan park, but dismisses the idea immediately. He can just imagine Mandy's reaction if the flirtatious American moved in. 'Well, there is one place, but it's a bit out of the way. Hummingbird Beach.'

Topaz's eyes light up. 'The sex party place?'

Martin laughs, which incites a flash of pain in his jaw. 'You've heard of it then?'

'Shit yeah. Everyone at the hostel was talking about it last night. They run a bus out on Friday nights. We were all planning to go.'

'Really?'

'You bet. That arsehole sells tickets. Could you drop me out there?'

Martin wonders if Jay Jay Hayes or the swami know of Harry the Lad's entrepreneurship. 'You sure? It's the opposite direction from the hospital.'

'I'll work it out.'

Martin is hesitant, but he wouldn't mind another look at Hummingbird Beach himself.

'Okay. Wait here. I need to get the car.'

Martin carries Liam back onto The Boulevarde and along to Mandy's Subaru. He'll need to borrow it; the Corolla doesn't have a baby seat. As he walks, he uses his phone. His first call is to Nick.

'Martin, shit. I forgot you were coming. Where are you?'

'The Boulevarde. Something's come up. We might have to postpone.'

'Suits me. I'm up to my ears in it round here.'

'A few flatties over the bag limit, then?'

'Ha. I wish.' Martin can hear something in his lawyer's voice, below the superficial lightness. 'It's something else, something more serious. Buggered if I know what they're looking for. Abalone or lobsters or something.'

Martin grins; there aren't too many abalone this far north. His eye hurts again. Maybe the damage is worse than he realised. 'I'll leave you with it then.'

Next he calls Mandy, but the call goes through to voicemail. She must still be with the police. So he texts, saying he's taking her car. Then, as an afterthought, he sends a message of support, dressed up with a couple of heart emojis. He calls Winifred. Again the call goes through to voicemail. No text for her, no emojis.

Mandy's Subaru is new. It smells new, it feels new, there are no rattles. The radio works. And compared to his Corolla, it's grot-free.

Martin picks up Topaz from the hostel car park, helps her put the packs in the back next to Liam's stroller and baby carrier. He shifts the rest of the boy's supplies onto the back seat to make room. The boy himself is wide-eyed and no longer complaining, taking everything in as Martin and Topaz rearrange the load. The young American takes the passenger seat and starts jostling her breasts about. 'What's up with this seatbelt? Can you help me out?'

The act is wearing thin. Martin's eye throbs, not his groin. 'You can manage.' And she does, offering the grin of a naughty child, unrepentant.

Martin pulls into the traffic, driving carefully through town; his vision somehow adrift. Liam falls silent, lulled by the sense of movement. By the time they cross the bridge spanning the Argyle, he's asleep. Topaz lifts her feet up on the dashboard, legs flashing in the sun, golden and smooth, extending out from cut-off jeans. If she's worried about Royce, she's not showing it. Her boyfriend has been taken to hospital yet she's driving in the opposite direction, apparently without a care in the world. She has her window down, the wind moving her long hair around her tanned face. She becomes aware of Martin's attention and smiles back at him, but it seems to him there is something fragile in her expression, as if she's unconvinced by herself.

'So why were they fighting?' he asks. 'Royce and Harry?'

'Harry hit on me. Royce thought he'd defend my honour. You know what idiots men can be.'

Martin recalls how Royce had seemed oblivious to Topaz's flirtations previously. 'I don't believe you,' he says, not so much challenging her as stating a fact.

She looks at him as if seeing something for the first time. Then she looks straight ahead and sighs as Martin passes the off-square crossroads, the caravan park to the left, the track up to Hartigan's to the right. He accelerates up towards a hundred kilometres per hour. 'Promise you won't tell the cops?' she says eventually.

'Sure,' says Martin.

'Drugs,' says Topaz. 'Royce has shit for brains. He tried to sell some eccies at the bar in the hostel. Harry took exception.'

'Really? Harry's anti-drugs?'

Topaz laughs. 'You kidding? Of course not. But *he* sells them. Royce was on his patch, the moron.'

'Right,' says Martin. It has the ring of truth about it. He wonders how much Johnson Pear knows of Harry's sideline business.

'It's no big deal,' says Topaz. 'All those backpackers, they're all out for a good time. There's always drugs if you want them. If the hostels don't deal themselves, they'll point you to the people who do. Royce should have scoped it first. He's a sweet guy and well endowed—just not with brains.'

'So he got what he deserved?'

'Depends on how bad he's hurt.'

'Have you heard from him?'

'Yeah, while you were fetching the car. Sounds like they're going to admit him for a few days' observation.'

'What will you do? Still try and find work?'

'No. As soon as he's discharged we'll move on, probably head back to Sydney.'

'What about your visa?'

'Sorry?'

'I thought you needed to get regional work.'

'Yeah. But there are heaps of places up and down the coast. And out west, on the rivers, they tell me. I don't want anything more to do with this shit town and that shitty hostel.'

They drive on in silence, the road straight, shearing its way through the watery scrub surrounding Mackenzie's, the top of the mangroves at eye level. The tide must be in; the smell has abated. A pelican, then two more, glide effortlessly across above the car, heading towards the lagoon. Martin tries to imagine the landscape if St Clair's development were to go ahead. According to the developer, enough of the scrub would be left to shield the golf course and marina from the road, so it should be no different driving through here. But somehow Martin feels it wouldn't be the same, that it would be better if the native title claim were to succeed.

He passes by the white flash of the cross off to the right, lonely amid the scrub. How old would his sisters be now? Thirty-five? Thirty-six? In their prime, with families of their own, Martin's mother—still alive—doting on her grandchildren. The thought saddens him and astonishes him: he has never before made that calculation, not since their deaths. Only since his return have such thoughts come to him, memories of his family bubbling up into his consciousness, quietly insisting on recognition like his own personal land claim, their ghosts asserting a continuous and uninterrupted connection with him. His mind might argue its case, assert that it's all in the past, that today's Port Silver is terra nullius, but there is no High Court here, no Court of Appeal. Mandy's words return to him, asking if he believes in fate or karma. He shakes his head. Maybe he should be driving towards Longton Hospital, not away from it. And then the memorial to his mother and sisters is behind him and the Court of Human

Emotions rises, temporarily adjourned. He drives on towards the turn-off to Hummingbird Beach.

—

'Oh my God!' exclaims Topaz, the archetypal American. Martin has pulled into the rough-and-ready car park and Topaz has leapt out. 'Oh my God!' She's looking down at the beach. 'This is heaven!'

'The office is down there in the old house,' says Martin, pointing. 'Let me fetch Liam and I'll see you there.' The boy has started to wake now the car has come to a standstill. Martin gives him a hug, holds him aloft to smell his bum, then carries him one-handed as he opens the back up, feeling as if he is getting the hang of it. He even manages to extract the baby carrier and lower the child into it, strapping him in, without dropping him. Liam is looking at him quizzically, as if unsure what's going on. He reaches out, as if to point at Martin's face. Perhaps he's seen the creeping bruise.

By the time they get down to the office, Topaz is already deep in negotiations with Jay Jay Hayes.

'Martin, back so soon. Not looking for a place to stay as well?' asks Jay Jay.

'No. But I did want to apologise for before.'

'He gave me a lift out here,' Topaz explains.

'Did you now?' says Jay Jay, cocking an amused eyebrow. 'What happened to your face?'

'That thug who runs the hostel, Harry the Lad. He hit me.'

The eyebrow falls, the amusement fades. 'Really? Don't get on the wrong side of him.'

'Why's that?'

'He's got a temper.' She's frowning, but smiles when she turns back to the young American. 'Now, let me get Topaz here sorted.'

The cheapest option is a bunk bed in a dorm, followed by renting a tent. Instead, the American decides to hire a cabin. While Jay Jay gets her kitted out with linen, Martin goes and gets the two packs from the car, Topaz's and Royce's. He can only haul one to the office with him, encumbered as he is with Liam's weight on his own back.

He reaches the deck as Topaz is heading off towards her cabin; he drops the pack and tells her the other one is up by the cars. 'Good on you, Martin,' she says, planting a provocative kiss on his lips, smirking at his discomfort as she ruffles Liam's head.

Martin returns to the office, where Jay Jay is sitting behind her desk. He looks; the box with the scans is nowhere to be seen.

'I wanted to apologise,' he says.

'So you said.'

'I wasn't looking for anything. Not really. I was just curious. An occupational habit.'

'Okay, forget about it.'

'I can't,' he says. 'Jay Jay, I need to do everything I can to help Mandy. I think Jasper's death is tied up somehow with the plans to develop your land and Mackenzie's Swamp. I just can't work out how.'

Jay Jay considers him for a moment before letting her breath out in a long sigh, as if giving in to Martin's imperative. 'What do you want to know?'

Martin lowers the carrier, lifting Liam out, holding the boy against his chest as he sits, all the while wondering how to frame his next question. In the end, he's blunt. 'What happens when you die?' he asks her.

Jay Jay's eyes widen at the question and she studies him intently for a moment, then she bursts out laughing, surprising Martin. It's a proper laugh, belly deep, not some pretence. 'I'm not going to die, Martin. Not any time soon.'

'The scans,' says Martin. 'Healthy people don't have scans. Not like that, not that many.'

The humour drops from the surfer's face. 'Did you look at them?'

'No, just the envelopes.' He spreads one arm wide, a gesture of innocence. 'They were just sitting there. I wouldn't be the first to see them.'

'Oh, for fuck's sake,' says Jay Jay. She stands, turns her back, reaches down and lifts her singlet over her head. And there on her back, running under her bra strap, are two large triangles of scar tissue, smooth and pink, recessed into the freckled skin, each about twelve centimetres long and half as wide. 'There,' she says, 'cop an eyeful.' Then she drops the top, turns, and resumes her seat.

'Skin cancer,' says Martin.

'Melanomas,' says Jay Jay. 'All those years surfing without a wetsuit. It catches up with you.'

Martin is unsure how to proceed. 'Are you . . . ?'

'Am I all right? Yes. They were cut out six years ago. After five years you're clear. If I sprout another one now, it will almost certainly be new, not a relapse. I get a visual check every three months, and up until last year I got a scan every six. But I'm done with scans now. I put them all in that box to chuck them out. I don't need them anymore.'

'So you're okay?'

'Never better.'

'That's great, Jay Jay. It really is. And I'm sorry to pry.'

She laughs at that. 'Right. Says the journo.'

Martin smiles, as if she's paying him a compliment. 'Tell me, though: who knew you were sick?'

Jay Jay shrugs. 'My doctor. The pharmacist. Some people up at Longton Hospital. A few friends.'

'Jasper Speight?'

'No. Not that I know of. I didn't discuss it with him.'

'Tyson St Clair seems convinced you will sell.'

'Does he now? Well, sorry to disappoint him, but who sells paradise?'

She's right. He imagines himself in her position. Maybe he wouldn't run a campground, maybe he wouldn't house a guru, maybe he wouldn't host bacchanalian parties, but he definitely wouldn't sell. Not if he could avoid it. 'I'm sorry, Jay Jay,' he says, standing, careful not to drop Liam.

'Let me know how you go, Martin. If I can help you, I will. I owe that to Jasper.'

'Right,' says Martin. 'There is one thing. What do you know about the disappearance of Amory Ashton?'

The smiles eases from Jay Jay's face. 'Ashton? What about him?'

'There's a TV crew over at the old cheese factory looking for his body.'

'What TV crew?'

'Channel Ten. Up from Sydney. Filming a cold-case crime special.'

'I don't know anything more than anyone else,' she says. 'He went missing years ago. His car was found burnt out somewhere up on Treachery Bay. There was speculation he was murdered, but nobody knows why.'

'Say he was dead. Any idea who would inherit his property?'

She shakes her head, frowning. 'No. I don't think he had any family. I never heard of one, anyway.'

———

Martin drives out of the campsite, his mind awash with questions. Jay Jay is not selling and she's not ill, so the plans of Tyson St Clair or anybody else to develop Hummingbird Beach and the swamp are going nowhere. So why does Doug Thunkleton think St Clair is about to demolish the cheese factory? And why does St Clair seem so confident Jay Jay will sell Hummingbird? And why was Jasper Speight killed? Did someone make the same mistake as Martin, believe that Jay Jay was seriously ill and the whole development plan was back in play?

The bruise on his cheek is beginning to pulse, connected by some tendril to the headache threatening to re-emerge at the base of his skull. He feels as if he's gathering more and more information that's meaning less and less. It's flowing in a torrent, but threatening to drown him rather than float him, the water growing murkier and murkier, full of cross-currents and rips.

The Subaru rattles across the cattle grid, the whole car vibrating. Liam issues an ominous howl. Martin slows down a tad. Where the track merges with the larger road, he stops. The signpost at the fork has him reconsidering. Fingers point towards the clifftop properties: Sergi, Cromwell and Hartigan. Liam gives an impatient squawk, wanting the car to resume its motion. Martin turns left.

The gravel road is runnelled and corrugated, in need of grading. It winds up the hill beneath a canopy of spotted gums, tall and imperious, interspersed with lesser trees cloaked in creepers and vines, while ferns and grass trees compete in the undergrowth, a remnant of coastal rainforest from back before the logging trucks and the dairy farms. He drives with the window open, breathing in the warm air, bird call bouncing all around. A wallaby, small and dark-furred, watches him approach from a bank above the road before bounding unhurried into the scrub. The track winds upwards for a kilometre or two before curling southwards. Martin can't be sure, surrounded by the forest, but he feels that he must be close to the clifftop. There's a sense of altitude. He checks his phone: one bar, the signal creeping up the coast. He passes a small clearing to the left where there's a break in the trees. There's a distant sound; it might be surf hitting the base of the cliff or it might be wind in the treetops.

He's always loved this feeling, this exploration of a new pathway, following it for the first time. As a kid, walking or riding a bike, trying to find shortcuts through the cane fields or paths along the base of the escarpment; as a reporter, entering a new country, a new conflict, discovering a new reality. And this track is new to him; he was never aware Ridge Road existed. As boys, they rarely ventured out along the long flat road towards the cheese factory. There was no destination back then, just twenty kilometres to nowhere: a swamp, a cheese factory and, beyond them, the rip-riven beaches of Treachery Bay.

The forest gives way abruptly at a fence line, replaced by the vibrant green of pasture, dairy cows raising their heads from grazing, curious at the intrusion. The road crosses a cattle grid and runs through the middle of a paddock. He slows right down. Cows saunter across in front of him, asserting their ownership, forcing him to give way. Liam vocalises his wonderment. 'Cows, Liam,' says Martin. 'Cows.' Liam answers with some strange articulation of his own. To the left, up towards the horizon, Martin can see a house nestled into a hollow below the lip of the hill, surrounded by farm buildings. To his right the land flows downwards, to a distant fence line and a screen of trees. A driveway for the house forks off the road. A sign says SERGI. Martin keeps driving, passing across another grid, through the fence line and back into forest. The road narrows: it's single lane now, grass sprouting on the rise between the wheel tracks. Another kilometre or two and it veers left, through a gate. There's a sign: CROMWELL-PARKES. He pushes on, the track twisting upwards. He emerges from the bush, arriving at a house. It's new, architect designed. Not big, not built to impress, but light and airy, a mixture of wood and stone and pre-rusted steel, with wide windows protected by strategically positioned awnings. And instead of sheltering from the weather like the Sergi farmhouse, this house lifts into it, perching on the clifftop, with nothing beyond it but the open sky and, presumably, the ocean. Martin is confused: the track leads to the house and no further. He pushes on, the Subaru in low gear. A figure appears in the doorway, a silver mop of hair.

Martin cuts the engine, climbs out, walks up towards the man who has descended some stairs to meet him. He's tall, almost gaunt, twenty or twenty-five years older than Martin. He's wearing canvas pants and an old blue shirt, both spattered with paint, as are his hands. A painter, at a guess, an artist.

'Hello there,' says the man as they converge. 'Can I help you?' His voice is rich and resonant and self-confident, a voice born of old-school privilege.

'Yes,' says Martin. 'I was trying to get through to the Hartigan place.'

'Can't be done,' says the man. 'At least not in that.' He gestures towards Martin's car, as if it lacks the pedigree.

'I saw a signpost,' replies Martin. 'Down near Hummingbird Beach. Said the road went through to Hartigan's.'

'It used to, but there's a bridge halfway along. It collapsed years ago. So no cars. The occasional bushwalker, dirt bikes and push bikes, an intrepid fisherman or two, but that's it. The track is still there. Down in the bush there, right next to our gate.'

'You don't want the council to fix it up? Shorten your drive to town?'

'Certainly not.' The man pauses, examining Martin more closely. 'Why are you so interested?'

'My name is Martin Scarsden. My partner, Mandalay Blonde, has inherited the Hartigan house. We're going to move into it.'

'Ah, I see,' says the man. 'Well, we'll be neighbours then. I'm Bede Cromwell.' He has a smile on his face; if he likes his solitude he obviously sees little threat in his prospective neighbour. The men shake hands.

'So you're an artist?' asks Martin.

'You've heard of me?' Bede says.

'Yes, I think I might have.'

But the man laughs, amused at Martin's polite lie. 'Yes. I can imagine.' His eyes are bright with humour, brown and warm.

Martin likes him. Then Bede becomes more serious. 'You don't want to open the old road, do you?'

Martin shakes his head. 'Can't imagine why we would. We can access Dunes Road directly. Sounds like it's better left the way it is.'

'That's good to hear. Just what I told that other fellow.'

'What other fellow?'

'Jasper Speight. The real estate chap.'

⁓

Bede Cromwell is most forthcoming, any residual aloofness dissolved by the knowledge Martin is to be his neighbour. He invites him in, curious rather than indulgent at the sight of Liam. They pass through a lounge room of bohemian chic, wall space at a premium: large abstract canvases compete with overflowing bookshelves and, trumping them both, an entire wall of glass, filled with sky and sea, a panorama of blues. Bede's partner, a taciturn bloke named Alexander, some sort of writer, is busy in the lounge staring at a computer screen and is not to be disturbed, so Bede leads Martin and Liam out onto the deck. And what a deck, more like a nest, perched right on the lip of the cliff. There's a one-hundred-and-eighty-degree view out to sea and along the clifftops, eighty metres above the surf. To the north the cliff line runs for kilometres, folding back and forth, rising and falling, while to the south it cuts inwards before doubling back out towards a point. 'That's you out there, on the point, almost hidden by the trees,' says Bede. 'The other side of the ravine. About two or three kilometres.'

Martin is standing, rocking Liam. 'It must be wild out here in a storm,' he says.

'Like the bridge of a ship,' says Bede, eyes alive. 'It moves. Sideways, up and down. Like a living thing. We love it.'

'Sounds scary.'

'Not if you know the engineering. It's designed to sway. It's all wood up top here, but underneath it's high-tech composites and aircraft-grade aluminium.'

Bede offers afternoon tea and seems pleased when Martin plumps for espresso over herbal teas. While his host is inside, Martin takes the opportunity to change Liam's nappy—how many can the boy go through? Bede serves olive bread with homemade dips and pâté. Martin feeds Liam a little dip from his finger. The boy loves it. He's clearly hungry and Martin belatedly remembers the food Mandy packed, a container of vegetable mash still in the back seat of the car. But the boy can't get enough of the spread, giving Martin's finger an unintended nip with his new front teeth. Bede brings out a jug of rainwater and Martin makes up a new bottle of formula.

'You know Jasper Speight is dead?' Martin queries.

'No. Is that right?' The man looks surprised. 'What happened?'

'He was murdered.'

'Murdered? Are you sure?'

'There's no doubt. Stabbed to death.'

'That's terrible.'

'At the place my partner is renting—was renting—in town.'

Bede turns away, looking out to sea, shaking his head as if in disbelief. 'Even here. There's no getting away from it, is there? The violence.'

'What violence?' asks Martin, not quite following the artist's train of thought.

Bede shrugs. 'Violence. It just seems ubiquitous. It's why we moved here from Sydney. Alexander won't even have a television.'

'I see,' offers Martin, not sure that he does.

Bede turns back to him. 'Alexander was bashed in Sydney. Twice.'

There's not much to say to that, so they sit in silence for a while before Martin restarts the conversation. 'So what was Jasper proposing?'

'Oh, he had plans to subdivide the properties up here. Our place, your place, Sergi's and Jay Jay Hayes's. Five-hectare plots, all with houses on the cliff. I think he had plans for about twenty in all. But none of us were interested. I know Bert Sergi isn't and he's got the most land. I heard Jay Jay Hayes wasn't interested either.'

'What was Jasper offering?'

'Money, of course. Good money, as a matter of fact. And we'd keep our own houses. The idea was that each house would be screened from its neighbours. Not sure how he intended to achieve that, but we really didn't get that far. None of us were interested.'

'I understand. You like it how it is. But was there anything about the proposal that was . . .' he searches for the right word and is not sure he's found it '. . . offensive?'

Bede gives a droll smile. 'I guess that's a matter of opinion.' Then he holds his paint-spattered hands wide. 'To be fair, if you were going to develop the clifftops, you could do a lot worse. He wanted to open the through road, which we didn't like, but below that would be given over to a dedicated nature reserve running down to the shores of the wetlands. I forget what he called it.'

'An environmental covenant?'

'Yes, that's it.'

Martin is considering his next question when his phone trills in his pocket. 'You have reception?'

'It's the elevation,' says Bede.

Sure enough, one bar. It's a text message from Winifred. *6 pm. Breakwater Hotel.* Martin smiles: the world's least verbose lawyer. He checks his watch. It's already gone five; time to get going. He thanks Bede, promising to invite him and Alexander over when Mandy and he have made Hartigan's habitable.

Easing the Subaru back down the drive, Martin wonders why Jay Jay had said nothing of Jasper's proposal. She mentioned the clifftop land, but not the real estate agent's offer. Surely he would have at least suggested it? And Martin will have to ask Mandy about Hartigan's. Jasper knew she'd inherited the house. If he had approached Bede and Alexander, Bert Sergi and Jay Jay, then surely he had approached her. So why hasn't she told him? Maybe by the time Mandy arrived in town, Jasper had already been rejected by the others and had abandoned the scheme. Or maybe it was the other way around, and Mandy's arrival and her inheritance had been the catalyst for Jasper: a way to make money, a way to protect the swamplands, a way to trump Tyson St Clair. So why hasn't Mandy mentioned it? If the cops suspected she was hiding something, no matter how irrelevant, their suspicions would rise again. Has she told them? Has she confided in Winifred? If so, why not in him?

He's just passing through Bede and Alexander's gate, threading the car through an obstacle course of potholes, when he sees the turn to the left, the continuation of the road. Coming down the hill, it's easier to see. He noses the Subaru into it. It's more like a fire trail than any sort of road; he's glad he's in Mandy's all-wheel drive, not his temperamental Toyota. Trees reach across the track, scratching at the windscreen and roof, forming a tunnel above the car. He inches forward. He should probably stop, but now he's started there's nowhere to turn; he'd have to reverse all the way. He checks his watch. Five-twenty. He should be heading back. But he nudges the car forward, curiosity getting the better of him. The track is red clay, damp and slippery, so different from the dusty drive into the cheese factory just a few kilometres away. *Microclimate*, thinks Martin.

A hundred metres further into the forest, the track opens up a bit to a kind of a clearing. There's enough room to turn the car around, maybe a five-point turn. And there, in front of him, barring their way, a gate. He cuts the engine, climbs out into the silence. The air is cool and damp, the rainforest smelling of nature and echoing with birdsong. In the back of the car, Liam emits a small wail, as if concerned he is being left behind. Martin searches the ground. There are tyre marks set into the clay, leading through the gate. They can't be that old, not with the amount of rain the forest would attract. He checks the gate. It's galvanised steel, grown old and rusty, threatening to fall from its hinges, but held shut with a new chain and a shiny brass lock. Who has the key? Who drives along a dead-end track? Who locks the gate on a track to nowhere? The trail on the other side of the gate looks passable, two concave paths running off through the trees, no more deteriorated than the track Martin has just traversed. Maybe it's the local volunteer fire brigade, maintaining the track as a fire trail. Makes sense. Martin considers getting Liam and the baby carrier, climbing the fence and continuing on foot, at least until he reaches the collapsed bridge. But to what end? He'd satisfy his love of new paths, but what would that achieve? He checks his watch again: half past five. He's already going to be late. Winifred will be punctual; people who bill in six-minute increments usually are. He looks past the gate, but there is nothing else to see—the track and the bush, that's all. By one side of the track, in the undergrowth, he spies an old tin sign. He bends down, scrapes away dirt and leaf litter. HARTIGAN. The fence line and the gate must mark the border between properties.

There is silence, a momentary pause, and then two events occur almost simultaneously. Liam lets out an ear-piercing wail and Martin's phone rings. He checks the screen. Mandy. But Liam will brook no delay; he screams again, a real scream. Panicking, hearing the pain in the boy's voice, fearing he has been bitten by some insidious creature, Martin rushes back to the car, unbuckling the boy from his booster seat, letting the phone ring out. He lifts Liam, tries to soothe him, rocking him. There is a moment's respite, Liam red-faced and sucking air, seeming puzzled at his own distress, looking to Martin for help, only to be overwhelmed by another soul-wrenching wail. There is no doubt: he is in pain. The phone rings again. Martin, desperate, answers. 'Mandy!'

'Hi, Martin . . .' She gets no further, hears her boy's anguished call. 'Is that Liam?'

'Yes. He was fine and then . . .' His voice is drowned out by another cry. The boy is writhing in his grip and the phone slips, falls to the ground.

'What the fuck, Martin? What have you done?' Mandy's voice sounds distant but no less anguished.

'What do I do?' he yells, feeling utterly useless.

But the phone has cut out. Either that or Mandy has hung up.

Liam sucks in a huge lungful of air, as if preparing for the mother of all screams, when suddenly he pauses and a curious, almost beatific look passes across his radish-red face. And that's when the diarrhoea begins.

chapter fourteen

MARTIN FINDS WINIFRED BARBICOMBE CONTEMPLATING THE REMAINS OF A LONG
drink by the window in the bar of her hotel, the Breakwater, overlooking the port. In Martin's youth, the place was a hybrid: the
front bar home to the fishermen and dockhands, the fish-gutters
and the mechanics, the mill workers and the retired whalers, while
upstairs, accessed through a separate entrance, were low-key holiday
apartments. It had always seemed a bit suspect, a bit English: why
would anyone want a view overlooking a fishing port when they
could have one overlooking a beach? But those days are gone.
Since the introduction of the marine reserves, the fishing fleet has
shrunk to an ornamental size. The port has begun to gentrify;
there are yachts, motor launches and charter boats dotted among
the empty berths and mothballed trawlers. The docks boast a cafe,
a retail outlet run by the fishermen's cooperative and a wine bar.
The hotel itself is lagging behind: the carpet in the bar is sticky

in parts, threadbare in others; the seats on some of the bar stools have begun to spring leaks, exposing yellow foam innards; there is the smell of stale beer and long-gone revelries. If this is part of Tyson St Clair's new tourism-driven Port Silver, it's badly in need of a facelift. There's a banner above the bar—UNDER NEW MANAGEMENT—so maybe a renovation is on its way.

'Hello, Winifred.'

As the lawyer looks up, Martin thinks she's showing her age. 'Hello, Martin. You okay? That's quite a bruise.'

'Nothing that won't heal.'

'How's the boy?'

'Okay, I think. Mandy has him.'

'Where?'

'She rented a room upstairs so she could give him a bath.'

'Good idea. He needs it; she can afford it.'

Martin stays standing. He's still feeling a little shell-shocked from the rivers of shit—how could such a small child contain such volume?—and from Mandy's tongue-lashing. 'What's that you're drinking?' he asks Winifred.

'Long Island iced tea.'

'Care for another one?'

'No, one's more than enough. But please get yourself something. Put it on my tab.'

Martin detours via the bathroom, finding a chipped ceramic basin where he scrubs his hands clean for the third or fourth time, still struggling to rid the smell from his nostrils. At the bar, waiting to order, Martin looks back at the solicitor. Winifred is staring at her near-empty glass, pushing ice around the bottom of it with her straw. Something is troubling her.

'Have you learnt anything more of use?' she asks as soon as he returns with his beer.

'Maybe, but nothing I can make much sense of.' He tells her of his second visit to Hummingbird Beach, of the road running through Mandy's land, and Jasper Speight's proposal to subdivide the clifftop properties—and his suspicion that Jasper must have approached Mandy with his development proposal.

Winifred listens intently, giving an occasional nod of comprehension. But when Martin finishes, she grimaces and shakes her head. 'It doesn't help. If Jasper Speight canvassed subdividing or upgrading the old road or anything else, all it does is tie them more closely together. I don't want them closer; I want them as far apart as I can get them.'

'Did she tell the police, though, about Jasper and the subdivision? Did she tell you?'

Winifred stares him down. 'It's called lawyer–client privilege.'

Martin bristles. 'She didn't tell them, or us, about her spat with Jasper at the lifesavers.'

'What are you insinuating?'

Martin swallows, unsure of himself, speaking anyway. 'That she's hiding something. Something to do with Jasper.'

'Are you going to broach that with her?'

Martin can't hold the solicitor's gaze, looks down at his beer instead. He'd done it once before: accused Mandy of misleading him. That was back in Riversend. It almost ended their relationship before it started. 'I don't see how I can.'

'I think that might be wise,' Winifred says drily.

'Maybe you should ask her about it. Lawyer–client privilege and all.'

'Maybe,' says Winifred. 'But remember Jasper Speight's dying words; he gasped your name. He was coming to see you, or to see both of you. It has to be something more. Something else.'

'St Myron the Wonderworker?'

Winifred just shakes her head again, looking disconsolate. 'I don't know what it means. I don't think the police do either. They've been through his collection; thousands of postcards. They can't see anything significant about that one.'

An elderly man approaches, his cheeks twin webs of burst capillaries, selling tickets for a raffle, a meat tray, proceeds to the local nippers. After Liam's performance, Martin has no appetite for meat trays or anything else and politely declines.

'You're a journalist, Martin, so tell me: Jasper Speight's murder has barely rated a mention in the metropolitan media. Why not? Is that unusual?'

Martin shrugs. 'Not really. There's no news hook. A real estate agent is killed in a provincial town. Worth a mention, but not much more.'

'Just say Mandy were to be arrested . . . what then?'

'Arrested for what?'

'I don't know. Arrested in connection with the murder.'

'That could be different.' He thinks it through. 'Maybe very different. Maybe even a media storm, like Riversend. After what happened down there, she's public property. An object of fascination. Christ, if Lindy Chamberlain got arrested for shoplifting it would be news. And another murder, in another town? The circus would be here before we could scratch ourselves.'

Winifred stares out the window. 'Sometimes I wish she wasn't so photogenic. That's part of it, isn't it?'

'Sure. But it's also the backstory, what she went through down there. She's perfect news fodder: some people will still think she's guilty of something; others will go to the barricades for her. Social media would light up like a Christmas tree. It doesn't matter that none of them even know her.' He looks down at his beer, then up at Winifred. 'So don't let her get arrested.'

Winifred returns serve with a sardonic smile. 'That's the plan.' But soon enough her frown is back, her concern. 'What do you know of Morris Montifore? You helped him out of a hole down in the Riverina.'

'That doesn't mean I know him. He plays his cards pretty close to his chest.'

'I checked him out,' says Winifred bluntly. 'With some of my New South Wales colleagues.'

'And?'

'He's one of the best, one of the state's leading investigators, with a reputation for thoroughness, professionalism and getting results. He's straight; there's no suggestion of him being involved in anything untoward. He also has a reputation for being politically astute, of conducting investigations and getting results in a way that doesn't rile the powers that be.'

'What does that mean?'

'That investigations remain focused and don't spill over into politically sensitive areas. That the identities of influential people are kept confidential. That the media are either shut out and kept in the dark, or receive tip-offs and full access. He gets the job done, but in a way that suits the priorities of the political establishment.'

'What are you driving at?'

'So why is he investigating a death that hasn't even made the metropolitan media? What's so sensitive that it requires their go-to guy?'

Martin hasn't thought along these lines, hadn't known of Montifore's reputation. It made sense for the authorities to send their best man to Riversend, but why send him here? 'Mandy?'

'Must be,' says Winifred. 'If Jasper Speight was killed anywhere else in this town and not her place, I wonder if Montifore would be the investigating officer.'

The meat-tray guy is back, saying that the raffle can't be drawn until the last of the tickets are sold. Martin buys the rest, twenty bucks worth, just to get rid of him.

He finishes his beer as the man assiduously writes the details on each and every ticket, first name and mobile number. When he's finally gone, Martin revives the conversation. 'Do you think Montifore is trying to keep Mandy out of the media? That they don't want the investigation to get any prominence?'

Winifred doesn't answer the question directly. 'Today was strange. Montifore had Mandy and me at the police station for a good five hours. He questioned her three times, about half an hour at a time. Left her there cooling her heels between times.'

'What are you thinking?'

The solicitor grimaces. 'The interviews were strange. At times I couldn't fathom Montifore's line of questioning. He was using an unusual interrogation technique. I've encountered it before, but not often. He kept changing the focus of his questioning, jumping around in time and place as if to disorientate her, to catch her out. I'm not even sure whether it's about Jasper's murder or something else. Every now and then he'd ask if she knew such and such a person. At first I thought they were all locals: Harrold Drake, Tyson St Clair, the mayor, the baker, the candlestick maker. But I've checked them out. There were one or two who aren't locals.'

'Who are they then?'

'No idea. It's got me worried. There's something going on here and I don't know what it is. They only asked briefly about her confrontation with Jasper Speight at the lifesavers, as if they'd already dismissed it as inconsequential.'

'You think Montifore is investigating something else? Something unconnected to Jasper?'

'I don't know.'

'Have you asked her? Does she know?'

'If she does, she's not telling me.'

There's more silence, more contemplation. Martin trawls through his mind, hoping for some spark, some inspiration, but nothing comes.

Any further deliberations are interrupted by Mandy herself, pushing Liam's stroller through the bar. She looks exhausted. And gorgeous. Martin leaps to his feet. She sizes him up for a moment, then smiles and falls into him, not so much an embrace as a bid for support.

'Are you okay?' he asks.

'Yeah. Just zonked.'

'Liam?'

'Fine now. They get sick, they get better.'

'Something to drink?'

'God, yes. Gin and tonic. Lots of gin.'

Martin orders at the bar and, with Mandy's permission, buys bottled water and apple juice to help Liam rehydrate. He makes up a weak mixture in a sterilised bottle and hands it to Liam. The boy's eyes light up as Martin squats. 'Marn,' he says. 'Marn!' Martin looks up at Mandy, but she's deep in conversation with Winifred and hasn't heard. Martin gives Liam the bottle, silencing him, then stares at him chugging on his bottle for a long moment. He stands, collects Mandy's drink from the barman and hands it to her. She doesn't muck about, ditching the straw and taking a healthy slug, then sighing with exaggerated relief. 'Thanks. I can't tell you how much I needed that.'

'Right,' says Martin. He slides onto his stool, glancing back at Liam, busy with his bottle in the stroller. 'Tough day?'

'Pointless day. A waste of time. Fuck-knuckles.' She looks at Winifred, who nods her accord. Mandy takes another drink. 'Let's get takeaway, Martin. Then an early night.'

'Sounds good to me.'

Across the bar, behind Mandy, Martin can see the meat-tray man preparing to draw the raffle. 'Let's get out of here,' he says to her.

⁓

Later, back at the caravan park, Mandy is dozing on the couch but Liam is wide awake, as if he's extracted the last energy out of his mother and is now joyfully squandering it, sliding along the linoleum floor on his bum, pushing himself backwards with puffy piston legs, looking for things to attack. He finds a magazine, tries sucking on it, then starts ripping at it instead.

'Backpack, Liam? Carrier?'

The child beams back at Martin. Is there comprehension there, or is Martin imagining it? Whatever, the boy doesn't stop chirping as he's lifted into the contraption and strapped in. Martin swings the pack up and onto his back. He's growing fond of the carrier; he likes the weight, the load supported by his shoulders and hips, the sense of impetus it gives him. It's like a remnant from an earlier life as a correspondent, the sensation of going somewhere, of forging ahead. And so it is with the boy: he and Liam are heading into an uncertain future, but for now they are travelling together.

He walks out the door of the cabin, leaving Mandy sleeping. And almost immediately a memory comes to him. Perhaps it's the heft on his back that invokes it, perhaps the angle of the sun cutting through the trees as it sinks towards the distant escarpment. Martin stands still, letting the memory come, closing his eyes, as if trying to capture a dream. His father. He's following his father. Martin has a backpack, his father too, and Ron Scarsden is carrying another bag in his strong hands. Where? When? Martin keeps his eyes closed, shutting out the present, willing the past to return. Camping. Camping with his father. There is sand, the sun low. Camping. Night-time, mosquitoes, unable to sleep, his father snoring. His father, hands imbued with competence, erecting the tent with speed and skill. Martin awed, worried he could never manage such a feat. Fishing. His father casting, reeling in. A fish on the coals of the fire. The wild beaches. Treachery Bay. He'd been there with his father, back before it all went wrong.

Liam shifts his weight, no longer mesmerised by the sunlight through the trees, urging him on, a jockey on his horse. Martin opens his eyes but doesn't move. Treachery Bay. He'd tried to remember earlier if he'd been there and could recall nothing. And yet now, unbidden, this memory surfaces. But that's not what shakes him. It's the memory itself. The flavour of it, the feeling of it. His feeling towards his father, the feelings he had back then, *before*. Admiration. Respect. Love. He draws a shallow breath. He has spent so long submerging the memories of after, he's never considered what it was like before. He stands for a moment more, the western sky turning vivid, infused with gold and pink and orange, until Liam starts to grumble.

Martin heads to the river, attracted by the water, the reflected sunset. Colours ripple in the wake of a passing boat, Liam vocal in his admiration. Another recollection, vague and nebulous, of light fascinating him as a small child, when he was too young for words and comprehension. And another memory, an early experience with fireworks: Vern and his dad lighting them, skyrockets held vertical in empty beer bottles, sending them up to explode in the heavens above the Settlement. He recalls how magical they looked, how they evoked a collective 'aahh' from onlookers. The Settlement. He remembers now; each year there was a giant bonfire on a vacant lot, the whole community there, united in a desire to watch it burn. He wonders if Liam has seen fireworks; he hopes he might be with him for the first time.

They walk along the shore, coming to the wharf where Vern dropped him last night. Two old men sit hunched over their fishing rods, side by side on a wooden bench, dark against the sunset shifting on the river.

One looks up, takes a suck on his beer. 'Hello, Martin, fancy seeing you here.'

Martin peers at the man's face, recognising something familiar in the golden light, taking a moment more to fathom its provenance. 'Sergeant Mackie?'

The man harrumphs. 'Long time since I was a sergeant, son. Just plain old Clyde nowadays.'

'Who's this?' the other man interjects, his voice like gravel. Martin sees nothing familiar about him. Whereas age has thickened Mackie and lowered his centre of gravity, this other man is wiry and without fat, his face folded in on itself: no jowls, just wrinkles as deep as crevices.

'It's Martin Scarsden—Ron Scarsden's son,' says Clyde Mackie.

'Is that right? Well, in that case, I'm glad to meet you. Brian's the name. Brian Jinjerik.' Brian doesn't stand, just holds out his hand. Martin shakes it, but cannot recall him.

'It's okay, Martin,' says Mackie, as if reading his thoughts. 'You wouldn't remember Brian. He was inside most of the time you were growing up.'

'Only 'cos you put me there, you old bastard,' says Brian without rancour.

'Only 'cos you deserved it.'

There is fondness in the banter; the former copper and the former crim, fishing together in the twilight waters of Port Silver.

'Catching anything?' asks Martin, unsure of what else he might say.

'Fuck all,' says Brian. 'Good time of day, bad time of tide.' And with that he reels in his line. 'Time I got going. Missus will have the dinner on and it's an early morning tomorrow. Nice to meet you, mate.' The man stands, sprightly on spindly legs, taking his rod and his tackle box, flicking his head towards Liam. 'And who's this young fella? Ron Scarsden's grandson?'

'Near enough,' says Martin, a touch of pride in his voice. 'My partner's son. Liam.'

'Fine-looking fellow. Look after him.'

Martin watches Brian go, bandy-legged, as if he's spent a lifetime on horseback instead of serving at Her Majesty's pleasure. The man heads into the gloaming, towards the line of trees separating the permanent residents from the tourist park.

'Take a seat,' says Mackie. 'Brian's right about the tide, but it's still better sitting here than up at the shack. Bloody beautiful, isn't it?'

'Sure is.' Martin eases the backpack from his shoulders, lowering it so Liam can look out across the sparkling water. He sits next to Mackie, wrapping his legs around the backpack to keep it steady. 'So no Mrs Mackie waiting with your dinner?'

'Not anymore. Died last year.'

'Oh. I'm sorry. I didn't mean to be flippant.'

'No harm done. She died easy. One stroke to let her know it was coming, another to carry her off. She led a good life; she died a good death.'

They're quiet then, looking out across the moving water as it eases towards the sea. Even Liam is quiet, transfixed by the water and the shimmering light. Somewhere behind them a frog calls and a cricket answers. A squadron of fruit bats heads up the river into the fading sunset, off to infiltrate the defences of the orchards, greenhouses and market gardens. A strange feeling comes upon Martin. It's not nostalgia, not that. It's something else. A sense of belonging; that this is home after all. That some part of him never left Port Silver.

As the sunset loses its colour, the streetlights on the bridge hover in the eastern sky and the glow of Port Silver rises like an aura, he breathes in the sense of the place. On the opposite bank the lights of individual houses grow stronger. The frogs are getting bolder, growing louder. Between his legs Liam is joining in, vocalising, as if experimenting, enjoying the sound for its own sake. The air is warm and moist and forgiving.

'Strange,' says Martin. 'You and Brian Jinjerik. Being mates and all.'

'No, not so strange. We moved in the same world, knew the same people, lived by the same rules. Tough times, tough men. Tough women, tough kids. Out in the Settlement.'

'You were from the Settlement?'

'Grew up there. I was one of the lucky ones—my mum knew which way was up. Got through school, joined the force. People like Brian didn't get the same chances.' Mackie pauses for a while, reels in his line, checks his bait, recasts it. 'He was tough, Brian. Him and his mates. Your father wasn't as tough, but he was smarter.'

'How do you mean?'

'He worked out pretty soon that warehouse robberies, repurposing cars and hijacking trucks was a mug's game.'

'He was a criminal?'

'Never convicted.'

'Arrested?'

'Plenty of times. Especially after your mum and sisters died. Drunk and disorderly, most weeks.'

'I remember. But before that?'

'Brian went to prison, a warehouse job up in Brisbane. I suspected your father was in on it but couldn't prove anything. Your mum, she straightened him out, and he moved on to more sensible lines of work.'

'I can't remember him working that much. Even before.'

'Nah. He hurt his back working a shift out at the sugar mill. Got workers compo, quite a sum, then went on an invalid pension.'

'I don't remember him with a bad back.'

'Funny that.'

Martin laughs. 'You didn't report him to the insurance company?'

'Me? Fuck no. Not my problem. If it kept him out of trouble, that was good enough for me. Every now and then I'd pull him into line, tell him not to be too blatant about the other stuff.'

'Other stuff?'

'Working. Casual stuff. On building sites or a night trawler or a shift at the cheese factory.'

'Right.' Martin wonders if the sugar mill ever discovered the truth.

'And when Brian got out, your dad showed him the ropes. Got him on a pension as well. Helped him onto the straight and narrow.'

The two men fall silent. In the backpack, Liam has slumped to one side, drifting towards sleep.

Suddenly Mackie is alert, his rod jerking in his hands. 'Oh fuck it, I've caught a fish.' Martin uses his smartphone as a torch while the old copper reels it in, silver and thrashing as it emerges from the water. The commotion wakens Liam. Something about the flapping fish upsets the boy; he begins to cry. Martin kneels, smiles, calming the child with soft words. Then he hoists the baby carrier up and onto his back, says his farewells and leaves the old policeman to gut his fish in peace.

———

Mandy is awake, waiting for them. She watches as Martin lowers Liam and gently removes the sleeping boy from the carrier. She takes her son, holds him close, rocking him before settling him in his travel cot, the boy oblivious. And then she comes to Martin, threading her arms around his neck.

'I'm sorry,' she says.

'For what?'

'For everything. It isn't how I imagined it.'

'I'm sorry, too,' he says, pulling her closer, his good cheek resting on her head, aware of the electric softness of her newly darkened hair.

'You have nothing to be sorry for.'

'You think?'

'I am so glad you're here.' And she kisses him, the first slow kiss of many.

But in the night, afterwards, Martin can't sleep. He lies awake next to Mandy's sleeping form, thinking of his father, trying to remember after more than half a lifetime trying to forget. What had he been like before the lottery win, before the deaths of Martin's mother and sisters, back before the alcohol took him? Martin finds it impossible to visualise him. The enduring memory is of the drunkard, couch-bound and television-addicted, closed to the world and closed to his son, wasting his money and squandering his health. He survived his wife by eight years; that's all it took to go from a fit and charming thirty-six-year-old to a cirrhotic, diabetic deadbeat. That's all it took to go through all that money, to feed it through the pokies and send it around the racecourses of Australia on the backs of no-hoper horses, leaving nothing to his son other than debts. Unpaid utility bills, unpaid rent, unpaid loans. No wonder he had died; he had nothing left to live for.

The guilt returns, now, in the middle of this sleepless night. The residual guilt Martin feels about his father's death, his reaction to

245

the unexpected news. His father had died, a single-vehicle accident, running off the road and into a tree, his blood alcohol level three times the legal limit. A stupid accident to end a stupid life. The guilt surges again as Martin remembers his reaction: of relief, of escape. Of joy. His father dead. And him laughing. And in the following days, even after discovering that all the money was gone, the enduring sense of freedom, his gratitude that he could live with Vern, that the shackles had fallen and he could re-create himself.

But there had been another Ron Scarsden, the man Clyde Mackie had recalled; the Ron Scarsden who took his son camping and fishing at Treachery Bay. Now Martin tries to conjure him, tries to push aside the memory of the bloated alcoholic. The first thing that comes to mind is his hands, strong and callused, agile and capable, the one image that had never fully deserted him. That most certainly must come from *before*, when Ron Scarsden was still working casually on the fishing boats and building sites and at the cheese factory, topping up his invalid pension. But there are other recollections, lurking dreamlike. Driving with him in the old van, Martin by his side, his father laughing and chiacking and telling jokes, taking him along for company up and down the winding escarpment to Longton. *Can you see the sea?* Another memory, a refinement. His father ruffling his hair, asking him if he wants to come for a ride up to Longton. He remembers that now, and a tear comes to his eye. He tries to remember more, but fatigue washes in like a tide, floating him back towards sleep.

THURSDAY

chapter fifteen

MARTIN LIES DOZING, TROUBLED NIGHT THOUGHTS LEFT BEHIND, THE CABIN'S mattress over-soft, the morning light filtering through the lilac of the plastic blind. He's finding it difficult to summon the impetus to move. Yesterday was a long and exhausting day, and sleep had come in fits and starts; now all he wants is to fall back down its comforting well. Somewhere a phone rings. He stretches out an arm; Mandy is already up. There are no sleep-ins for the mothers of young children. The phone persists; hers not his. He hears her soft voice, considerately low, and a warm wave of emotion passes through him. He still can't fathom what she sees in him, but the bed feels all the warmer for her affection. He hears her voice again and then her laughter, and again the warmth comes to him, even as her laughter brings him fully to consciousness. He no longer wants to sleep, he wants to be with her: what is making her laugh, what is bringing her joy?

In the kitchen, flooded with morning light, he finds her dancing, waltzing around the small space holding Liam. The child is laughing, understanding his mother's mood even without comprehending her words. For a moment Martin watches, spellbound, not wanting to disrupt the magic. Then Mandy sees him, glides over and kisses him. 'Good morning, sir.' There is light playing in her eyes and dimples dance on her cheeks. 'It's come through. Hartigan's.'

'The house?'

'Yes. We just need to go in, sign some final papers and pick up the keys. It's ours.'

Martin moves to her, holds her, her and her son, the three of them swaying together.

'It's going to be our home, our refuge. Liam's castle.' And she beams at Liam, starts dancing again. 'Did you hear that, Sir Liam? Your castle.'

———

There's a celebratory air out of keeping with Drake and Associates' clinical conference room, the decor unable to dull the mood. Mandy is still buzzing with pleasure; even Winifred is breaking out a tight-lipped smile. Liam has been liberated from his stroller and has crawled under the conference table, from where he emits intermittent squeals, half words and half laughs, much to the consternation of Harrold Drake. Martin sees himself reflected in one of the dark glass walls and is surprised to find that he too is smiling. For once, there is a sense that fate is on their side, the axis of the world really has tilted. He considers removing Liam's nappy, just to ramp up Drake's discomfort.

There is not a lot to discuss: Mandy signs, Martin witnesses, Harrold Drake shakes their hands. He presents them with two sets of keys, as if bestowing a gift.

'Ha!' Mandy exclaims, taking Martin's hand. 'Let's go.' And she drops to her knees, crawling in under the table to extract Liam.

But Winifred clears her throat, smile easing away. She turns to their host. 'Harrold, we've a few minor things to discuss. Housekeeping. I wonder if you might give us a few minutes?'

'Of course,' says Harrold smoothly, but he can't help stealing a glance under the conference table as he leaves.

'What gives?' asks Mandy, back on her feet, holding Liam.

'Let's sit,' says Winifred. 'My legs aren't so young anymore.'

Martin takes a seat, unconvinced; he's sure that Winifred could outsprint him if needs be. 'What is it? What's happened?'

Mandy hears the concern in his voice and her smile begins to waver. She places Liam back under the table, takes a seat. 'Winifred?'

But the lawyer is offering a reassuring smile. 'I did a bit of research into the cheese factory and its owner, Amory Ashton. There's a fair chance Mandy is going to inherit that as well.'

Mandy frowns. 'The one on the lagoon that Martin was telling us about yesterday? Really? How?'

'Amory Ashton was your great-uncle—Siobhan Hartigan's half-brother.'

'He left it to me?'

'Not exactly. You weren't even born when he wrote his will. He bequeathed everything to his sister and her heirs. When Siobhan died, her property passed to her husband Eric, your grandfather, who bequeathed practically his entire estate to you.'

'So it's mine,' says Mandy, still sounding unsure.

'Not yet. Ashton hasn't been declared dead, not officially. There's no body, he just vanished. That was a bit over five years ago, and in New South Wales he has to be missing seven years before he can legally be declared dead.'

'What are you driving at?' asks Mandy. 'At some point I'm likely to inherit. Is there some other significance?'

Winifred's voice is calm, her fingers steepled in a pose Martin is growing familiar with, a gesture of judicial judgement. 'Harrold Drake holds Amory Ashton's will here in this office.'

'Drake knows Mandy is the heir?' asks Martin.

'Probably.'

'Why only probably?' asks Mandy. 'Surely he's read it.'

'Here's how it works,' says Winifred, taking on something of the air of a maths teacher broaching a new concept. 'Drake could have accessed Ashton's will at any time, but probably had no reason to do so until he disappeared. When he did, he would have seen Siobhan Hartigan as the heir, and that her heir in turn was Mandy's grandfather, Eric Snouch.'

Martin interrupts. 'Hang on. He had Ashton's will, but surely your firm held Siobhan Snouch's will and her husband's.'

'Correct. Within a week of Ashton's disappearance, Drake inquired after Siobhan's will and then Eric's. We have records.'

'And you let him look?'

'He had every right to look. Wills are not secret documents.'

Now it's Mandy's turn. 'But I thought Eric's will was kept sealed or something until I turned thirty?'

'No, not the will. But the major beneficiary of the will is a testamentary trust. So Drake learnt of the trust and found out that, upon Eric's death, most of the Snouch family fortune passed into it. But he had no way of knowing who the beneficiary of the trust was. Nobody did until you turned thirty—except for the trustees, of course.'

'In other words, you.'

'Correct.'

'And did Drake ask who the beneficiary was?' Martin wants to know.

'I've checked. Yes, he did.'

Martin smiles. 'But you were legally obliged not to tell him.'

'I understand we were very polite,' says Winifred.

'But now?' asks Mandy.

Winifred gives a shrug. 'He still can't access it. Nothing has changed, not legally. But we effectively told him who the beneficiary was the moment we informed him that Mandy had inherited Siobhan Hartigan's house from the Snouch estate. It's the same line of inheritance.'

Martin feels a puzzle piece fall into place. 'That's why St Clair contacted Channel Ten and initiated the search for Ashton's body. He told me straight up he doesn't care who killed Ashton or how he died, he just wants him declared dead and the ownership decided. And now he knows the chain of inheritance and he can offer to buy Mandy out.'

'Precisely,' says Winifred. 'But why the rush? Another two years and Ashton can be declared dead anyway.'

It's Mandy who answers. 'Because in two years' time the land at Hummingbird Beach could be sold and the development underway. He's convinced himself Jay Jay Hayes will sell. And by then, I would know I didn't own a derelict factory on the side of a swamp in the middle of nowhere but a valuable piece of land. So he's hoping to get in early, get the land for a song from the dumb blonde.'

'Has St Clair approached you?' asks Martin.

Mandy shakes her head. 'No. I've never met him.'

The three of them trade looks as they consider the possibilities, but it's Martin who spells out the contradiction. 'It doesn't make sense. He's made no approach to Mandy. More importantly, he was falling over himself to tell me about his plans for the factory and its land. He knew I was Mandy's partner when he told me that.' The two women nod, agreeing with his assessment.

'Did Jasper Speight ever mention him?' Winifred asks Mandy.

Again, Mandy shakes her head, but now her voice is not so sure. 'Jasper definitely mentioned plans to develop Hummingbird Beach, and I seem to remember him saying something about a swamp, wanting to save it. He might have mentioned St Clair's name, I don't remember.' She shrugs. 'I wasn't interested in any development. I just wanted my house up on the point.'

Martin sees his opportunity. 'Did Jasper Speight ever mention a plan to develop the land up along the clifftops? Five-hectare lots, stretching from Hartigan's all the way north to the point near Hummingbird Beach?'

'Yeah, he did once. He was very enthusiastic. He said the other landowners were considering their options, but I said I wasn't subdividing.'

'He said the others were considering it?'

'That's right. But I don't even know who they are yet.'

'I do,' says Martin. 'None of them want to subdivide.'

'I wouldn't read too much into that,' observes Winifred. 'A real estate agent bending the truth. If no one was interested in selling, his proposal was going nowhere.'

'We're missing something,' says Mandy. 'If Jay Jay Hayes isn't selling Hummingbird Beach, then why was Jasper investigating a subdivision? And why is St Clair so keen to find the body of Amory Ashton? Surely it can't be because I've emerged as the heir to Hartigan's and the factory. Can it?'

There's silence then. They can all feel it: this new information is important, but they can't work out how. Mandy bends down and lifts Liam onto her lap. The boy looks around expectantly, waiting for the next contribution.

It's his mother who speaks. 'Is that what Jasper wanted to tell us? To tell Martin?' she whispers. 'Did he know who killed Ashton? Did he find his body?'

The three of them drive to Hartigan's: Mandy, Martin and Liam. Like a real family, a proper one. Behind the wheel, Mandy seems determined to recapture the morning's elation. She's declared the search at the cheese factory a positive: if Doug Thunkleton finds a body, if it somehow provides a motive for Jasper Speight's murder, that can only help clear her name. It reminds Martin of his twin priorities: clearing Mandy and starting their new life. The rest is superfluous. Or it should be, but he can't quite shake his journalistic curiosity. It's part of him. Somewhere in all of this, there is a terrific story, one that's screaming to be told. It's not the staggering criminality of Riversend, but it's certainly something to capture the imagination: murder and mystery, drugs and sex, celebrity and religion, all unfolding against a background of real estate speculation, small-town ambitions and big-time money. He smiles to himself; clearing Mandy still comes first and foremost, plus building their new life together. But if there is a story, a big, compelling story, well, so much the better.

He feels a weight lifting. He imagines Vern's elation when he and Josie learn of the good news: if Mandy owns the cheese factory, she can block the golf course development, if not the marina. He recalls what Jay Jay Hayes had told him about environmental covenants. If Mandy placed one on the cheese factory site, that would go a long way to cruelling the golf course development for all time. And that, in turn, would undermine the basis for St Clair's neighbouring riverside housing subdivision. Martin allows himself a private smile; he's starting to enjoy himself.

'Can you see the sea?'

It's Mandy, talking to Liam. They're on the drive to Hartigan's, winding up through the rainforest towards the house.

'Can you see the sea, Liam?'

Can you see the sea? His father's voice comes to him unbidden, silencing his thoughts, dampening his enthusiasm. The tall trees, the strobing sunlight, the precipitous land; Martin is back inside the van, on the escarpment. *Can you see the sea?* A memory, clear as day. Not some distant echo, not some fleeting image, but as if it happened yesterday. From before the accident; before Ron Scarsden's disintegration, when Martin was six or seven, when his dad was still his dad. Still his hero. It's not a memory he struggles to recall; it's within him as it's always been within him. He closes his eyes, returns to his younger self. The car, the sounds, his father beside him, laughing. Happy. Big and strong, his tradesman's hands, one on the oversize steering wheel, guiding the van smoothly through the hairpins, the other on the stick shift, running up and down through the gears with practised ease. *Can you see the sea?* He can hear the tone of his father's voice, the throaty timbre. The self-assurance, the natural confidence. And emotions return, bound to the memory: his love, his elation, his joy that it is just the two of them, the men together, driving down towards home, father and son. *See the sea, get home free.*

'Martin?' It's Mandy, jerking him back to the present. 'You okay?'

The car has stopped. They've reached a gate. HARTIGAN, says the faded sign, this one still attached to its gate. 'Sorry,' he says, shaking his head, climbing out.

The place seems smaller, a scale model of the storm-blasted house of Martin's memory, but still impressive, even with its back to them. It sits on the highest point, subordinate to nothing, two storeys tall, its weatherboard walls flaking white paint, display-ing patches of yellow undercoat and bare wood, neglect made beautiful on this sunny morning, windows shuttered, ocean-blue paint peeling away in solidarity with the surrounding walls. It looks vaguely American under its gabled roof of corrugated iron, with dormer windows peering away to the north and south. Martin sees the two doors on either end of the wall facing them, knowing already where they lead: into the kitchen and into the hallway. And the window is still there, the one Scotty and he escaped through. This side of the house, facing the bush, seems blank, only the small portico over the front door extending any sort of welcome. Martin knows why: the Hartigans built their home to face the sea, not the land.

Mandy parks and they walk towards it, Mandy carrying Liam. The wind is in their faces, clean and fresh, full of salt and promise.

They ignore the front door, drawn instead to the house's seaward side. Mandy leads the way, the design revealing itself as they progress. Extending from the two-storey block is a large single-storey room the width of the building: the lounge where Martin once sheltered from the storm with Jasper and Scotty. This seaward extension is surrounded entirely by a verandah, its far end curved like the prow of a ship. Indeed, there is something nautical about the design of the building, as if inspired by a boat putting to sea. And sitting on the roof of the lounge, like the bridge of a ship, a large balcony with wooden balustrades reaching out from an upstairs room.

They climb a short set of steps onto the verandah. The boards are weathered, fraying, broken altogether in spots. But it's the view that commands their attention, not the house. To the south, the ground falls away, taking the foliage and trees with it so that they can look down towards the mouth of the Argyle and the foaming sandbar, across the breakwater to Town Beach, to Nobb Hill and the lighthouse. To the right, glimpsed above the trees, is the port and the town. Martin hadn't realised this headland was so high; it's like Nobb Hill without the nobs. To the east, the view is out to sea. Container ships sit on the horizon, rendered motionless by distance. Martin continues by himself around the verandah. To the north, the cliffs fold, softened by sea mist, sheer sandstone and headlands, rainforest reaching down to the sea. There is a reflection of sunlight from a far headland; Bede Cromwell and Alexander Parkes's home, perched atop the cliff like an insect poised for flight. Beyond that, the cliffs continue, past Sergi's dairy farm, all the way to the point where Jay Jay

Hayes surfs, rounding into Hummingbird Beach and, finally, the estuary leading to Mackenzie's Swamp and the site of the old cheese factory. Martin feels a swell of exhilaration—this house is part of the town, part of the landscape, but aloof from it. Their future, safely quarantined from his youth by the wide waters of the Argyle River. Who would have thought it; the haunted house come to rescue him, offering him something he never imagined possessing: a family of his own.

Mandy joins him. 'The whales will be coming north again soon,' she says. 'We can sit out here and toast them on their way.' Her eyes are shining, her early morning elation back for real.

They stand on the verandah for a moment longer, silenced by the magnitude of the ocean. He takes her hand as he scans the vastness, hoping to spot an early whale among the white caps; instead there are only the container ships and a coal carrier, edging against the end of the world, an idle fishing boat closer to shore and a fisherman's tinnie approaching the cliff. It would be a good spot, Martin imagines, in close to the rocks, inaccessible from land. Provided the swell doesn't grow too large.

They enter through the French doors off the verandah, screen door scraping its protest, the lock initially unsure of the provenance of their keys. Inside, the house presents as a strange hybrid of a holiday home, a time capsule and a promise of the future. There's a tube television, a stereo with a turntable, a rotary telephone, all coated with a fine layer of dust. They explore, they plan, they begin to imagine a life together. Mandy's arms grow tired so Martin takes Liam as they explore upstairs and down. The kitchen, the larder and the laundry, a bathroom with a claw-foot tub. The dining room, the table cleared. Stairs down to a wine cellar, sadly pillaged.

Upstairs, bedrooms, the two largest at either end, one with views over the forest, the other looking out to sea with access to the bridge-like balcony, the third and fourth rooms with twin dormer windows.

They leave the way they came, out onto the verandah, taking with them a burgeoning list of what needs to be done: solar panels, roof repairs, a new bathroom, a room for Liam. Water tanks cleaned and septic tanks serviced. Before he locks the door, Martin takes a final look around the lounge. It's almost thirty years since he was last here, sheltering with Jasper and Scotty. The fireplace is the same, although it has been cleaned of ashes; the two-seater couch where Jasper held his cut foot aloft is still there, tattered and destined for the tip; the window they entered through has been repaired, the boarding gone, the glass replaced. Mandy's grandfather, Eric Snouch, only died five years ago; he must have kept up some level of maintenance. Martin checks the bookshelf. The encyclopaedias are all there, volume U–V intact. So are the Phantom comics. He smiles. Perhaps he can read them with Liam.

On the drive down the hill, Martin opens the gate, half carrying it as it scrapes into the soil on its loose hinges. He's got it fully open when he hears a shrill whine, the sound of a two-stroke. His first thought is that it's a chainsaw, someone come to desecrate the forest. He holds his hand up, signalling Mandy to keep the car where it is as he tries to locate the source of the sound. There's a louder buzz and a trail bike breaks out of the bush, not more than thirty metres down the hill from where he's standing. The back wheel showers gravel as the rider flicks it out expertly, giving the throttle another burst to accelerate away and out of sight. Martin is left with fleeting impressions: a rider in black, panniers, a yellow L-plate. The sound recedes and Martin catches the oily smell of exhaust on the wind.

chapter sixteen

MANDY DROPS MARTIN BACK AT THE CARAVAN PARK TO COLLECT HIS CAR. SHE'S taking Liam to child care and then going shopping for brooms, mops and a vacuum cleaner, intent on cleaning up Hartigan's. She needs to get the power on and start checking out architects and tradespeople. Martin gives her Vern's number, telling her his uncle knows all the local tradies, that Lucy May might be able to help. He's kissing her goodbye, happy that she's happy, when his phone rings. It's Nick Poulos, his voice urgent. 'Martin. Can we meet?'

'Sure. What is it?'

'I've got something for you. Surf club in half an hour?'

'Don't you have an office?'

'Of course. But see you at the lifesavers at eleven.' The phone goes dead.

Martin is there on time, but his lawyer is a good twenty minutes late. Nick Poulos doesn't apologise. He takes a seat opposite Martin. 'What happened to you?'

Martin touches his cheek. 'Harry the Lad hit me.'

'You want to sue?'

'No.'

'Good.' Nick leans in conspiratorially. 'I heard they're searching the cheese factory.'

'Yeah, I know.'

Poulos is taken aback. 'You know?'

'Yes. I was there yesterday. It's Channel Ten filming a cold-case true-crime doco.'

'Not the police?'

'Not that I know of.'

'Right.'

'Nick, is that why you wanted to see me? You could have told me that on the phone.'

The lawyer looks sheepish. 'Sorry.' But he quickly regains his intensity. 'You think that's what Jasper discovered?'

'It's one possibility.' Martin is beginning to think the meeting is a waste of time. 'Did you manage to track down Jasper's ex-wife?'

'Yeah, I did. Lives in New Zealand—Wellington. Didn't I text you?'

'No, Nick, you didn't.'

'Oh, here then.' Nick pulls out his phone, messages the contact through to Martin.

Martin makes sure he has it before continuing. 'Did you know Amory Ashton yourself?'

'Me? No, never met him. He was gone by the time I got here. But I caught the aftermath, or the end of it. He was as dodgy as all get out. I did a bit of work for some of the employees. The place wasn't unionised and they were after their entitlements: unpaid wages, leave pay, superannuation, that sort of thing.'

'And?'

'There wasn't any. The place was a mess. The bookkeeping, what there was of it, was a complete shambles.'

'How did the workers fare?'

'Got screwed, as usual.'

'And you?'

'I didn't get paid either. Thanks for your concern.' Nick offers a sardonic grin. 'But I was new in town; it helped engender trust and goodwill.'

'So what happened? Was Ashton bankrupted? Was an administrator appointed?'

'Yeah, administrators. They took one look at the books and closed the factory. But any final distribution can't be settled until he's declared dead and the land sold.'

'Can't that happen anyway? Can't he be bankrupted in absentia and the land sold?'

'Usually that could happen, if it was in his name, but it's not. It's all tied up in trusts.'

'And if he's declared dead?'

'Then we find out who controls the trusts, get a court order to sell the factory and the land, and distribute any proceeds. But it would be cents in the dollar. Sweet FA.'

'Nick, I know who the owner will be.'

Nick blinks. 'Who?'

'Mandalay. She inherited at the same time she inherited Hartigan's.'

Nick looks down, rubs his hands together, thinking. 'Right. I probably should have worked that out. But she hasn't inherited yet.'

Martin nods. 'Yes, but what happens once Ashton is declared dead and she gains control? Can the creditors team together to force a sale to get whatever they can?'

'I guess.'

'And is there a dominant creditor?'

'Yeah, his bank. Westpac.'

'Who knows that?'

'The bank, the administrators, me, Harrold Drake, some of the larger creditors. Half the town. Why?'

'So if someone desperately wanted to buy the land, they wouldn't need to wait for Ashton to be declared dead, they wouldn't need to negotiate with Mandy. They could come to an arrangement directly with Westpac.'

Nick Poulos sits upright, thinking it through, as if surprised by the suggestion. 'Yes. I think that's right. They couldn't take formal ownership, of course but, yes, all the mechanisms could already be in place. Technically, Mandalay could still stymie it, but she'd have to pay out all the creditors. She'd be mad to do that.'

'Can we find out if someone has approached Westpac, cut a deal? Tyson St Clair, for example?'

Nick is nodding slowly, following Martin's logic. 'Harrold Drake—he's St Clair's lawyer—so he won't be talking, but I had a bit to do with the administrators. Let me see what I can find out.'

Once Nick has left, Martin calls Vern, seeking more information about Ashton.

His uncle answers, his voice breezy. 'Martin. How's tricks?'

'Good, Vern. What do you know about Amory Ashton?'

'That prick. What about him?'

'There's a camera crew searching the cheese factory. They think his body might be buried out there.'

'Really? They want a hand?'

'You want to help?'

'I want to piss on his grave.'

Martin laughs. 'Sounds like you're familiar with him then.'

'Fucking oath I am. Owes me money. Me and half the town.'

'Can I meet you somewhere?'

'Not now, mate. I'm down at the dock. The fishing inspectors are in town. I'll call you later, when I'm free.'

Martin looks around the surf club. Somewhere here, among the locals, among the retirees in their cargo shorts and chinos, their beer-swollen polo shirts, their feet encased in socks and sandals, their age-spotted hands clutching the day's first schooners, dentures present and correct, will undoubtedly be men who knew Amory Ashton. But by now, opinion would have solidified: the man was a bastard of a boss and a crook; he drove a big car and flashed his cash around even as he ripped off his workers and dudded his creditors. Martin needs facts, not opinions. And facts look pretty thin on the ground here. He could ask about the altercation between Mandy and Jasper; some of the staff might have witnessed it. But to what end? Mandy wasn't contesting it.

Instead, he rings the former Susan Speight in New Zealand. The voice that answers is bright, cheerful. 'Hello?'

'Susan Speight?'

'This is she.'

'Susan, this is Martin Scarsden. I'm a—'

She cuts him off. 'I know who you are. The great man, Martin Scarsden.' Now the voice is tainted by hostility. 'Where were you when we needed you?' Martin doesn't know what to say, is still searching for words when the woman speaks again. 'What do you want?'

'I'm trying to find out who killed Jasper.'

'Is this for your paper?'

'No, it's for me. For me and my family. For Jasper. I want to find the killer.'

Another pause before she speaks again, the edge coming off her words. 'What do you need to know?'

'What sort of man was Jasper?'

Susan Speight sighs. 'He was complex. A mixture. Good and bad. You never quite knew which one you were dealing with.'

'Was he a good husband and father?' Martin winces as he finishes the question; it sounds like a reporter's query.

'He was an amazing father.'

'And husband?'

A bitter little laugh comes down the phone. 'You mean was he faithful? No, he wasn't. He was a player. Half the town knew it. A small place like Port Silver, full of gossips and small-minded deadshits.'

'That's why you divorced him?'

'Part of the reason. That, the money and the mother.'

'The money?'

'He was a gambler. He never destroyed us, never went too far, but every now and then he'd break out. He could lose thousands in a week. He'd try to hide it, but I'd find out and he'd be full of remorse. Then he wouldn't do it for a year or two until the pressure got too much.'

'What pressure?'

'His mother.'

'Denise?'

'Yeah, the arch bitch herself.'

Now it's Martin's turn to pause. 'Can you explain that?' An image of Denise comes to him, the grieving mother, collapsing in on herself in her real estate agency. 'I've been away a long time.'

'Oh, come on, you must remember how she controlled his every move. How she stopped him from going to uni. That used to come up all the time, how you and that other friend of yours went. What was his name?'

'Scotty.'

'Yeah, you and Scotty. How you guys got away and never came back, and she wouldn't let him go. Especially you, coming from the Settlement and all. Vern could find the money for you, but she wouldn't give him a dime.'

The mention of Vern's selflessness twists another knife into him. 'Jasper would talk about that?'

'All the time. You want to know what ended our marriage? That woman, that's what. The cheating I could live with, the gambling outbreaks I could endure. But not that. I'd try to get him to leave, restart somewhere else, and he'd be all for it. But it never happened. When she started trying the same thing with our kids—deciding where they'd go to school, insisting on braces when they didn't need them—when he wouldn't stand up to her, that's when I left.' She stops speaking almost abruptly; Martin wonders if that's a suppressed sob he hears. 'It wasn't Jasper I left. I wanted him to come with us. He couldn't.'

'When was this?'

'About three years ago.'

'Did his gambling get worse once you'd gone?'

'I don't know. He was good with his support payments. And he sent some nice stuff over for the kids.'

'He had access to the kids?'

'In theory. He promised them he'd visit, but he never made it.' And this time Martin is sure he hears something akin to a sob. 'He never did travel. Just collected all those fucking postcards. He couldn't even get away to see his kids. It broke my heart all over again.'

'So she controlled him.' Martin isn't asking a question: it's a statement, a summary.

'Yes. And every now and then, when he was under pressure, he'd break out. A fling, an inappropriate proposition, a splurge on the horses. A stupid, impotent rebellion. But he never got away.'

Martin is out of questions, consumed by the thoughts flowing through his mind, building a new understanding of his old friend. 'Thanks for talking to me, Susan. You've been incredibly helpful. And I'm sorry for your loss. Truly.' Martin knows it's too little, too late.

'Just catch the bastard, Martin. Write another spectacular exclusive. A front-page screamer. Jasper would have liked that.' The phone cuts out.

He sits alone in the club, the call still reverberating through his mind, recollecting the Jasper Speight of his childhood. He'd never considered Denise to be that overbearing, that controlling, but Susan Speight's depiction rings true. Denise had disapproved of Scotty and Martin, especially Martin, had never hidden the fact that she thought they weren't good enough for her boy. And what was it Susan had said? That the flings, the inappropriate propositions came when Jasper was under pressure. So what pressure was he under when he slid his hand up Mandy's leg at the lifesavers?

Martin looks about him, and suddenly he no longer wants to be in the club. He heads out onto The Boulevarde, walks towards Speight's Real Estate. He wants to see Denise again, reassess her. At the very least, she may know about the cheese factory, know if Ashton had tried to unload it before it all went pear-shaped. Compared to her, Nick is a blow-in. But when he gets to the shopfront, it's still closed, the handwritten note still taped to the inside of the door. Martin rereads the last line. *Funeral arrangements—Longton Observer.*

The *Longton Observer.* It's worth a try. A big employer like the cheese factory going out of business, the owner disappearing under mysterious circumstances, that would be a massive story. The editor would know the facts—and the scuttlebutt. Martin returns to his car, left baking in the sun in the car park above the former supermarket, and begins the forty-five-minute drive to Longton.

———

The highway town wears its prosperity more comfortably than Port Silver. There's none of the bling, none of the pretence, no compulsion to appeal to tourists. But Australia's quarter-century of uninterrupted economic growth has left its mark. That and being located in perennially marginal seats, state and federal. The main street is full of cars, there are no empty shops, no vacant lots. There are signs to the hospital, the airport, to the mall, to Longton Grammar. To an industrial estate, to a retirement home, to an aquatic centre. But when he enters the air-conditioned relief of the newspaper office, there's little sign that the affluence has filtered into the local media. An elderly receptionist looks up at him, decidedly unimpressed. Her hair is permed into a tightly woven helmet, tinted mauve and lacquered into place. Cat's-eye glasses hang from a chain around her neck.

'Listen, love, if someone hit you, tell the police, not us.'

Martin touches his cheek. The pain is diminishing even as the bruise grows more prominent. 'It's not that. I was looking for the editor.'

'That makes two of us.'

'He's not here?'

The old woman sizes him up. 'You don't know much about journalism, do you, love?'

'What do you mean?' asks Martin, taken aback.

'The real ones don't sit around on their arses; they go out chasing stories.'

'Right,' says Martin, feeling strangely wrong-footed. 'So you know where he's gone?'

'I do.'

'Could you give me his mobile number?' He tries to smile, knows it's not impressing anyone. 'Please. It's important. A story. A cracker.'

She stares at him, a living bullshit detector. He holds her gaze. 'Righto, here then,' she says, making up her mind. She takes a business card, one of many stacked on top of the counter right in front of him, and passes it over. 'Not that it will do you any good.'

'Why's that?' asks Martin through his embarrassment.

'He's most likely out of mobile range.'

'Why? Where is he?'

'Old cheese factory down near Port Silver. Don't know why.'

'Right. Fair enough.' Of course he is.

'Have a nice day.' She dismisses him, chalking up another victory against the riffraff of the world.

But Martin isn't done. 'Say, did he ever write anything about a murder down in Port Silver on Monday? Jasper Speight, a real estate agent?'

The old dear looks at him, a mix of pity and contempt. All she says is: 'Yesterday's paper.' She goes to hand him a copy then withdraws it as he reaches for it. 'Three bucks.'

Martin doesn't bite. 'EFTPOS?'

'Cash.'

He searches his wallet, hands over five bucks. 'Keep the change. For your medication.'

He walks outside. The front page is an advertorial for a local hardware store, but the murder is the first real news story, the page-three lead.

POLICE INVESTIGATE LOCAL DEATH
By Paulo Robb in Port Silver

Sydney homicide police, including a crack team of forensic experts, are investigating the death of Port Silver real estate agent Jasper Speight.

It's believed the body of Mr Speight, 41, was found inside a townhouse at 15 Riverside Place, Port Silver, about eleven o'clock on Monday morning.

Police have not confirmed how Mr Speight met his death, but have not ruled out foul play. As of Tuesday afternoon, police were still collecting evidence at the crime scene.

Police have called for any witnesses who saw Mr Speight at any time on Monday morning, or had contact with him in any way over the weekend, to come forward.

It's believed the real estate firm Mr Speight ran with his mother, Denise Speight, managed the property at Riverside Place on behalf of out-of-town investors.

Mr Speight was a well-known local identity . . .

As an afterthought, he checks the editorial page to find who owns the paper. The publisher is listed as St Clair Holdings.

Martin chucks the paper in a nearby bin and texts Paulo Robb, asking him to call. He's about to head across the road to the library when he hears laughter, a voice somehow familiar. Sitting outside a cafe, drinking coffee, is Tyson St Clair. He's talking to someone, a large man wearing a broad Panama hat, who has his back to Martin. St Clair sees Martin, waves his good hand in acknowledgement. St Clair's companion turns, sees him, turns back. The two men continue their conversation, but Martin hasn't moved. The other man; a broad brown face. Martin struggles for a moment before he places him: the swami from Hummingbird Beach, dressed in street clothes. The holy man and St Clair? Together? What does that mean?

Martin is still trying to think that through as he enters the Longton library. The building is new, spacious, its air-conditioning ducting a shiny, sinuous feature curling above the room. There's a desk, a young librarian, hair dyed red, shaved on one side, long on the other. Oversized glasses teeter on the end of her nose, her eyes darting back and forth between her computer screen and a form in front of her. She senses Martin's presence and looks up, smiling. 'How can I help?'

'I'm interested in back copies of the *Longton Observer.*'

'Seriously?'

'Yep.'

'Your funeral,' she says, but the warmth of her smile takes the edge from her words. She stands. She's wearing a torn t-shirt, tartan pants and Doc Martens. 'Follow me.'

She leads him through an open reading area, through some book-filled stacks to a back wall where that day's papers are spread out across the top of a long chest of old map drawers, surely rescued from the building's predecessor. The *Sydney Morning Herald* and the *Daily Telegraph* are here, the *Courier-Mail* from Brisbane, plus the *Financial Review*, *The Australian* and *The Land*. In pride of place is the *Longton Observer* as well as a free throwaway, the *Rivers Real Estate and Restaurant Review*. Top marks for alliteration.

'Today's papers are on top, recent editions in the drawers underneath. Anything more than a few months old is online,' the young librarian informs him.

'Can you show me that?'

'Sure.'

She takes him back through the stacks to a row of cubicles, each with its own monitor and keyboard. 'The metros are on a national database. The *Observer* is there as well, but it's quicker to access through our own server. No delay.' She shows him the interface. He thanks her and she smiles radiantly. Martin wonders if she's just fallen in love with someone and takes a seat.

He sets a date range—from six years ago to four years ago—
and types in the name 'Ashton' as a search term. Over a hundred
results appear, but nine out of the first ten refer to a young girl
cracking an appearance on a television talent show—Elaine Ashton,
aged ten. A death metal guitarist. He refines his search to 'Amory
Ashton', which cuts the results to twenty-four. In the first year, there
are only three articles. The first reports that Mackenzie's Cheese
and Pickles has won a trophy at the Tamworth show for its Port
Silver Blue. Martin shakes his head and moves on. The next article
reports Ashton and the cheese factory have secured a development
grant from a federal government regional development initiative.
The report reads like a press release and it probably is: the local
federal MP, a member of the National Party, claiming credit for
the half-million dollars for 'environmental enhancements'. There's
a photo of four men in suits: Amory Ashton, fat and beaming,
flanked by Cyril Klapper, mayor of the Argyle River Shire, and
Darryl 'Dazzer' Duncan, the National Party's federal member.
Next to the mayor stands Tyson St Clair, credited as the head of
the Port Silver Chamber of Commerce. Martin looks at Ashton;
perhaps the man had eaten his factory's profits. Not only is he
grossly overweight, but there is an unhealthy sheen to his face,
like a heart attack waiting to happen, even compared to the MP,
whose own head resembles a beetroot gone wrong. Tyson St Clair,
by contrast, looks slim, fit and tanned, like a half-back posing
alongside the front row of a veteran's rugby scrum.

The two other reports from that first year are perfunctory.
The state Environmental Protection Authority has agreed to
investigate the cheese factory; Ashton is quoted as saying it's a
formality and that he initiated the visit. There is no mention of

what, exactly, the EPA intends to investigate. And there's a report about a cheese factory truck crashing on the escarpment road. Tyson St Clair is quoted, again in his capacity as head of the Chamber of Commerce, calling on all and sundry—the federal government, the state government, the local council and anyone else—to fund the upgrading of the road.

For the next four months there's nothing, then reports come in a burst. The first is a brief on page seven.

Police are requesting information concerning the whereabouts of Port Silver resident Amory Ashton, last seen on Friday afternoon at the Mackenzie's Cheese and Pickles plant. The police say their inquiries are routine at this stage, but would like to hear from Mr Ashton or anyone with knowledge of his whereabouts.

Martin looks at the date. The newspaper is the Wednesday edition, so Ashton was last seen the previous Friday. Five years and three months ago.

By the Saturday edition, Amory Ashton is no longer a brief; he's the front page. FOUL PLAY SUSPECTED—SEARCH FOR BUSINESSMAN. There's a large head-and-shoulders photograph, apparently taken at the same time as the report of the federal grant. Ashton is wearing the same shit-eating grin, the same suit, the same unhealthy sheen, flabby face creased around pebble eyes. Dead eyes. The article reports Ashton's Mercedes had been found burnt out in an isolated spot amid the dunes behind Treachery Bay. The car was found by fishermen the same day the factory owner was reported missing, but they thought little of their find and didn't report it until returning to town two days later. The paper again reports that Ashton was last seen on the previous Friday by workers leaving for the day. Mackenzie's Cheese and Pickles had cut weekend shifts three years before, so Ashton wasn't noticed missing until the following Monday. The plant manager had thought it strange when his employer wasn't at the factory first thing, and grew concerned after Ashton failed to attend a late-morning meeting. Even so, the manager didn't contact police until that afternoon, after his boss failed to return phone calls.

The next Wednesday's paper and Ashton is still missing. The headline asks: WHAT HAPPENED TO AMORY ASHTON? The article states that police are probing the financial health of Mackenzie's Cheese and Pickles, quoting unnamed sources. There is also an unconfirmed report of Ashton being spotted in transit at Auckland airport. The following Saturday's edition has moved on: Ashton is still missing but the focus has shifted to the future of the cheese factory, with concerns about its ownership and viability. The plant is still operating, but its future is uncertain. And that continues to be the main thrust over the next several weeks as the plant closes, at first temporarily. The workers complain about back pay and being fleeced of entitlements, creditors call in the administrators, the plant shuts for good. The fate of Ashton becomes the footnote, relegated to the bottom of the copy, with nothing new to report.

Slowly the stories ebb away, with short pieces to mark each anniversary cut and pasted from one year to the next. Then, during the past year, a new series of reports declare that 'eminent local businessman Tyson St Clair' is developing 'visionary plans' for the factory site, including a golf course. The opposition of local Aboriginal groups is noted; Josie Jones is quoted, saying the land is subject to an ongoing native title claim. Martin is impressed:

Observer owner Tyson St Clair hasn't shut out the opposing voices. Ashton and his disappearance are noted far down in the copy, enough to trigger the library's search engine, but nothing more.

Martin finishes his search. Ashton is either dead—possibly murdered, possibly killing himself—or he's fled, a fugitive from his creditors and aggrieved workers. It's entirely possible. If he knew the plant was beyond saving, he might well have pocketed the five-hundred-thousand-dollar federal grant and anything else he could pilfer from the company's accounts and skipped the country. Nick Poulos had said the books were a mess and the *Longton Observer* had intimated impropriety. Perhaps he is overseas somewhere, living the life of Riley, the burnt-out car a clever ploy. It occurs to Martin that if Ashton torched his car and fled, then he would have needed an accomplice to drive him back out.

He's about to leave when a new idea comes to him. How far back do the digitised records go?

He sets the date parameters: a two-week window, thirty-three years ago. He hesitates for a moment, lump in his throat, before entering his own surname in the search field: 'Scarsden'.

And there it is, emerging from the past, hitting him with newly minted clarity.

TRAGEDY IN SWAMPLANDS

A young Port Silver mother and her twin daughters have lost their lives in a tragic accident on Dunes Road, three kilometres south of Mackenzie's Cheese and Pickles.

Mrs Hilary Scarsden and her three-year-old daughters Amber and Enid lost their lives when the car driven by Mrs Scarsden left Dunes Road and sank in Mackenzie's Swamp.

Police say no other vehicles were involved. They are not ruling out mechanical failure.

There is more copy but Martin's gaze is drawn to a photo, the death car emerging from the lip of the water, winched by a tow truck, a man signalling back to the winch operator. It is a respectful photograph, taken from a distance, with only the winch man to animate it. Nevertheless, it's enough to inspire morbid imaginings. Were the bodies still in the car, or had they already been retrieved? Thoughts flood into Martin's head as if through an open window. Did the crash kill them, or did they drown? Did they suffer, or was it quick and painless? Did his mother die still elated by the lottery win or with the terror of drowning, of her precious girls being taken?

He shakes his head, trying to clear away the speculation, the waves of unwelcome and unfamiliar emotion. He looks at the photo. The car appears unharmed, intact. No sign of damage, apart from a broken rear brake light. It hadn't rolled, shows no sign of any visible impact. It had left the road and driven straight into the water.

Inside the paper, the story continues. There is no more fresh information about the crash, just background, reporting that Mrs Scarsden and her daughters are survived by her husband, Ronald Scarsden, and their eight-year-old son Martin, long-term residents of the Settlement. There is another photo of the accident scene, a wide shot, taken from further back: the tow truck and the emerging car at its centre. The central drama is framed by vehicles on each side. To the left, a police car, with an officer talking to a man. Martin looks closely, trying to see beyond the dot matrix of the newspaper screen. Is the policeman Clyde Mackie? Is he talking to the person who discovered the accident? Martin is about to look away, the pit in his stomach growing, when it suddenly grows larger again. To the right, another vehicle. A Morris van. His father's car. Martin looks back at the two men by the police car. Is that his father, back to the camera, helping the police? Had he driven out there, having heard the gut-wrenching news? But if the Morris belonged to his father, whose car had his mother been driving? They had never owned two cars, he's sure of that. People in the Settlement were lucky to have one.

He flips back to the front page, to the closer photograph. The car looks somehow familiar. Of course—Vern's car. She had borrowed it to tell her husband of their bonanza. But why was she on Dunes Road? Of course: the cheese factory. His father must have been working a casual shift. Martin flicks back to the wider photograph. And there in the distance, another detail: the Port Silver lighthouse, a white vertical shaft, sitting on the horizon above the rear of Vern's car. So the cross is definitely on the correct side of the road. Which meant she was driving back into town, not away from it, when she crashed. Had she already told his father the news of the lottery, been heading for Port Silver, full of joy and excitement, when something had gone terribly wrong? Vern's car. Had he maintained it properly? Had the brakes been good? Martin thinks of his uncle: not good with writing, not good with numbers, but always good with his hands, always tinkering. If the brakes needed work, Vern would have fixed them himself, done it right. And it was a straight road; there would be no need to brake anyway. Maybe a wallaby, bounding out from the scrub?

The questions keep coming, unbidden and insistent. His father. Had he been the first on the scene, following them back into town for their fish and chips and champagne celebration? Had he witnessed the accident? Good Lord, no wonder he had taken up drinking, his life unravelling before his eyes. Martin examines the thirty-three-year-old photograph once more, the wide shot. It's not hard to see, now that he knows what he's looking for: the man, back to the camera, the one talking to the policeman, has a dark ring around his torso. From the water. From where he had waded in, trying to save them.

The voice of the librarian disturbs his train of thought. 'Are you okay?'

Martin looks up, startled, trying to pull himself back into the present. 'Yes. Fine. Why?'

She blinks, hesitant. 'You're crying.'

⸺

The surf on Town Beach is rougher than usual, the flatness of the previous days pushed to one side by a tropical low drifting south towards New Zealand. There are no clouds here, not in Port Silver, but the swell is high, the waves churning. An offshore breeze is adding chop, turning the waves ragged and unpredictable, not deterring the swarm of surfers off the point, but discouraging swimmers from venturing more than waist deep. Not Martin; he's out among the breaking waves, diving under, emerging only in time to dive again, feeling the wash pull him one way and then the other as the cylinders cascade over him. He's not used to it: his body remembers the patterns of the waves, his mind recalls the tactics, but his muscles have lost the easy endurance of his teenage years.

Abruptly, he's short of breath, hardly able to suck in enough air before needing to dive under the next wave. But still he persists. He needs this, the pounding of the surf, the cleansing, the second-by-second decision-making, the concentration on survival banishing all other thoughts. He surfaces, copping a mouthful of water as one wave catches its predecessor in a double peak. He coughs, attempting to draw breath, merely ducking under the next break rather than diving towards the sand, feeling himself shaken by the power, pushed violently towards the beach, lucky the wave caught him before it started breaking. Now his arms are weak and protesting, and his lungs hurt. He needs to get back into shore, not much more than fifty metres away. But some knowledge comes to him, some instinct. There's a gap in the waves, and he starts swimming out to sea, as hard as his arms will allow, away from the break zone. Out the back.

He dives through a final wave just before it shatters, his body threatening to go into lockdown. Instead he wills calm upon it, kicking his legs up, floating on his back, forcing himself to relax. Another wave comes through under him, no longer a threat, bobbing him up and down like a cork. He drops his legs again, treading water, regaining his strength, regaining his breath. Then, when he's ready, he pushes back into the break zone. He fails to catch the first wave, but it's enough to return him to the surf. He dives under the next, but knows he can't wait too long. The next is perfect, breaking in a curl, slow motion, left to right, the timing perfect, the place perfect. He starts swimming towards shore, two or three quick strokes, and then the wave has him, lifting and carrying him shorewards atop its rushing wall of water, riding it, above the foaming white front as the wave completes its break, its power almost spent, propelling him forward a few more metres before finally relaxing its grip. He tries to stand, his feet touching the bottom. Another wave comes through, foaming around his head, a final caress. Martin swims along with the remnants of the next one, borrowing its residual energy. A few more strokes, then wading, the waves little more than froth. His legs are rubbery, his bladder suddenly demanding. He walks up onto the sand, trying not to lurch. A lifesaver watches him pass without a word, eyes full of knowing.

Lying on the beach, sun on his back, towel beneath his stomach, the sensory memories of his teenage years return. Toes digging into the sand, the hovering shadows of seagulls. But not just sensory memories. Real memories as well. His father. Drinking. Always drinking. Drinking away the lottery, like chipping at a mountain. The hero of his boyhood disappearing into stupefied oblivion, his only communication to demand another beer from the fridge or takeaway food. And always the Veuve Clicquot, glowing like a lighthouse in its alcove above the television, promising to guide Martin to a safe harbour, away from the sea monsters that prowl the depths.

He's still there, lying on the sand, wondering if even the most powerful surf could ever cleanse him of his past, when Mandy finds him and wrenches him back to the present. She's crying, her beautiful face contorted in pain.

chapter seventeen

MARTIN IS ON HIS FEET IMMEDIATELY. 'WHAT IS IT? WHAT'S WRONG?'

'Martin,' is all she can manage.

He wraps his arms around her, pulls her close. 'Is it Liam? Is he okay?'

She's shaking her head, eyes closed. 'He's fine. At child care.' She draws a breath. 'Fuck, Martin. I don't believe it. I— Shit. Pure shit.'

He says nothing, waiting.

She takes another deep breath, gathers herself. 'I went to see Tyson St Clair.'

'And?'

'The bastard,' she says. The tremor has gone from her voice, replaced by determination. 'The utter bastard.'

'What happened?'

And then she laughs, taking Martin by surprise. She steps back, looking at him and shaking her head as if in disbelief. Laughs again, not a real laugh but a facsimile, feeble and humourless. 'The bastard. The contemptible shit.'

'Tell me.'

She breathes deep, tries to compose herself. 'I went to see him. I wanted to see him up close, to see what I could tease out of him. I thought I could suss out his interest in the cheese factory. I'm the new owner, or might be soon, and he wants to buy it.'

Martin nods his understanding. He's not sure Mandy approaching St Clair is so wise, given the police are yet to exonerate her of Jasper Speight's murder, but he keeps his opinion to himself. 'What happened?'

'He doesn't work from his office; he works from his home up near the lighthouse.'

'I know. I've been there.'

She looks at him, assimilating this fact. 'Right. Did he show you his office upstairs, with the views and the models? His eyrie?'

'He did. But what happened?'

'So he answers the door, as if he's been expecting me. I figured it was a bluff, you know, that he was trying to unsettle me, make me seem predictable. Anyway, he sends me upstairs, says he'll be straight up. So I'm waiting up there, admiring the view, checking out the models. There's one of Hummingbird Beach, the cheese factory, all his plans. And then he comes up the stairs, wearing a robe. And suddenly he's pissed off. "What are you doing?" he says. I start asking what he means and . . .' Her voice trails off, she pauses to gather herself, then continues with renewed determination. 'He kind of barks at me, "Get your gear off and bend over."'

'*What?*'

'You heard. He . . .' And again her voice breaks.

'What the fuck? What did you do?'

'I kicked him in the balls.' And the smile cracks again, so now she's laughing and crying at the same time, fighting both. 'And then I got out of there. I headed for the stairs. He grabbed me by the arm, so I slapped him. In the face. Not as hard as I wanted. I was off balance. And I told him to fuck off. He was angry, so angry. I think he was about to hit me. And then it was like he got it. He looked horrified and let me go.'

'What do you mean he got it?'

'I think he mistook me for someone else. Someone he'd been expecting.'

'What? Who?'

And the distress is back in Mandy's eyes, the tremor in her voice. 'Don't you see, Martin? He thought I was a hooker.'

———

Martin's synapses are firing, neurons connecting, as facts and imaginings mix and blend with hunches and journalistic instinct to simmer and bubble in the intuitive soup of his mind. Tyson St Clair, property schemes, a mistaken identity: the ingredients churn inside his cranium, steaming and stewing. It's a familiar feeling, an intoxicating one, the sensation he's on the cusp of discovery, that a big story is brewing. It's there, he can sense it, taste it, the thrill that so often presages a scoop. But he keeps himself in check, says nothing to Mandy, not in her distraught state. And he remembers Riversend, where he had leapt to incorrect conclusions and been sacked as a result. Not this time. This time he'll double-check; this time he will stand the story up.

First, he drops Mandy at Drakes. She's composed herself, steel replacing distress, eager to see Winifred, eager to press charges, eager to spit roast St Clair on a legal rotisserie. He gives her a final hug of support, kisses her and watches her stride in through the automatic doors. She's right: St Clair must have mistaken her for someone else; it's the only possible explanation. Mandy and St Clair had never previously met. He must not have seen any of the coverage of the Riversend murders, didn't make the connection. Or her auburn hair had fooled him. Not just an arsehole then, but a dumb arsehole. Now, with Liam at child care and Mandy plotting with Winifred, Martin is free to follow his intuition. Twenty minutes later he's parking the Corolla at Hummingbird Beach.

He finds Topaz lying on the beach, flanked by a couple of young men. She's topless, sunbaking on her back with her eyes closed, her breasts perfect globes, her admirers unable to look away for long. Martin shakes his head; they're like putty in her hands. He realises that one of the men is the soapie star Garth McGrath, his hair grown long but his stubble-covered chin as sharp as ever.

'Topaz?' says Martin.

'Who are you?' asks McGrath as she opens her eyes and smiles.

'That's Martin Scarsden,' says Topaz mischievously. 'The famous reporter.'

'Scarsden? Another grub journo?' McGrath spits into the sand.

'That'd be me.'

'Fuck, don't you people ever get enough? This is harassment. Where's your photographer? Off in the bushes with a long lens?'

'There is no photographer, sunshine. You're yesterday's news.'

'What?'

'Yeah. Sorry about that.' He turns to Topaz, who is smirking happily. 'Can we talk? Somewhere private?'

She raises an eyebrow. 'Really?'

'Yes. It won't take long.'

Martin is hoping she'll get up and follow him, but instead she addresses her companions. 'Fellas, can you give us a moment?' And they do, they obey, standing and walking off down the beach together, such is the power of a pair of perfectly formed tits. Martin watches them go, McGrath still swivelling about, trying to spot paparazzi among the bushes.

Martin crouches. 'Yesterday morning I went and saw a man called Tyson St Clair. He lives in a big house up by the lighthouse.'

'If you say so.'

'Just before I got there, when I was walking down from the light house, I saw you leaving.'

She says nothing.

'What were you doing there?'

'None of your business.'

'Topaz, I'm not a cop, I'm not going to tell anyone. But it's important that I know.'

'Why? So you can write a story? Sorry, pal, I don't think so.'

'It's not for a story. I'm trying to help my partner Mandy stay out of prison.'

Topaz frowns. 'That murder, the one we gave you the alibi for, that was her?'

'It was her house. She's still a suspect; I'm helping her.'

Topaz sighs, looks out at the water. 'I don't see how I can help. I already spoke to the cops.'

Martin won't be deflected, but he tries to ease some of the urgency from his approach. He sits, moderating his voice. 'She's a bit like you, you know: young and very good-looking. Sexy. She went to see St Clair. He told her to strip.'

Topaz bursts out laughing. 'I bet he did, randy old rooster. What was she expecting?'

'She went to talk business. He mistook her for someone else.'

'Sounds like it. But sorry, Martin, I really can't help you.'

'Why not? What do you owe them?'

'Them?'

'Them.' He lets the word and its implications settle. 'The man who bashed Royce and the men behind him. St Clair owns the hostel; he's Harry the Lad's boss.' That has her attention. 'Tell me the real reason Harry the Lad beat up Royce, or it's all going in the paper. It was nothing to do with drugs, was it?'

Topaz stares at him, lip curling with distaste. 'You do that, do you? Threaten people? Is that how you get your stories?' She starts to stand.

But Martin isn't wearing that. 'They bashed your boyfriend. He's in hospital with a serious head injury. Surely you want to settle the score? You have my word no one will ever know who told me.'

Something in her changes then, the veneer of brightness falls away, the carefree backpacker vanishes. She looks older, more world-weary. She sits down again, saying nothing, holding her breath. She takes a towel, wraps it around herself. She stares at the breaking waves. Martin lets her think. A young couple, surely still teenagers, amble slowly past, arms around each other, oblivious to anything but their own existence, the youth with the blond curls and his beautiful girlfriend who were kayaking when Martin first visited Hummingbird. Martin and Topaz watch them pass.

'Okay,' she says finally. 'But will you take me up to see Royce today or tomorrow? I'll need to talk to him. And then we'll have to leave. You promise you won't publish anything?'

'Absolutely.'

She sighs again before speaking. 'Okay. It's true that Harry sells drugs out of the backpackers, no big deal, but the hostel also runs a kind of employment service. They have a bus—you probably saw it—and they drive anyone who's interested out to the market gardens and greenhouses and orchards to pick fruit, whatever. The backpackers earn some money, and if they do it for three months they can get a one-year extension on their visa. It's good business for the hostel if they can lock people into a three-month stay. Harry also arranges apartments.' She pauses, swallows, considers what to say next. Martin stays quiet, knowing any prompt could be counterproductive. 'But there's a short cut; Harry told me about it the day we arrived. Some of the farmers out there, they'll sign the paperwork, get you the visa, if you sleep with them a couple of times. It's a pretty popular option. All the girls know about it. It's an open secret. No harm done.'

'And Tyson St Clair?'

'Just the once. He only wants each girl once. It's the shortest of short cuts.'

'And only the prettiest girls.'

She flicks him a bitter smile. 'Yeah, something like that. Harry the Lad vets them, chooses them, sends them up there. Tells them what's expected of them.'

'Quite the honour.'

She turns to him then, eyes flaring. 'Don't be an arsehole. I'm not proud of it.'

'Sorry. Can you tell me what happened?'

'Are you going to write a story, tell people what he does?'

'Do you want me to?'

She considers this. 'I don't know. Maybe. But you can't use my name. Even if he sues you, you can't reveal my name, not even in court. I'm not testifying.'

Martin is surprised by her knowledge of defamation and courts. 'I've been a journalist for twenty years. I know how to protect a source. Tell me.'

'He sent me upstairs to this office. There was no small talk. Harry had told me what to do: to strip, so I was naked when the old man arrived. St Clair came up the stairs, told me to twirl around so he could check me out. He was practically salivating, the old perve. Gross. Then he told me to bend over across this desk, next to a model of Port Silver. So I did, looking out the window over the town. It was a hell of a lot better than looking at him. And then he banged me from behind.' And she lets out a brittle laugh. 'And get this, he's talking the whole time, boasting about how he owns the town, as he's banging away. *I built it* and *I'll show the bastards* and shit like that, and the model of the town is shaking like there's some sort of earthquake, and it doesn't even sound like he's enjoying himself. And as soon as he's done he tells me to get dressed and get out.'

'Quite the gentleman.'

'Quite the arsehole.'

'But you got your visa?'

'Yeah, I got the paperwork.'

'And Royce? What happened there?'

'Royce was not so thrilled about what I'd done. My fault for telling him. So he decided to scoop some cream off the top. He threatened Harry, said he'd expose their nice little sex-for-visas scam, demanded a commission. Worked a treat, didn't it?'

'That's why Harry the Lad bashed him?'

'Yep. Royce said he knew a reporter and if they didn't pay it was all going in the paper.'

'He knew a journo? He didn't mention my name, did he?'

'Why do you think Harry whacked you on the beach?'

'Oh, for fuck's sake.'

They pause then, considering the waves, the way they line up to break on the shore.

'Here comes the great man,' says Topaz.

'Sorry?'

'Over there.' And she flicks her head to indicate back behind Martin. He turns and sees the swami walking along the beach with a small group of followers.

'Check it out,' says Topaz sardonically, 'the seer and his disciples.'

'Not a convert, then?'

'Fuck that. He should be back wandering around the Punjab with his begging bowl, not fleecing Aussies.' And she adds, with the contempt of the eternally thin, 'Look how fucking fat he is.'

They watch as the holy man leads his followers into the shallows, stopping when they are knee deep. They kneel in the water and he dunks them under, holding their heads as he does so.

Martin laughs. 'Looks more like a christening than a Hindu ritual. It's not exactly the Ganges.'

But Topaz doesn't respond and, when he turns, she's staring at the swami and his followers with contempt.

'Are you okay?' he asks.

'The arsehole. At least St Clair gives you a visa.'

As they watch, the faux baptism comes to an end and the group walks back past them, before sitting in a circle on the grass above the beach. They begin to chant softly.

Topaz stands, apparently intrigued. 'What are they doing?'

On the grass, the devotees are taking turns to sit before the swami and have their foreheads daubed with a red-brown dye, not a bindi so much as a circle containing dots. Martin recognises it as the symbol on the sign at the turn-off from Ridge Road.

'They've been here for a fortnight,' he says, recalling what Jay Jay had told him. 'They must be preparing to graduate. A big party tomorrow night. Could be fun.'

But Topaz is saying nothing, all humour drained from her face. She looks troubled.

'Topaz?'

'I've told you what you wanted,' she says, voice sharp. 'Don't you need to go save your girlfriend?'

He leaves the young American, heading towards the car park. As he walks, the importance of what she has revealed begins to swell within him, growing clearer, writing itself across his mind's eye like an old-fashioned ticker tape. St Clair and his henchman Harry 'the Lad' Drake are running a sex-for-visas scam out of the backpacker hostel. If Jasper Speight discovered this, it could have endangered the property developer's ambitions. If St Clair were to be convicted of visa fraud, he would no longer be a fit and proper person to run a company. That's the law. If Jasper exposed him, the international proponents of the Hummingbird Beach resort would have washed their hands of him and turned to Jasper instead. Which gives St Clair and Harry the Lad a clear motive to kill Jasper Speight. Martin needs to tell Montifore. He quickens his pace.

Perhaps Jasper had sought leverage over St Clair, had threatened to expose him. Perhaps he'd even informed Johnson Pear, the same police officer who went soft on Harry the Lad after the beach brawl with Royce. Perhaps, instead of acting on the allegation, Pear had sent word back to St Clair and Harry the Lad. Perhaps. And so Jasper had turned to Martin, coming to the townhouse to tell his old friend of another small-town scandal. Perhaps.

Now a new and urgent concern emerges from Martin's speculation. If he's right and Jasper was killed to keep the visa fraud secret, then Mandy could be in danger. Martin had left her with Winifred, intent on prosecuting St Clair for his outrage. His chest tightens, a sense of panic growing. He needs to warn Winifred not to threaten St Clair with legal action. Harry the Lad had put Royce into hospital when the young backpacker had threatened exposure; what violence might he visit upon Mandy? Martin changes course, heads for the office; with his mobile out of range, he needs to use the landline. He needs to call Montifore, and he needs to warn Mandy.

But Jay Jay Hayes isn't in her office and the door is locked. He has no idea if she's nearby or surfing off the point or gone into town to get supplies. It doesn't matter; he doesn't have time to search her out. He needs to get word to Mandy and Winifred. He runs up the hill to his car.

He drives on a knife edge: too slowly and he may be too late, too quickly and he risks crashing, being stuck with no way to get his message to Port Silver. His mind is telling him to take care, that a minute or two either way won't make a difference, but his heart is telling him otherwise. He guns the engine, swerves to avoid a pothole, crashes into the next one, as wide as the car itself, suspension bottoming out, sump hitting gravel. Trees scrape the Toyota's flanks, ruts catch at its wheels, rocks thunder into the floor. He almost loses it on a corner, lucky to glance off a roadside stump instead of ploughing into it. Around a bend, a stopped van blocks most of the track: a man holding a jack, a woman staring at a flat tyre; Martin hits the horn, doesn't slow as the couple scrambles to safety, sending a stream of profanities in his wake. As he nears the junction with the cliff road his mind, having lost the debate over speed, inserts a new calculation: he won't get a signal on Dunes Road until he reaches the caravan park, a good fifteen or twenty minutes away. But he recalls getting a signal up on Ridge Road, one bar. Where was that? Before Sergi's? Maybe five minutes away, maybe ten. He hits the cattle grid at speed, becoming momentarily airborne, the steel rails left ringing in the still air. At the cliff road he swings left. The rainforest it is.

It's difficult enough to negotiate the wild road steering with two hands, but as he approaches the top of the first hill he slows, steers with just his right hand, holding his phone aloft with the other, the 'no signal' message taunting him. He's almost at the top, starting to wonder if the signal will ever come through, if the previous day was just some anomaly of the weather, clouds bouncing signals, when as if by magic one bar appears. He hits the brakes and it disappears again. He's not yet at the summit; surely it must work better up there, a few hundred metres further. And it does. Miracle of miracles, it does. Two bars. The phone pings in celebration as texts and emails arrive. He ignores them all. He rings Mandy and, to his relief, she answers straight away. She's at Drakes, she tells him, alone with Winifred. He asks to be put on speaker, realising he's breathing hard, as if he's been running, not driving. He calms his thoughts, takes a breath and tells them what he knows. There are no interruptions.

Only when he is finished does Winifred speak. 'You will tell this to the police?'

'My next call. But only to Morris Montifore. I don't trust the locals, not Johnson Pear.'

'Understood. And the name of this witness? The young woman?'

'I gave her my word I wouldn't identify her.'

'Okay. Montifore won't like it, but that's your battle not mine.'

'Have you got his number?'

'I'll text it. Don't say you got it from me. He'll know, but there's no need to confirm it.'

'Thank you, Winifred. Just make sure St Clair remains unaware we've discovered the visa fraud. He might be dangerous.'

Winifred forwards the contact, but Morris Montifore isn't answering his phone. Martin leaves a voicemail: 'Morris, it's Martin Scarsden. I've discovered something important, a motive to kill Jasper Speight. It involves Tyson St Clair and Harrold Drake Junior. Call me.'

And now? Now nothing. He's sitting in his car, still breathing hard, adrenaline still pumping. He gets out, checks the car. There are scratches along its sides, but there always have been, and mud and dirt and dust. The cover of his front indicator is smashed, part of the orange plastic missing from when he glanced the tree stump, but nothing more. He gets back in, moves slowly forward, looking for a place to turn. His engine has developed a deeper, more masculine sound; somewhere along the way he's managed to put a hole in his muffler. He turns the car around and heads back the way he came. He still needs to get back to town, needs to see Montifore, but the urgency has gone from his mission.

He mulls over what he's discovered, what a story it might make, the link between the visa scam and Jasper's murder more evident by the minute. The old journalistic imperative is back, coursing through his veins, the need to peel away perceptions and get to the bottom of things. St Clair, the predatory bastard, and Harry the Lad, his thuggish accomplice, most likely protected by the corrupt local plod, Johnson Pear, killing Jasper Speight to avoid exposure; exposure by Martin Scarsden, investigative journalist par excellence. It's a great story. Not quite the body count of Riversend, but not bad. A further burnishing of the Scarsden reputation, a further poke in the eye for the gutless bastards who sacked him from the *Herald*. Doug Thunkleton will be begging for forgiveness, pleading for an interview. Martin touches his eye, still swollen, still sore. He looks at it in the rear-view mirror. The bruise is a deep purple with the first hints of less savoury colours. It's healing, if slowly. Maybe he should get some photographs taken: the seeker of truth beaten by the murderer's accomplice. Maybe it could be the image on the back cover of his next book.

As he nurses the Corolla down into a shallow gully and then up again, up where his phone got its first bar, just before the track swings left and down the hill, he reaches a small plateau. Beside the road, on the shoulder, there's room to park a couple of cars. Curious, he pulls the car over and kills the engine. Climbing out, he's greeted by the coolness of the forest, the wind nothing more than a breeze at ground level, but hushing through the top of the canopy. The space for the cars is no accident; there's a walking trail heading into the undergrowth. This must still be Jay Jay's property, part of the bush block, never developed for dairy. Maybe it's the section Jasper Speight was interested in developing. No longer in a rush, Martin decides to have a quick look.

He walks briskly along the track, which soon splits into two, the left fork heading down towards Hummingbird Beach. He follows the right fork, and after a hundred metres or so the sound of the surf starts coming through the trees and he can smell the salt in the air. And then he's free of the trees, the path leading another dozen metres to a level sandstone shelf, a natural platform above the ocean. The point is not as high as he might have imagined, not as high as Hartigan's or Bede and Alexander's, but the view is possibly more spectacular, stretching up the coast to the wild beaches and crashing surf of Treachery Bay. Looking landwards, he can see where the beaches start, at the northern shore of the Mackenzie's Swamp estuary. He can't see Hummingbird Beach, but it must only be a few hundred metres from where he stands, hidden by a headland. Below, maybe thirty metres down, there is a flat rock shelf a metre or two above the ocean. He can see rock pools, channels where waves flush water in and out, and large sandstone boulders, dislodged from the clifftop by long-ago storms. And as Martin watches, a figure, all in black and carrying a surfboard, rounds the headland from Hummingbird. It's Jay Jay Hayes, wetsuit to protect her from the sun as much as it is to keep her warm. He thinks of calling out, but lets her walk undisturbed. She doesn't look up, doesn't see him. She appears deep in thought or, more likely, she is so used to this landscape that she feels no need to re-examine it.

As Martin watches she walks to the edge of the rock plateau. She attaches her leg rope, then stands dead still, assessing the rhythms of the sea, choosing her moment, then launching herself catlike into the swell. Martin is mesmerised by her mastery, paddling with assurance out through the heaving ocean, unconcerned by the nearby rocks, at home in her environment. In no time, she is positioning herself off the point, waiting barely a moment before she is paddling forward, onto the wave, onto her feet, carving across the wave towards Martin. He holds his breath; she is practically on top of the rocks, almost touching them, before switching direction in a heartbeat. The wave starts breaking away from the point and she glides away along it, momentarily out of sight as she crouches within its curling cylinder, reappearing to carve up to the top of it and cutting back down, the board obedient to her will, part of her. The wave starts to lose its power as it moves towards Hummingbird Beach and the estuary; Jay Jay comes off the back of it, board already pointing oceanwards, and she drops with feline agility onto her stomach and is immediately paddling seawards. Only now, almost back to her take-off point, does she look up and see Martin. She waves, he waves back. Her own private surf break; no wonder she doesn't want to sell.

—

Morris Montifore doesn't look happy. The detective's face looks worn, his eyes hooded. He's behind a desk in an open-plan office, some sort of meeting room turned into a temporary headquarters for the Sydney homicide detectives. His deputy, Ivan Lucic, is with him, eyeing Martin with scepticism.

'Martin Scarsden, journalist,' says Montifore, his voice carrying not so much annoyance as weariness.

'Martin Scarsden, witness. Martin Scarsden, source of information.'

Montifore looks unimpressed. 'Whatever. Tell me what you know. But if this is some stunt to extract information from me, I'm not in the mood. Leave now.'

'Can I sit?'

'Of course you can sit.'

Martin takes a seat and recounts what he and Mandy have discovered about Tyson St Clair, his penchant for young back-packers and the sex-for-visa racket. Lucic smirks salaciously when Martin describes St Clair's behaviour, but Montifore merely listens, face stern, giving nothing away. From time to time he nods his encouragement for Martin to continue, the slightest of frowns extending twin creases from his nose up across his forehead. Martin recounts finding a corroborating witness, a backpacker, who has confirmed St Clair's predilections and that visas are available in return for sex.

When Martin finishes, Montifore says nothing for a long moment, then he turns to his offsider. 'Ivan, let me talk to Mr Scarsden here in private.' Lucic nods his compliance and goes to leave. 'And, Ivan, not a word to anyone. Not yet. Okay?'

'Of course.'

Montifore waits until his subordinate has left the room and closed the door behind him, before speaking. 'So your theory is that Jasper Speight knew of this scam and was threatening to expose St Clair?'

'Yes. That may have been why he wanted to see me the morning he was killed.'

'Why expose St Clair?'

'To get the inside running with the consortium wanting to develop Hummingbird Beach. There's a million-dollar spotter's fee, according to St Clair himself, plus a commission on the sale if Jay Jay Hayes agrees to sell. Not to mention becoming the consortium's man in Port Silver. On top of that, if St Clair was convicted, it would stop him developing Mackenzie's Swamp. Jasper was opposed to the development. You know about that, right?'

'I do,' says Montifore. He ponders his options a little longer. 'I assume Mandalay Blonde is willing to make a statement as to what occurred with St Clair?'

'You would have to ask her, but I'm sure she would.'

'How about your backpacker source? What's her name?'

Martin takes a deep breath. 'I can't tell you. I promised her she would remain anonymous.'

Montifore shakes his head. 'Of course you fucking did.' The exasperation is evident on the policeman's face, his voice flat. 'You journos and protecting your sources. I don't have to remind you that has no standing in law. None whatsoever.'

Martin shrugs. 'I can't give you her name. Not without her consent.'

'Well, in that case, we've got nothing. Mandalay Blonde's evidence is next to useless without corroboration, you must see that. At the most, St Clair made an indecent suggestion. Gross, but not unlawful. And he made no mention of visas or any other quid pro quo, not to Mandalay Blonde, am I right?'

Martin nods.

'Right. And she's hardly an impartial witness. Speight died in her home and she's still a person of interest. So any statement she does make can easily be construed as self-serving, an attempt to deflect suspicions. St Clair's counsel would eat her alive.'

'But you can investigate, surely. You're a police officer. You don't need my witness; you can find others.'

'You think? If St Clair gives them a visa after one root, why would they hang around? And why talk to us and incriminate themselves? Remember, we're asking them to admit to breaking the law. They'll be afraid of jail or deportation or both. And whatever others at the hostel have heard would be hearsay, inadmissible. We need your witness, or someone just like her: someone who has received the paperwork for a visa.'

Martin doesn't know what to say. He thinks there is something not quite right, that Montifore should be more enthusiastic. He's come offering a solid lead, a potential breakthrough, and the policeman appears more irritated than grateful. 'What is it, Morris? What aren't you telling me?'

That does little to calm the detective. 'First, we are not on a first-name basis. Second, I am a homicide detective and you're a journalist; I am not obliged to tell you anything. Just the opposite.'

'So why send Ivan Lucic out of the room?'

'What do you mean by that?'

'No witnesses. No recordings.'

Montifore leans back in his chair, laughing. 'Jesus. You really are a dumb cunt, aren't you?'

'What? Tell me.' But Montifore is shaking his head, still smiling. At least the policeman is engaging. 'Listen,' says Martin, 'you know why I'm here. I'm not hiding anything. I want to help clear Mandy of suspicion. And yes, if this ends up being a good story, all the better. But I am being absolutely transparent. You know where I stand.'

Montifore nods, seems to come to some conclusion. 'All right, here's what I can tell you. Not for publication. Got that?'

'Of course.'

'The first thing is that you hold information vital to an ongoing homicide investigation: the identity of a vital witness. Information you are withholding from police. That is a criminal offence. I could arrest you here and now. If you continued to withhold that information when I put you before a magistrate, let's say tomorrow, then you will also be in contempt of court. Prison time. That's what I can tell you.'

Martin looks into the policeman's unsmiling eyes, keeping his own face impassive, resisting the temptation to give voice to the slurry of invective storming through his mind. He's thinking of how to respond when Montifore speaks again.

'But I'm not going to do that. Instead, I want you to find this source of yours and persuade her to talk to me. In private. I will keep her identity confidential. If your theory proves to be correct, then it's entirely likely we won't need her in court; we can leverage her statement to gather more compelling evidence. Search warrants. Phone records. The works. But we need her statement to get those warrants.'

Martin smiles. 'You're worried about Johnson Pear.'

'No comment,' says Montifore, but now there's the hint of acknowledgement edging his eyes.

Of course, thinks Martin, that's why he sent Lucic out; he doesn't want his subordinate to see him questioning the propriety of a fellow officer.

'Here's the situation,' Montifore continues. 'As of tomorrow, it will be just Ivan Lucic and me here, plus one inexperienced constable. Forensics and the rest of the unit will be heading back to Sydney. I am reliant on Pear and his goodwill to operate out of this station, for administrative help and any additional manpower. I can't afford to get him offside, and I certainly can't tip him off. You need to get me that witness; until then my hands are tied. And you need to make sure anyone else who knows, including your girlfriend and her pain-in-the-arse lawyer, understands it too.'

Martin doesn't say anything, knowing he needs to tread carefully.

'I will pursue this theory of yours,' Montifore says, 'but I want to do it discreetly. If Jasper Speight discovered St Clair engaged in criminal activity, he may well have gone to Johnson Pear in the first instance, only to have nothing happen, which is why Speight decided to come to you. You can see the implication as clearly as I can: Pear didn't investigate.'

The men stare at each other for a moment before Martin speaks again. 'You don't think Pear could be implicated in the murder?'

'Go find your source, Martin. Tell her to speak to me. Tell her not to talk to anyone else. Let's not put her in danger.'

chapter eighteen

MARTIN DRIVES ALONG THE BOULEVARDE, HIS DAMAGED MUFFLER EMITTING A LOW roar, bouncing back from the shopfronts through his open window. He wants to return to Hummingbird and convince Topaz to talk to Montifore. But first he wants to reassure himself Mandy has recovered from her encounter with St Clair. She's left Drakes, gone to pick up Liam from child care and take him to the caravan park. He'll wait for her there, then head to Hummingbird Beach.

He motors across the bridge, the Argyle languid below. He's slowing to turn left into the caravan park when his mirrors light up. Blue and red lights. The police. Shit. Just what he needs. He indicates meticulously, eases the car off the blacktop into the entry of the caravan park, the dolphin hanging by its nose, still threatening to fall. He cuts his engine and sits waiting for the police officer to approach him. He's pretty sure that's what's expected nowadays, that you wait for the police, no jumping out to meet them like when he was a kid. An American thing, he thinks: fear of guns. Sit in the car with your hands on the wheel.

He sees movement in his mirror and his heart drops a beat. It's Johnson Pear walking towards him, hands hitched into his belt, gun prominent. Gun prominent. Martin attaches his hands to the top of the steering wheel in clear view. Shit. He takes a deep breath, paints his face with neutrality.

'Oh, well. Here's a surprise. The celebrated journalist himself.' Pear's smile leaks malice like a Liberian tanker. He leans over, places his hands on the windowsill.

Martin looks him in the eye, smiles. 'Afternoon, Officer.'

'Licence and rego.'

Martin knows Pear will have already checked the registration through the police car's computer, but he's not about to argue. He leaves his hands on the steering wheel. 'My licence is in my wallet in my pocket. The papers are in the glove box.'

Pear's smile broadens. 'Good. Get them.' And he takes his hands off the door, stands straight, hitching his hands back into his belt. Near his gun.

Martin has no choice: he must comply. Slowly he reaches down with his left hand, arching his back and extracting his wallet from the left front pocket of his pants. He watches Pear as he does so, seeing the bully's grin, seeing the casual movement of his hand onto the stock of his gun. Martin has his wallet out, holds it in clear sight, up near the top of the steering wheel, using both hands to open it and retrieve his licence. He hands it to Pear, who gives it the most cursory of glances before handing it back. 'Rego.'

Martin slides the licence into his wallet and places the wallet on the dashboard before turning away, leaning over to open the glove compartment. He's about to grab the papers when Pear speaks, low and hostile. 'Stop. Hands up where I can see them.'

Martin does what he's told, turns, and flinches involuntarily. Pear has his pistol out and is pointing it at him, the mouth of its barrel a black hole, sucking in Martin's attention, emitting fear like X-rays. The moment lasts a few seconds and forever.

'My mistake,' says Pear. 'Thought I saw something.' He smiles, eyebrow cocked. 'Tell you what, don't worry about the papers.' He returns his gun to its holster, but he's not finished. 'Turn it over—the engine.'

Martin starts the car.

'Give it a good rev, will you?'

Martin obeys.

Pear nods in mock seriousness. 'Muffler's fucked. You know that?'

'Just happened this morning,' says Martin, then bites his tongue, recognising the game Pear is playing, knowing nothing he says is going to help.

'Is that right?' says Pear, cocking his other eyebrow. He starts walking around the car, moving to the back first, Martin following him in the mirrors, his hands back in clear view on the steering wheel. Pear continues past the boot and along the car's far side, before stopping in front of the grille. He grins at Martin, draws a finger across his throat, an instruction to kill the engine. Martin complies.

'Come and have a look at this,' commands Pear.

Martin climbs out, knowing what's coming.

'Your left front indicator is smashed. Were you aware of that?'

Martin nods. 'Also this morning.'

'Rough day,' says Pear. 'Okay. You can get back in.' And then he adds, 'Hands where I can see them.'

Martin returns to the driver's seat. Pear makes a great show of walking back to his car, returning with a handheld device like an EFTPOS machine, prodding at it with a stylus. Martin tries to maintain his poker face while he waits, wondering just how many offences he's about to be ticketed for. As many as Pear fancies, he supposes. The policeman is taking his time, ticking off items like it's a hotel breakfast menu and he's on company expenses. A van passes with no muffler at all by the sounds of it, gaskets gone, black smoke pouring out the exhaust. Pear watches it go and smiles at Martin. A black Range Rover coming from town slows and turns in front of them, passing into the caravan park, tinted windows concealing its interior. Martin feels a surge of adrenaline kick in. It's a car that doesn't belong anywhere near the caravan park. Almost too late, Martin thinks of the number plate, only gets a glance, but it's enough. There are just three letters: TSC. Shit. His imagination fills in what his eyes couldn't see: Tyson St Clair and Harry the Lad and the thug from the cheese factory, bent on no good. He wants to get going, to get in there, before Mandy and Liam return, but knows he's powerless; if he attempts to drive off now Pear will arrest him on the spot. And if he uses his phone, the policeman might shoot him, claim he thought Martin was going for a weapon. So he sits there emasculated, at Pear's mercy, knowing any attempt to hurry the policeman along will only have the opposite effect. He closes his eyes, urging calm upon himself.

But now, in his side mirror, he sees more movement, another vehicle approaching. Fear folds into reality: it's the Subaru. He can see Mandy's face now, in the mirror. She slows, indicating to turn into the caravan park, easing her car to a stop alongside them, engine running.

Pear turns to her. 'Keep going.'

She ignores him, God bless her. 'You okay?' she calls to Martin.

'Get going,' Pear repeats, 'or I'll book you as well.'

'Wait for me by reception,' calls Martin.

Mandy frowns, shaking her head, signalling she hasn't heard. She moves off, her car disappearing through the rusted arch of the entry, the dolphin hanging like the sword of Damocles, Martin consumed by stomach-gnawing trepidation.

Pear leans down, hands back on the windowsill. 'Tell you what: seeing as you're a local again, I'm going to let you off with a warning. A welcome home gesture.'

If there is anything welcoming in Pear's demeanour, Martin can't see it. But he's anxious to move, to follow Mandy; he's not going to derail that now. 'Thank you. That's very generous.'

But Pear isn't done. He leans even closer, head almost through the window. His breath doesn't smell good. 'You know what a warning is, don't you?' He pauses for Martin's nod. 'Excellent. This is a warning. First and last.' He withdraws his head, stands erect. 'Now, get the fuck out of my sight.'

Martin does what he's told, starting the Corolla, indicating carefully, crawling forward and through the gates under the precarious dolphin. Once through the entry way and out of sight of Pear, he accelerates, ignoring the cacophony of speed limit signs, impatient to get to Mandy. He gets to the fork in the road at reception only to be brought to a stop by the owner moving across the drive, her prosthetic leg shining in the sun, as if she's just given it a good polish. She stops in the middle of the drive, blocking his way, signalling with both hands for him to slow down before moving off to one side. 'Slow down, mate. Can't you read? There are kids and oldies galore in here.'

Martin wants to swear, to vent his frustration at the woman, but he suppresses it. 'Right you are,' he says. 'Old car; sounds faster than it is.'

The owner looks unimpressed; Martin doesn't care. He's on his way again, heading towards their cabin.

He arrives just in time to see it end. Parked outside their cabin is the Range Rover, a large and lustrous machine. If it's ever been off-road, he sees no evidence of it. He pulls over, jumps out, starts to run. And then stops. Standing on the steps to the cabin is Tyson St Clair. There's no sign of Harry the Lad, no sign of the menacing Islander. The developer is armed only with a bouquet of flowers and a gift-wrapped box—and he has a startled look on his face. Mandy's standing at the door, delivering a tongue lashing. Martin is in time to hear its culmination, spoken quietly but with passion to spare: 'Just fuck off and die, you miserable, pathetic, loathsome creep.' And with that, she steps back into the cabin, delivers St Clair a devastating smile and closes the door.

For a moment, St Clair doesn't move; he just stands there, flowers held limply in one hand, gift in the other.

'That went well,' says Martin, mischief bubbling, his fear and trepidation replaced by relief and victory.

St Clair turns to him. 'I just wanted to explain, to apologise. That's all.'

Martin smiles. 'Good luck with that.'

'She told you?'

'That you thought she was on the game? Indeed she did.'

St Clair comes down off the steps, looks at the useless flowers, and tosses them on the bonnet of the Range Rover, followed by the gift-wrapped package. He walks over to Martin. 'Look, it was an honest mistake.'

Martin shrugs. 'It's not me you need to convince.'

'I don't need to convince anyone,' St Clair replies tersely. 'I didn't need to come here. I wanted to make amends, that's all.'

Martin makes a rapid assessment. St Clair hasn't realised Martin knows about the visa scam. Good. But by now he surely knows that Mandy is the new owner of the cheese factory. Martin tries to sound earnest. 'I'm sorry, I can't take up your job offer, Tyson.'

St Clair's eyes blaze like twin blue gemstones, but he says nothing.

Martin pushes it. 'I'm going to stick with journalism.'

St Clair is squinting, face hard. 'What do you want?'

'Tell me why you instigated the search of the cheese factory,' says Martin. 'Why you tipped off Channel Ten. Why now?'

A smile births itself on the hard face of Tyson St Clair; the businessman can smell a deal. 'All right, I'll tell you all about it, but I want something in return.'

'I'm all ears.'

'You give me your word that the incident with young Mandalay stays between the three of us. It does not, under any circumstances, go in the papers or into any sordid little book of small-town intrigues.'

Martin frowns, as if pondering the journalistic code of ethics. But it's an act; inside he's smirking. At some point he will write the story, but it won't be about St Clair mistaking an upright citizen for a prostitute; it will detail his participation in visa fraud and coercive sex. So when Martin speaks, he's not making a serious commitment, despite his sober voice. 'You have my word. I won't write it. It's not in her interest.'

St Clair grins. 'Correct. It makes me look bad, but it does her no favours either. Where there's smoke, there's fire. That's what people will think.'

Martin gestures, as if in agreement. 'Tell me. What makes you think Ashton was murdered and that he's buried at the cheese factory?'

St Clair shrugs, as if to indicate he's not saying anything new. 'He had a lot of enemies. He owed a lot of people money. There were rumours he had come to a sticky end and the last place he was seen alive was at the cheese factory. It's worth a look.'

'Did Ashton owe *you* money?'

'Too right he did. Bastard. And get this: I got a whiff, before he disappeared, that he was in strife. He offered to sell me the lot. I didn't realise how much he needed the money. I could have got it for a song.'

Martin frowns. 'So why didn't you buy it?'

'Because five or six years ago it was a shithole in the middle of nowhere. And if I'd bought it, I risked having the EPA insist I pay for its clean-up. Not to mention a bunch of creditors chasing me. No thanks.'

'What's changed?'

'The French and Hummingbird Beach. If he can be declared dead, I can find the owner and buy it from them.'

'You don't know who the prospective owner is?'

St Clair offers a derisory little snort, looks sadly at the flowers and the gift. 'Of course I do.'

'Are you paying Channel Ten to search the factory?'

'No. They're staying for free in one of my properties. That's it.'

'Have they found anything?'

St Clair sizes him up. 'I've been sworn to secrecy. But off the record, Thunkleton says he's making progress.'

'What does that mean?'

'You'll have to ask him. Now do we have a deal?'

Martin is shaking St Clair's hand when Mandy emerges from the cabin. She's holding Liam and she's looking daggers. Seeing them, she turns on her heel and returns inside.

Once St Clair has gone, the Range Rover heading back towards its habitat on Nobb Hill, Martin goes after her to explain himself, fearing the worst. Instead he finds Mandy smiling.

'He doesn't know, does he?' she says. 'That we know about the visas?'

'No, I don't think he does. But he's definitely worked out you are the likely owner of the cheese factory, or soon will be.'

She shakes her head. 'What a prize dick. He treats me like that and then thinks flowers and a trinket will smooth it over?' She moves to Martin, takes his arm. 'I hope like hell you're going to write something. An exposé.'

'All in good time.'

And she smiles some more. And so does he. Maybe they're getting somewhere. Maybe. But it's a fleeting moment of satisfaction. He needs to get to Hummingbird and convince Topaz to help. But first, before he leaves mobile range, he calls Morris Montifore. This time the detective answers promptly.

'Martin? How'd it go with your source?'

'I'm not there yet. But I need to check something with you first.'

It's not what Montifore wants to hear; his reply is curt. 'I'm listening.'

'Did you know that Channel Ten is searching for a body at the abandoned cheese factory on Dunes Road?'

'I'm aware of that. What about it?'

'I just ran into Tyson St Clair. He claims the television team is making progress.'

'Progress? What does that mean?'

'I don't know. That's why I'm telling you. Perhaps you can find out.' Montifore says nothing; Martin persists. 'If Jasper discovered who killed Ashton, the murderer could have killed Jasper to keep him quiet.'

'You should be a policeman.'

'You've spoken to St Clair?'

'Of course.'

'You could have told me.'

'Told you what? A rumour about a cold case?'

'Did St Clair say anything else? Does he know who killed Ashton?'

Now there is a touch of anger to the policeman's voice. 'You think I'd be sitting here on my arse if I knew that?' There's the briefest of pauses. 'Martin, go talk to your source. We need her onside and on the record.' And Montifore hangs up.

The policeman is right; Martin's priority has to be persuading Topaz to speak to the detective. He bids Mandy goodbye and gets going. Out on Dunes Road, he tries to think through how he will convince the American, but instead the unmuffled sound of the Corolla, its throaty growl, reverberating around him, enters his head through the open windows, arousing memory.

Jasper and his hotted-up Mazda. The Beast. Fanging along Dunes Road, shattering the speed limit, Jasper and Martin in the front, Scotty in the back, arms out the windows, hooting their delight. It's a graduation present from Denise; either that or a bribe to stop Jasper following his friends to Sydney. It's an old car with a new paint job: day-glo yellow with black racing stripes, front lowered, back raised, a burbling, gurgling concoction of chrome and hormones. A chick magnet, according to Jasper. He only gets it a month before Martin leaves Port Silver for good, but in that month the three of them do it all: endless laps around The Boulevarde, hill climbs against the clock up the escarpment, challenging the land speed record after midnight on Dunes Road. And getting pulled over on three separate occasions by Clyde Mackie.

Martin smiles. The Beast. Not all memories are bad. And then he's passing his family's cross, alone by the roadside, and he's wrenched back into the present, reminded that most memories are not good.

—

Martin finds Topaz on the beach with a small group of admirers, sitting around an unlit fire, passing around a joint. Some of the more industrious campers are bringing firewood down from the forest in preparation for night time. The last golden shafts of sunlight are carving through the trees, the wind has dropped, waves punctuate the late afternoon like a heartbeat.

'Hi, Topaz. Can I have a word?'

'Sure,' she says, handing him the reefer like a challenge. 'We're all friends here.'

He takes a perfunctory toke. He already feels like an outsider, wearing shoes on the sand, a forty-one-year-old in street clothes; no need to behave like one. He passes the joint on to the youth next to him. 'Seriously. It's important.'

She smiles, moves away from the circle, hips swaying for the benefit of the eyes she knows will be following her. She climbs up the ledge and onto the grass above the beach, where she turns to face him, eyes sparking with the last of the sunlight. 'What is it?' she asks.

'The police. They need to speak to you.'

She frowns. 'You said you wouldn't tell them my name.'

'I haven't. That's why I'm here. But they don't know if I'm telling the truth. From me it's only hearsay.'

'What about your girlfriend? Don't they believe her?'

'No. She stormed out of St Clair's place the moment he told her to strip. There was no mention of visas.'

But Topaz is already shaking her head. 'No. I can't. I won't.'

'Please. Someone killed my best friend. You understand? Without your help, the killer may well go free, kill again. There's a chance my innocent girlfriend will go to prison. Is that what you want?'

'You say that, but you don't know that. And if the police knew I was scamming a visa, they could arrest me, deport me. I'm not risking that, not with Royce lying helpless up in that hospital.'

'So you've already applied then?' he asks.

'Applied for what? The visa extension?'

'Yes.'

She frowns, as if they're talking at cross-purposes. 'No, not yet. When I get back to Sydney.'

'So you still have the paperwork, the form or letter or whatever it is?'

'Yes.'

'Then you haven't done anything wrong yet, nothing illegal. If you haven't submitted the application, you haven't broken any law.'

Topaz looks unsure. 'What are you saying?'

'If you talk to the police, then they can't charge you, even if they wanted to. All you have to say is that you had second thoughts and couldn't go through with it. You'd be in the clear. No arrest, no charges, no deportation. Just the opposite; they'll be grateful for your help.'

'And no visa.'

'No. But if you do submit that form, try to get a visa extension after less than a week in Port Silver, what do you think is going to happen?'

'You're threatening me?'

'No. Helping you. You can't use that form. Not now. Not with the police aware of what's going on. But if you give it to the police, they'll have the evidence they need.'

'I told you, I'm not testifying.'

'You won't have to. If the police can talk to you, see that form, they'll have enough evidence to get search warrants, pull up all the past records, find cases where visa extensions were actually granted on fraudulent documents. They may not even care about the recipients; they'll go after St Clair and Harry Drake and the farmers. Surely you'd like to see Drake get his comeuppance after what he did to Royce?'

Topaz stares into his eyes, thinking. The flirt has gone, the happy-go-lucky persona stowed for the moment. 'Okay, I'll talk to them. If they want the form they can have it, but I will not appear in court. That's my condition. I want anonymity and I want immunity.'

'Okay. Let's call them. Only they can make those assurances.'

They walk together to the office, Martin hoping Jay Jay is there and the landline is free.

There's a low light coming through the windows of the office. Martin is about to try the door, when Topaz grabs his forearm. 'Listen,' she hisses.

Martin stops, holds his breath, listens: the waves breaking, distant music and laughter, and, closer, someone groaning. Adrenaline catches Martin, taking the edge off the dope: there's someone in pain, someone inside the office. He reaches for the handle, but again Topaz grabs his arm, stops him. He turns to her; she is smiling, shaking her head. She removes her hand, combines it with her other to make a crude gesture, a finger moving in and out of a hole. Suddenly Martin understands.

Topaz moves to a window, presses her face to it, looks back at Martin, eyes wide, a huge smile on her face. 'Check it out,' she whispers.

Maybe it's the dope, maybe it's his innate curiosity, but Martin doesn't resist the invitation to voyeurism. He presses his face to the window, holding up his hands to cut out the glare from the setting sun.

The couple are on the floor in front of the desk, candles glowing along its edge. A pair of feet, a plump brown shape: a man lying on his back, head obscured by the woman riding him enthusiast-ically, her back to the window. Her skin is white, glowing in the candlelight. Two diamonds are carved into her back, moving as if alive as she writhes on top of her lover.

'Jay Jay,' whispers Martin.

'And the swami.' Topaz laughs. 'God, he's like a trampoline.'

But Martin is not answering. He's transfixed. The twin skin-cancer scars dance in the candlelight and below, curving around one buttock, is a ragged crescent, flashing purple and crimson in the flickering light. 'What's that on her bum?' he asks.

'Spanking,' says Topaz, an element of awe in her voice. 'God, they're really going for it.'

Martin takes a last look. The backpacker isn't wrong. Jay Jay's arms are now high in the air, her back arching, her moaning louder and more emphatic. He's seen enough and looks away.

Back on the beach, the sun has set and the fire has been lit, flames bright in the diminishing light. A portable speaker is playing this decade's take on folk music. Martin really wants Topaz to talk to Montifore tonight, before she changes her mind. She's already declined his invitation to drive up the cliff road into mobile range. So the phone in reception is the only option; he'll have to wait till Jay Jay and the swami reappear before he asks to use it. He looks at Topaz, across the fire. She's got an arm draped around the neck of a gorgeous young Polynesian woman dressed in a tank top and a tiny denim skirt. The woman is laughing too much, obviously stoned. Martin is offered a joint; he takes a long toke and passes it on. He removes his shoes and socks.

Gradually more people gather and the music steps up a notch, no longer acoustic. He accepts a drink of orange juice, quickly realising it's more than juice. Alcohol. Vodka. He finishes the drink, the sweetness cloying. There is beer. A young fellow asks him if he wants to join the pool. Twenty dollars in, as much as you can drink. And smoke. Martin only wants one beer, but hands over the money anyway, buying his licence to be here, to linger, to wait for Jay Jay and the guru and to persist with Topaz. She's up dancing with the young Polynesian woman now, their hips grinding. Others are dancing as well, some just watching. Garth McGrath the soap star arrives, chugs back some beer, eyes fixed on Topaz. Martin fears he may have to engage the randy prick in conversation; he doesn't want him making a move on Topaz before Jay Jay and the swami return.

And then they arrive, the guru and the surfer. The spiritual leader is wearing a look of divine peace; Jay Jay merely looks smug. She sees Martin; their eyes lock. She moves around the fire to him. 'Didn't think I'd see you here,' she says, voice questioning.

'Discovering my inner hippie,' he says, laughing at his own quip, then catching himself. The blend of alcohol and dope must be stronger than he'd realised.

Jay Jay shakes her head as if in disbelief. 'Give me your phone then. And any cameras you've got with you.'

'What? Why?'

'You're not the first, sweetheart. I had half the press corps dancing around my fire one night.'

'Jay Jay, I swear—that's not why I'm here.'

'Of course not. But just to be safe, I'll put them in the office. You can get them back when you leave.'

Martin nods, sees the opportunity. 'Sure. But while you're there, can I make a call on your landline?'

She shrugs. 'I guess. Telling your girlfriend where you are?'

'No, not exactly.'

She laughs. 'Didn't think so. But tell her to come join us, if you want. She enjoyed it last time. Might help her chill a bit.'

Martin blinks. Mandy? Last time?

'Phone,' says Jay Jay, hand out.

Martin hands over his smartphone. 'I'll be right with you,' he says. 'I need to bring someone with me.'

'Whatever,' says Jay Jay. 'But don't leave it too long. I want to have a swim before it's totally dark.'

But it's too late; Topaz isn't interested. Martin can't convince her to leave the dance floor, where she is becoming increasingly entwined with not only the Polynesian girl but with Garth McGrath, his eyes alive with lechery, his hands all over them.

Martin gives up, walks over to the office alone, feeling himself swaying a little. In the gloom, he misjudges one of the steps leading up to the office, trips, almost falls. Inside, the office smells of extinguished candle, incense and more earthy odours. Jay Jay is leaning against her desk, drinking.

'You want a beer?' she asks. 'Colder than the ones down there.'

'Sure,' says Martin, accepting a bottle. 'Okay to make that call?'

'Go for your life. Not international, right?'

'No. Local. I just need my phone to check the number.'

Jay Jay hands over the phone. Martin finds Montifore's number, makes the call.

'Yes?'

'It's Martin Scarsden.'

'Martin.'

'Just a moment.' Martin turns to Jay Jay, who is putting his phone in the drawer of her desk. 'I'll lock up after I'm done, if you like.'

Jay Jay casts a quick eye over her office. Clearly, she doesn't trust him. He doesn't blame her. 'Okay,' she says. 'Slam the door behind you.' She points up towards one corner of the ceiling. 'Security camera. It's recording.'

Martin nods his understanding then turns his attention back to the phone. 'Morris, you still there?'

'I am.'

'I found the witness. I think she'll talk to you. Can you assure her that she won't be arrested?'

'What for?'

'Visa fraud.'

'Has she already applied?'

'No. She has the form signed and ready to go, but she hasn't submitted it.'

'In that case, I can assure her she won't be charged, provided she doesn't submit the paperwork. But I need to see it.'

'I understand. I'm going to try to convince her to talk to you on the phone first, anonymously. Are you okay with that?'

'Anonymously?'

'As a first step. So you can persuade her to go on the record, hand over the paperwork.'

'Okay, sure. Failing that, just get the form.'

Martin wonders if the policeman is suggesting he steal it, decides to ignore the idea. 'I'll get back to you.'

At the fire, the party has stepped up another notch, the music louder, the flames higher. A few more people have wandered down from their campsites. There's maybe two dozen now, mainly backpackers, plus a few older couples in their thirties. The same teenage couple Martin recalls from the beach are dancing together, as if trying to meld into each other. Martin is relieved to see he's not the oldest person there; some hippies in their fifties or sixties are standing in a group, swaying to the music, watching the dancers and passing around a huge reefer. The smell of dope is rich, mixing with the sea air, the music, the noise of laughter and talking. People are entering the moment, letting their worries go and their inhibitions fall. Martin sees it, hears it, wonders if he could ever be so relaxed as to experience it.

Then Topaz is next to him, pulling him over to dance with her. She sways close. He's about to push away, to withdraw, when he sees Garth McGrath glaring, eyes lit with anger. Martin can't help himself; he starts dancing.

It leaves him hot, sweating in the still evening. He drinks more beer and some punch. He's exhausted. Exhilarated.

The swami is sitting cross-legged, lotus-like, with a huge grin on his face, his bare belly shimmering in the firelight. Opposite him, a pretty young girl with blonde hair has replicated the position. She holds her hands out, palms upwards, and the swami is tracing patterns gently across them with the tips of his middle and forefinger. He reaches out, touches her forehead. She opens her eyes, beaming. He has a large Coke bottle by his side. He pours a couple of nips into a plastic cup and hands it to her. She smiles her gratitude and stands, taking the plastic cup with her. She's replaced by an old hippie woman with pendulous breasts.

'What's that?' Martin asks Topaz.

'Huh? What?'

'The swami. He's dispensing.' Martin laughs. 'Let's get some.'

'Fuck that,' says Topaz.

'Your loss.'

Martin looks into the guru's eyes. They are like deep pools, profound and inscrutable. He closes his own eyes, feels a surge as if some tide has him, is carrying him with it.

Then he and Topaz are dancing again, and the pretty young blonde and the old hippies and McGrath and the Polynesian girl and the teenage lovers. Later, there's a memory of swimming, of stars so bright they hurt his eyes, stars so alive they dance in time with the music. And the taste of a kiss, sweet and treacherous.

FRIDAY

chapter nineteen

MARTIN DREAMS. A BEE, BUZZING, YELLOW AND BLACK, CIRCLING HIS HEAD. IT wants to tell him something; something important. The buzzing is words, but he can't make them out, it's the wrong language, he regrets not paying attention in school. Now the bee is growing bigger and bigger, too heavy to fly. It lands, its furry coat turning shiny as it transforms into a car, shimmering gold with black stripes. Jasper's car. Now he's inside, Jasper is driving, excited, declaring the car is amphibious. And it is: they're driving in the water, down the Argyle. They're laughing. Through the rear window Martin can see Scotty waterskiing, towed by the car, and he wants a turn. Then it's Mandy behind the wheel, Jasper and Scotty have gone, and the mood changes. They're heading towards the sandbar, the deadly surf. He tries to warn her, but she's not listening. Liam is sleeping in the back, buckled into his booster seat. He can't swim! Martin panics, grabs the wheel, yanking at it, trying to reach the secret beach and safety. The wheel comes off in his hand. Dread washes through him. Now he's alone in the car, not Jasper's car, his own. It's limping along Dunes Road, exhaust scraping on the road. In the rear-view mirror he sees a car approaching, blue and red lights flashing. He pushes on the accelerator as hard as he can, but there is no response. He looks down; the foot pedals have fallen out the bottom of the car onto the road. He looks in the mirror; the approaching vehicle is no longer a police car. It's going too fast, it's going to rear end him. He's helpless. It's going to kill him.

Martin wakes. A mosquito is buzzing around his ear, but he feels unable to move. His eyes are sticky, his vision blurry. Sunlight is stabbing at him like blades, jabbing him into wakefulness. His mouth is dry, and he feels hot, too hot; he's slept too long. His limbs are stiff, parts of him ache. Where is he? The bed is unfamiliar, the smells strange, the room unknown. The caravan park? No. What's that sound, that distant beat? Waves? Shit, he's at Hummingbird Beach. He eases himself into a sitting position. There's a glass of water beside the bed; he gulps it down. A wave of nausea catches him unawares, his stomach revolting against the water. It's all he can do to avoid vomiting. More parts of his far-flung body start reporting for duty. He pulls back the sheet, looks down: his arms and chest are covered in mosquito bites, itching and inflamed the moment he sees them. His legs start complaining. He pulls the sheet away altogether. He's naked. His knees are grazed, already scabbing with dried blood. How did that happen? Now his head joins the orchestra of complaint, the lead instrument: a pulsating throb consolidating and intensifying, a scalpel inserted behind his left eye, a sickening pain in the back of his neck. He closes his eyes, trying to calm himself, to will away the pain and nausea, but it does nothing to ease his affliction. Instead he starts shaking, trembling involuntarily. He feels like he's been fed through a machine and extruded.

He tries to stand, can't maintain the posture, sits back down again. Shit. He can't stand; he can barely think. What sort of hangover is this? Nothing like he's ever experienced. He remembers the previous night clearly enough up until a point, dancing on the beach, but then his recollections grow disjointed. Swimming in the ocean. Snogging. Snogging whom? And then no memories at all. Nothing.

He looks down at himself, realises again that he's naked. Where are his clothes? He looks around. No sign. What does he do now? He needs to move, he knows that, but just the thought of standing sends a new wave of nausea crashing through him. His left knee is oozing blood. He lifts his arms, exciting his excruciating neck. His elbows are also grazed, but he can't hear them; the rest of the orchestra is too loud. Christ, the swami and his jungle juice. It started going downhill after that, his memory increasingly frayed and tattered. Shit. Naked. He reaches down, feels his crotch. Sticky. He smells his hand. Christ.

Topaz staggers into the room, light shattering through the doorway, her hair a mess, her face fragmented by emotion, a towel wrapped around her. 'You,' she says.

Martin can't talk, just nods.

'Move over,' she says, crawling onto the bed next to him, lying face down. The towel falls from her; she's also naked, back scraped and bruised.

'Jesus,' says Martin, able to articulate at last.

'Did we?' asks Topaz.

'I can't remember. I think I did with someone, but it's a black hole. I can't remember a thing.'

'You too, then.' Her voice is a whisper, hoarse and quiet.

Martin tries to ease himself up, feels sick again, stifles a cough.

'Go and puke,' says Topaz. 'Get it out of you. If there's anything left. Drink water, as much as you can.'

'Can I borrow your towel?'

'Goddamn,' she says, but rolls over, freeing the towel. Martin sees hickies on her neck, touches his own neck, feels something there. He hopes it's a mosquito bite. He touches his cheek, the top of his jaw, the bruise that Harry the Lad gave him. Compared to the rest of him, it feels fine.

'Are you all right?' he asks.

The question triggers tears, washing into her eyes. She shakes her head, no longer able to speak. Martin's eyes sweep down her naked body, not excited by her nudity or tantalised by her breasts but horrified by the bruises on her thighs. Had he done that? Was he capable of that? Surely not.

He gets upright, still unsteady on his feet, holds her towel unconvincingly over his genitals. He makes the door, but the sunlight ignites the full dynamic range of the orchestra, kettle drums crashing, and he rushes off the steps, just getting clear before vomiting, towel thrown aside, not a thread of clothes, not a fibre of dignity. He throws up over and over, well beyond the point where there is anything left to expel, yet still he retches, until his throat burns with residual acid and his stomach muscles cramp.

Eventually he stands. Topaz is at the door to the cabin. 'Here.' She tosses him a plastic bottle of water. He bends to retrieve it, the blood rushing to his head and stepping up the pressure, the orchestra thundering its discordant refrain. He rinses his mouth, gargles, spits the water out, then tries to stomach a few gulps. The water feels wonderful as he swallows, but there is still revolution in his innards.

'Someone gave you a good work-out,' says Topaz. 'Hope it wasn't me.'

'What do you mean?'

'Your arse is red raw.'

Martin looks at her in shock. Tentatively he passes a hand behind him. She's right, his buttocks are sore to the touch, as if he has been beaten. A nightmare thought comes to mind; he threads his hand through his legs, touches his anus, feels a rush of relief when there is no pain, no blood on his fingers. It didn't happen, but it could have.

'Now you know how we feel,' says Topaz, her eyes full of contempt.

'What the fuck did they give us?'

'I thought it was eccies. That's what the others said.'

'Not to me.'

'No one forced you to take it.'

'No one forced you, either.'

They stare at each other for a moment, but Martin is incapable of confrontation. 'So what was it then?' he asks.

Topaz shakes her head. 'Fuck knows. Eccies for sure. And that other shit. Rohies.'

'Rohypnol?' The date rape drug. Known to reduce inhibitions, notorious for blacking out memories. He thinks she's right. 'Have you ever had it before?' he asks.

'Yeah.'

'And?'

'And yeah. Same memory loss.'

'Shit,' says Martin. Suddenly, as if self-awareness is coming back in stages, he realises he's standing there naked. He picks up the towel, wraps it around his waist.

'Wondered when you'd remember that,' says Topaz, a faded smile on her lips.

'What now?' asks Martin.

'Can you drive?'

He blinks at the suggestion of re-entering the world. 'Not yet.' He takes another tentative swig of water. 'But soon. If I have to. Why?'

'We should go to the hospital.'

'You want to see Royce?'

'I do,' she says. She blinks away another tear. 'And I want to take every antibiotic and antiviral known to man. You should too.'

Martin looks out across the beach. There are a few people about, but the morning is silent, kangaroos grazing, birds quiet, only the metronome of the waves keeping time. So much for paradise.

———

They don't leave for another two hours. The first is spent lying on the bed, drinking water, dozing, slowly surfacing. Topaz has painkillers: ibuprofen, paracetamol, codeine, aspirin. Martin swallows two of each, relieved when they stay down. The second hour is lost finding his clothes, scattered down on the beach near the remains of the fire. His wallet—credit cards and cash intact—is miraculously still in his pants pocket. They eat toast and bananas and drink milk in the communal kitchen, and normality starts washing back.

'I feel like complete shit,' he says to the room in general, to the other three or four people present. But they just shrug, as if nothing out of the ordinary has happened. Martin recognises some of them from the previous evening, before the blackout. They were there, partying with everyone else. Yet this morning they look fine. He watches as a couple, laughing congenially together, head out down to the beach and into the water. Martin looks at Topaz, wonders if she has noticed: not everyone has been affected the same way. They're just about to leave when Garth McGrath enters, walking on tiptoes as if the ground is covered in glass shards. One look at his face is enough: it's saying what they feel. He's unshaven, eyes red, face pallid under his tan, his t-shirt on back to front.

'You too?' asks Martin.

'What?'

'Last night. I can't remember the last part of the night.'

McGrath looks at him, unsteady on his feet, emotions unsteady across his face. He nods. 'Yeah. Me too.'

'Has it happened before? You've been here a lot longer than us.'

He shakes his head. 'No. Never like this.'

They sit in momentary silence.

McGrath speaks again. 'Sometimes it's just grog and dope. Sometimes something more, in the punch. But it's always been good. Fun. Not like this. Not losing my memory.' He looks like he's about to cry. He runs his hand up through his lustrous TV-star hair, his knuckles bruised and flecked with dried blood. 'Do you think they did it to me on purpose?'

'What do you mean?'

'Drugged me. Did you see a photographer?'

Martin and Topaz exchange a look. Neither bothers to respond.

'I think they set me up,' mutters the soap star.

Topaz stands, walks slowly up to McGrath. 'I woke up in your bed,' she says, voice knife sharp.

'Right,' says McGrath, at first confused, then a smile begins breaking across his face. It doesn't get far. Topaz punches him once in the guts, abruptly. The celebrity doubles over, heaving, only just making it out onto the grass.

'C'mon,' says Topaz, 'let's go.'

They leave the kitchen, the actor staring after them like a kicked dog.

'Look,' says Martin, gesturing with a nod. The swami is sitting in a lotus position, surrounded by a circle of his followers, their eyes closed. He's solemn and tranquil; the followers seem serene. Topaz looks at them with loathing.

'His potion. Did you drink any?'

'No,' says Topaz. 'Not that I remember.'

Almost too late Martin remembers his phone. Jay Jay isn't at the office, but a young man is minding the shop. Martin's phone is on the desk waiting for him, and his car keys have been handed in. They're on the desk, next to his phone. What else has he forgotten?

'Topaz, the paperwork. Can we take it?'

'You really want to do that now?'

'I do.'

She responds with an acidic smile. 'Sure. Let's get one back on the fuckers.'

The drive towards Port Silver is silent until Martin's phone starts shaking and chirping as they approach the caravan park, back in mobile range. He pulls off to the left, into the drive to Hartigan's, not far before the road reaches the bridge. There is a flurry of texts from Mandy. At first, they're encouraging. *Take care. So lucky to have you.* And then they're routine. *Cooking. How long?* and, *Eating now. Will leave some.* And then worried: *R U OKAY?* and, *Going to bed. Please tell me u OK.* There's one from Montifore sent that morning: *Any progress?* And another: *Where are you? Need to talk.* And finally, from Mandy: *WTF? Where r u? Police coming.*

'Shit,' says Martin. The police. The caravan park's entry is right there, on the other side of Dunes Road. 'This won't take a minute,' he says to Topaz.

Mandy is waiting, standing on the steps to the cabin, clutching her phone as if she is willing it to communicate with him, to lure him back.

He drives right up, pulls over next to her.

Her face is fragile, a tremor in her voice. 'Where have you been?'

'Long story. What's happened?'

'The police are coming. They want to interview me again.' She looks shaken, as if she's had her own night of excess.

'Why? What do they want?'

'I don't know.'

'Does Winifred know?'

'No. She's waiting there for me.'

'Why didn't you drive in?'

'They told me not to. I was waiting for you.' Her eyes drift to the car, to Topaz in the front seat.

'Where's Liam?' asks Martin.

'Child care. I took him in early. Then the police called, they were looking for me. So I came back here.' She smiles weakly, stifles the expression. 'I wanted to see you. I was worried.'

'I'm fine.'

Her eyes drift back to Topaz in the car. 'Did you sleep with her?'

Martin feels panic in his guts. 'No. It's not like that.'

But she sees the evasion in his eyes, the lie. She slaps him, hard, across his still-bruised cheek. She says nothing, just stares him down, the words unsaid more excoriating than any profanity. He stares at her, desperate for a way to explain, to pull them back together.

The tableau is broken by the arrival of the police, their patrol car easing shark-like up to them. Mandy walks to it without saying anything else. She's carrying an overnight bag. The sight of it shakes Martin. What is she expecting? What does she know? He wants to go after her, to reassure her, but he's frozen to the spot. She gets into the police car and it pulls away and he's still standing there.

Winifred Barbicombe doesn't answer her phone and Martin is forced to leave an awkward message, asking why the police are questioning Mandy and if he can help. When he calls Nick Poulos, his lawyer lets his phone ring and ring, then answers just as Martin is about to hang up.

'Martin, what gives?'

'They've arrested Mandy.'

'Arrested? You sure?'

'Detained then. They've just come out to the caravan park and taken her in for questioning. They didn't want her to drive herself.'

Poulos says nothing for a moment. 'Leave it with me, I'll see what I can find out. What about you? Did they want to speak with you?'

'No. They more or less ignored me.'

'That's good,' says Nick. 'I'll call you back when I know more.'

Reluctantly, he gets back into his car. He wants to be with Mandy at the police station, to find out what's happening, to be there when she's released. Driving to Longton is the last thing he feels like, as if somehow ascending the escarpment is a dereliction. But waiting in the foyer of a police station, possibly for hours, will do no one any good. He starts the car, begins the journey to Longton.

As they drive, Topaz is silent, eyes either closed or staring out her side window. There is no flirting; she's like a different person. Martin concentrates on the road. The edges of the world seem blurry, as if threatening to peel away. He knows he can't afford to slip up, that he probably shouldn't be driving. The last thing he wants is Johnson Pear breathalysing him. Or ordering a blood test.

———

Longton Hospital comes in two parts: the original building of brick and wood, erected some time in the early twentieth century, is now overshadowed by a two-storey building of concrete-laden functionality. A sign informs them that administration, physiotherapy and out-patient services are housed in the older building, while casualty and emergency as well as general wards are in the newer building. Casualty is quiet enough: a ginger-headed kid, eyes red, with a damaged arm in a homemade sling, sits next to his mother. An elderly Asian man has fallen asleep three places along.

The triage nurse casts an eye over Martin and Topaz, expressing her scepticism with nothing more than a raised eyebrow, before taking their details and telling them to be seated. Martin slumps into one of the plastic chairs next to Topaz, gives a desultory look at the magazines on offer. *Woman's Day*, *Women's Weekly*, *New Idea*, *Who*. Royalty, Britain's and Hollywood's; babies on their way, divorces imminent, affairs rumoured. For a moment he longs for a life so boring that a celebrity's baby bump could interest him. Topaz is still alternating between staring into the middle distance and closing her eyes for minutes on end. Her forehead is creased; Martin wonders if she's in pain. He asks at the counter how long the wait might be. The nurse says he is fourth in line, but that could change. He has a yearning for a newspaper and coffee; he risks leaving. First he tells the nurse that he'll be right back, that the doctors should see Topaz first. The eyebrow rises once more.

When he returns with two coffees, two doughnuts and a *Sydney Morning Herald*, Topaz is still waiting. She takes the drink and snack with a quiet thank you.

'You okay?' asks Martin.

'I'm really not,' she says.

Martin doesn't know how to respond. At least the coffee and doughnut taste good, especially the icing, providing much-needed ballast. He starts feeling a suggestion of what it might be to be human for the first time since waking at Hummingbird.

The doctor, an intern with a face from the Subcontinent and an accent from Parramatta, calls him before Topaz. She leads him into a small consulting room. 'When did this happen?' she asks, looking at his eye.

'The day before yesterday. It seems to be healing.'

'Let me see.' She examines him quickly, pulling back gently on the eyelid. She has a torch, uses a magnifying glass. 'How's your vision?'

'Good. No problem.'

She looks puzzled. 'Then why did you come in?'

'It's not the eye.' He explains the party, the possibility of unprotected sex with multiple partners.

'The possibility?' Is that the hint of a smile cracking through her professional veneer?

'I'm not sure,' he says.

Professionalism regains control of her face, but the smile remains in her eyes. 'So why the rush to come in?'

'I have a partner,' he says, shame in his voice. 'She wasn't there.'

The amusement vanishes from her eyes, but Martin can detect no judgement. 'That is very wise of you. Considerate.' She prescribes him a slew of drugs, tells him to refrain from unprotected sex for a week. He requests painkillers, something strong. She agrees to some low-level codeine tablets.

'One more thing,' he says. 'I feel like I might have been given something illegal. Some sort of drug. Is it possible to have a blood test?'

The intern frowns. 'I can take some blood, but I'm not sure pathology is really set up for that sort of thing.'

'Could you take some anyway, just in case they can find something?'

The intern shrugs. 'It's probably not a bad idea anyway. Check out your liver function.'

When he's done, Topaz is still outside waiting.

'I'm going to the chemist,' he says. 'I'll be right back.'

'It's okay, you don't have to wait for me. I'll go visit Royce when I'm done here.'

'You sure?'

'Yeah. There'll be a bus to Port Silver. Or I might splurge on a motel up here.'

'All right. And the visa form—I can give that to the police?'

There is a hardness to her eyes. 'Yeah. Do it. Fuck 'em.'

The sun has picked up its intensity, baking the town, away from the moderating effects of the ocean. The light hurts his eyes, the heat comes as an affront. A dry wind is coming from the west, carrying the dust of drought and the threat of fire. Officially it's autumn, but the danger is unabated, with the bush tinder-dry even this far east. Especially this far east, where fuel loads are higher. He sniffs at the breeze, but there is no smoke in the air, only the windblown topsoil of the interior.

He finds a chemist, but the pharmacist is out for a few minutes. They take his prescription, tell him to return in half an hour. Jesus. Half an hour. He tries ringing Nick, but the call cuts off. He's wondering why when a text appears: *Working on it. Call soon.* Martin texts Montifore: *Have visa form. There shortly.*

Martin looks about. What can he do? What can he possibly do? He sits in the shade. It's all going awry. Maybe it's the drugs, maybe it's him. Mandy must be in some sort of trouble, but he has no idea what it is. Just when she needs him, he's stuck in Longton, waiting for his prescription.

He pulls out the visa form, examines it. The sponsor isn't Tyson St Clair, but someone he's never heard of: John Prentice. The address, up along the Argyle, suggests Prentice is a farmer. Makes sense. Topaz's name and passport details are there. Topaz

Jade Throssel, born in Sacramento, aged twenty-nine. Older than she looks.

He tries again to remember the previous night, but fails to extract anything new. He suspects it's not coming back, ever, that the drug stopped the memories being created in the first place. There are just the same shards: memories of dancing, swimming, feeling so very, very good. Then there's just a void, and nothing's going to fill it except his lurid imagination. He thinks of this morning, how bad he felt. Topaz, himself, Garth McGrath. But no one else. Maybe there were others, still sleeping it off in their cabins and tents, unable to face the day. And yet he saw some revellers from the night before out and about in the morning, swimming and walking and laughing and attending to the swami. The swami himself had appeared unaffected. So what had happened? Had he, Topaz and Garth been targeted? Why them?

A memory returns from earlier in the night, before the drugs: Jay Jay and the swami having sex on the floor of her office. Martin recalls the diamond-shaped melanoma scars rising and falling, the red crescent on the surfer's buttock bouncing in the candlelight. Jay Jay and the swami. What a strange combination. No stranger than the swami, dressed in western clothes, chatting with Tyson St Clair here in Longton. But Topaz didn't drink any of the guru's potion; he can't have been the one responsible.

Martin looks at his phone. Still twenty-five minutes to wait. An idea comes to him, through the fog and the orchestra of pain.

In the Longton library, he goes directly to the computers with access to the digital newspaper archive. He closes his eyes for a moment, gathering himself. The last thing he feels like is looking at a screen. He fires up the catalogue, enters 'Jay Jay Hayes', sets the dates way back, forty years, and hits search. The first hit is from thirty-seven years ago and shows a trio, three women standing proudly with their surfboards. Jay Jay is the youngest of the three, just thirteen, but already in the centre, flanked by the others. The copy, more of an extended caption than a story, identifies the young women, reporting they have won the local surfing competition and are heading to Ballina for a regional competition. The following year Jay Jay wins the regionals at Ballina, gets to the last round of heats in the statewide championships. After that, there's plenty more: Jay Jay carving along waves, Jay Jay smiling shyly at the camera, Jay Jay bikini-clad and growing in confidence, rising through the amateur ranks, turning professional at age eighteen. All so very promising. The nature of the reports change, from locally written puff pieces to matter-of-fact wire copy from distant shores: South Africa, California, Chile, Hawaii. Cracking the world tour. Then they start to fade, petering out about twenty-five years ago. And then she's gone. Martin does a quick calculation. She would have been about twenty-five or twenty-six. No stories of retirement, no reports of injury. Just gone. He leans back in his chair. She'd given up surfing, at least the world tour. There could be all sorts of reasons for that: injury, marriage, even children. Or the most common reason of all: she wasn't good enough. Martin knows that there's outstanding money to be made in surfing, as there is in most sports, but only for a small elite, the ones winning the big prize money and scoring the lucrative product endorsements. After that the prize money would fall away pretty rapidly, and any endorsements would be paid in kind: free surfboards and wetsuits and beachwear, not the money needed for airfares and hotel rooms and food. And that's now; twenty-five years ago, the women's circuit would have been running on next to nothing. He thinks about it and decides there is little definitive to be discerned: she was a promising amateur, she turned pro, gave it her best shot, then it ended.

He brings the search dates forward. Nothing. Nothing for years, nothing for decades. Then, seven years ago, an obituary. Her father. Dead at eighty-three, his wife predeceasing him by twenty years, his sole survivor his daughter Jennifer 'Jay Jay' Hayes, the former surf champion. Was that when she had returned to Port Silver? For his funeral, to inherit the old dairy farm? Or had she returned earlier, to care for him in his decline? Martin thinks of Hummingbird. Signs of the dairy are few and far between. Maybe her dad had given it away well before his death, had simply lived out his retirement at the old farm. There were worse places to do it.

He continues his search, moving the date forward, not expecting to learn much more. Instead, the next story hits him straight between the eyes, a front-page splash: CHAMPION SURFER IN SHARK ATTACK. Martin feels awake for the first time in the day, alertness coming with adrenaline, cutting through his headache and dullness of mind. He reads.

Former professional surfer Jennifer 'Jay Jay' Hayes is recovering in Coffs Harbour Base Hospital after fighting off a shark that mauled her leg at Hummingbird Point, 20 kilometres north of Port Silver.

It's believed Hayes was surfing alone, just after dawn, when her board was struck from below by a large shark. It then mauled her upper thigh before she fought it off.

Locals say a number of bull sharks have been seen in the vicinity of the attack recently.

Ms Hayes was able to scramble to safety on rocks before staggering several hundred metres to raise the alarm. She was airlifted to Coffs Harbour suffering from deep gashes and extensive blood loss.

Ambulance officers say she is extremely fortunate no major arteries were severed. 'It's quite remarkable, really, that she fought off the shark and then had the presence of mind to stem the bleeding and summon help.'

Ms Hayes first came to prominence two decades ago . . .

Martin smiles grimly. Now he understands the angry mark he saw on the woman's buttock when she was having it off with the swami. Not spanking, but scars from the shark attack. And it explains her insistence on wearing a wetsuit in the March seas, when the water is at its warmest: not just for sun protection, but also to hide her injuries.

Martin is about to continue his search when his phone rings, loud in the quiet of the library. It's Nick Poulos. 'Mate, I'm with Inspector Montifore. You'd better get down here.'

chapter twenty

NICK POULOS IS NOWHERE TO BE SEEN AS MARTIN ENTERS THE PORT SILVER POLICE station, but Ivan Lucic is sitting waiting, his face breaking into a grin as he sees Martin. 'This way,' he says.

'What's happened?' asks Martin. 'Where's Mandy?'

'Relax. You're about to find out.'

But Martin doesn't relax. Lucic is in control: confident, serious, malevolent. Martin feels as if he's walking into some sort of trap. He shakes his head, trying to free it of paranoia. It's a police station, for God's sake. He needs to clear his mind, be on his guard, think before he speaks. He just wishes his head were clearer; he wishes he hadn't been so quick to swallow the painkillers from the Longton pharmacist.

Lucic leads him to an interview room that looks like something from a television drama—one with a low budget. A plastic-topped table, cheap office chairs, a concrete floor, brick walls. Clean, smelling of disinfectant, as if awful things have occurred here, things requiring sanitising. But it's cool. At least it's cool.

Martin sits, places his head in his hands, closes his eyes, tries to gather himself. The headache has been driven back, pacified by the codeine, but it's still there, plotting its return like a guerrilla in the hills. A fundamental ache remains in his bones, but his stomach has signed some sort of armistice. He breathes, tries to centre himself. It's not easy: something is coming for him, he can sense it, something worse than a headache. He is in a police interview room and he has no idea why.

The young constable enters. She has her video camera. Martin looks around him. It's the same interview room as Monday, when Johnson Pear interviewed him. Why hadn't he recognised it? Christ, he's not prepared for this. The constable busies herself with the camera, mounting it on a tripod, plugging in a lead to a microphone built into the table, checking that everything is in readiness, not once looking at Martin or acknowledging his existence. She leaves.

Some minutes later Montifore enters, followed by Lucic and the constable. Montifore gives him a cursory look, face serious, then busies himself with a file, opening it on the desk. Lucic, by contrast, does nothing but look at Martin, grinning. If it's meant to be intimidating, it's working. 'Recording,' says the constable, but Montifore remains entranced by his paperwork. Lucic smiles as if he's trying to break a record.

The door opens. Nick Poulos.

'What's going on, Nick?'

His lawyer grimaces. 'The police have some questions for you.' He flicks a glance at Montifore before returning his gaze to Martin.

'It is important that you answer absolutely honestly. I strongly advise you to do so.'

Martin stares incredulously. Whose side is this guy on?

Poulos sits next to him, placing his hand on his client's shoulder, a supportive gesture, as if to reassure Martin of his loyalty.

'Let's get started,' says Montifore. 'Constable?'

'Still recording, sir.'

Montifore reels through the formalities: the time of day, the names of those present. Then he pauses, gathering his thoughts. Or increasing the pressure.

'Martin, I want you to cast your mind back to your arrival in Port Silver four days ago, this past Monday. You have already given a signed statement that you arrived at the townhouse rented by Mandalay Susan Blonde at around eleven o'clock in the morning. You claimed that Jasper Speight was already dead when you arrived. I want you to think carefully. Is there anything about that statement you would like to revise? Anything you would like to change? Anything you would like to add?'

Martin glances at Poulos, who does nothing but raise his eyebrows, whatever that is meant to convey. 'No,' says Martin. 'Nothing.' What is the detective driving at?

'Understood,' says Montifore, his voice measured. 'But for the record, would you mind repeating now how the events unfolded from the time you entered the townhouse?'

Nick Poulos interjects. 'Just a moment. He gave his statement, has said he doesn't want to alter or add to it. That should be enough.'

Montifore looks at Poulos, considers his position. 'All right. Mr Scarsden, in your statement you said that after discovering the body of Jasper Speight and ascertaining he was deceased, you saw Mandalay Blonde sitting in the lounge, mere metres away, her hands covered in blood. Is that still your memory?'

'Yes. There was blood on her hands; I wouldn't say covered. They're your words.'

'Thank you,' says Montifore. 'And you didn't go to her? You rang triple zero and waited where you were for the police and ambulance?'

Martin looks at Poulos but gets no response. Why is Montifore going over this? 'That's correct,' says Martin. 'I think she was in shock. I think I was as well.'

'You say Jasper Speight was dead. You checked for a pulse. Was there any sign of the weapon that killed him?'

'No. I wasn't looking but, no, I didn't see anything.'

'From where you were on the floor, did you have a clear view of Ms Blonde?'

'Yes, I did.'

'And at any stage, from the time you first saw her to the time the ambulance and the police arrived, was she ever out of your sight?'

'No. She was kind of frozen there. Almost trance-like. As I said, in shock.'

'You say you were sitting on the floor. Did you remain there for the entire time, until the police and ambulance came?'

Martin tries to remember. 'For most of it. But I think I must have stood when I heard the siren stop outside. I was standing when they came in the door.'

'You're sure of that?'

'Yes.'

'And did you, once standing, look back towards Mandalay Blonde?'

'I'm sure I must have. I can't imagine I wouldn't have done so. I was concerned about her.'

'But you can't be absolutely sure?'

Martin closes his eyes. The image of Mandy sitting on the couch, hands bloodied, is burnt into his mind. But from what angle is he looking? The floor or standing? Some mixture of the two. He shakes his head. 'I can't be one hundred per cent sure; I can't recall precisely. But it would have been bizarre if I didn't. And I would absolutely remember if she had moved from the couch. Why?'

Montifore nods, as if in understanding. 'That's fine, Martin. From your position on the floor, when you can be absolutely sure that you saw Ms Blonde, were you in a position to see if anything was on the sofa next to her?'

Martin casts his mind back. He shrugs. 'I can't remember seeing anything else. Nothing of consequence.'

'Cushions?'

'What?'

'Cushions. Were there cushions on the sofa?'

Martin blinks. Then a flash of memory, the white of the sofa contrasting with her hands, like blood on the snow. 'Yes. There were two cushions, one in each corner of the sofa.'

Nick Poulos shifts next to him. Martin glances over; his lawyer has a small smile.

'And nothing else?'

Martin thinks. 'No, that's all I recall.'

'So no sign of the weapon? There or anywhere else?'

The weapon. The knife. Is that what this is all about? 'No. I saw no sign.'

'And you didn't talk to Ms Blonde?'

'No.'

'That's strange, isn't it?'

Martin looks him in the eye, pushes some anger into his voice, some assertiveness. 'You think so? You have a guidebook of how to behave when you find a man bled out on your girlfriend's floor?'

'No need to get aggressive, Mr Scarsden.' It's Lucic, his smirk back.

Martin jabs his finger at the sergeant. 'I checked his pulse, then I rang the ambulance and the police, within seconds of finding him. Are you telling me that was the wrong thing to do? You want to put that on the record?'

Montifore grimaces, Lucic lets his smile talk for him, Nick places a restraining hand on Martin's leg.

'Let's move on,' says Montifore. He examines his notes. If he's allowing time for the tension in the room to ease, it's not working. 'According to the timeline I have here, you and Mandalay Blonde returned to the townhouse on Tuesday afternoon, the day after the murder. Is that correct?'

'Yes.'

'And why were you there?'

'We went to collect Mandy's stuff. Clothes and toiletries and whatnot. Equipment for her boy, for Liam—bottles and blenders and blankets. There's a lot of stuff.'

'And during this time, was Ms Blonde ever out of your sight?'

'Yes. Several times.'

'So you can't be completely sure exactly what she collected?'

Martin is shaking his head. Jesus, they're still on about the knife. 'No, I can't. But the police had been there for more than twenty-four hours. They'd searched the place thoroughly. There was fingerprint dust everywhere, on every available surface.'

'You're an expert on forensic techniques and police searches then?' It's Lucic, needle in his voice.

'No, but I'm sure the police must be. Is Sergeant Lucic really questioning the competence of his colleagues?' Martin looks directly into the lens of the camera.

Montifore smiles. 'Okay, settle down, you two. Let's move on.'

Another pause, while the detective regards his next piece of paper. Nick Poulos places a hand on Martin's shoulder to get his attention, then nods encouragement. Martin breathes out. He shouldn't let that prick Lucic get under his skin. Not when he's this tired and hungover.

'Right,' says Montifore. 'The things you collected from the town-house, Mandalay Blonde's possessions. What did you do with them?'

'We've rented a cabin at the caravan park across the river. We took everything there.'

'Everything? Did you throw anything out? Take it to the tip? Throw it in a kerbside bin?'

'Not that I recall.'

'And you used Ms Blonde's vehicle?'

'And mine. We used both cars.'

'And where was the boy, Liam?'

'He was with us.'

'You're sure?'

'Yes. He's quite a handful.' Martin catches the constable smiling behind her camera. 'Mandy picked him up from child care an hour or two before we went to the townhouse. You can check with the childcare centre. I assume they have a sign-out.'

'So how long were you at the townhouse?'

Martin shrugs. 'Forty-five minutes. An hour. Something like that.'

'Before sunset?'

'Yes. Well before.'

'When you arrived at the caravan park, who unloaded the possessions from the cars?'

'We both did.'

'You worked together?'

'Yes.'

'The possessions belonged mostly to Mandalay Blonde and her child?'

'Yes.'

'So was it the case that you unloaded the cars while Ms Blonde arranged her possessions inside your cabin?'

'I'd say so. For the most part.'

'I see,' Montifore continues, voice relaxed, non-confrontational. 'And that afternoon you and Mandalay Blonde and the boy walked together by the river, watched the sunset, and then had dinner at your cabin.'

'No.'

'Sorry? No?' Montifore appears surprised by the response.

'No.'

'Where were the two of you then?'

Martin looks at Nick Poulos, who is staring down at his hands and won't make eye contact. Martin returns his gaze to Montifore. Lucic is no longer smiling, just looking at him intently. The constable operating the video camera has grown still, giving no sign she is breathing. Martin senses this is the pivot of the interview, the point it has been leading to. He doesn't know what to say, how he can help Mandy, so he tells the truth.

'I went to dinner at my uncle's place, up along the river. I got there around seven, maybe a little later.'

'Before sunset?'

'Yes. Maybe fifteen minutes before.'

'And returned when?'

'Not sure. Maybe ten-thirty, maybe later.'

'What is your uncle's name?'

'Vern Jones. Vernon, I guess.'

'And your uncle can confirm those times?'

'Yes. And his wife. And a swag of kids. My uncle and his son gave me a lift back to the caravan park in his boat.'

'Why?'

'I'd had a bit to drink. Didn't want to drive.'

'And your uncle? He doesn't drink?' There's a glint of humour in Montifore's eyes.

'His son steered the boat.'

Montifore smiles, but Lucic is dead serious as he poses the next question. 'Just for the record, let me get this straight: the evening of the day after Jasper Speight was murdered, after he died in front of your partner, instead of remaining with her you went to your uncle's place and got drunk?'

'Correct,' says Martin.

Montifore looks disappointed, although Martin doesn't know if it's in him or his sergeant. 'Thank you for your assistance, Mr Scarsden. You're free to go.' And he announces, for the benefit of the camera, that the interview is officially over.

'Just a moment,' says Martin, standing. 'I have something for you.' He pulls Topaz's visa application form from his pocket and hands it to Montifore. 'A few hours ago, you were desperate to get your hands on this.'

Montifore unfolds the form, scans it quickly. 'Thank you, Martin. I promise you this will get the attention it deserves.' There is sincerity in his eyes, but Martin can't help but hear irony in the policeman's words.

Martin waits until he and Nick Poulos are out of the station and down the steps before he turns on his lawyer. 'What the fuck was that all about?'

'Let's get a coffee,' says Poulos, his tone conciliatory.

'Let's not. Tell me what just happened. And tell me why you did nothing to help me.' Martin is jabbing his finger at Poulos, millimetres from his chest.

Nick puts his hands up, as if to surrender. 'They were trying to trap you. To see if you would lie.'

'About what?'

'They have a witness who says they saw Mandalay throw something into the river at the caravan park at sunset on Tuesday, while you were at your uncle's place. The police think it may have been the knife. The murder weapon. Police divers are on their way from Sydney.'

Martin stands and stares at Nick for a frozen moment even while his mind is already off and racing.

'There's something else,' says Nick. 'About the cheese factory.'

But Martin's not listening, he's already moving. 'Tell me later. I'll ring you!' he yells over his shoulder.

⸻

The traffic along The Boulevarde is clogged. He is consumed by frustration, resisting the urge to shout, to bellow at all these people sleepwalking their way through normalcy. And then he's away, over the bridge, to the caravan park.

At the fork by reception, he turns right towards the section reserved for permanent residents. He passes a hedge, enters a small self-contained world of HardiePlank cottages, originally the same, now rendered unique by their residents. It's like a village in miniature: roads shrunk to the size of bike paths, houses reduced to large kennels, lives reduced to a bonsai scale. But there is life here: a couple of young mums stand smoking cigarettes and chatting amiably, their babies in cheap strollers; a bloke in a blue singlet and tats is ducking his head in and out of the gizzards of a muscle car; and there, a group of older men, playing boules on a patch of grass. Martin parks his Corolla, the old car at home in the low-rent community. He walks over to the men playing boules, asks for directions.

Clyde Mackie is gardening, weeding in among the potted flowers on his tiny deck. There is a radio murmuring; it sounds like the races. 'Martin?' he says. 'What is it?' He must see the urgency on Martin's face.

'Can we talk, Clyde?'

'Of course. Come up.'

Martin climbs up onto the small deck. There is just enough room for a couple of chairs sitting side by side, a small table between them. Mackie turns off the radio. 'You want something? Tea, coffee? Something to eat?'

The suggestion of food elicits a pang of appetite; his body wants more than Hummingbird toast and a Longton doughnut. 'Water. A glass of water would be good. And yes, some food if you have something.'

'Righto,' says Clyde, removing his gardening gloves and entering his small home. A moment later he's back with two glasses of water and a white-bread sandwich of devon and tomato sauce. 'Sit down, Martin. This place is too small for pacing around like that.'

Martin sits, drinks some water, launches into it. 'Clyde, how often do you and Brian fish down there at the wharf?'

'Most days, I guess, if the weather's good,' says the former policeman, eyes canny.

'You always fish around sunset?'

'That's our routine.'

'Can you remember if you were fishing on Tuesday?'

'I'd say so. I think I've been there every day this week.' Mackie is concentrating, trying to remember. 'Maybe had one day off. Monday, I think, but it's hard to be sure. The days kind of melt into one another.'

Martin bites his lip. 'Clyde, it's important. Can we ask Brian?'

The old policeman is about to respond when a light sparks in his eye. 'Hang about. Tuesday, you say? Was that the cricket, the one-dayer?'

Martin looks at Clyde, blinks, smiles. 'Let's see.' He has his phone out, searches, confirms that Australia did indeed play on Tuesday. A day-nighter at the MCG. 'Yes. The cricket was on.'

'Well, we were both there then. We had the radio on from the start of Australia's innings. So that's about six-thirty or seven through until it was too dark to fish. It was a corker of a match. We watched the end at the hall. Finished about ten or ten-thirty.'

Martin can feel a smile trying to break free, but he's not done yet. 'So you were down at the wharf from six-thirty or seven until about an hour after sunset?'

'That's right. What is it, Martin? Why do you need to know?'

'Did you see anyone else down there?'

'I'm sure we must have. Plenty of people head down to the river at that time of day.'

'What about my partner, Mandy Blonde?'

'No. I would have remembered seeing her. She's quite the looker, you know.'

'Are you sure?'

'Of course. I didn't even know you were staying here then, if I recall correctly.'

'You do, Clyde, you do recall correctly. We only moved here that afternoon.' His smile has broken through, but he keeps his focus; this is too serious. 'If Mandy had come down to the river around sunset, is there any chance you could have missed her? You know, too busy fishing, looking out at the river, wickets falling in the cricket?'

Mackie is shaking his head before Martin can even finish the question. 'No, mate. If she came down, we would have seen her.'

'Can we check with Brian?'

'Of course we can, son. But not until you tell me what's going on.'

So Martin tells him about the allegation made by a mystery witness, accusing Mandy of throwing something into the river some time close to sunset on Tuesday.

Mackie shakes his head. 'That's bullshit. I'm sure we would have seen her—or anyone else tossing evidence into the water. Any idea who this so-called witness is?'

'No.'

'Tuesday, you say. So who knew you were staying here then?'

Martin looks at the policeman, mind starting to hare off in different directions. It's a valid point; they'd only just arrived.

'Come on, son, let's find Brian.'

———

Brian Jinjerik is outside his own cottage, lifting a large galvanised toolbox from the tray of an ancient ute. Martin gives him a hand.

'Thanks, mate,' says Brian. 'Back's killing me.'

'You been working?'

'Yeah. Up on a roof in the heat. Broken skylight. Can I help you with something?'

'You can.'

And he does, corroborating his friend's recollection. Mandy wasn't by the river at sunset on Tuesday.

Martin rings Winifred. The call goes through to voicemail. Martin swallows a swear word, texts Winifred, uses capitals. *TWO WITNESSES CONFIRM MANDY NOT AT RIVER TUESDAY SUNSET. CALL ME.*

It takes the lawyer less than two minutes to respond.

'Martin. Are you sure?'

'Yes. I'm with them now. Two residents of the caravan park. They fish at sunset every day. From the wharf. They were there Tuesday. Swear they would have seen Mandy if she went anywhere near the river.'

'They're reliable?'

'One is a former policeman. Served for decades.'

There's a pause. Then: 'Can I speak to the policeman?'

Martin hands the phone to Clyde Mackie, who takes Winifred through his recollection, his voice dropping half an octave, full of courtroom-honed authority. Martin hears him explain about listening to the cricket, describe where they were sitting, what they saw. Mackie assures Winifred he is willing to make a formal statement.

The call finishes. Mackie's eyes are gleaming. 'You know what that lawyer told me? The so-called witness alleged your girl threw whatever it was, presumably the murder weapon, from the wharf, not the riverbank. That's impossible. We were sitting on the wharf the whole time.'

Martin feels tears well in his eyes, unbidden. 'Thank you, Clyde. I'm more grateful than I can ever say.'

Mackie looks embarrassed. 'It's all right, son. I'm not doing you any special favours. Just telling the truth.'

'You want a beer?' asks Brian Jinjerik. 'Sounds like you've had a win.'

But Martin is already thinking ahead. 'No, thanks. I've still got a few loose ends to tie up.'

'Well, come on then,' says Mackie to Brian. 'Sunset isn't that far away. We can have a cold one down at the wharf.'

———

Back in his car, a thought niggles at Martin, something that Clyde Mackie had said. That on Tuesday afternoon he hadn't even known that Martin and Mandy had checked into the caravan park.

So who had known? Winifred. The owner of the park. Who else? Nick? But the false witness had only just come forward. By now, all sorts of people would know they were staying here. He shakes his head. The line of thought is going nowhere.

His phone rings. Nick Poulos.

'Nick.'

'What's happened? Why is Winifred so fired up?'

Martin explains.

'Holy shit, that's brilliant,' says the lawyer. 'A false witness? Montifore will crucify them.'

'Let's hope so. But does he know who it is?'

'Don't know. The coppers said it was anonymous, so probably not. Although that could be a ruse to protect their source.'

'Not now, not if they know it's bullshit.'

'They're getting divers up from Sydney. They're going to search the river.'

'What? Why? Won't they cancel that now?'

'Think it through, Martin. The knife might still be there. If someone is trying to frame Mandy, they might have chucked the knife in there themselves, from the bank or from a boat, then given their false tip-off.'

'Do you think it could lead them to the killer?'

'Or an accomplice. If they find the knife. And if they know who tipped them off.'

'What about Mandy? Have they let her go?'

'Not yet. But it shouldn't be long.'

Martin checks his watch. Shit. Liam.

'Nick, her boy—our boy—he's at child care.'

'You want me to collect him?'

'Could you?'

'I'll let you know. They'll need signed consent from Mandy.'

'Really?'

'Yes. Really. Hang on.' Martin can hear Nick talking to someone. Then: 'It's okay, the police are letting her go. She'll get him herself.'

'Can I talk to her?' Martin waits; he can hear muffled voices in the background.

Then Nick is back with him. 'Sorry, mate, she has to race. The place will be closed already.'

Martin ends the call and starts driving back out of the permanent settlement, back past the reception. The owner is out on the deck, smoking her pipe. Martins stops, walks up.

'G'day,' he says.

'It is. How's your woman?'

'How do you mean?'

'I saw the police take her away.'

'All good. She's been giving them a hand. She's on her way back now.'

'Glad to hear it.'

'Police tell you they're sending some divers over to check out the river?'

The owner frowns. 'How did you know that? They only told me five minutes ago.'

'As I said, we're helping with the investigation.'

'Is that right?'

'It is,' Martin lies. 'Tell me, this drive, is it the only way into the park?'

'I guess. You can come by boat to the wharf, or walk in along the river, but this is the only way in with a car.'

Martin nods. 'Have you seen anyone unusual hanging about these last few days? Someone other than residents or guests?'

She shakes her head. 'Nah. Nothing like that. A motorbike or two along the riverbank, but that happens from time to time.'

'Motorbikes? Like bikies or something?'

'Fuck no. Little shitheads on trail bikes. Two-strokes: sound like a cross between a sewing machine and a Mixmaster.'

'When was that?'

'All the time. Not today, but yesterday, the day before. Early in the morning. Too early. You get walkers and mountain bikers as well, but they don't bother anyone.'

'Thanks,' says Martin, thinking he needs to pass this on to Montifore. What was it the police were always saying in their public appeals for information—any detail, no matter how insignificant?

The owner leans over, retrieves her prosthetic leg, goes about reattaching it before standing. 'Sounds like we're going to be busy. All those cops.' From inside the office, a phone starts to ring.

'Tell me,' Martin says, 'if you don't mind—what happened to your leg?'

'Shark attack,' she says. 'Lucky it didn't get more of me.'

'When was that?'

She shrugs. 'About ten years ago.' She moves into the office to answer the phone.

Martin returns to his Corolla, sits thinking. Trail bikes by the river, shark attacks, bogus witnesses. Puzzle pieces that don't quite fit, certainly not to each other. He leans forward to turn the key in the ignition, when another thought comes to him. Nick Poulos. What did he say? If the murder weapon had been planted in the river, it could have been thrown from the riverbank or from a boat.

An image comes to Martin's mind, unbidden and unwelcome. Vern and Levi dropping him at the wharf. Another image. Martin cutting a string of sausages beside his uncle's barbecue, the knife glistening in the firelight. Jesus. He feels a surge of nausea. Another image. A knife slicing through Jasper Speight's abdomen. And a motorbike, a two-stroke trail bike with yellow L-plates.

chapter twenty-one

'YOU CAN'T STAY HERE,' SHE SAYS, LOOKING HIM IN THE EYE BEFORE BENDING TO unbuckle Liam. The boy is asleep in his car seat.

Martin deflates, the air escaping from him, taking his optimism with it. 'Didn't Winifred tell you what I found out? That I'm the one who cleared you?'

She stands up, leaving Liam where he is for the moment. 'She did. Thank you.' But there is little gratitude in her voice and no warmth.

'Mandy?'

She shakes her head. 'You slept with that backpacker. That tart. I can't just forget that.'

Martin spreads his hands in conciliation. 'I was drugged. I don't even know if I slept with her or not. I can't remember.'

Now there is real anger in her face, prosecution in her voice. 'I've just been subjected to a four-hour interrogation by the police about where I was and what I did on Tuesday afternoon and evening.

By the time I got to the childcare centre, Liam was hysterical. And why was I at the police station for so long? Because there was no one to verify what I was saying. Because on Tuesday night you were with your uncle, boozing it up and smoking dope. The day after Jasper Speight was murdered. Then, last night, you were off partying again, taking drugs, sticking your dick who knows where. All night. You are unreliable, Martin. I've had plenty of unreliable men, I don't want another one. Liam deserves better than a part-time father.'

At his name, the boy comes awake, lets out a cry. Mandy breaks eye contact with Martin, bends again to extract the boy from the car, lifts him, holds him.

'Marn!' says the boy, extending an arm towards Martin.

Mandy shakes her head; there are tears in her eyes. 'You stayed in Sydney, writing your book, when you should have been here. And now you are here, you're still missing in action.'

'Mandy . . .'

'No. You can't stay here. Go to Hartigan's. Stay there. Work out how to fix the place up. Work out how to fix *us* up.'

'What did Winifred say?'

'Fuck Winifred. She's happy. I'm not. Now go.' And with that she takes Liam into the cabin.

Martin is still standing there when she emerges some minutes later. She has Liam in his carrier. She throws him some keys. Hartigan's. 'I'm taking him for a walk. Don't be here when I get back.' She moves away, then stops, looks back. 'I'll call you,' she says, her anger now tinged with regret. But she still turns and walks off towards the river.

Martin looks at his hands, but they hold no answers. He has little choice. He enters the cabin, collecting his clothes and possessions. It doesn't take long; he's had plenty of practice. The itinerant correspondent, he of a thousand hotel rooms, packing up and moving on once again. *Shit.*

He leaves the caravan park, crosses Dunes Road and drives up towards Hartigan's, his mind at once weary and restless. Montifore is closing in on the killer. There is a false witness, someone claiming to have seen Mandy throw the knife into the river. Find the witness, find the knife, find the killer. How hard can it be? And Montifore has Topaz's visa form, the necessary catalyst for a court order, search warrants and police investigations. If St Clair is involved, Montifore will root him out. So why does Martin feel so empty, so despondent? There is a hollowness, a sense of life gone awry. He fears he's losing Mandy and Liam, that he's lost her trust, all mixed up and compounded by last night's excesses. Fatigue washes over him, the weight of the past pressing down.

He reaches the gate to Hartigan's, stops the car, sits for a moment, unable to summon the energy to move. He closes his eyes. An image comes to him: the Settlement laid out before him, the Settlement of his youth, as if seen from above, an impossible vantage point. He jerks his eyes open, pushes the image away, looks around. Memories lay hidden in this landscape like a minefield, everywhere he looks, threatening to explode beneath him at any time, no matter how carefully he steps. Something has happened; there's no containing them. Pandora's box is open for business.

He knows he needs to sleep, to restore his psychic balance, but now he fears the images, the memories. He blinks, widens his eyes, as if to tap some vestige of vigour: the sun is flaring in his rear-view mirror, low in the sky, heading towards the western horizon and the darkening line of the escarpment. There will be no electricity at Hartigan's, he has no torch, only his iPhone to guide him. He checks the battery level. It's half empty, just like himself. He should get to the house, see if he can find some candles or some sort of lamp. It's too warm to light a fire, but the idea of the fireplace stirs something in his stomach: hunger. It occurs to him to return to Port Silver, pick up some takeaway, some candles.

There is nowhere to turn the car. The sensible thing would be to open the gate, drive to the house, turn around there and come back down. But the thought of getting out of the car is too much for him. He puts it in reverse, starts easing it down the hill, looking for somewhere to turn. The sun is in the mirror; he squints into the light, uses his side mirrors. He's making progress when another thought comes to him: the motorbike bursting from the bush yesterday morning.

He stops the car, swinging the wheels across the slope, pulling the handbrake hard and putting it in first gear before cutting the engine. He breathes deep, gets out. Looking back up the hill, he can see the gate. The motorbike had appeared close by, maybe a little further down the slope. Now that he's searching for it, the track's not hard to find, emerging over the top of a bank. He climbs over, edging down onto the remains of the original road. It's overgrown, save for a single track formed by trail bikers, bush-walkers and mountain bikers. Above him, the canopy is thinner over the old road. He can see a tree has been felled, disguising the juncture of the road and the drive up to Hartigan's. Bushes have started growing around it. No wonder he missed it when they drove up yesterday.

He wants to follow the path, find out where it leads. He's travelled Ridge Road from the Hummingbird Beach end, and now here he stands at the other end. It irritates him: he has the two ends in his mind, but the middle is missing. He wants to join them, fill in the gap, knows he won't be satisfied until he does. But it won't be long before the sun drops below the escarpment. There's no time to explore Ridge Road, not now. It's too late, and he's too tired. But first thing tomorrow, he'll take a look. Maybe Jasper Speight found something up along the road that got him killed.

———

Martin sleeps. No candles, no fire, no food. The only things he's eaten since Clyde Mackie's devon sandwich are painkillers, antibiotics and antivirals. Flattened by the day's efforts, asleep in the shell of Hartigan's, adrift on the same couch where Jasper Speight once nursed his cut foot. His gear is still in the car, his clothes are still on his back, his body is still unwashed. His sleep is so profound the first helicopter barely wakes him. Its searchlight penetrates the windows, bathing him in light, the pressure from its blades rattling the shutters and stirring the roof. Even then, it's already passed by the time he's emerging into full consciousness, his molasses brain struggling to establish what just happened. He closes his eyes, recommencing the downward drift, until the chopper once again rattles the house and sucks him into wakefulness. He gets up, opens the French doors, walks onto the verandah. The helicopter has already moved north, running along the top of the cliffs. It's not alone. There are two of them. More sound: he turns in time to see a third helicopter power past, pursuing the other two.

Helicopters. Here. Why? Maybe some wealthy Hollywood A-listers, heading for Byron, are strafing the cliffs with their searchlights just for the hell of it. Entitled shits. In the middle of the night.

Inside, his phone rings. The caller ID reads *Bethanie Glass*. Bethanie, his former colleague at the *Sydney Morning Herald*, the paper's star police reporter.

'Martin, is that you?' There is urgency in her voice.

'Bethanie, hi.'

'Where are you?'

'I'm up the coast. With Mandy.'

'Port Silver? You told me you were moving to Port Silver.'

'Yes. Port Silver.'

'Fantastic. Have you heard what's happened?'

'What? No.'

'Turn on the television. ABC News.'

'I can't. No TV, no power. Tell me.'

'There are reports coming in, some sort of mass murder-suicide. A lot of victims. Like Jonestown. At a hippie commune called Hummingbird. Do you know it?'

'Yes.' Suddenly he's fully awake, his mind alight. Murder-suicide. Hummingbird.

'Can you get there? File copy? It's a seven-hour drive from here. We're hiring a light plane, but it will still take forever.'

Jonestown? Who's the murderer? The swami? Who are the victims? File some copy? 'Bethanie, I don't work for the *Herald* anymore.'

'Hang on, I'll put you on to Terri.'

Martin can hear the hubbub of the newsroom at the other end of the phone line as he waits for the editor. He checks his watch. Ten-thirty at night. Not so late then, but late for the *Herald*, in these days of single editions and skeleton staff. It must be a big story.

'Martin, Terri Preswell. You know this place, Hummingbird?'

'I was there this morning.'

'What? Really?'

'Who's dead, Terri? Who killed them?'

'We don't know. We've got fuck all. The cops aren't saying. The teevs have got their choppers up there but there's nowhere to land, so it's just aerial shots. We're on the phones. We're hearing at least a half-a-dozen dead, but we can't confirm anything. Can you get out there?'

'I don't work for the *Herald*,' he reminds her.

'Fuck, Martin. It's a freelance job. We'll pay top dollar, whatever you like. It's the biggest story in Australia, but we need it now. By tomorrow every news outlet in Australia will have people crawling all over it.'

'I still get a by-line?'

'Jesus, Martin, of course you still get a by-line. If it was up to me, you'd still have your job.'

'Good enough. I'm on my way. But there's no mobile reception at Hummingbird. I'll have to get in, get what I can, then drive back into range before I can file.'

'Right. Well, call as soon as you can. Ring through the main points and we'll get something up while you write the rest.'

'Okay,' says Martin. 'Talk soon.' He hangs up. For a second, he wonders what he's just committed himself to. But only for a second: the adrenaline is coursing through him, the old feeling is back. He can feel his focus narrowing, everything else becoming extraneous, his attention closing in on one thing and one thing only: the story. *The biggest story in Australia.*

Martin almost crashes the Corolla into the gate on his way out, locking up the brakes, the car skidding before coming to rest with centimetres to spare. He gets the gate unlocked, throws it open, guns down the hill. But at the junction with Dunes Road, he's forced to stop as an ambulance, lights flashing, comes hurtling across the bridge from Port Silver, a quick burst from the siren warning him. It's followed by a twin-cab ute, a flashing roof light proclaiming its authority. Martin squints against its headlights, preparing to follow. But an arm emerges from the back window of the ute, waving madly, and the vehicle brakes hard and pulls off onto the verge. A figure is out of the vehicle, running towards him. It's Nick Poulos, wearing a high-vis vest.

'You heard?' asks his lawyer.

'Hummingbird? Multiple deaths?'

'Yeah. Leave your car, come with us. The police have called in the SES.'

Martin reverses his car back into the drive, then runs after Nick to the ute. He can't believe his luck as he's handed his own fluoro-orange vest. The SES is going to take him right into the middle of the action.

There are rapid introductions: the driver, Phil, is Goori; next to him is a small Asian woman, Lee; in the back Nick is now in the middle, and on the far side is an old bloke smelling of grog and animals, with a lazy eye and a fleece covered in dog hairs: Paddles.

They pelt along Dunes Road, taking no time to reach Ridge Road and, moments later, the turn into Hummingbird Beach. There are cars strewn all around, abandoned by the side of the road in the urgency of the moment. Martin can see a television crew pulling gear from a plumber's van; he wonders where the choppers have landed. More media will be on their way, chartering planes, flying in from Brisbane and Sydney, landing up at Longton airport, commandeering cars to get down the escarpment. He has a jump of a good few hours on most of them.

There is a roadblock, a police car angled across the track next to a commandeered barrier still bearing the signage ROADWORKS AHEAD. The headlights carve out the scene: Doug Thunkleton waving his hands, imploring the constable for access; Martin recognises the young officer who'd served him breakfast. The policeman leaves Thunkleton standing, talks briefly to Phil, waves them through. Martin keeps his head down.

Phil pushes the ute hard, and by the time they get to the Hummingbird car park, they've almost caught the ambulance, its flashing lights flooding the dark trees with moving impressions of red and blue, shadows made mobile like some macabre disco.

The young policewoman is there, the video camera operator. Her voice is urgent, no-nonsense, addressing the paramedics. 'Down there by the beach, where the lights are. The Port Silver crew have set up triage.' She turns to the SES volunteers. 'Phil, good timing. You blokes help the ambos. Do whatever they want.' The ambulance officers, a man and a woman, are already pulling gear from their vehicle: oxygen bottles, a defibrillator, bags of equipment, stretchers. The SES team load up and head towards the pool of light under the open shelter, down by the beach, Martin with them.

They descend into a painting by Hieronymus Bosch: some people dressed, others half naked; some wandering in shock, others

being violently ill; some helping others, others helpless. They pass
Harry the Lad, eyes glazed and passive, being led by the hand
up towards the car park. Johnson Pear is in charge, assisted by
the middle-aged couple Martin recalls from the beach, no longer
naked, no longer smiling. The man is standing, gazing around
with a dazed look, but the woman is all business. There is a single
paramedic here; the Port Silver ambulance must already be ferrying
victims to Longton, leaving her. A man with dreadlocks is kneeling
beside a young woman, holding her hand, talking to her even
though the girl appears to be unconscious. As Martin watches, she
goes into spasms, some sort of convulsion. The ambulance officers
don't hesitate, moving to take over straight away. All around other
bodies are strewn. At least half-a-dozen are unconscious, others
are awake but incoherent, muttering and rambling. Martin can
see Topaz and Jay Jay among the unconscious, plus a couple of
other faces familiar from the previous night. There is the smell
of vomit, of shit. A young man starts screaming something and
Lee moves to him, crouches, trying to calm him, trying to reason
with him through the veil of drugs.

'You lot,' says Pear to the remaining SES volunteers. 'Two of
you help the ambulance officers. Help get the most serious cases
to the ambulance. Phil, you driving?'

'Yep,' says Phil.

'Right. Tell the ambos. If they want you to drive less severe
cases to Longton Hospital, you do it, okay?' Pear doesn't wait for
a response, turning to Nick and Martin. 'You two?' He hesitates,
but only for a split second. 'You have torches? Phones?'

Martin and Nick reply in unison: 'Yes.'

'Right. Search the beach, the tents, the cabins. People may have wandered off, become disorientated, passed out. You need to find them, get them back here.'

'What about those guys?' asks Martin. Over to one side, lying beyond the shelter at the edge of the spray of light, are the dark humps of four people.

'Too late. Leave them.'

'Okay, listen up!' It's one of the ambulance officers, a young woman, her voice clear and authoritative. 'They've overdosed from drinking something. They may be getting worse, not better. They need to void, get any remaining substance out of their stomach. Anyone who is still conscious, get them to throw up. Fingers down the throat, sea water, whatever it takes.'

Pear turns his back on Nick and Martin, returns to assist the living.

'Beach first,' says Nick, 'then we search the cabins and tents.'

'Split up?' asks Martin.

'No. If we find someone, we'll need to carry them back here as quickly as possible.'

'Right. Beach first.' But before Nick can respond Martin has walked across to the four dark shapes spread on the ground, away from the frantic rescue attempts. In the dim light, he can see their faces, devoid of life: the swami, Garth McGrath, a young woman and an old man, shirt ripped where someone has attempted to resuscitate him. The last two still have red-brown bindis smudged across their foreheads.

'Shit,' says Nick.

A voice penetrates their thoughts: Johnson Pear. 'Get going, you guys. The chopper will be back any time.'

They head away from the pool of light, down onto the beach, the waves maintaining their metronomic rhythm, unhurried by the drama unfolding on land. In the half-light spilling from the shelter, Martin can see someone across the sand, standing by the remnants of a fire. 'Look,' he says to Nick Poulos. As they walk towards the figure, it turns on a torch, sweeping the sand, shining the beam directly at them.

'Woah,' says Nick, 'you're blinding us.'

The light drops. 'What are you two doing here?' Martin recognises the voice: Morris Montifore.

'SES,' says Nick. 'Pear sent us searching for more victims. You seen any?'

'No,' says Montifore. 'I haven't looked.'

Martin looks past Montifore. The fire, still burning, red coals glowing below orange-yellow flames. Logs and stumps still surround it, where people have been sitting. All around, the detritus of a party: empty plastic cups, water bottles, pieces of clothing. An empty wooden bowl, banded with gold. The smell of vomit.

'Don't go anywhere near the fire,' says Montifore. 'It's a crime scene.'

A new noise imposes itself in a rush, a helicopter bursting into view above the headland, spotlight scouring the sand. It catches them in its blinding glare, Montifore waving it away from the fire. At first Martin thinks it's media, but then he sees a figure winching down, helmet and goggles. The man unbuckles as Montifore runs to him. The man nods his comprehension, talks into his shoulder, guides the chopper in to land at the western end of the beach, away from the fire.

'Look!' says Nick Poulos. 'There.'

And Martin can see it too. At the opposite end of the beach, up towards the point, a dark shape, a body lying prone, down by the water. They run towards it.

———

It's two o'clock in the morning. Mandy has let him back into the cabin, persuaded by the urgency in his voice, the magnitude of the story and his need for electricity. The television is on, the sound muted. Martin is on the phone, his voice hushed but intense, relaying the facts to the Sydney newsroom as quickly as he can. Terri Preswell has gone home, Bethanie Glass is in the air, but Martin knows the man on the other end of the phone well. Cormac Connors, a true newspaperman, volunteering to coordinate the breaking story. Martin recounts the salient information as best he can. As many as seven people believed dead, including Swami Hawananda and Garth McGrath. Martin can hear Connors' sharp intake of breath. The death of the soapie star is like pouring petrol on the bonfire; the huge story just got exponentially bigger.

'You sure about McGrath? Your source is reliable?'

'I'm the source. He's dead. I saw his body with my own eyes.'

'Okay. So the police haven't released any names?'

'No, I wouldn't think so.'

'Right. I'll need to call Terri. It's her call if she wants to run with it before relatives are notified. I'll call you right back.'

Mandy is watching him from the bedroom doorway, her arms crossed, her face creased with concern. They stare at each other across the abyss of the lounge. Martin can't see what she's thinking, can't divine her feelings.

The phone rings. It's Terri Preswell. 'Martin. Tell me what you know.'

He recounts the events of the evening.

'You have absolutely no doubt it was Garth McGrath?'

'None.'

'Okay. Fuck the formalities. We can't sit on it. He's a public figure. We go with it.'

'Your call,' says Martin.

'Your by-line,' says Terri.

'I'm okay with that.'

'Good man. So what happened up there? What are the police saying?'

'It's definitely poisoning. Either a drug party gone wrong or murder. Or a murder-suicide. We need to canvass all possibilities. The police will be thinking along the same lines.' He quickly recounts Montifore guarding the fire and the aftermath of the party surrounding it.

'Photos?' asks Terri.

'Couldn't. The police were there. They only let me stay because I was with the SES, helping.'

'Okay, here's how we're going to play it. We'll get a story up asap; Cormac can write it. The lead will be seven believed dead, up to a dozen more airlifted out or taken by ambulance. A drug party gone wrong or a murder-suicide, with the finger pointed at the dead swami. We'll run it with your by-line. Cormac will ring and read it back to you before it goes out. But we'll leave McGrath out for now; no one will be reading at this hour except our competitors. I want to leave that until about seven or eight am, so everyone knows it's our exclusive. Can you file that story? You have your laptop?'

'Yep.'

'Good. I want a news piece and your first-hand account. The competitors will scavenge the news report in no time, but your first-hand account, being there, that will set us apart. You good with that?'

'Sure. Cops won't like it.'

'Sure as shit won't. Does that bother you?'

'No.'

The editor laughs. 'Good to hear you're still one of us. Call me on the mobile when you're filing. I'm going to head back in.'

Martin is smiling when he hangs up, amused by Terri's compliment. Then he sees Mandy, arms crossed tightly, frowning. She shakes her head. 'Seven people dead. And you're smiling.' She turns on her heel, closes the door of the bedroom behind her.

Martin wonders what to do, how he can explain, then concludes that two o'clock in the morning is not the right time to try. Instead, he gets out his laptop and starts writing.

He's finished by four but sleeps only fitfully after that on the lumpy lounge, his phone ringing every half an hour or so: sub-editors checking facts. And Bethanie will be arriving at Longton, wanting to meet. He shuts his eyes to gather his strength for a moment, only to be shaken awake. He opens his eyes. Mandy.

It's morning and she has a cup of coffee for him.

He sits up. His neck hurts. Sun is pouring in through the windows. The first taste of coffee makes him want to believe in God.

'Thanks,' he says, searching her face.

'I read your story,' she says. 'You saved that boy's life.'

She hands him her iPad.

A sub has given his first-hand account a suitably emotive headline.

WE FOUGHT DEATH IN THE NIGHT
By Martin Scarsden at Hummingbird Beach

We found him on the beach. Dying, alone in the dark.

The waves were lapping at his feet, death just moments away. He was beginning to convulse, going into cardiac arrest. We thought we were too late.

I don't know his name. It didn't matter then, it doesn't matter now . . .

He looks up at Mandy. She isn't smiling, but she seems calm. 'Go on. Do what you have to do. We can talk when it's over.' She turns away, then back again. 'And for God's sake, have a shower and change your clothes.'

But Martin doesn't move. He scans down to the last lines of his story, wishing it might be different, as if somehow he might have dreamt it.

We found them inside their cabin, still entwined, still in love.

But we were too late.

Not everyone could be saved.

SATURDAY

chapter twenty-two

LONGTON HOSPITAL IS UNDER SIEGE, THE CAR PARK CHURNING WITH CAMERA crews and photographers, radio journos and television link trucks, a moving clot of ambition, hungry for facts, ravenous for news. With Hummingbird Beach locked down, the crime scene inaccessible, the media have congealed here outside the hospital where half-a-dozen people are fighting for their lives. It's life and death and it's live to air, news as it happens, when it happens, the news you need right now.

Martin circles the scene, searching for somewhere to park. He leaves the Corolla a block away, in the sun, unable to find anything closer. He should have known it would be like this. If any news outlet had hesitated to send reporters, that hesitation had been quickly erased by his own stories, now metastasising across the country and around the world. A religious cult, drug-fuelled orgies, seven dead, a television star. Plus the X factor:

the mystery surrounding what happened and who was responsible. It doesn't get much bigger than that. The British, with their peculiar penchant for Australian television soaps, have gone nuclear; Garth McGrath, star of *Paradise Waters*, is dead at thirty-four, victim of a sex and drug cult. Unconstrained by any jurisdictional concerns, the London tabloids are already spiralling towards absurdity, competing with social media to vent the most ludicrous, salacious and far-fetched theories. Social media itself has turned feral, with blurry phone shots of the death scene multiplying, spawning fakes and dark humour. A mound of floral tributes is building outside the hospital entrance, climbing up the plain brick sign reading LONGTON BASE HOSPITAL. A group of middle-aged women huddle tearfully by the tribute, supporting each other in their grief, surrounded by hungry lenses.

'Martin Scarsden, well met.' He turns towards the voice, a voice resonant with timbre and authority. Doug Thunkleton, television reporter. 'Should have known you'd have the jump on the rest of us.'

'Hi, Doug.'

'Fantastic piece. Fucking brilliant.'

'Thanks. You back on news?'

'Johnny-on-the-spot, just like you. I got some terrific stuff.'

'You got in?'

'Didn't have to. Got the best of the phone footage, plus an interview with the hippie who filmed it.'

'Right. So what's happening now?'

'Medical staff promising a press conference at ten. An update on the victims. Latest we've heard, there are four still critical, four serious, a dozen more in for observation. A couple airlifted to Brisbane, but the rest they'll treat here.'

'Why Brisbane?'

'Closer than Sydney.'

Martin turns back to look at the hospital. There's a policeman and a security guard standing at the entrance. 'Anyone getting in?'

'Not a chance. We tried dressing a cameraman as a male nurse. No luck.'

'Chequebook?'

'What do you take me for?'

'Didn't work, huh?'

'Nah. So we're all stuck out here waiting. I've heard it's bedlam in there. They're discharging anyone they can, just to make room.'

'Really?'

'Yeah. We're doorstopping people as they leave.'

'Getting anything?'

'Not a lot.'

'Okay. Thanks, Doug. See you round.'

'Hey, Martin, while we're waiting, any chance of knocking off a quick interview? As far as I know, you're the only journo who made it into Hummingbird Beach.'

Martin sighs. It's the last thing he needs. 'Sure, mate, but let's make it a bit later.'

He has only gone a few steps when another voice bails him up. 'Martin!' It's Bethanie Glass.

'Bethanie. Didn't take you long to get here. Get any sleep?'

'Not a lot. You have anything new?'

'No. You?'

'Nope. I went down to the commune, but it's sealed off, no access. Then I came up here. Have you spoken to Terri?'

'Not this morning.'

'You should. She's singing your praises. Loves your pieces. Wants you to stay with us. You should call her. Get a good rate out of her while you're still in favour.' Bethanie smiles.

'Thanks. I will.'

'How do you want to play this?'

'How do you mean?'

'Division of labour.'

'Well, one of us needs to stay here for this press conference.'

'I'll do it,' says Bethanie. 'You're the one with the local contacts.'

'Thanks, Bethanie. Joint by-lines?'

'Absolutely.'

Martin looks at the hospital, at the security guard and police officer. 'I'll see you in a moment.' He walks across to the entrance.

'You media?' asks the beefy-looking security guard, puffed up by the importance of his role.

'I'm a local. Port Silver,' says Martin, deflecting the question. 'I've come to help a mate. He's being discharged.'

'What's his name?'

'Royce McAlister. Got in a brawl down at the beach the other day. He's been in for observation.'

'Is that where you got that shiner?'

'Yeah. I tried to break it up.'

'Wait here,' says the security officer and moves inside.

Martin turns to the policeman. 'You a local?'

'Glenn Innes,' says the constable.

'Didn't think I recognised you. Long way to come to guard a door.'

'You're telling me. Sooner I'm out of here the better.'

'Must be under control by now. You won't be here much longer.'

The policeman regards him warily. 'I wouldn't know.'

The security guard re-emerges, addresses the constable. 'Yeah, he's good.' And then to Martin, 'Follow me.'

Martin trails the security guard through the foyer to the reception desk. There is a hum of efficiency, of things being done, of well-controlled urgency; a complete contrast to the provincial inertia of the previous day and the chaos at Hummingbird during the night.

'You're here for Royce McAlister?' asks an older nurse in a voice of matronly command.

'That's right.'

'Good. Follow me.'

Royce is sitting up in bed. He doesn't look surprised to see Martin, and doesn't look surprised when the nurse announces his friend is here to pick him up. 'Good on you, mate,' says Royce.

'I'll let you get dressed and collect your stuff. Sign out at the desk downstairs when you go,' says the nurse.

They wait till she's gone before either of them speaks.

'What the fuck is going on around here?' whispers Royce. He points across the ward. 'There was an old bloke there this morning. They kicked him out, put that girl in there as soon as his wife turned up.' Martin looks across at the young woman sleeping peacefully, monitors connected, two separate IV drips feeding her arm. 'It's a blokes' ward,' whispers Royce. 'But they put her in here, told me I had to leave, to find someone to collect me. I've been calling Topaz. I saw her yesterday and she said we were leaving. Now she's not answering.'

Martin moves closer to the young man, keeping his voice low. 'She's in hospital, Royce. Here or in Brisbane.' And Martin recounts as quickly as he can what occurred at Hummingbird. Well before he's finished, Royce has looked away and is staring at a wall, shaking his head. 'I don't fucking believe it. She knows how to handle drugs.'

Martin doesn't know how to respond to that.

'Come on. I'll get dressed. We can find her.'

'No, don't get dressed,' says Martin. 'The place is crawling with cops and security; they'll kick us out. Leave your gown on, lean on me. If they think you belong here, they won't challenge us.'

Royce looks at him approvingly. 'Good thinking.' There's a pole on wheels by the entry to the ward, a fresh bag of saline attached to its top. Royce commandeers it, looping the bag's tube around his arm. But they don't need to go far. Just the next ward. Four beds, four women, curtains surrounding the beds drawn back. When lives are at risk, privacy comes a distant second.

'Topaz,' whispers Royce. He's seen her in one of the beds closest to the door, asleep or unconscious or comatose, a monitor tapping time to the slow beat of her heart. He moves to her, the pole and Martin forgotten. 'Topaz?' He sits on her bed, reaches out, strokes her hair.

Two of the other beds also contain sleeping women, but the occupant of the final bed is awake and sitting up, staring out the adjacent window. Jay Jay Hayes. Martin walks to her, sits next to her on a plastic chair, back to the door.

She turns to him. 'Hello, Martin,' she says.

'Jay Jay. How you feeling?'

'Fucking awful. They pumped my stomach. Filled me up with charcoal.' She's clearly upset, her hands kneading the blanket. There are tears in her eyes when she looks back up. 'Is it true?

Did people die?' She must see the answer in his expression, closing her eyes, dread creasing her face. 'My God. How many?'

'Seven.'

'Seven? Oh no. Who?'

Martin reaches out, takes her hand. It's trembling. 'Garth McGrath. A man, two devotees, a young couple.' At the thought of the young lovers, so innocent and so dead, his own eyes start to tear. 'And Swami Hawananda.'

'Dev? Oh God.' Her eyes are wide with the horror of it, the death of her lover. 'He's passed?'

'I'm afraid so.'

'And you were there? You saw?'

'Afterwards. With Nick Poulos and the SES. We helped. Did what we could.'

Jay Jay nods, eyes hollow. 'I see.'

'What happened, Jay Jay? What went wrong?'

'I have no idea. The potion was poisoned. Spiked. That's all I can think of. A mistake. A tragedy.'

'The punch is always spiked. Everyone knows it.'

'No.' Her eyes are filled with conviction. 'No. Dev is—was—always so careful. Controlled the amounts, made sure everyone knew what they were doing, what they were taking.'

'Which was what?'

'Alcohol. That's all it was, mixed with spices. He may have added drugs in the past, but not recently. After Garth turned up and the media followed, I spoke to him. He saw the risk. So in recent months it was just grog, spices and fruit juice.'

Martin grimaces. 'No. I was there on Thursday night, remember? People were taking more than just alcohol.'

Jay Jay sighs. 'You're right. There are still drugs—weed and pills and whatever—but that doesn't mean he was supplying them.'

'Not just party drugs. There was Rohypnol, or something similar.'

The dismay hasn't left Jay Jay's face, but now it has a focus. 'The date rape drug? On Thursday? Are you sure?' Her voice has softened to a whisper.

'Yes. I was affected. So was Topaz. So was Garth McGrath. Maybe others.'

Jay Jay shakes her head in disbelief. 'I was there on Thursday. I didn't have any.' A line creases her forehead, confusion gathers at the corner of her eyes. 'Garth? Why would he back up the very next night?' She looks across the ward. 'And Topaz? She was there both nights as well.'

Martin follows her gaze: Topaz is still unconscious, Royce sitting on her bed, holding her hand, whispering to her. It's a good question: why indeed? He turns back to Jay Jay Hayes. The tears have escaped her eyes, are rolling down her cheeks. She wipes at them messily, smearing her face with the back of her hand. He looks at her; she's grief-stricken, the reality of her lover's death gouging her emotions. He knows he should leave her to mourn, or stay and comfort her. Those are the decent options. Instead he persists, knowing he may not get another chance. 'Has anything like that ever happened before with Rohypnol?'

She nods. 'It did. Just the once that I know of. A month or two ago. I only heard about it afterwards.' She looks down, breaking eye contact. 'Same thing, just a few people affected.'

'Is it possible that the swami was not being completely honest with you?'

'Dev?' Her eyes flare, momentarily defensive. 'No. No way. And whoever was spiking drinks with rohies, it can't have been in the potion.'

'You sure?'

'If it was, everyone would have been affected.'

'Who was affected the first time?'

She looks up at him, offers a smile, out of place on her ravaged face. 'There's a rule: what happens at Hummingbird stays at Hummingbird.'

'You think that's going to cut it with the police?'

The smile fades. 'No. That was Garth's rule. But he's dead now.'

'So who was affected?' he asks again.

'Garth. Jasper Speight.' And now she does look up at him. 'And maybe your girlfriend, Mandalay.'

That stops him dead, derailing his line of thought. Mandy at Hummingbird Beach. With Jasper; with Garth. His chest feels constricted; for a moment it's hard to breathe. Jay Jay had said before that Mandy had been at Hummingbird, but he'd pushed it aside, glossed over it, telling himself she'd just been there to check out the scene, not to participate. *Christ.* He presses on, pushing his emotions down into a box like he has done so many times before, suppressing them, reverting to intellect alone, like a pilot on one engine.

'As you say, it sounds as if the Rohypnol is unconnected,' he continues. 'Both times, just a few people affected, no one poisoned. But this time everyone was poisoned. The potion is the obvious vector. Who made it?'

'Dev. He serves it from a ceremonial bowl.'

'I can't remember that. Not on Thursday night.'

'No, the potion is only dispensed every second Friday, at the end of a two-week intensive. He ladles it into small glasses from his bowl. It's meant to be a release after two weeks of abstinence, a celebration of re-entering the world.'

'He was there on Thursday. There was no bowl, but he was doling out something from a big Coke bottle. I had some.'

Jay Jay cracks a weak smile. 'What can I say? He liked to party.'

'Seriously?'

'Yeah. There wouldn't have been any of the intensive people there, not on Thursday. You'd remember them. They'd all have henna symbols on their foreheads by then. They get bigger as the fortnight passes.'

Martin thinks for a moment, trawling his suspect memory. He remembers the guru sitting in a lotus position, opposite a pretty girl, but he can't remember any markings on her face.

'So who got this potion of his? Only those doing the course?'

'No. They went first, then anyone who wanted to could join in. The idea was the participants were re-entering the world, so it helped if the world was partaking. I think that was the theory. On the off weeks, there'd always be a party. It wasn't really connected to him, but he often showed up. Just like Thursday.'

'So, there are two types of parties? Is that what you're telling me?'

'I guess. The ceremony took place every fortnight. At first it was just the swami and a couple of followers, then people camping started joining in. Then word got out and people would bus in from the hostel in town. So now there's a party every Friday, even on the alternate weeks when the intensive people don't participate.'

'But the swami would still attend?'

'Most times. He was a bit of a drawcard.' She smiles moment-arily, as if some fond memory has come to her.

'So who organised these parties?'

'No one. They just became a regular thing.'

'But a bus would come out from the hostel—driven by Harry Drake junior.'

Jay Jay nods, frowning. 'That's right.'

'Did Harry supply drugs?'

'I don't know for sure, but the people from the hostel are always out of it, more than anyone else. So probably.'

Martin lowers his voice, attempting tact, knowing he fails. 'The police will wonder if the swami did it on purpose.'

'What do you mean?'

'Murder. Suicide. Some elements of the media are already reporting it that way.'

She shakes her head, keeps shaking it, expressing her disbelief long after he gets the message, as if to convince herself as much as him. 'No. There was no sign. Nothing like that. He said he wanted to stay at Hummingbird for the long term.'

'Where did he mix the potion? In the communal kitchen?'

'No. Up at his retreat or in his cabin, by himself. He'd bring it down in a big Coke bottle, like the one you saw, then pour it into the bowl.' She's about to continue when some thought comes to her, causing her to lift both hands to her mouth, eyes wide. 'He told me someone had been going through his things.'

'When? Yesterday?'

'No. A week or two ago.'

'You should tell the police. They'll want to know.' She nods. 'But tell me: two parties in two nights; two drug parties in two nights. Is that usual?'

'No. I can't remember that happening before.'

'Do you think he was genuine?' Martin asks.

'What do you mean?'

Martin is recalling the swami, dressed in street clothes, wearing a Panama hat, meeting with Tyson St Clair in Longton. 'Did he believe in what he was doing?'

She smiles wryly. 'Absolutely. He was very genuine. He helped me.'

'How's that?'

'Meditation. Reflection. Forgiveness.'

Martin glances out the window. Put like that, it sounds almost attractive. 'So he was the real thing?'

'In his own way. Unorthodox, but sincere.'

'Unorthodox how?'

'After I quit surfing, I spent a bit of time in India, at ashrams. Trying to find myself.'

'And?'

'Didn't do me any harm, except for the dysentery.'

'What's that got to do with him?'

'He's not from that heritage. He's got a few chants, but none of the scriptures. If he'd trained under a guru, he'd have been more like the rest of them. But that doesn't mean he was a fraud.'

'I guess not,' says Martin, deciding not to debate the definition of fraud.

They sit in silence for a while, each consumed by their own thoughts.

'What the fuck are you doing in here?' It's Morris Montifore, standing in the doorway, angry and indignant.

'Morris, I need to tell you something,' says Martin, standing.

'No you don't,' hisses Montifore, taking him by the arm and leading him out into the corridor. 'Get this straight: we are not on speaking terms, you don't call me by my first name, and as sure as fuck you don't ring my mobile.'

'I'm trying to help.'

'By infiltrating a crime scene and then reporting it in the *Herald*? You told me you were done with journalism.'

'I saved a life at that crime scene.'

Montifore stops, stilled by anger. 'Is that a threat?'

'What?'

Montifore stares at his shoes, as if counting to ten. He calms down a little. 'Okay. Tell me. What is so important?'

'The drug parties. They've been going for months. Sometimes just alcohol and marijuana. Sometimes ecstasy. But maybe not supplied by the swami, not recently.'

'We know.'

'I was at one Thursday night. There was something else. Rohypnol.'

That gets Montifore's attention. 'You can't know that for sure.'

'Maybe not, but I know how you can find out. I was here yesterday. At this hospital. Me and that comatose young woman in there, the one with the doting boyfriend. Her name is Topaz. They took blood samples from us. You have my permission to test mine. I'll give you written permission if you need it. Compare it with whatever you've got from last night.'

Montifore sees the logic. 'You're suggesting that this was an escalation, two nights in a row?'

'Maybe. Or maybe totally unconnected.' He's about to go on, to tell the policeman about the previous incident, then decides against it. Jasper and Mandy together at Hummingbird: that's not a fact he wants to drop into the bear trap mind of Montifore.

The detective doesn't pick up on Martin's hesitation. 'Okay. Good. But leave now. You can't be here.' The instruction is clear, but his voice has softened, lost its acrimony.

Martin goes to move, then says, 'I need to take that guy with me. They've discharged him, given his bed away.'

'Okay. Get him quick. And Martin?'

'Yes?'

'That boy on the beach—the one you saved. Thank you. I didn't see him.'

'Of course.'

Montifore nods, a curt, almost imperceptible expression of gratitude.

Martin re-enters the ward. 'C'mon, Royce, we need to get going.'

'Can't I stay with her?'

Martin shrugs. 'I suppose. But you'll still need to get changed and collect your stuff. They're taking your bed.'

Outside, in the car park, the day is hot and growing hotter. There is no wind, no sea breeze, not even a dry exhalation from the hinterland. Summer is extending its reach, stretching into March, its power undiminished.

Martin sees Doug Thunkleton hovering and retreats into the shade of a jacaranda tree. He punches a name into his phone, calls the number. Jack Goffing. ASIO agent. The two men bonded during the investigations down in Riversend, each helping the other out of difficult situations. Maybe Jack can help now.

'Martin. I see you're back in the thick of it.'

'That's one way of putting it.'

'What can I do for you?'

'You've seen the news reports?'

'Australia's Jonestown?'

'Jesus. We used that?'

'Who hasn't?'

'Jack, about the dead swami—Dev Hawananda—he used to dole out this potion at the parties. He might have poisoned it, or someone else might have tampered with it. You know what I'm talking about?'

'Yeah. I read your story, among others. Good job, by the way.'

'Is it possible he's a fake?'

'You mean not actually divine?'

Martin can hear the sardonic barb in the intelligence officer's comment, but he shares none of Goffing's amusement: he was there, he saw the dead and the dying. 'No, I mean not actually a swami. Is there any way to check him out, to see if he was who he claimed to be? Maybe check out his background in India?'

There's a pause. Then: 'Morris Montifore is there. Tell him your suspicions. You don't need me.'

'Montifore is run off his feet, head like a pressure cooker. I can't get near him and, if I did, he's likely to explode. If you find something, then I guarantee I'll pass it on to him.'

'Before or after you publish?' The amused tone has returned to Goffing's voice.

'Before, of course. I'd want his quote.'

This time Goffing laughs aloud. 'Okay, I'll see what I can do. But you do realise it's a Saturday? You're lucky I'm going in to work this afternoon.'

'Oh, and Jack, one other thing.' It has come to him as an afterthought. 'There's a young couple here—an Australian called Royce McAlister and his American girlfriend, Topaz Throssel. They're young, in their twenties. There's something not quite right there.'

'Like what?'

'They got caught out trying to extort money. The boyfriend says Topaz knows her way around drugs, but she was at the Hummingbird parties on Thursday and Friday nights. She's in hospital now, comatose and on a drip.'

Goffing doesn't speak at first. With anyone else Martin might grow impatient, but he's learnt to value the intelligence man's cautious assessments. 'I don't get it,' he says finally. 'What am I looking for?'

'I'm not sure. Past criminality. Any convictions. Maybe this whole disaster is a result of some scam gone wrong.'

'Have you told Montifore?'

'I don't have anything to tell him. Not yet.'

Goffing promises to do what he can and ends the call.

Martin starts to walk away, but doesn't get far before he's intercepted by Doug Thunkleton, camera crew hovering with intent. 'That was smooth. How did you get in?' asks the TV newsman, flicking his head towards the hospital.

'Native charm.'

'You got time for a quick interview?'

'Shouldn't we wait until after the press conference?'

Thunkleton glances at his watch, frowns. 'I guess you're right. Straight afterwards then?'

'Sure. Just come find me.'

Martin looks as Thunkleton rejoins the pack. It's growing larger by the minute as more and more journalists arrive from Sydney and interstate. It's the biggest story in the land and getting bigger. It's in his nostrils; he has got the scent. He wants to get to Port Silver as fast as he can, to stay focused, to chase down the facts and spread them to the world. First he finds Bethanie, confirms she will cover the press conference. Then he hurries back to his car and, muffler growling, drives towards the escarpment and Port Silver.

But the road won't indulge him: it cares nothing for stories and deadlines and journalistic egos. It's too narrow, there's too much traffic percolating up through its hairpin bends, there's nowhere to overtake. He finds himself stuck behind a semitrailer grinding its way down the mountain in first gear. Tyson St Clair is right about one thing: Port Silver is not going to get much bigger without a new access road. Just when he thinks he couldn't be moving any more slowly, the truck wheezes to a stop altogether, air brakes hissing. Hesitantly, Martin pulls out, contemplating overtaking, but then sees the issue. Below them, another truck, the twin of the one in front of him, is coming up the mountain. It's negotiating a precarious three-point turn around a hairpin corner, a helpful motorist waving directions to the driver. Martin pulls back in, stops and turns his hazard lights on. This is going to take forever: first the truck coming up, then the one in front of him going down; it will need to execute the same manoeuvre to get around the corner—and then the two or three hairpins below that. Martin lets out a sigh, tries to convince himself it doesn't matter, that he's not on deadline. But the lack of motion tugs at his focus, at his single-minded pursuit. He wants to concentrate on the poisoning, he wants to question the swami's bona fides, he wants to ascertain the source of the Rohypnol, he wants to ponder the mysterious disappearance of Amory Ashton, he wants to speculate about Royce and Topaz and the role played by Harry the Lad. He wants to think about anything other than Mandy at Hummingbird with Jasper and Garth. But the traffic is stopped; there is no escape. Jay Jay's revelation has sprung back out of its box, no longer compartmentalised. What does it mean? That Mandy's been unfaithful? Had she misled him and Winifred about the fight with Jasper at the lifesavers? Had she lied to the police? Back in Riversend, she'd also been slow with the truth, about her relationship with the homicidal priest. He'd been blinded by her beauty, believing her. But that was then, back before she knew him, back before they were lovers, back before they'd started planning a future together. Surely it was different now. But why hadn't she told him she'd been to Hummingbird? Instead, she'd slapped his face after she learnt he spent the night there. And now he can't ask Jasper, he can't ask Garth, and the thought of confronting her turns his stomach.

Made restless by his roiling thoughts, he gets out of the car, as if he might leave them inside. The Longton-bound truck crawls up the hill and past him, followed by a slow-moving caravan of cars. He'll be stuck here for a while yet as the driver of the truck in front waits for the traffic to pass before attempting his own hairpin pirouette. Martin walks off to the side of the road. The sun moves with him, flickering through the trees, a slow-motion strobe. *Can you see the sea?* his father asks him. He stares into the distance, above the spreading green of the ferns, through the vertical gaps in the spotted gums. And there it is: the sea, a thin horizontal line dividing one shade of blue from another. The sea. He can see the sea. All he had to do was stop long enough to look for it.

chapter twenty-three

THERE ARE NO FLORAL TRIBUTES AT THE ENTRY TO HUMMINGBIRD, JUST A SURLY-looking police constable standing with her arms crossed, her car parked across the narrow track behind the cattle grid. Martin cuts the Corolla's engine, silencing its increasingly delinquent muffler, and approaches the officer. She's young, hair cut in a dark bob, eyes hidden behind sunglasses. She doesn't wait for him to speak.

'It's a crime scene. No entrance.'

'I've been staying here,' says Martin, voice conciliatory. 'I just came to collect some of my stuff and my friend's.'

The constable removes her sunglasses, not blinking. 'You're Martin Scarsden. You're a journalist. Go any further and I'll arrest you.'

'I was here last night. I was part of the SES team. Saving lives. They told me I could get my stuff.'

Her eyes bore into his, not a skerrick of sympathy in them. 'I'm a graduate of the Goulburn police academy,' she says quietly.

Martin blinks. Why is she telling him that?

'I graduated the same year as Robbie Haus-Jones. The most decent man I ever met.' Her voice is even and unemotional.

Fuck. Now he has it. Robbie Haus-Jones, the young constable who had befriended him out west, who did so much to help him; the young constable now recovering from third-degree burns, suspended from the force and facing criminal charges. Robbie. Poor Robbie.

Martin doesn't even try to respond. He gets back in the car, reverses precariously, cowed by the policewoman's unwavering gaze. Once he's out of sight of her righteousness, he manages to turn the car around and drive out. What now? He's unsure. For a moment he contemplates driving to the cheese factory, finding a canoe or a kayak and paddling along the shore of the swamp and out through the estuary to Hummingbird. But what canoe, what kayak? Easier to park at the bridge and wade along the stream, swim around the headland to the beach. And then what? Emerge like the monster from the black lagoon and get himself arrested? Terrific. They could parade him for Doug Thunkleton and the media: Exhibit A—dickhead. He gets to the juncture of the drive, where it meets Ridge Road. Ridge Road . . . He recalls the walking track between the road and the lookout on the point. There was another path forking from it, leading down towards Hummingbird Beach, to the side of the campground where the guru's followers were housed. What had Jay Jay said about the guru mixing his potion? *Up at his retreat or in his cabin, by himself. He brought it down in a big Coke bottle.* Up at his retreat? Brought it down? It's worth a look.

A few minutes later he leaves the car at the entry to the walking track, the same place he'd parked three days ago. The track is the same, the sound of the surf is the same, but today nature isn't so impressive, not so present. There's no wind; maybe that's it, nothing to ease the growing heat. The path leading down towards Hummingbird's campsite is exactly where he remembers it. He starts to descend and there, still some way above the campsite proper, as if he has imagined it into existence, a sole cabin sits off to the right on a shelf of bare sandstone, shielded from the track behind a screen of foliage. He follows a narrow walkway leading to the side of the cabin and up some steps onto a small deck. If the cabin itself is modest, the view is extravagant: to stand on the deck is to breathe exhilaration. The panorama extends right up the coast, to the dunes, the endless beaches and the thunderous surf of Treachery Bay, all the way to a distant green-blue line where the escarpment meets the sea.

At first, he can't get the door open. He's reluctant to use his hands, to leave any evidence he's been here. He steps off the deck, finds a couple of sticks, returns to the door and uses them to prise it open.

It's a one-room cabin, even smaller than the guest cabins down closer to the beach. There is the smell of incense and spices, cloying in the enclosed space. A large bed dominates the room, raised high, draped with multi-coloured cloths of silk rather than a mosquito net. On the floor, there's a discarded condom packet. Martin pauses, realising the police haven't been here yet. They mustn't know about the cabin. Is that possible?

He puts his hands in his pockets, not wanting to leave evidence of his presence. Before the bed is a prayer mat. Martin can imagine the guru here, in the lotus position, the door flung wide, the world stretched before him, like a god surveying the earth below. A carving of Shiva hangs from the wall on one side, Krishna on the other. Martin uses his phone as a camera. There is a wooden wardrobe—Balinese, at a guess—with a Panama hat sitting on top. Inside, various robes and, incongruously, business shirts and chinos. Street clothes like the swami had been wearing at Longton, talking with Tyson St Clair. Martin photographs the clothes. At the bottom of the wardrobe he finds a pile of footwear, eastern sandals and western shoes and boots, and next to them an old-fashioned suitcase, a relic, lacquered cardboard with dark brown ribs of polished wood, adorned with fading stickers. Martin takes a rag, lifts the case clear, photographs the outside. The stickers say *Madras*, *London* and *Bombay*. How long since Chennai was Madras and Mumbai Bombay?

Martin places the case on the bed and, with a silk cloth protecting his hands, eases it open. There are some clothes: thick jumpers and winter vestments. Martin sifts through the contents. Under the clothes he finds a well-thumbed guidebook, an old Lonely Planet guide to India. He lifts it out. Its pages are interspersed with several postcards. Postcards. Martin feels his breath catch. Carefully, his hands awkward behind their silk shield, he opens the book, examining each postcard in turn, before returning them to the same page. There is a black-and-white portrait of an Indian holy man, identified on the flip side as Swami Brahmananda Saraswati, another of the Beatles with Maharishi Mahesh Yogi, a third of Bhagwan Shree Rajneesh wearing orange robes and looking like the cat that swallowed the cream. The remaining three postcards are paintings of Hindu deities: Brahma, Vishnu and Ganesh. None of the cards have handwriting on their flip sides. Religious postcards. He racks his brain, trying to find some link with the postcard Jasper Speight gripped in his dying hand, the postcard of a Greek saint. But there is no link, nothing substantial. He eases the book back into the bottom of the case and closes the lid. He's just about to place it in the wardrobe when a thought flashes through his mind, a suspicion. He again settles the case on the bed, opens it. There: inside the lid, on a piece of blue adhesive tape, is the name of the owner, written in pen. *Swami Dev Hawananda.* But why write his name on a piece of tape, so easy to remove? Martin tries to peel the tape back, but it's too difficult with his hands impaired by the silk cloth. He discards the cloth, uses his finger-nails. He works slowly, not wanting to tear the tape or damage the case beneath it. Soon he has peeled enough back to see the beginnings of writing: another name. Gently, but with mounting excitement, he pulls the tape back until the name is revealed. It's not English, but nor is it Hindi or Sanskrit. Instead it's Cyrillic, or maybe Greek. Martin takes his phone, photographs the name: *Μύρον Παπαδόπουλος.*

For a moment, he considers taking the case. Once he wouldn't have hesitated. As a younger man, a foreign correspondent, he would have stolen it, heedless of consequences, contemptuous of local laws. But now that's impossible. He can't remove evidence useful to the police. What has changed: himself or merely the jurisdiction? If he were in India, would he be so respectful of the police? Or fearful? It doesn't matter; he can't take it. Instead he smooths the tape back into place, rubbing it with the silk cloth to make sure it's holding fast and to remove his fingerprints. He closes the lid, places the case on the floor and photographs it from several angles before placing it back in the wardrobe. He needs to leave, he knows there can be no excuses should the police discover him here, yet he understands this is his only chance, he's never going to be allowed back in here, not with the dead man's worldly goods still in situ.

He scans the room. What is he looking for? What has he missed? And then it comes to him. He lifts the silk draping the bed, climbs onto it. And there it is, on a shelf above the bedhead: a mortar and pestle. He stands on the bed, excited by his find. Next to the stone implements are a brown glass bottle and a narrow sandalwood box. He doesn't move the box, just opens it where it is, lifting its brass latch, his hands still cloaked in silk. An array of six small medicine bottles with metal lids and a clear plastic bag containing pills. The bottles have old labels, hard to decipher. Martin gets his phone out, takes multiple shots, moving the lens in as close as he can. Fuck he loves his phone. Then he lowers the lid, gets off the bed and leaves the cabin, heart pounding.

Exhilaration has him. This is shit hot. A scoop. Inside the inner-sanctum of a cult leader, the poisons arrayed, the images carrying the story. Martin Scarsden, out ahead of the pack, out ahead of the police. He starts skipping, swept along the path, headlines forming in his mind. Wait until Terri and the back-stabbers at the *Herald* see what he's got. The front page awaits. He stops for a moment, takes a deep breath. It tastes of sea salt and vindication. And he's free to write whatever he likes, to assert whatever he likes; the dead can't sue. Yet as he stands there, the first doubts shade him. He's safe here, he knows. Even if the police climb the track from the beach he is well clear of them.

So why is he hesitating? Something passes through him. Guilt? No, not that. Responsibility? No. Culpability? Possibly. Can he really find such evidence and keep it for his articles? Not tell the police before publication? Can he get away with it? He's frozen to the spot, the urge to skip gone. He has to tell them, or how can he use it? Otherwise he risks being charged with withholding evidence and becoming the story himself. His rivals wouldn't hesitate to pile on, condemning him for unethical behaviour: the man who jeopardised a murder investigation. Is there anyone as righteous as a journalist who has been scooped? Hell, how can he finesse this? And that's when it comes to him, the real reason he's hesitating. It's not about the story or how the police may react. It's not even about the impact on Mandy. It's not about practicalities; it's about the deaths of seven people and who killed them. The image returns: the beautiful couple, laid out like meat on their bed, their innocence gone, their lives stolen. It's about Jay Jay Hayes, grieving for her dead lover. He trembles. As always, he's been putting the story first, not considering the consequences. And at that moment he knows what he has to do; how could he ever have thought any different?

Hesitation dispelled, he strides to his car, uses his key to open the boot. He lifts the tatty carpet, revealing the spare tyre compartment, then he powers his phone off and slides it down next to the tyre. He closes the boot, makes sure it's locked, makes sure the car is locked, then hurries back down the track, past the retreat, down towards the Hummingbird Beach campsite. At the bottom, still sheltered by the rainforest, he stops, recovers his breath, settles himself like an actor waiting in the wings for his cue. And then he steps out into the clearing.

The look on Ivan Lucic's face is worth the price of admission. He looks appalled as he watches Martin sauntering towards him, suddenly deaf to the discussion he's been having with three officers dressed in disposable plastic overalls, FORENSIC SERVICES in large letters on their backs.

'How's it going?' Martin asks breezily. 'Need a hand?'

But Lucic isn't smiling. 'Martin Scarsden, I'm placing you under arrest for wilfully disobeying a lawful instruction.' He turns to the other police officers. 'Can someone go and get some cuffs from the car, please?' One of the forensics officers shrugs and walks away, clearly not used to arresting people.

Martin suddenly finds his bravado difficult to sustain. 'Seriously, I'm here to help. I have vital information.'

Lucic shakes his head. 'The constable at the gate warned you off. You should have followed her instructions.'

'Exactly what I was doing. Until I realised you might be about to miss vital evidence. Make a fool of yourself.' The words are provocative, but Martin is keeping his voice as mild as he can.

Lucic bites. 'What evidence?'

Martin swallows. Lucic wants to crucify him; he needs to make this convincing. 'I was obeying her instructions. I just went up onto the point, not onto the site. I didn't cross any police barriers. I just wanted to see if I could see the beach from up there, in case our photographer could get a shot of you guys working. You know, long lens, paparazzi-style.' He turns around, gestures vaguely in the direction of the point.

Lucic is controlled. 'Keep digging.'

'There's a track winding down. A walking path. I was looking

for a vantage point for the snapper. And that's when I found it.'
He pauses for effect.

'Found what?'

'The swami's cabin.'

'What?'

'His cabin.'

'Bullshit. We've searched his cabin. It's over there.' Lucic indicates somewhere behind Martin.

'He had two. Up there is his retreat. It's kind of hidden away. Easy to miss.' Martin spreads his hands. 'No police tape. Nothing.'

'How do you know it's his?'

'Jay Jay Hayes, the owner of this place, told me he had a retreat to himself as well as a cabin. I glanced inside. It's full of Indian paraphernalia. Silk robes, incense, carvings of Hindu gods. It looked like nothing had been searched. I was about to head off when I heard your voices, figured you'd want to know. Before I wrote the story.'

Lucic stares at him as if trying to vaporise him. 'You went inside. Did you touch anything?'

'Yeah, I went in. That's how I knew it was his. Then I knew you needed to know, so I came down.'

Lucic glares at him, considering the situation, then smiles maliciously. 'I'm still arresting you.'

Martin experiences a surge of desperation. He can't get arrested, not now. Mandy needs him, the *Herald* needs him. Time to play a few cards. 'No you're not,' he says calmly, impressed at his own bluster.

'And why's that?' asks Lucic.

'Because I will tell the magistrate exactly what happened: that despite being told not to enter this site, I felt obliged to inform the police of vital information they had overlooked.'

That does it. Lucic is seething now, it's there in his eyes, but he's still keeping a lid on his emotions. 'Why would a magistrate side with a journalist instead of a detective sergeant?'

Martin shakes his head, as if in pity. 'It doesn't really matter what the magistrate says, this is one for the court of public opinion. The *Sydney Morning Herald* will report my testimony, so will the rest of the media. I will recount how I assisted police and was persecuted in return. Your bosses can read all about it.'

Lucic says nothing. They are still for a moment, a stand-off, a test of wills. The impasse is broken by one of the forensics team. 'Isn't that like, um, a breach of journalistic ethics or something?'

Lucic and Martin both stare at him with contempt, but it's Lucic who speaks. 'Why don't you go and help your mate look for those handcuffs?' The young man blushes, looks at his older colleague, presumably his superior. 'Actually,' says Lucic, 'cancel that. Go and get the equipment you'll need to search this cabin.' He waits for the young man to walk away before he turns to the remaining technician. Martin recognises him: the man who was so understanding when he and Mandy collected her things from the townhouse. 'You have anything to add?'

'No, sir,' says the forensics expert, looking uncomfortable.

Lucic turns to Martin. 'Give me your phone.'

'It doesn't work out here. No signal.'

'I don't care. Give me your phone.'

'I don't have it. It's back at the caravan park charging. I knew it would be useless here.'

Lucic turns to the forensics officer. 'Search him.'

The man looks shocked. 'No, thanks,' he says, and walks away.

Demarcation dispute, thinks Martin, *insubordination in the ranks.* But he's wise enough not to say it.

'Spread your arms and legs,' says Lucic.

'Really?'

'Really.'

Martin does what he's told. Lucic takes his time about frisking him, but takes no uncalled-for liberties, content with the unspoken threat the search entails.

'Okay. You can go.'

'Thank you,' says Martin. 'And, seriously, I hope you find something useful.'

'Get lost before I have second thoughts.'

Martin turns, starts walking, is beginning to congratulate himself when Lucic speaks again. 'No. Not that way. You might contaminate the site.'

'I've already been up there. My car's up there.'

'Too bad. Out the main track. You can follow the road up.'

A two-kilometre walk, closer to three. But there's nothing useful to say, so Martin says nothing.

But when he gets up past Jay Jay's house and reception, he pauses. The three forensic officers are collecting bags of equipment from the car park. There are two uniformed officers sitting on the deck of the house, drinking tea, looking out to sea. He can't see anyone else. He slows his pace. The blue-clad technical officers head down, passing him, not making eye contact. Martin walks higher, out of sight of the deck. He stops, looks, listens. Just the unhurried collapse of the waves on the beach and the white noise of distant surf. Nothing. He looks down at the site, makes a quick calculation, a quicker decision.

He moves rapidly across behind the cabins on the western side of the path, the cabins occupied by the fun-seekers, the backpackers and the swingers. There are only five huts, all with police tape across their doors. Martin recognises the one rented by Topaz, so he discounts it. The young couple who died were one along, so not that one. Martin looks closely; the cabin at the end of the row, up against the bushland, looks a little larger and has its own water tank. Garth McGrath would have wanted the best cabin.

He walks quickly, not looking back, ducking under the police tape, moving up the stairs onto the small deck. He uses the heel of his palm to ease the door open, again conscious of fingerprints. He has no reason to be here, no ready-made excuse. He feels a strong sense of trespass. The man is dead, and he is transgressing.

The room is a mess, clothes everywhere. On a wide shelf beneath a side window there's a framed photo of McGrath receiving some sort of award, a Logie perhaps, placed to impress visitors or maybe to reassure McGrath his star still shone. Next to it is a toiletries bag. Martin opens it, careful not to leave prints, hands wrapped in a t-shirt. Toothpaste, wrinkle cream, some sort of fake tan cream. But no pills, nothing incriminating. Surely if they were here, the police would have taken them for testing. There's a cardboard box on the floor beneath the shelf. Martin tips its contents onto the floor. There's a wallet, a set of BMW car keys and a gold Rolex, still ticking away. A packet of condoms, extra-large. Martin doesn't touch anything, surprised the personal items haven't been removed. There's another photo: McGrath with a blonde woman, good-looking, like a model, and two young children. The family, abandoned in Sydney, relegated to the box. Again, the feeling of trespass sweeps him. He is unsure what he's looking for: perhaps an explanation for why someone like McGrath would end up in a place like this. Carefully, hands still covered, Martin replaces the bits and pieces into the box. He takes a last look around. What's he doing here? What's he looking for? Maybe for the reason he's still alive and McGrath is dead. One night earlier and he could be up in the Longton morgue now, in the drawer next to McGrath, with someone else—Mandy most probably—considering his personal belongings, the last flotsam of his life, floating to the surface in his wake.

He's about to leave when he sees it, hanging from a hook on the shelf below the window. The thin silver thread of a necklace, a single pearl at the end. Just like the one Mandy used to wear.

chapter twenty-four

AWAY FROM THE WATER, THE HEAT IS OPPRESSIVE. THERE IS NO WIND, NOTHING to stir the swampy humidity. His shirt is soon sweat soaked, small bush flies coat his back and land on his face, getting at his eyes, taunting him, undeterred by his swatting hands. He trudges up Ridge Road, the shade from the trees ineffectual. He's had two nights in a row with insufficient sleep; his legs grow heavy with the effort. But the uphill slog is the easy part; it's his own thoughts, his sense of betrayal, that weigh most heavily upon him. Mandy. How could she? Garth McGrath. Of all people. He needs to stop and rest, to regather his strength. And, soon, he's chastising himself: how hypocritical he is, how childish. He had slept with Topaz, or the Polynesian girl, or someone. Probably. But only because he'd been drugged. And if it happened to him, most likely the same thing happened to her. Jay Jay had intimated as much. Garth McGrath, predator. He has no proof it was the actor, of course, except that he was the only person affected, or claiming to be affected, on both occasions the date rape drug was suspected. Could a soapie star act that well? And on both occasions, McGrath had clear targets: Mandy in the first instance, Topaz in the second. And, Martin realises, on each occasion there were other men there, men who might have been protectors or who might have been competitors: Jasper and himself, men who might have intervened. Men who also got drugged. He recommences walking, his growing anger helping to propel him up the hill. By the time he gets to his car, the matter is settled in his mind: McGrath was the low-life drugging women with Rohypnol, using the swami as a cover. The evidence may be circumstantial, but Martin can't imagine any other scenario that fits the facts.

He desperately wants to write this story now; he wants to hold up McGrath for the ridicule he so richly deserves. He wants the mountain of floral tributes building outside Longton Hospital to turn to ash. And yet—the acknowledgement comes reluctantly—if McGrath was guilty of those crimes, no matter how abhorrent, most likely he was not responsible for the deaths of seven people, including himself. Rohypnol did not kill the victims. No, the two incidents must be unrelated. A grim determination comes over Martin. He wants to avenge Mandy, but clearing her of murder is the priority: he needs to find Jasper's killer. Garth McGrath's deprivations are not the main story.

And he needs to see Mandy. He has no idea what he's going to say, how to approach it. Maybe he should make a full confession, explain what had happened on his own evening of misadventure. Surely she would take the opportunity to reveal what had befallen her at Hummingbird Beach. Surely.

These are the thoughts filling his mind as he steers the car down the hill and back onto the reliable asphalt of Dunes Road, heading for the caravan park. He's almost there when his phone, recovered from the boot, begins to chirp. He's back in range. He pulls over a little before the entry track to Hartigan's. There are messages and missed calls. The first two calls were from a blocked number, no message left. He calls Jack Goffing.

'Jack, was that you?'

A short pause. 'Martin.'

'Any information?'

'Yes. Your guru. His passport is genuine, his details check out. He's a bona fide Indian.'

'Okay,' says Martin, trying to keep the disappointment from his voice. 'Thanks for that.'

'Your two young grifters, on the other hand, are less straightforward.'

'Grifters? Topaz and Royce?'

'Correct. They were investigated in Melbourne last year, caught out pulling a scam. But in the end their mark didn't want the embarrassment of going to trial.'

'What did they do?'

'Oldest swindle in the book. I assume the girl is a bit of a looker.'

'She is. And knows how to use it.'

'That sounds right. It works like this: she seduces a married guy. They're going at it when her so-called husband bursts in, catches them in flagrante delicto, threatens to beat up the mark or expose him. The mark then pays them off to keep the peace. An oldie but a goodie.'

'Shit. That works, does it?'

'All too often. And in this case, the guy was drugged, which made him easier to seduce, easier to manipulate.'

'Drugged? What with?'

'Rohypnol, probably. Something like that.'

Rohypnol? Martin joins the dots. But the dots don't align. Topaz wasn't around when Mandy was drugged, and she wouldn't have drugged herself and let McGrath molest her. At most, it would give her some knowledge of the drug and its effects. 'Thanks, Jack. I really appreciate it, you going out on a limb for me like this.'

Goffing laughs, an unexpected response. 'It's okay, Martin. I've listed you.'

'What does that mean?'

'You're officially listed as one of my sources.'

'Really?' Martin shifts uncomfortably in his car seat. Somewhere, in the subterranean vaults of the secret police, he is now listed as an informant, a source. It doesn't sit well with him. 'I'm not sure I'm comfortable with that.'

'Relax. You're not the first journo on our books and you won't be the last.'

'Why doesn't that make me feel any better?'

Goffing laughs again, knowing he has Martin where he wants him. 'Oh, and Martin? Your grifters, Royce and Topaz—she's not his girlfriend; they're married.'

'Married? She has permanent residency?'

'Better than that. She's a citizen, has an Australian passport. And an American one too. Why?'

'Nothing. I've got to go. Thanks, Jack.'

But Martin doesn't start driving again. The story they fed him that first day when he picked them up hitchhiking was bullshit.

Topaz has a passport; she didn't need a visa, she didn't need to work in the regions. They were simply rehearsing their cover story with Martin. They'd come to Port Silver specifically to scam the visa scheme, a variation on their regular swindle. They must have heard about it in Sydney. Not a bad idea: someone involved in illegality is unlikely to complain to the police. And might be willing to pay more money. Higher risk, higher reward.

He rings Bethanie. She answers immediately. 'Martin. I tried calling. You been out of range?'

'That's right. At Hummingbird. How was the presser?'

'Nothing out of the ordinary. The doctors went first. Seven confirmed dead, all at the beach last night. Four still in a serious condition in Brisbane, but all expected to recover. The ones here are expected to be released over the next day or two. The doctors anticipate no permanent organ damage.'

'That's good news. And the cops?'

'Treating Hummingbird as a crime scene, but not ready to declare it a crime. They say it may have been unintentional, an accidental overdose. They say comparisons with Jonestown are, quote, far-fetched, unsubstantiated and inappropriate, unquote.'

'Right. Can't argue with that. Anything else?'

'Yeah. They're pissed off at us for revealing McGrath's identity. They say normal procedures should have been followed. But I get the feeling they won't be losing any sleep over it.'

'What else could they say? You filing?'

'Doing it now. You have anything to add?'

Martin thinks of what he has found at Hummingbird, what Jack Goffing has told him. 'No. Nothing substantial. Not yet. Hopefully something for tomorrow's paper, if it pans out. But apparently there was a lot of coverage of Hummingbird a month or two ago, when I was stuck down in the Riverina—Garth McGrath leaving his wife, bacchanalia on the beach, that sort of thing. Can we get the clippings from the library?'

'I've already downloaded them. I'll send you a link.'

Martin ends the call and starts his car, but he doesn't pull onto the road just yet. He can see the entrance to the caravan park, just a hundred metres ahead of him, the dolphin hanging by its nose. He needs to talk to Mandy, ask her about McGrath. He sits for a moment, indecision weighing on him. He takes the idea and tries pushing it back in its box, a rational part of his mind insisting a confrontation won't help.

His phone rings; he's grateful for the distraction. *Nick Poulos*, says the screen.

'Nick.'

'Martin. Where are you?'

'Dunes Road.'

'Right. Well, the police are after you.'

'Me? Why?'

'They suspect you of tampering with a crime scene.'

'Seriously?'

'Yes, Martin. Very seriously. Come straight to the lifesavers.'

Martin can't help himself: 'You really don't have an office, do you?'

'The surf club, Martin. Now.' The call goes dead. Martin wonders at his lawyer's assertiveness.

———

This time Nick is not late. When Martin arrives he's waiting inside for him. Everybody else is out on the deck, enjoying the view, hoping the sight of the ocean might cool them. Without a sea breeze, the club is uncomfortably warm, roof fans merely stirring the humidity. Nick is dressed like a beach bum, not a lawyer, his five o'clock shadow wound forward to a midnight mat, but his laptop is open and the look on his face is one of concentration and sober assessment. Martin sits without shaking his hand.

'So tell me,' says Nick.

'I went looking for information. I'm back writing for the *Herald*.'

'So I see. But you know as well as I do that is no excuse.'

'I didn't tamper with any evidence.'

Nick wears a look of pity, as if listening to the excuses of an infant. 'You were there. You circumvented a police roadblock. Montifore is spitting chips. He's going to hang you out to dry.'

'I was trying to help.'

Nick looks unconvinced. He has a notebook. 'Take me through it.' Martin recounts what he found at Hummingbird Beach, leaving out his search of Garth McGrath's cabin, describing his discoveries in the swami's hut, emphasising how he immediately informed Ivan Lucic. When he's done, the lawyer leans back, shakes his head again. 'Sorry, this isn't going to cut it. You shouldn't have gone inside, not after the constable warned you off. They can charge you, haul you before a magistrate.'

'Nick, seriously, I was trying to help. I could have kept the information to myself.'

But Nick is not appeased. 'You may or may not have compromised a crime scene, but that's not the point. You're a journo; they're law enforcement. The magistrate will see an opportunity to set an example, to send a clear message: under no circumstances should a journalist or anyone else disobey police instructions and enter a crime scene.' He pauses, sighs and summarises. 'You're fucked.'

'What do you suggest?'

'Grovelling. Go to Morris Montifore before he escalates it, before it gets near a court.'

'Maybe I can trade. Give them what I found.'

'You found something?'

'Several things. The first is a young woman, an apparent victim, currently in Longton hospital. Name of Topaz Throssel. She and her husband are small-time con artists. The police may know of them. There's a possibility the deaths resulted from some sort of extortion gone wrong. A scam.'

'Who were they trying to extort?'

'Don't know. Maybe Jay Jay Hayes. Maybe the swami. Apparently, his Indian passport is genuine, but I still think there's something suss about him. He had a guidebook to India. Why would an Indian carry one of those? And here, check this out.' Martin pulls up one of the photos on his phone. It's of the name written inside the case, under the tape. He passes it to Nick.

The lawyer frowns, his eyes widening with surprise. 'That's Greek.'

'Can you read it?'

The lawyer's brow momentarily furrows in concentration. 'Holy shit,' he says. 'Myron. Myron Papadopoulos.'

The two men stare at each other.

'Myron,' says Nick.

'Myron the Wonderworker,' says Martin. 'The swami had post-cards in his case.'

'Jesus,' says Nick. 'We've got to tell Montifore. He needs to know this.'

'Agreed. But who is Myron Papadopoulos?'

'How should I know?'

'You don't think it could be Hawananda's real name?'

'You just said he was definitely Indian,' says Nick.

'With a guidebook to India.'

Nick looks at him, face blank while his mind churns. 'I'll google it.' He starts typing into his laptop. 'God, there are thousands of them. Papadopoulos is the most common name in Greece. Like Smith is here.'

'So good for an alias?'

'I guess. Listen, do you have a photo of this guy? The swami?' he asks Martin.

'No.' And then a thought occurs to him. 'Can I borrow your laptop?' Nick pushes it across the table to him. Martin logs into his webmail. Sure enough, Bethanie has come through. 'Hummingbird articles' says the subject line and, in the body, there's a link to a file-sharing service. Martin clicks through, opening articles. Before long he finds one with a photo of the swami sitting in the lotus position, radiating beneficence.

Nick takes the computer back. 'I just want to try something.' He taps away for a few minutes, intensity spreading across his face before suddenly it lifts, swept aside by a smile of tidal power. 'Bingo!' He twists the laptop towards Martin. 'Here's our man.'

Martin looks at a Facebook page. It's in Greek; he recognises nothing. Nothing except for a photo of a man who has to be the swami. The swami, just much younger. 'How did you do that?'

'Facebook facial recognition. I put the photo in my feed. I tagged him and started with Myron, and up popped a few suggestions. I found this guy, Myron Florakis.'

'Florakis? So Papadopoulos is an alias? Can you confirm that's him?'

'Give me a moment.'

Nick types and, as he types, his features begin to distort: first his eyes widen, then his eyebrows lift, and then his jaw drops, until his whole face is united in an expression of astonishment, with nothing left but to voice his surprise. 'Fuck me,' he whispers.

'What?' demands Martin.

'Fucking hell.'

'What is it, Nick?'

'Here.' Nick swivels the laptop back around. It's a newspaper report, a pdf, black and white, poor quality, like a fax that has been scanned into a computer. It's all in Greek.

'What's it say?' asks Martin.

Nick takes the computer back, starts reading from the screen, translating hesitantly as he goes.

'It's from almost eight years ago. The headline is WITCH'S BREW MANHUNT WIDENS. The story reads: *Police have extended the dragnet in the so-called Witch's Brew case to the mainland, believing a number of people with important information may have fled Crete on a ferry to Piraeus, including self-styled religious healer Myron Florakis.*'

'He's a fugitive?'

'Yeah. Was,' says Nick. He reads more. 'Okay, here it is. *The religious ceremony went bad, with several disciples overdosing, resulting in three deaths.*' Nick looks up at Martin, no further words necessary.

'Let's go see Montifore,' says Martin.

'Hang on, there's more. *Florakis, the son of a Greek father and an Indian mother, returned to Crete about five years ago and set up his controversial healing centre, a mixture of Christian and eastern beliefs.*' Nick stops reading, looks up at Martin. 'Indian mother. It's him,' he says matter-of-factly. 'Let's go.'

'Hang on, I just want to make one call.'

Martin heads out onto the deck, but it's too crowded and too hot, so he returns inside, finding a quiet corner. He rings Goffing, quickly telling him what they've discovered, that he's in trouble with the law, that he's on his way to beg forgiveness from Montifore. He asks Goffing to see what he can find out about Myron Florakis, if he was indeed a fugitive.

'And you're going to hand all of this over to Montifore?'

'Shit yeah. I need to save my arse.'

When he finishes the call, Martin checks his watch. It's almost five. It's true he needs to throw himself on Montifore's mercy, but before that he needs to file for the *Herald*; the policeman is just as likely to lock him up and gag him. And this story is too big to sit on.

⌣

They find Montifore and Lucic inside a dimly lit Chinese restaurant in Longton, the Heavenly Dragon, sitting at a round table big enough for twelve. Outside, the light is golden, the town awash with the late-afternoon sun, but inside the light is low wattage. Maybe all the power is being fed through the air conditioner. The detective inspector has his paper napkin on his lap, the detective sergeant has his tucked into his collar. All class. They say nothing as Martin and Nick walk towards them. Montifore's stare could

carve marble; Lucic's smirk could curdle milk. There are no greet-
ings from either party. Nick Poulos gets straight down to business.

'My client is extremely apologetic. He is willing to fully cooperate
and hand over critical evidence he has gathered.'

Montifore grunts, if only to express his contempt.

'Can we sit?' asks Nick.

Another grunt without a word attached to it, but it sounds
close enough to permission. Martin and Nick exchange a glance
and sit. The policemen continue eating, ignoring them, making
sure they know how insignificant they are, how completely they
are at Montifore's mercy. Montifore finishes masticating a honey
prawn, looks up, slowly moving his gaze from journalist to lawyer.
'Tell me,' he says.

Nick does the talking, as earlier agreed with Martin. 'My
client suspected there was something suspicious about Swami
Hawananda. He wanted to share his suspicions with you, but he
had nothing concrete. So, he went to Hummingbird Beach and
searched the guru's cabin.'

Lucic almost chokes. 'He's admitting to that?'

'I am,' says Martin.

'He removed nothing, he changed nothing,' says Nick.

Montifore turns his gaze to Martin. 'Cut to the chase. What
did you find?'

'My client . . .' Nick starts, but Montifore shakes his head.

'Him. Not you.'

Nick shuts up; Martin swallows. 'There's a suitcase. You can
find it. It's—'

Montifore turns to Lucic. 'We've got it,' says the junior officer.

'What's in it?' Montifore asks Martin.

'His name. In Greek. Under some adhesive tape on the inside of the lid.'

Montifore turns to Lucic. The sergeant shrugs and Montifore turns back to Nick. 'In Greek? You sure?'

'Yes.'

'He's Indian,' says Lucic. 'His passport is genuine. We've checked.'

'That's true,' says Martin. 'Indian mother, Greek father.'

Montifore is looking at him intently. 'Go on.'

'We've identified him,' says Nick. 'His real name is Myron Florakis.'

'Myron?' repeats Montifore. 'As in the Wonderworker?'

'That's right. He's a fugitive. Or was. We have newspaper clippings. I can forward them to you, but they're in Greek.' Nick explains the essentials of the reports: Florakis was a self-styled religious leader, three of his followers died, others were hospitalised in a drug overdose, and he fled. The overdose was most likely accidental, but police still believed Florakis was culpable. Martin scrutinises the policemen's faces as his lawyer lays out the evidence, seeing the scepticism waver and fold, replaced by calculation. Lucic leans back in his chair, squinting with concentration. Montifore maintains his intensity. He turns his attention back to Martin. 'Is this in tomorrow's paper?'

Martin nods silently.

'Highlighting your role. One step ahead of the police, finding the evidence. Tipping off the slow-footed investigators. That all there?'

Martin holds the policeman's gaze. 'No. Not in the first edition.'

'Do you cite police sources?'

'No.'

'What sources do you quote?'

'Greek newspapers.'

Montifore nods. 'Good for you.'

It's only once they get outside that Martin feels he can breathe again. By the look of Nick Poulos's face, the lawyer feels the same.

'Fuck me. Well played,' says Nick.

'Yeah,' says Martin. 'Just let me call the editor.'

They're almost at the top of the escarpment, driving back towards Port Silver, Nick at the wheel of a ten-year-old family wagon, when Martin finishes his call and lets out a long sigh of relief. Terri has managed to change the copy in time; Martin's first-hand account of finding the suitcase has been expunged, as has the reference to being out in front of the official investigation. But before he can speak his phone breaks the silence. It's an unidentified number.

'Hello?' says Martin, voice uncommitted.

'Martin, it's Jack. You alone?'

'No. I'm in the car with my lawyer. He's driving.'

'Can he hear me?' asks Goffing. 'I'm not on speaker, am I?'

Martin looks across at Nick. 'No. We're good.'

'I just read your article. Please tell me you've told Montifore.'

'My article? It hasn't been published yet.'

'So what?'

'So what? The secret police spying on the free press. That's so what.'

'Yeah, whatever. Listen, I have something for you. You need to tell Montifore. It's important.'

'I'm all ears. Hang on.' He puts his hand over the phone. 'Nick, pull over. We might have to go back.'

Nick looks doubtful, but pulls off the road, still a good kilometre before the escarpment.

Martin is back on the phone. 'Okay, I'm listening.'

'First, your information looks spot on. I assume your lawyer helped you with that?'

'That's right.'

'Good. So, last the Greek police knew Myron Florakis was still in the wind. Montifore will be able to identify him within hours from fingerprints.'

'Good,' says Martin. 'Is that all?'

'No. Get this: two of the victims in Crete were tourists, a Canadian and his American girlfriend. The American's name was Cascade Throssel.' Goffing pauses, perhaps for effect.

Martin blinks. 'You're shitting me.'

'They were sisters. Topaz was two years older. And she was there.'

'On Crete?'

'Yeah. But she left around the time her sister went to the retreat with her boyfriend. Looks like she's been travelling ever since.'

'I'll be damned,' says Martin into the phone, then turns to Nick. 'We're going back. Turn around.'

'Martin. You there?' asks Goffing.

'Yes.'

'For now, tell Montifore you and your lawyer discovered this in the Greek press archives. I'll text you a link you can use.'

'You don't want to be involved?'

'Fuck no. Keep me out of it.'

⌒

Montifore and Lucic are still at the round table, eating banana fritters and ice cream, washing them down with beer, when Martin and Nick walk back in.

CHRIS HAMMER

'Get your copy changed in time?' asks Montifore, not missing
a beat.

'Hope so.'

'So what now?'

'We think we know who the killer is,' says Martin. 'The killer
at Hummingbird. It wasn't the swami.'

Montifore says nothing. Lucic pushes his plate away, drains his
beer and waves towards the counter for the bill.

Five minutes later the four men leave the restaurant, walking
purposefully towards the hospital, the two police in front, Martin
and Nick following. The lawyer's puppy-dog enthusiasm has long
deserted him, replaced by a quiet determination.

The police stop, turn to confront Martin. 'We don't need your
help,' says Lucic. 'Beat it.'

'Police breakthrough,' says Martin. 'Homicide crack baffling
case wide open. Front page. Surely you'd want that reported.'

'Not until I give the say-so,' says Montifore. 'I want this
controlled.'

'You got it.'

'Okay. Let them come,' Montifore says to Lucic. But at the
hospital, Montifore turns again. 'Wait outside. I can't have you in
there with us. But we'll be coming out this door. We won't dodge
you; the story is yours.' The police enter through casualty.

Martin gets straight on the phone to Bethanie, castigating
himself for not thinking ahead.

'Martin? What is it?'

'Do you have a snapper with you?'

'Yeah. I'm with him now. Baxter James.'

'Baxter? Is he sober?'

'For now. What's up?'

'Where are you?'

'Port Silver. We've set up at the Breakwater Hotel. Bit shabby but great views.'

'Okay, listen. I'm in Longton. The police are about to make an arrest at the hospital.'

'An arrest? Right. We're on our way. See you there.' She ends the call.

Martin looks at his watch. Port Silver is forty-five minutes away. The photographer will thrash the guts out of his rental; he might make it in half an hour if the escarpment is free of trucks, but he's still unlikely to make it in time. Martin checks the camera app on his phone, making sure the flash is switched on. Next, he calls Terri Preswell, updates her.

'Too late, Martin, the paper's gone. We'll rejig the lead for online, say we believe an arrest is imminent.'

Martin is about to respond when Montifore and Lucic burst out of the doors, like peas squeezed from a pod. Empty-handed.

'Terri, I got to go.' And he hangs up on the editor of the *Sydney Morning Herald*.

'They've gone,' says Montifore. 'Did you see them?'

'Us? No,' says Nick.

'They've only just left. Scarpered.'

'They don't have a car,' says Martin. 'Do they know you're after them?'

'What difference does that make?' spits Lucic.

'If they know you're on to them, they'll make themselves scarce. Otherwise they might still be in the open. Hitching on the highway or checking into a hotel.'

'Right,' says Montifore, taking charge, talking to Lucic. 'Get everyone up here from Port Silver. Get patrols out on the highway checking for hitchhikers. Everyone else to the Longton police station. We'll coordinate from there.' He turns to Martin. 'Here's the deal. We don't want to alert them that we're on to them, so nothing in the paper, nothing online until we nab them. Understand? Nothing. In return, when we get the bastards, it's all yours—you'll get the pics, an exclusive. You got it?'

'Deal.'

Montifore and Lucic storm off towards the police station.

'What next?' asks Nick.

'Give us a moment.' Martin calls Terri at the *Herald*.

'What is it now, Martin?' she answers.

'We need to cut the imminent arrest line. The Myron Florakis exposé is strong enough by itself.'

'You serious?'

'Yeah. The suspects have done a runner. The police don't want us to alert them.'

'Do we care?'

'They've promised exclusive access if we hold off, eternal pain if we don't.'

There's a long pause. 'You think it's worth it?'

'Yes.'

'Okay. Done. But when you get a chance, file as much as you can with a hold on it. As soon as they arrest them, I want it up online. You good with that?'

'Perfect.' He ends the call.

'Port Silver?' asks Nick.

'No. Train station. It's how they got up here from Sydney.'

Nick looks shocked, then smiles. 'Quick thinking.'

———

Martin finds a phone app for the state railways and it hurries them along: the Sydney-bound train is scheduled to pass through Longton in less than ten minutes. Topaz and Royce have timed their run well. Nick drives, Martin texts Bethanie. *Longton train station. Tell Baxter. Look for me. Approach with stealth.*

Night is almost complete by the time Nick pulls off the road a hundred metres from the station. The heat remains, trapped by an unmoving mass of air, the stars hazy.

'You wait here,' instructs Martin, climbing out of the car. 'If they're not there, I'll be back inside two minutes. Any longer, it means I'm talking to them. You'll need to call Montifore. If we let them get on the train without telling him, we're fucked.'

'Got it,' says Nick.

It's a small-town station, a whistlestop on the slow train from Brisbane, nineteenth-century brick and stone, now painted heritage colours, well-maintained in denial of its decline. The drive to Sydney is now less than seven hours, the train still takes more than ten.

There is no one on the platform. Not a soul. Just moths, excited by the late season warmth, circling lamp posts. His heart skips a beat. He starts running, mind churning. Where could they be? Is there an overnight bus instead? Is he wrong about the train? Then he finds them, in a small waiting room, backpacks at their feet, sitting in silence. Alone. Royce smiles when he enters, laughing at the sight of him. 'Martin! Come to say farewell?' He's on his feet, seemingly oblivious to what is happening. Either that, or he's a good actor. A good con man.

But Topaz is past acting. She simply looks at Martin, face impassive, eyes hollow.

Martin has her now, has the fugitive, the killer. For a five-minute exclusive.

'I know,' he says. 'Crete.'

Topaz merely nods, eyes closed.

'What does that mean?' asks Royce.

Martin gets out his phone, stands there, takes a photo of the woman, shrunken, her vivacity gone and her eyes empty, sitting on a bench in a waiting room in a small country town staring into the camera. He takes another two shots before Royce is back in frame, sitting beside his wife, putting his arm around her. 'Topaz?'

'It wasn't planned, was it?' asks Martin. 'You didn't even know he was here when I picked you guys up on Monday.'

Topaz shakes her head, her voice a whisper. 'No.'

'So when did you know?'

'Sitting on the beach with you and Garth. I saw him dunking those followers in the water. It looked like a baptism. Then the marks on the forehead. Something clicked, some connection.'

'But seven dead?' says Martin.

'Baby?' asks Royce, arm around her, concern in his eyes and the first hint of tears.

Topaz appears devoid of emotion as she addresses Martin. 'It wasn't meant to happen like that. Just him. Him and me.'

Martin recalls seeing Topaz, laid out and unconscious, covered in vomit. She'd taken a lethal dose, but hadn't kept it down for long enough.

'So what happened?'

'I don't know.'

'What was the poison?'

'Doesn't matter.' And she falls into the protective hollow of her husband's shoulder, the distress in his eyes and his alone.

There's a distant hum. The train is approaching. Martin ducks his head out of the doorway. He can see a single light in the distance. It's almost here.

'C'mon, babe, let's go,' says Royce, standing. 'The train. Let's go.'

But Topaz doesn't move. She sits, deflated, eyes again closed. 'He deserved to die. I deserved to die. But not the others. I'm so sorry.' She doesn't say anything more, and Martin finds himself unable to ask another question.

The train eases into the station, comes to a stop and sits waiting, breathing, expectant. If anyone is getting on or getting off, Martin doesn't know. His back is to the train, his attention on the two fugitives.

Nick Poulos enters the waiting room. He walks across to Topaz and Royce. She doesn't acknowledge him, so he silently hands Royce his card. The young man reads it, looks up, still not entirely comprehending. 'Please help her,' he says to Nick, voice weak and cracking.

Then Montifore is with them, breathing hard, Lucic at his side, with the constable from Hummingbird Beach, her pistol drawn, pointed at the ground. Montifore stops, considering the tableau in front of him. He ignores Martin and Nick, having eyes only for Topaz and Royce.

'Topaz Throssel,' he says formally, 'I'm arresting you for the murder of Myron Florakis, also known as Swami Dev Hawananda.'

He turns to her husband. 'Royce McAlister, I'm arresting you for being an accessory after the fact of murder.' Royce looks astonished, Topaz looks resigned, but both allow themselves to be handcuffed. The train pulls out, oblivious, continuing its journey south. Two more police arrive and are instructed to bring the backpacks.

It's a sad little procession that leaves the station, consigning it to its long night of well-illuminated desolation: two uniformed officers, one each guiding Topaz and Royce; then Montifore and Lucic and the constable; then Martin and Nick; and, last of all, the two policemen carrying the backpacks with latex-gloved hands. There is no hurry, no rush, all is calm. Until the night is suddenly broken with lightning: Baxter James's flash gun.

Montifore doesn't try to close it down. Instead he steps forward into frame as Topaz is placed into the back of a marked car. Only after the car pulls away does he speak, looking at Baxter and Bethanie but addressing Martin. 'Are they with you?'

'Yes. From the *Herald.*'

'Okay. I've arrested them, but we won't charge them until lunch-time at the earliest.' He cracks a smile. 'Thanks, Martin.' And he walks to a waiting car.

'I'm going to the station; they need representation,' says Nick, more of a statement than a question.

'Of course,' says Martin. And then, almost as an afterthought, 'Hey, Nick?'

'Yeah?'

'Thanks. I wouldn't have worked it out, not without you.'

'Maybe,' says the lawyer, but he's not smiling.

'What was all that?' asks Baxter, already checking his shots on the back of his camera. 'Not charging them?'

It's Bethanie who explains. 'We can report it all for now. Once they're charged, it's sub judice.'

'Too late for the paper, though,' says Baxter, looking at his watch.

'Yeah, let me call Terri. She's not going to want to sit on this,' she says, reaching for her phone.

⌒

There's a McDonald's on the highway with free wi-fi, but it's way too slow; they use their phones instead, hooking up their laptops. Baxter has his photos away in no time, getting them out through his tablet. Martin works on his laptop while Bethanie coordinates with the production team at the *Herald*.

'They want it by nine, otherwise they'll hold it till morning,' she says.

And so Martin writes as quickly as he can, not bothering with rereading, not concerned with typos or grammar or style, the words flowing out of him in a catharsis, forming themselves. Bethanie is reading over his shoulder, suggesting improvements and correcting errors as he goes. They're finished within fifteen minutes.

EXCLUSIVE
By Martin Scarsden and Bethanie Glass in Longton

A young Australian-American woman, Topaz Throssel, is under arrest and is expected to be charged with the murder of seven people, including actor Garth McGrath and self-proclaimed religious leader Swami Dev Hawananda.

A team of *Herald* investigators intercepted Ms Throssel and her husband, Australian Royce McAlister, as they attempted to flee Longton in northern New South Wales by train.

The couple attempted to escape as a *Herald* probe uncovered dramatic new evidence that Swami Hawananda was an imposter with his own dark history.

In a sensational development, the *Herald* can reveal that Hawananda was in fact a Greek–Indian fugitive named Myron Florakis, wanted in connection with the deaths of three people on Crete eight years ago.

It's believed one of the victims on Crete was Topaz Throssel's younger sister, Cascade Throssel. It will be alleged this was her motive for killing Florakis.

Seven people died at a beach party at the secluded resort and religious retreat Hummingbird Beach near Port Silver on Saturday night after an unknown poison was added to a ceremonial potion.

It's believed Ms Throssel attempted to suicide by drinking the same lethal mix, but was saved by the quick actions of police and ambulance officers.

Royce McAlister is being held under suspicion of being an accessory after the fact. It's believed he was not aware of his wife's actions until confronted by an investigative team from the *Herald* . . .

Martin and Bethanie give it a last read through, a final tweak, and hit send, propelling their copy out through the ether and onto a computer screen in the newsroom of the *Sydney Morning Herald*. A text message confirms receipt. 'It's there,' says Bethanie. 'Let's get a drink.'

Martin smiles. 'I'll be right with you.'

He steps outside into the car park, still radiating heat. He rings Mandy, his heart glad.

She answers, voice uncertain. 'Martin?'

'We've cracked it. We know who killed the people at Hummingbird. The police have arrested Topaz, the backpacker from Hummingbird.'

'That's good,' says Mandy, but there's no joy in her voice. 'I guess that gets her out of your life.'

Martin ignores the barb. 'And we think we know who killed Jasper—and why.'

There's a pause. 'Really?'

'We've nothing conclusive, but I'm pretty sure it was the swami. His real name was Myron. He was half Greek, half Indian.'

'Myron. The same as the postcard.'

'Exactly. Jasper worked it out. I don't think the postcard was part of his collection; I think he found it in the swami's cabin. He worked out Hawananda was an imposter. And was wanted in connection with drug deaths in Greece.'

They talk some more, but Mandy sounds flat and Martin's mind keeps returning to the necklace he found in McGrath's cabin.

'Thank you, Martin. Thank you so much,' Mandy says finally, her diction strangely formal, before she ends the call.

Martin, Bethanie and Baxter celebrate in the beer garden of a pub in Longton. Martin has fish and chips, Baxter has steak, Bethanie has a schnitzel. They share a salad and a bottle of white wine. And then a second bottle, and the necklace is forgotten. Martin loves it, being back in the fold, back with the colleagues, like a sports team celebrating a big win. They've pulled down a screamer, booted a goal after the siren, won the grand final. They've landed the biggest story in Australia and he's gone a long way towards clearing Mandy of murder. It doesn't get much better than this.

'It's like winning the lottery,' says Bethanie. But not even that can dampen Martin's spirits.

Terri Preswell calls. 'It's online now,' she says. 'Excellent work, you three. Outstanding fucking work. Great copy, great photos.' There is exhilaration in her voice, the adrenaline high every journalist knows and covets, the drug that keeps them coming back for more. 'We're running it all over the home page; I've pulled the social media team in to give it maximum exposure.'

'Wow,' says Martin. 'Thanks, Terri. For everything.'

'No problem. But we're not done yet.'

'What are you thinking?'

'I've got the lawyers here. They're worried about when this Topaz woman will be charged.'

'The cops said not until noon at the earliest.'

'You believe them?'

'Sure. They want the story out there.'

'Okay, but it means that we can't hold anything else for Monday's paper—particularly anything about her past, her sister's death in Greece. That may be ruled prejudicial. We need to get it up online before she's charged.'

'Yeah, I get it. I can do a piece focused on Topaz. On her and the swami, paths colliding, something like that. On their pasts.'

'Okay. But concentrate on her. I'm commissioning another piece from a stringer in Athens on Florakis and the deaths in Crete.'

'Makes sense.'

'Good. So the timing is the same as last night. We don't want to put anything else up online yet, but we'll need fresh material for the morning. Write overnight, get it to us as soon as you can. But it has to be here by six tomorrow morning. The lawyers can give it a once over and we'll get it up by around seven, after everyone has seen what we've already got and the competitors are catching up. We'll do another social media storm, make sure the whole country sees it. Then we can close it back down when she's charged.'

Martin agrees and they spend several more minutes working through details of how to coordinate the coverage. And the whole time he's thinking about the implications of Terri Preswell strategising with him—Martin Scarsden, freelancer—and not with Bethanie Glass, the rising star of the *Herald*. It's as if he's never left. Before ending the call, he sows the seed for another follow-up, maybe for Monday's paper: the murder of a local real estate agent, connected to the deaths at Hummingbird, probably killed by the swami. Terri is enthusiastic.

Martin, Bethanie and Baxter find a hotel, check in. Martin and Bethanie get a two-bedroom suite with a separate lounge. Baxter gets a room to himself. They set up their computers and get started while Baxter takes his camera and goes out scouting for pictures, promising to bring back supplies of coffee and snacks.

'Tell no one what we've got,' says Martin.

'Mate,' says Baxter, as if insulted by the suggestion. 'Won't stop me finding out what they know, though.'

'And don't drink too much,' says Bethanie.

'*Moi?*' And he cracks a Baxter grin.

SUNDAY

chapter twenty-five

THE LONGTON DAWN MAY BE SMOOTH AND CALM, THE SKY OUTSIDE THE HOTEL window a luminous gradient between pink and blue, but Martin Scarsden is haggard and jittery, powered by caffeine, nerves and too little sleep. Terri and the lawyers have the story, the designers have his photo of Topaz Throssel sitting forlorn in the waiting room of a railway station, the train about to leave. Her eyes are haunted, staring back at his phone. Baxter wasn't happy when he saw it, immediately recognising the power of the image.

Bethanie is asleep, catching what she can before the day begins. But Martin is restless; he needs to walk. The police have arrested Topaz for the deaths at Hummingbird; the swami almost certainly killed Jasper Speight. Mandy is in the clear. His story is all over the internet, spawning imitations and driving the news cycle. He should be feeling elated, but he doesn't. Some time in the night, some time during the fitful hours, from his stolen sleep and fleeting dreams, something has come to niggle at him. He reaches into his pocket; the necklace is still there. How is it that journalism can be so easy, and life so difficult?

So he walks. A train comes through, a thunderous reminder that life doesn't have a pause button. The rising sun flickers through the trees. Memories come flickering with it: a cricket ball, camping near a beach, an empty bottle of champagne. A beautiful woman in a bookshop in the middle of nowhere. Suddenly he feels very tired, can sense age spreading through his limbs, the irreversible process. He feels vulnerable, exposed to whatever his subconscious may elect to throw up at him.

A car crawls down Longton's main street, as if apologetic about disturbing the new day. Further down the street Martin spies a gaggle of tables and chairs on the footpath. A bakery, here as everywhere, the first business of the day to open. Martin walks towards it, thinking of yet more coffee, maybe breakfast. Bacon and eggs would work, a few moments by himself, to eat, to put his thinking on pause. But when he enters the shop he finds Royce McAlister and Nick Poulos sitting at an inside table, sipping coffee, eyes blank. Nick sees him, gestures for him to join them. Royce looks at him without emotion. Martin orders a coffee at the counter and some breakfast; there is no bacon and eggs, he has to make do with a day-old quiche. He sits at the end of the table, Nick on one side, Royce on the other.

'You okay?' Martin asks Royce.

The young man just shakes his head.

'He's in the clear,' says Nick. 'He knew nothing of it. He was in hospital the whole time. The police have dropped the charges.'

Martin studies Royce's face, still wearing the bruises of the beating Harry the Lad gave him; there is no sign of relief.

'Topaz?' Martin directs the question to Nick.

'She's confessed. She poisoned herself and the guru. She's adamant she intended no harm to anyone else.'

'You believe her?'

'It's kind of academic. One case of murder, six cases of manslaughter. Not a lot I can do for her.'

'You're representing her?'

'For now.'

Martin turns to Royce. 'Did you know? About her past? What happened to her sister?'

Royce shakes his head again. 'None of it.' They're the first words he's spoken. They fall with the weight of truth. The once-vibrant young man is gone, replaced by a husk. A wave of reality has swept over him and he's lost his footing, no longer able to con anyone, himself included. 'All that time, not a word.' He's staring into space, not at Nick or Martin, talking to himself more than to them. 'I thought we were a team, us against the world. I meant it; I guess she didn't.'

'More like she never trusted herself,' says Martin.

'What do you mean?'

'She was running, Royce. Trying to distance herself. It's not your fault.'

'That's easy for you to say.' The pain is clear on his face.

Silence falls upon the table. Martin abandons the quiche; it's stale and close to inedible, its filling exhibiting a suggestion of greyness. Nick gets more coffee for himself and Royce. A truck comes to a standstill outside, air brakes wheezing, engine left idling as the driver, with his greasy hair, tats and a well-tended gut, orders his breakfast: a sausage roll, a sachet of tomato sauce and a bottle of chocolate milk. He pays and leaves. The gears crunch, the truck moves off.

'Royce,' says Martin, 'the other day, Monday, when I gave the two of you a lift, you said you'd come all the way from Sydney on the train. Port Silver was not a random destination.'

Royce says nothing. Nick is alert. Martin might be his client but so too is Royce.

Martin presses on. 'I know why you came. You'd heard of the sex-for-visas fraud that Harry the Lad was running. You thought you could scam him. You had it planned, even before you arrived.'

Royce looks him in the eye, shrugs. 'I'm not admitting to anything.'

'You don't have to.'

'Then you don't have to ask me.'

'And I know you're married. Topaz has an Australian passport; she doesn't need a visa.'

Royce still isn't engaging. 'And?'

'How did you know about the visa scam?'

'Mate, every second backpacker knows about it. And not just here. It's rife. All those river towns out west? There's randy farmers everywhere. Not an organised racket like here, though. We should have stuck to swindling them.'

'So you'd done it before? Scammed farmers?'

Nick interrupts. 'You don't have to answer that.' He turns to Martin. 'Ease up, will you, for Christ's sake.'

Martin looks at Nick, back to Royce, softening his voice. 'Listen, anything you tell Nick is protected by client–lawyer privilege. You know about that, right? The police and the courts can't force him to reveal what you tell him. I'm offering something similar. There's no legal protection, but if you tell me information in confidence, I won't reveal who told me. Journalists protect their sources.'

Royce turns to Nick, who shrugs.

'It was your mate,' says Royce. 'Jasper Speight.'

Martin doesn't move. His mouth hangs open, his next word stillborn, his line of questioning forgotten. 'Jasper Speight?' It's all he can manage.

'He was the one who told us about St Clair.'

'St Clair? How? You've been to Port Silver before?'

'No. We tried scamming Speight in Sydney. We thought he was married—he was wearing a wedding band. But when I walked in on him and Topaz having it off, he just laughed, offered us his former wife's email address and phone number. He saw straight through us.'

'When was this?'

'About a month ago.'

'I don't understand. Why would he tell you about St Clair?'

Royce shrugs. 'He had it in for the guy and that bastard who works for him, Harry the Lad.' Unconsciously Martin lifts his hand, touches his still-bruised eye. Will it ever get better? 'Yeah, sorry about that,' says Royce, but he doesn't look sorry at all.

'So what was the deal with Jasper? He wanted you to con St Clair? Why?'

'Nah, it wasn't like that. He wanted Topaz to film it. Use a concealed camera.'

Martin sees it now. 'Blackmail.'

'I guess,' says Royce. 'We didn't give a shit what it was for. Speight said he'd give us ten grand for a video and the visa paper-work. Sounded like easy money.'

'And when you learnt he was dead—murdered—you still went ahead?'

'Didn't have much choice. We were low on money. Thought we'd just go it alone.'

'Which is why Harry the Lad beat you up.'

'That's right. Told me to shut the fuck up and get out of town.'

'What happened to the video?' asks Nick.

Royce shakes his head. 'There is no video. The Speight dude was going to give us the spy camera when we arrived but, you know, he was gone.'

They sit in silence again. A young man, too slim to have been a baker for long, emerges from the back of the store carrying a tray. 'Hey, mate,' he says to Martin. 'I've got some fresh quiches here if you're interested, straight out of the oven.'

Martin looks at the unfinished specimen on his plate. 'No, thanks,' he says.

Nick turns to him. 'There is one thing. I tried telling you on Friday, after the police quizzed you about the knife, but you ran off in a hurry. It probably doesn't matter now.'

'What is it?'

'You asked me to check with Westpac, to see if anyone had made an approach to buy the cheese factory site. Remember?'

Martin shrugs. 'Yeah. Doesn't seem too important now.'

'Probably not. But there were approaches. Recently.'

'Approaches? Plural?'

'Tyson St Clair.'

'I guess that comes as no surprise.'

'And then Denise Speight. She came in over the top.'

'What does that mean? Over the top?'

'She's signed a memorandum of undertaking to buy the land.'

Martin smiles. 'St Clair won't be happy. I didn't realise she was such a player.'

'I wonder if she'll still want it,' says Nick. 'Now that Jasper has gone.'

———

Outside again and Martin feels worse, regretting the quiche. His mind is still jangling with the unholy mixture of too much caffeine and too little sleep. The world has a washed-out quality to it, grainy and cinematic, the light too bright. He feels troubled by the unexpected link between the grifters and Jasper Speight, and surprised that Denise Speight has convinced Westpac to give her the rights to buy the cheese factory. But none of it's important; perhaps some background colour if he turns it all into a book. Still, it makes him think. Jasper Speight paying Topaz and Royce to film St Clair; Denise Speight gazumping St Clair on the cheese factory. Seems like Jasper and his mother may have been working together to best St Clair. So why was Jasper coming to see Martin with the postcard of St Myron the Wonderworker? Civic duty; wanting Martin to expose the swami as an imposter? Or to eliminate a rival and manipulate Martin? Royce's allegations have shaken Martin's view of his old school friend: honey traps, secret cameras and blackmail. As a teenager, Jasper was at times reckless, at times thoughtless, but never manipulative, never scheming. What had changed? Had his mother changed him, or had the lure of land and money, the whisper of silver, corrupted him? Maybe Jasper was at Hummingbird as a proxy for his mother; maybe the swami was there as a minion for St Clair. Martin recalls St Clair and the swami having coffee together in Longton. So exposing the swami would be in the interest of Jasper and Denise, removing the influence of the holy man and, through him, St Clair. The quiche sits uncomfortably in Martin's stomach, like a piece of lead. Something is wrong.

Denise Speight and Tyson St Clair are competitors, rivals. What had George said at the fish-and-chip shop? That the landholders of Nobb Hill behaved like they were in *Game of Thrones*? St Clair had his plans for the swamp, the cheese factory and the river-front; Jasper had plans to subdivide the clifftops. But Denise had gazumped St Clair on the cheese factory, going direct to Westpac, while her son Jasper had hired Topaz and Royce to film compromising footage of St Clair. What a rat's nest.

Martin checks the time. Still early. But fishermen are always up early. He rings Vern.

'Martin. G'day. Bit early in the day for journos, isn't it?'

'Are you at home, Vern? I need to speak to Josie.'

'No, mate. Already on the boat. I'll text you through her contacts.'

'Thanks.'

'No worries. Great reporting, by the way. Scooped the pool again. But are you okay? You sound anxious.'

'Sure. Fine.'

'Glad to hear it.' His uncle ends the call.

Can he? Hear the anxiety? No matter; his phone vibrates, Josie's contacts arriving. He rings her.

'Hello? Josie here.' Her voice is uncertain, not recognising Martin's number.

'Hi, Josie, it's Martin Scarsden. I hope I haven't woken you.'

She laughs at that. 'Not with this many kids. How can I help?'

'I'm just wondering about the native title claim on Mackenzie's Swamp. Has anyone tried to buy you out? Offer a deal?'

'Why do you want to know?'

'To be honest, I'm not sure. But something's not right.'

'Yeah. We've had some offers just in the last few months, out of the blue. Tyson St Clair and Denise Speight are both after it.'

'Right. Is there a frontrunner?'

'Not at this stage. It's our land. We'd like to keep it ourselves.'

'So there's no chance of you selling?'

There's a short pause, and then there's a sigh. 'It's not as simple as that. There's no guarantee our claim will be successful, and it'll probably take years to determine. This would be money upfront.'

'But you'd lose your land. It'd be turned into a marina and a golf course.'

'Only if St Clair got it.'

'Why? What does Denise Speight want to do with it?'

'Nothing. She says she wants to turn the cheese factory into an eco-resort, but will make sure the wetlands are preserved.'

'That's what she told you?'

'Yeah. She and Jasper.'

'Jasper?'

'That's right. He was always opposed to the golf course. We told you that.'

'So you might sell to Denise?'

'It's possible. If she's still interested, now that Jasper is dead. But it's not up to me. It would have to be a community decision.'

'Thanks, Josie. Thanks a lot.'

'Sure. Any time.'

He sits on the protruding ledge of a shop window. It's covered in dust, blown east from the drought-stricken interior, but he doesn't care. He's trying to remember what Denise Speight told him that morning he spoke with her, the day after her son's murder. He'd thought she was in shock, close to inconsolable. Yet she'd been quick to tell him of Tyson St Clair's plans to develop his marina and golf course, quick to tell him of Jasper's opposition. He had asked her what she wanted to happen to the swamp and she'd replied along the lines that she would like to see it developed, provided the Gooris received fair compensation and the promise of employment. He's sure that's what she said, or words to that effect. She had said nothing of her own interest, though. Why?

His phone rings, startling him. An unidentified caller. Jack Goffing, he presumes. But it's not Goffing.

'Martin? Martin, is that you? It's Wellington Smith.' The voice is assertive, edgy.

'Yeah, it's me,' replies Martin.

'What the fuck, Martin? That's all I have to say: what the fuck?'

This is all he needs. Wellington Smith, publisher of *This Week*, soon-to-be publisher of his true-crime book on the deaths in western New South Wales. Wellington Smith, the man who threw him a journalistic lifeline after the *Sydney Morning Herald* sacked him. 'Wellington, I haven't forgotten you. This story has it all: sex, drugs, murder. There's another book in it. It's a guaranteed bestseller.'

'I know that, Martin. I'm not a complete moron. So why the fuck are you publishing it all over the Fairfax websites? They boned you, remember?'

'I had no choice. The police are going to charge Topaz Throssel by lunchtime. The *Herald* will have to pull it all down. No one will be able to go there until after the trial, including us. Think of it as publicity. And when the case is over, we can have the book ready to go.'

That seems to calm the publisher down. Martin can hear him breathing heavily at the end of the phone, gathering his thoughts. 'So we're good for a magazine feature? And another book?'

'I would think so.'

'Good man, I'll hold you to that. Good man.' And he's gone, hanging up without another word.

The very idea of writing another book exhausts Martin; he longs for sleep. But first he decides to go to the police station to check for updates. He's just started walking when he sees an SUV, a television news car, circling like a shark. It pulls up next to him, tinted window descending.

'Martin fucking Scarsden! What a ball-tearer.' It's Doug Thunkleton, his voice too loud for the morning.

'Doug. Fancy seeing you.'

'Do you know when they're going to formally charge Topaz Throssel?'

'Not until lunchtime or so.'

'Excellent!' says Thunkleton. 'Thanks for that. I've got to go do a live eye. See you round.' The news car starts moving off.

'Doug! Hang on a moment.' The car stops, and Martin walks up to the open window. 'You back on news full-time?'

'Not yet. Might never go back. I'll wrap this up, then get back to the true crime.'

'So you're still going ahead with that?'

'Are you shitting me? It's a cracker. Walkley Award written all over it. You wouldn't believe the stuff we've got. You won't be the only one writing books.'

'Really? That good? That's fantastic. So you've worked out the identity of the killer?'

'Getting close.'

'Just one thing, Doug—it was Tyson St Clair who tipped you off to the story, wasn't it? Not Jasper Speight?'

'Yeah, that's right: St Clair. Why?'

'Nothing. Thanks for that.'

He walks through the slowly waking town, trying to think through the fate of the cheese factory and Mackenzie's Swamp. Tyson St Clair had tipped off Doug Thunkleton about the rumoured whereabouts of Amory Ashton's body, yet Denise Speight has managed to out-manoeuvre him; she'll most likely buy the land from Westpac as soon as Ashton's body is found. Martin is wondering if St Clair knows he's been gazumped.

He arrives at the police station, another fortress of a building, less concrete and more brick than in Port Silver, but imposing nevertheless. Must be in the same marginal seat. The old equation: law + order + pork barrelling = votes. He stands outside looking at it, indecision gripping him. If it holds any answers, it's not revealing them to him.

He's still there when the glass doors glide open and Morris Montifore walks out. The policeman looks like he's had no more sleep than Martin; his face is gaunt, his eyes bleary.

'Morning, Martin. I saw your reports.'

'And?'

Montifore shrugs, his voice deadpan. 'Nice photos. Got my good side for once.' He isn't smiling. Perhaps he's too tired.

'Morris, can I tell you something? I have no idea what it means or whether it's useful or not. I just can't tell you my source.'

Another shrug. 'Sure.' Any exhilaration the policeman may have garnered from the arrest of Topaz Throssel seems long gone.

'Ask Topaz why she and Royce came to Port Silver, if it's connected to Jasper Speight.'

This time Montifore does smile, a wan effort. 'You've been speaking to Royce.'

'I didn't say that.'

'Guess I'll never know then.' The detective grows serious. 'But thanks, Martin. She already told us, but thanks anyway.'

It's Martin's turn to shrug. 'You still not planning to charge her until lunchtime?'

'That's the agreement. That suit you?'

'Yeah. Thanks. We'll have some more stuff up online any moment. The *Herald* has commissioned a stringer to write up all the events from Greece.'

Montifore nods. Having the backstory aired in public will do the prosecution no harm. 'She's made a full confession. I don't think it's going to be much of a trial. The way things are heading, she'll plead guilty.'

'To all seven deaths or just the swami's?'

Montifore sighs. 'You're right. She's admitted to poisoning the swami and herself, that's all. Be sure to make that distinction in anything you write. She's claiming anything else was an accident. Who knows? Maybe we'll have to split the trials.'

'The poison—did she put it in the swami's bowl?'

Montifore shakes his head. 'I can't tell you that.'

'Please, it's important. I won't publish, not until you give me the all-clear.'

Montifore looks beyond caring. 'Okay, absolutely not for publication. She says she put it in the bowl right at the end, when only herself and the guru were left.'

Martin nods. He knows Topaz has no reason to lie; nor does Montifore. 'Will you do a press conference?'

'Yeah. Not that I want to, but Sydney wants it out there. Here, in about an hour, a short on-camera statement, no questions. A doorstop.'

'I might try and get some sleep then. Thanks, Morris.'

'Martin?'

'Yes?'

'You should know: we found the knife. The divers found it in the river yesterday afternoon. It's already in Sydney.'

'I see. Washed clean by the river, I'm guessing.'

The detective sighs. 'More than that. Scrubbed with bleach before it went in.'

'Well, that fucks that then.'

Montifore looks him in the eye. 'I guess so. Although those technical bods, they know their stuff. Amazing what they can come up with when they try.'

'What does that mean?'

'It might be a good idea for you to get down to Port Silver. Be with that girlfriend of yours.'

Martin blinks, the import of the words unmistakable. 'Why? You know who killed Jasper and why. It was Hawananda.'

'No. That's what we thought too. But he couldn't have killed Jasper Speight. He has an alibi.'

'He's dead. How can he have an alibi?'

'On Monday he was leading an intensive. All morning. There were twelve witnesses. Ten of them are still alive.'

Martin just stares. For a long moment he doesn't know what to say. And then he does. 'You've already interviewed Mandy twice. What more could you possibly think you could get from her?'

The detective sighs again, as if the weight of the world is upon him. 'It's the knife. The handle is covered in a brown stain. It's the same colour as her hair.'

Martin is speechless. He remembers the stain upstairs in the townhouse, all around the bathroom basin.

Montifore might look more sympathetic if he didn't look so tired. 'Drive her up here, will you? Get her to walk in by herself. If we have to bring her in, no one wins.'

———

Martin has left his car in Port Silver, so Baxter drives him down the escarpment, passing a steady stream of media heading in the opposite direction, alerted to Montifore's doorstop. The further down the hill they get, the heavier the air becomes, warm and humid, desperately in need of a cleansing sea breeze. Martin tries ringing Mandy and tries again, but she doesn't answer. He calls Winifred Barbicombe. He leaves a voicemail; she calls him back. He explains the knife; she says she'll head up to Longton, that Martin should drive Mandy up.

The knife. It has to be a plant. Clyde Mackie has already discredited the anonymous claim that Mandy threw it in the river at sunset on Tuesday. But does that matter? If the knife has retained forensic evidence, that would trump Mackie. DNA beats everything, the smoking gun of the twenty-first century. But this can't be DNA. The bleach and a couple of days at the bottom of the Argyle would eliminate that. It's just the hair dye. Is that enough to condemn her? His mind, deprived of sleep, is restless and ill-disciplined. Only sleep will sedate it. That and the identity of Jasper Speight's killer.

Baxter drops him at his car, still parked outside the surf club. It has a single parking ticket. Hell, since when did council start charging for parking? He starts the engine, gives it a good revving, the noise from the muffler bouncing back and forth between the yet-to-open stores of The Boulevarde.

At the caravan park, he finds Mandy sitting alone by the river.

'Hi,' he says.

'Hi,' she replies. 'I wondered if you might turn up.' There is no anger in her voice; if anything, it is shaded by something suggestive of regret.

'Where's Liam?'

'Still sleeping.' She holds up a baby monitor.

Martin sits next to her so they are both looking out over the water. 'Sorry, I couldn't get away earlier. We worked most of the night.'

'I know. I saw it online. That woman. Topaz.' There is no rancour in her words, no accusation. 'Seven dead. All to avenge her sister.'

'The swami was her target, the rest were unintentional, six innocents in the wrong place at the wrong time. I don't know their names. Just the swami and McGrath.' For some reason, this bothers him. He still doesn't know their names.

She shakes her head, a line of concern on her forehead. 'It's terrible. Unbelievable.'

Martin reaches into his pocket, retrieves her necklace. 'I found this.'

She looks at it as he pours it into her hand. She says nothing.

'I found it at Hummingbird. In his cabin. McGrath's.'

There's silence. She looks across the water. He waits. Seconds pass as if they are centuries.

Eventually she speaks, voice soft. 'I couldn't tell you. I was too ashamed.'

'What happened?'

'I went up there. I was interested. I heard the beach was beautiful.' She pauses. 'No, it wasn't that. Not just that. I was lonely. Stuck in that townhouse with only Liam for company. Day after day, night after night. I started to think you weren't coming, that you'd stay in Sydney. That you didn't want me.'

'I will always want you,' he says, taking her hand.

But she pulls it away. When she speaks again it's with sadness, not bitterness. 'You came to Riversend with all those grand gestures and big words. All that love. A better man than Byron Swift and all the others. And then you left again to write your book. You didn't even help me move here. The book was always more important to you than me and Liam. I didn't know if you were coming or not.'

'I was always coming. The book's finished. I'm here now.'

'Are you? You weren't here yesterday. The divers were, the police were, the gawkers were. All day yesterday, they were here and you weren't.' There are tears in her eyes. 'You were with the story. She's your real mistress.'

How can he respond to that? It's true, he'd concentrated on the Riversend book to the exclusion of everything else, written it in four weeks flat, seventy thousand words, pushing himself day and night. Wellington Smith had set an impossible deadline and he'd beaten it by five days just so he could get here, get back to her. But how can he say that? She'll just believe he worked nonstop because that's what he loves, his obsession. And in a way he knows that's true.

'He drugged you, Mandy. Garth McGrath drugged you.'

She turns to look at him, recognition in her eyes, but says nothing.

'Just as he drugged me. And Topaz Throssel.'

She still says nothing.

'Can you remember what happened? Or are bits blacked out?'

'How do you know that?' she asks, her voice a whisper.

'It's one of the effects of the drug. Rohypnol. It's what he used. The date rape drug.'

'Jesus,' she says, her eyes greener than the river water. But there is no relief in them. If she feels exonerated, she doesn't look it. Quite the opposite. Instead, she's unable to meet his gaze, appearing even more distressed. 'I was reading the story yesterday, your story, keeping up to date on my laptop. And then the divers arrived. I tried ringing you, but your phone was off. Too busy reporting. So I stood and watched them, Liam and me. Then others came down from up there in dribs and drabs.' She flicks her head towards the permanent residents. 'They watched the divers too. And then they started watching me instead. By the end, none of them were watching the divers; they were only watching me. I couldn't bear it. I took Liam and went driving. Way up Dunes Road, up to Treachery Bay.'

'They found it,' says Martin. 'The divers found it.'

'Found what?'

'The knife.'

She sighs. 'Good. What happens now?'

'It's in Sydney. They're running every possible test they can on it. Blood, DNA. Electron microscopes, the works. I've told Winifred.'

She turns to him. 'It wasn't me, Martin. I didn't do it.'

'I never said you did.'

'You don't have to.'

He doesn't know how to respond to that, so he pushes on, says the words he can't avoid saying. 'Your hair: when did you dye it?'

She looks at him curiously, perplexed by the gravity of his words. 'Sunday night. To surprise you. Why?'

'You did it yourself?'

'Yes.' She's frowning now, unsure of herself. 'What's going on?'

'You did it in the townhouse? Upstairs in the bathroom? The night before Jasper was killed?'

'Yes. Tell me. What is it?'

'The knife. Montifore says the handle has a stain on it.'

She says nothing, not responding, instead turning to look at the water.

'I spoke to the police in Longton. They want to interview you again.'

'I don't have anything to do with that knife. I never saw it, I never touched it.'

'I know. I believe you. I'm just the messenger.'

Another wave of distress moves across her face. 'Is that why you came here? Because the police told you to?'

'No, Mandy. I'm here to be with you, to support you.'

But her mind has leapt ahead. 'The media. Are the reporters there, the photographers? Like in Riversend?'

He hasn't thought of that, but it's true. They'll be staking out the police station, awaiting Montifore's doorstop on the deaths at Hummingbird. 'Yeah, they'll be there. But they don't care about Jasper, they don't care about the knife. All they care about are the deaths of Garth McGrath and the swami. Australia's Jonestown. You're not implicated in that.'

Mandy doesn't move. She's still, her face like wax, perfect, a sculpture. Only the tears animate it, running from first one eye then the other, single tears, her gaze locked on Martin, as if she is struggling to understand what is happening between them.

'I'll call the police,' he says. 'See if we can meet somewhere else. A hotel or something. But if we don't go up there, they might arrest you. Or issue a warrant. Or tip off the media pack. We have no choice; we have to go.'

Still Mandy doesn't move. When at last she speaks, her voice is low, almost a whisper. 'You were gone too long. You should have been here.'

There is something in her words, something low and fatalistic. The tone is not one of accusation, but of something more concerning. 'Mandy?'

And the dam breaks, she is overcome by sobbing, her body moving again, her face racked.

He moves to her, takes her arms. 'Mandy?'

'You weren't here. The story had taken you. I didn't know if you were coming back. I was alone. Afraid.'

And in that moment he fears he is losing her, he can feel it, her and her boy slipping away. But he can find no words to say, no comforting phrase. The writer of a million words, struck dumb.

A cry cuts through the morning, shrill and static-laden. It's the baby monitor, Liam imposing himself upon the stillness, the future attempting to assert its sovereignty over the past.

chapter twenty-six

THEY DRIVE IN SILENCE. THERE IS NOTHING TO SAY. JUST PLENTY TO THINK: UGLY thoughts colonise his mind, toying with his emotions. Mandy is driving; he doesn't even have that to distract him. What had he been thinking of, leaving her, abandoning her, while he wrote his precious book, winning his professional vindication, showing the naysayers even as he was losing her? A memory pierces him: he is in his Sydney flat, words pouring onto the page, and in the moments in between he's thinking of her, relishing his new feelings of love, his knowledge that absence does indeed make the heart grow fonder. How cruel that memory is now, for while his heart had grown fonder, hers had drifted, blown by uncertainty and his apparent indifference. She'd feared he was just one among many, one more thief in the night.

Another thought comes spearing in from some corner of his mind, skewering him. Jasper. His old friend, avid reader of his newspaper reports. He'd seen what was happening: Mandy, the partner of his old friend, beginning to drift, like a raft on the sea. They'd fought at the lifesavers, but why? Jasper seeing an opportunity to move in on Mandy, or angry at her for straying? Martin shakes his head, as if to rid himself of such speculation; these thoughts achieve nothing except torment.

She sits next to him, close enough to touch yet unreachable, inches away yet distant, concentrating on driving, heading towards the high school and the childcare centre, down the palm-lined road. In the back seat, Liam babbles in his capsule, the sound of innocence, proto-words filling the silence. It breaks Martin's heart. When Mandy takes her son into the centre Martin wonders if it will be the last time he will see the boy. He'd like to leap out, to hold him, to breathe in the wondrous smell of him. But when they arrive at the centre, he stays in his seat. If the police detain Mandy, then he'll be the one picking up Liam. He almost wishes that they do hold her, just so he can spend some time with her son, bathe in his goodness, his simple joys, for a little longer. He watches as Mandy carries Liam towards the centre, not the front door but somewhere around the back. Of course, it's Sunday. The owner is babysitting, a private arrangement.

They're almost to the base of the escarpment when her phone rings. She pulls off the road, crossing to the other side, where there's a turn-off to the sugar mill. The same place he picked up Topaz and Royce almost a week ago. By the time she's brought the car to a stop, the call has rung out. She calls the number back; he can hear her side of the conversation.

'I see,' and, 'About twenty minutes,' and, 'Can we meet them somewhere else?' and, 'Why not?' and, finally, 'Yes. Thank you.'

Martin waits a moment, hoping she might volunteer the information, but he's forced to ask: 'Not good news?'

'It was Winifred. The police want to talk at the station.'

'Really. Why?'

'She doesn't know. She'll meet us there.'

Again they fall into silence, their bond seeming more and more tenuous now that Liam is no longer with them. He tries again. 'Mandy, you need to know, I've got your back on this. I'm with you.'

At last she looks across at him. 'Thanks, Martin. Let's hope it's not too late.' But then she is concentrating on the narrow bends of the escarpment, her face troubled and her eyes apprehensive.

———

As they feared, the media are waiting outside the police station. Either his fellow journalists are being diligent, or they don't know what else to do, or they've been tipped off by the police. The floor of his stomach is hollow, eaten out by the thoughts pouring from his mind. *The police want this. They want her photographed. Even after their disgraceful treatment of her in Riversend, they're doubling down.* And then, worst of all: *They must know something.*

'Fuck this,' says Mandy. She drives straight up to the station, turns into the driveway beside it, past the twin signs saying POLICE VEHICLES ONLY PAST THIS POINT. She follows the drive around, pulling to a stop directly outside the back door, under another sign: STRICTLY NO PARKING. She's out of the car, leaving the motor running, keys in the ignition, but the glass door to the station is locked. Then Martin too is out of the car, hitting the intercom button next to the door, hitting it again.

'Who are you?' says a disembodied voice. 'You are not permitted to utilise that entry.'

'It's Martin Scarsden and Mandalay Blonde, here at the express demand of Detective Inspector Morris Montifore. Ms Blonde's lawyer, Winifred Barbicombe, should already be there.'

'One moment, please.' And nothing.

Mandy looks at him. 'They're doing it on purpose. They want me trapped out here.'

Martin hits the intercom button again. 'Open this door now, or we are leaving and it's your responsibility.'

There's no reply.

'Martin! Mandy!'

They turn. It's Baxter. Or not so much Baxter as the lens of his camera, the flare of his flash, rattling off a burst of shots. He lowers the camera, shrugs an apology, communicating that he's only doing his job, even as he's checking the screen on the back of the camera. Then he raises it again, fires off another staccato burst. Martin feels a surge of emotion: anger, frustration, betrayal.

There is the sound of the lock disengaging and the door opens. It's Winifred. 'Inside,' she says, voice calm. Then she looks at Martin. 'Not you, just Mandalay.'

Mandy exchanges a look with him, something of the old communication at last. And then she's gone. The door closes, the electronic lock re-engaging noisily.

'Martin!'

He turns. It's Doug Thunkleton, puffing and out of breath, followed by his camera crew.

Martin is sorely tempted to say something cutting, something sarcastic, to curl his lip and vent his spleen into the camera lens.

Instead he turns and climbs back into the Subaru, ignoring the pleas of Thunkleton to stop and talk. He drives out through the animated gauntlet of photographers and TV crews swarming along the side of the building, hungry for an image, even if they have no idea what it is and what it might mean.

He gets clear of the throng, checking in his rear-view mirror that none of them are desperate enough to tail him. Only when he's sure no one is following does he stop in the shade of a kerbside tree, double-checking he's alone before screaming, unleashing a three-minute torrent of obscenities, yelling until he's spent all his anger, all his frustration. Then he opens the windows, breathes deep. When he's calm again, he readjusts the seat for his longer legs and the mirrors for his greater height. But he doesn't know where to drive. He knows he has to do something, he's just not sure what. He needs to be helping Mandy. Or even chasing a story. Something. Anything.

His phone rings. It's Bethanie. 'Hi, Martin.'

'Bethanie.'

'Baxter showed me the photos.'

'Will you run them?'

There's a pause. At least she pays him that small courtesy, thinking it through before answering. 'Any reason why we shouldn't?'

'You have a story to go with them?'

'Is it connected to Hummingbird?' she asks.

'No. It's the other murder, the one at Mandy's townhouse.'

'Oh, right,' says Bethanie. 'They think the swami did it. Are you still doing that for tomorrow's paper?'

'Probably.' He says nothing about Hawananda's alibi and he says nothing about the knife.

Bethanie hesitates, weighing the newsworthiness of the story. 'You really don't want to expose her to publicity, do you?'

'No. Not after what happened down in the Riverina. Do you blame me?'

'Of course not. But Baxter has filed the pictures independent of me. You know their workflow.'

'Directly to the picture editor. Understood. Thanks, Bethanie.'

'What for?'

'Calling me. For not pushing it to them.'

'Don't thank me yet. We'll see what happens.' She ends the call.

He sits there, wondering what it is he has just done. If Bethanie finds out about the knife, or Hawananda's alibi, she'll know he's misled her. *Christ.* The police are questioning Mandy, the *Herald* has an exclusive photo, and he's done his best to nobble the story. For a moment he considers his career, just how good it felt to be back in harness, working with Bethanie and Baxter, filing their scoop, breaking open the biggest story in the land. And he knows that, no matter how unspoken the ambition, his hopes of re-employment had been kindled. Now he realises he won't be rehired, not when Terri learns of his subterfuge. And then he smiles. In the end, he didn't have to choose between Mandy and the paper; the choice was made for him. He needs to help Mandy, he needs to clear her. Everything else is secondary. He starts the car and gets going. He has to work out what happened at Hummingbird, who killed Jasper Speight and how to win back Mandy's trust. He turns the car around and drives towards Longton Base Hospital.

Jay Jay Hayes is sitting up, staring out her bedside window, eyes unfocused.

'Jay Jay?'

Her eyes regain their focus. She turns her head, looks at Martin. 'Oh. It's you.'

'Are you okay?'

'No.'

'Did you hear? The police arrested Topaz last night. They're charging her with murder.'

'I see.' Her eyes return to whatever space she was regarding when he entered, the news eliciting little response. 'So it was her.'

Martin sits down in the chair beside her bed. 'Swami Hawananda killed her sister. In Crete, eight years ago. An accident.' He recounts the story as best as he can.

Jay Jay shakes her head. 'But why did she have to kill the others?'

Martin takes the opportunity. 'That's what I want to talk to you about, Jay Jay. I'm like you; I can't see why she would want the others dead. She's confessed to the swami, but she denies the rest.'

Jay Jay is frowning. 'You mean she survived? I saw her drink the potion. She was the first to be sick.'

'How do you mean?'

'She started vomiting. Like really badly. That's why I called the ambulance.'

'You're the one who called them?'

'Yes. I was scared. I was suddenly feeling very ill, even though I just drank a token amount. Some of the others seemed fine, dancing and laughing like usual. But something was going wrong.

She was vomiting and then . . .' She closes her eyes for a moment. 'And then Dev collapsed. That never happened before. So I called the ambulance. Then I was spewing myself. I couldn't stop. I must have passed out.'

'She planned to die,' says Martin. 'But she vomited up the poison before it could kill her.'

'What was it?'

'I still don't know. She must have got it when I left her up here on Friday. The police scientists will have worked it out by now.'

'Right.'

'Jay Jay, how did it work? I was there on Thursday night. The swami was doling out drinks from a Coke bottle. Was it the same last Friday, the ceremony at the end of the intensive?'

'No, more formal. He'd ladle the potion out of a ceremonial bowl. The disciples first, then anyone else who wanted some. He made sure no one got more than one cup. It was dressed up as ritual, but it was also a safety thing. Once everyone had some, he would drink a little himself. Then he would tip any remainder into the sand. He was extremely careful about it.'

'I thought it was just alcohol, fruit juices and spices.'

'Yes, it was. Maybe after Greece, he was just being super careful.'

'And that's what happened on Friday, the same as usual?'

Her forehead creases. 'I guess so. I can't be sure. Topaz was heaving up, I was starting to feel ill, Dev collapsed. I ran for the phone.'

'And the swami? He always participated himself?'

'Yes. He said it was a connection with the divine.' She returns to staring out the window. 'The divine,' she whispers. And she just continues to stare, as if she has forgotten Martin is there.

'Jay Jay? Is there something else, something you're not telling me?'

She looks at him. Her face seems calm, almost serene, but there is something deep in her eyes, he sees it now. 'It's back, Martin.'

He says nothing, guessing at her meaning.

'The cancer. It's back.'

Martin still says nothing. What can he say?

'They were running tests, to make sure I was recovering. The blood markers are there. It didn't show up on the X-rays; they're not sensitive enough. I need to go to Sydney. Have an MRI and the rest.'

'I'm sorry, Jay Jay.'

'They searched every inch of my skin, even in my eyes, but they couldn't see anything. It could be a false positive, that's what they say. But I know it's there, it's melanoma. It's come back to kill me.'

Martin blinks. Late-stage melanoma. Until very recently, a death sentence. 'I hear there are new drugs, amazing results.'

'Yes. Perhaps.' She doesn't sound too confident in her luck. 'But I think I deserve it.'

'No one deserves cancer. You know that. It's a lottery,' he says, immediately regretting the analogy.

But she looks unconvinced. 'You wouldn't understand. It sits inside you, eats away at you, stresses you, keeps you awake at night. You can never rest. It wears you out. Leaves you vulnerable.' She stares straight ahead, eyes dry. 'I don't think the drugs will work. Not on me.'

There is a chill sitting on the crown of Martin's head; the follicles on the back of his neck are rising. He's heard this language before, this type of confessional. Not in Australia, but in war zones, in refugee camps, in the aftermath of ethnic cleansing. She's not talking about cancer; she's talking about guilt. 'Jay Jay, what have you done?'

'I'll tell you. I'll tell you everything. Put it in your paper if you like, once I'm gone.'

'You're not going to die.'

'All the better then. Deal?'

Martin nods. He doesn't know what he's agreeing to, but he wants to hear and she needs to tell him. If she's played some part in the Hummingbird deaths, then he needs to know it. 'Deal,' he says.

'Amory Ashton,' she says.

'Ashton? What about him?'

'I killed him. I didn't mean to, but I did.'

Martin is still, the air electric. 'What happened?'

'I had a fight with him, ugly man.'

A memory flashes into Martin's mind: Jay Jay riding the guru in her office, the scar like a red scythe around her buttock, the report in the *Longton Observer*. 'Sharks,' he says.

She nods. 'Sharks. I was attacked. Attacked on my own break. By his fucking sharks.'

'His sharks?'

'Might as well have been. Bull sharks. They'd come into the swamp, attracted by the factory, by the effluent.'

'So you killed him?'

'Not intentionally. I went over there after I got out of hospital. I was so angry. I wasn't the first, did you know that?'

Martin nods. 'The owner at the caravan park.'

'Good. You know. Put that in your paper.'

'I will.'

'It was a beautiful day, close to sunset. Calm, no wind, no chop to spoil the swell. I wanted to get back in, I felt ready. The wound had healed. But I couldn't. I was too scared. Scared of my own break. That's what he'd done to me. I was already thinking of what I might do with the place, thinking of some sort of low-key campground for surfers, a retreat, some yoga and some meditation, but I could hardly have people there if it was shark-infested. So I went to his factory to confront him. The place was empty, the last shift had clocked off, but his car was there, he was there. He was down on the jetty, fishing.'

'What happened?'

'We argued. It was ugly. He was ugly. His words were ugly. He tried to grab me. He had these horrible fat fingers, like sausages, clawing at me. I kicked him as hard as I could, tried to get away. I pushed him, pushed him in. Off the jetty, into the swamp.'

'What? He drowned?'

'Sharks got him.'

Martin doesn't know what to say. An image comes to him, thrashing arms, the water turning red. 'Sounds like self-defence. Why didn't you report it?'

'I should have, I realise that now. But I didn't have any real reason to be there. I thought the police would say it was premeditated, that I went there intending to kill him.'

'So what did you do?'

'I took his fishing gear, put it all in his car and drove it up to Treachery Bay. I torched it then walked back along the beach, in the dark—in the shallows, so there were no footprints. It took two hours.'

Martin doesn't know how to respond. A part of him is excited; it's another riveting revelation to be included in his next book. A separate chapter. But that's the problem: it is separate, unconnected to the deaths at Hummingbird and the murder of Jasper Speight. Unless . . .

'Am I the only person you've told about this?'

'Yes. Pretty much.'

'Did you tell Jasper Speight?'

'Jasper? No. Why would I tell him?'

'Who then?'

Jay Jay looks down, ripples of grief washing over her face. 'Dev. I told Dev.'

Martin sees it now; the relationship between the swami and Jay Jay wasn't casual, it wasn't hedonistic, it wasn't between a guru and his disciple. 'You were close,' he says, stating it as a fact. 'Partners.'

'Yes,' she says. 'Partners. Lovers.' She reaches out, takes Martin's hand. 'I miss him. Already, I miss him. And now to face this, the cancer, alone. I wish he were here.'

'You told him about killing Ashton. Did he ever mention his past? What happened in Crete?'

She doesn't speak, just shakes her head, her hands kneading the hospital blanket.

They sit in silence for a while, then: 'Martin?'

'Yes?'

'Can you drive me home? They can't do much more for me here. I need to get ready for Sydney. I need to pack my stuff.'

chapter twenty-seven

AT HUMMINGBIRD BEACH, THE ROADBLOCK IS GONE FROM THE CATTLE GRID, THE forensics team is gone from the car park, only the limp remains of police tape demonstrate they've been there at all. The site is almost deserted, the car park all but empty, just one old Holden and, off behind some trees, a forlorn BMW, still covered in bird shit. Garth McGrath's. The Holden belongs to the old couple, who have stayed on to keep an eye on the place. They hear the car arrive and come to help, embracing Jay Jay and assisting her down to her home.

Martin says a quiet farewell. They've hardly spoken the entire way from Longton. It's as if Jay Jay has folded in on herself, become elderly overnight. But before he leaves, he tries to ask the question that has been plaguing him for much of the drive. 'Jay Jay, I don't want to distress you, but I've been wondering about Hummingbird. The future.'

'What happens if I die, you mean?' she says matter-of-factly. 'You asked me that once before. I guess I'll have to see Nick Poulos, get a new will drawn up.'

'A new will? You already have one?'

'Of course. I've been sick before.'

'Who was the beneficiary? The swami?'

'That's right.'

'And now?'

She smiles wanly at that. 'Now? I don't know. We'll see.'

———

Back on Dunes Road he drives towards town, past the white cross, familiarity bleeding it of potency, through the tea-tree and mangrove landscape, swamp on the right, forested cliffs to the left, lighthouse afloat in the distance. He forces himself to concentrate, on guard against fatigue and microsleeps. He gets within range and his phone rings, as if on cue. He pulls off to the side of the road.

'Martin? It's Bethanie. Where have you been?'

'Hummingbird. What's happening?'

'They held their doorstop, the doctors and the cops.'

'Anything interesting?'

'Pretty routine. All the remaining victims are out of danger and making good progress. Your mate Montifore confirmed Topaz Marie Throssel as the woman they have arrested and intend to charge. He gave a blanket warning about publishing prejudicial material once charges are laid.'

'Good. He say anything we didn't know already?'

'Not a lot. He only took a few questions.'

'What did he say about Mandy? Anything?'

'Yeah. Thunkleton asked him how she was connected. Montifore was emphatic, saying there was no connection between her and what happened at Hummingbird, that she was helping out with a separate matter. He pretty much killed her as part of the story.'

Martin feels the tension leave him. Montifore hasn't told the media pack of the swami's alibi or about the knife. 'So we don't need to include her in our coverage?'

'It's not as simple as that, Martin.'

The tension returns: Bethanie is a good reporter. Maybe she senses something isn't adding up. 'How do you mean?'

'I told you, Baxter filed his photos of her.'

'And?'

'C'mon, Martin, they're exclusives. No one else got her going in. Plus, she's still a person of considerable public fascination after what happened in Riversend. Plus, the swami killed someone in her house. Plus, she's stunningly good-looking, in case you didn't notice. More like a catwalk model than a police informant. I mean, how the hell *does* she do that?'

Martin sighs. He knows it's no use arguing the toss with Bethanie; it's out of her control. If the editors in Sydney like the image, they'll use it. 'So what's next?'

'I've already filed the doorstop. Meanwhile, I've lined up a one-on-one with one of the victims. The coppers have taken the guard off the hospital. It's an exclusive. We're thinking she might be our breakout piece for the paper if your dead real estate agent story doesn't come together. Baxter was thinking about taking her back out to Hummingbird, photographing her at the scene of the crime. Do you know if we can get access yet?'

'Yeah, the cops have gone. It's a good idea. Once you've done, can you give me her number, just in case I need to follow something up?'

'What is it? What are you chasing?'

'I'm still trying to work out what happened, who was responsible. How it's all linked together. But it's early days. I might have something later in the week.'

There's a long silence on the other end of the phone before Bethanie speaks again. 'I don't follow. What do you mean, who was responsible? Topaz Throssel has confessed. You caught her, for goodness' sake. It was our exclusive, our scoop, all over the website, all over social media. You're not saying you got it wrong, are you?' Martin can hear the trepidation in her voice; after what happened at Riversend, he can't blame her.

'No. She's guilty all right. I meant the other murder, Jasper Speight.'

There's another pause. 'I thought the swami killed him, trying to cover his past. That's what you told me. That's what we told Terri.'

'Yes, but the police think there may be more to it than that.'

'So that's why they've pulled in Mandalay Blonde?'

Martin doesn't know what to say. He realises he's sweating despite the Subaru's air-conditioning. 'I guess so.'

'Jesus, Martin. Terri has Baxter's photo burning a hole in the comps desk, she's riding me to file something to go with it, and now the police are interrogating Mandy Blonde about a murder? And you don't tell me?' Martin can feel the heat of her anger coming through the ether. 'You can't expect me to sit on that.'

Martin breathes deep. 'We don't need to file it for today. We've got the whole Hummingbird aftermath to deal with. You have your interview with one of the victims.'

'No, Martin. No. We have the photo, we have her being questioned in the Longton police station in relation to a murder connected to the swami and possibly seven deaths at Hummingbird Beach. If we sit on it, someone else could get it. What do I tell Terri then? That I knew and didn't say anything?'

'Okay, okay. You're right. Of course you need to file it. But I can't be involved; the conflict of interest is obvious. And if my name is on the by-line, Mandy will never talk to me again.'

'That's fine by me.'

'But do me one favour?'

'What's that?'

'Don't beat it up. I'm positive Mandy is innocent. The police could clear her at any moment. Don't make the same mistake I did down in Riversend and go off half-cocked.'

Another pause. When she speaks, some of the heat has left Bethanie's voice. 'I guess that makes sense. But you realise it's Terri's call.'

'Sure. Just don't over-egg the pudding.'

'Shit, Martin.' He can hear a hint of regret. 'I'm sorry.' And she ends the call.

For a long time, Martin just sits there, parked off the side of Dunes Road. He's done what he can to protect Mandy, but he knows it's not enough. The media pack is in town, hungry for stories. And if the supply from the police dries up, they'll splinter, start chasing their own angles. And a photo of Mandalay Blonde on the *Herald* website will be irresistible, no matter how much

Bethanie plays it down. And once someone has revved it up, the rest will follow, each trying to outdo the other, replaying all the images from out west, the images Mandy has travelled to Port Silver to escape. He needs to act; he needs to help. And the best thing he can do now, the thing that would help her the most, is to find a new story, a bigger story, to drive the news cycle forward, to drive it in another direction, so Mandy is forgotten.

First question: if it wasn't the swami who opened up Jasper Speight with a filleting knife, who the hell was it?

His phone rings. It's Terri Preswell.

'Terri.'

'Martin. Bethanie has taken me through the situation with your girlfriend. I'm going to hold off publishing the photo. For now.'

'That's fantastic. Thank you so much.'

But she cuts him off. 'Don't thank me, Martin. If we don't get anything better, the photo will be the front page tomorrow morning.' And she hangs up.

Shit. It's already gone one. He has five hours until the front page is locked down. And if the *Herald* puts Mandy on the front, the rest of the media will swarm. And before long, one of the reporters is sure to uncover the swami's alibi and learn about the knife. Five hours. He has five hours to save Mandy's reputation; five hours to save their relationship; five hours to save face with Terri Preswell, Bethanie Glass and the *Sydney Morning Herald*. Five hours to find who really killed Jasper Speight. Five hours . . . at most.

But he has no idea what to do.

He's sitting there, trying to think, when a motorbike turns sharply in front of him, heading up the dirt track towards Hartigan's, the rider in black. A motorbike. Again. He remembers Ridge Road:

had Jasper Speight discovered something up there that had put his life at risk? Certainly someone didn't want people accessing the residual road: there was the old gate on the boundary of Bede and Alexander's place secured by a shiny new lock, but with tyre tracks beyond it. At this end, a tree felled, the entry to the track disguised. And down at the caravan park, someone had thrown a filleting knife into the Argyle. What had the park owner said? Trail bikes, riding along the river at all times of day. It's enough. He starts the car and follows. When he gets up towards the gate, there's no sign of the bike or its rider, just the distant squeal of a two-stroke engine and an oily smell hanging in the air. Martin leaves his car, finds the concealed entrance to Ridge Road, and pushes through the bushes, already running.

At first he's almost sprinting, carried by adrenaline and dread, but he soon slows to a jog as his lack of fitness and lack of sleep impose themselves. The path is narrow, carving through the under-growth, following what's left of Ridge Road. Around him the bush is silent, the rainforest expectant; the air is thick, the heat heavy. The track leads up, slanting more and more northwards the closer it gets to the high ground of the cliffs. He stops to catch his breath and thinks he can hear the surf, a distant white noise. He berates himself for rushing off in pursuit of the trail bike. What is he looking for? He runs again, as if trying to outdistance his doubts.

The land starts to slope down and no more than fifteen minutes after leaving the car he reaches a fallen bridge, collapsed into a gully. It must be the one Bede Cromwell mentioned. To one side of the moss-covered timbers, the path leads down into the gully and up the other side. He can see the tyre marks left by the motorbike, where the rider has manoeuvred down into the creek bed and up the other side. The rider must have skill. And guts. Martin scrambles down, pauses at the bottom, close by the pools of water, breathing hard by the trickling stream. He bends, cups some water, drinks. It's cool, clean on his palate. He looks at the flow, trickling out of one pool and into another. It's not flowing inland and down into Mackenzie's Swamp, as he might have expected. Instead, it's flowing the other way, towards the cliffs and the sea. He scrambles up from the gully and recommences jogging.

Only another hundred metres or so further, the track bursts out of the forest into a clearing, a wide circle of dirt. Martin stops, panting. Beyond the clearing he can see where the track continues, no longer a single lane, but twin furrows. He looks at the ground. There are other tyre tracks here, the parallel lines left by a car. The circle of dirt is not just a clearing but a turning circle. This is as far as a car can come after passing through the gate at the far end of the Hartigan block. But there is no car, and there is no motorbike. Christ. The rider must have continued on. Maybe he has a key to the gate. Martin looks at his watch. Four and a half hours to save Mandy from a newspaper lynching and he's stuck in the middle of a rainforest, out of breath, out of ideas, and running out of time. He looks to the heavens, as if seeking divine intervention, and that's when he sees it: the gap in the canopy. To the west side of the track, the trees are thick and obstructing the sun, the undergrowth dense and impenetrable. But to the east, the seaward side, while the undergrowth looks just as solid, there is a gap in the trees, the sky is clear and blue.

Martin investigates the roadside foliage. Now he knows what he's looking for, the path isn't difficult to locate, partially obscured by the shrubbery. He pushes through, and just ten metres in from the road it opens up into a wider track, clearly defined and easy to follow, even as the land begins to fall away. Another ten metres and, pushing through more shrubbery, there's concrete. Concrete, here. A concrete path, just wide enough for a vehicle, cracked and covered by dirt at its edges, with weeds and grass pushing through the lichen-lined cracks. It looks old, decades old, the pebbled surface rough where the cement has eroded over the years. The material reminds him of the gun emplacements from the Second World War still dotted along the coast and preserved as historic monuments. Could this be that old?

The path doesn't run straight down the slope but veers away to the right, at a diagonal, to minimise run-off and to render the gradient less steep, like an off-camber cricket pitch. Thirty metres further and it stops in a wall of vegetation. Martin looks up, finds again the telltale gap in the canopy slanting back down the slope the other way. He checks the wall of plants: sure enough, someone has pushed through the bushes. Martin follows, gaining access to another concrete slab, running across the hill at a complementary angle, the fall of the earth growing steeper. And on the concrete, the dirt tyre marks of the motorbike. He's heading in the right direction.

And when the concrete slab ends after another thirty metres he knows what to look for: the gap in the canopy, the small track at the apex of the angle between this slab and the next one, a third concrete segment, slanting back across the slope at a similar angle to the first section. He hurries on, taking care not to slip, eager to reach the bottom. He can hear the surf clearly now: the track is leading down towards the sea.

He's just starting the fourth slab, when the shrill snarl of the motorbike comes to life. It's coming his way, up the slope. He scrambles off the track into the bush, sharp leaves scratching at his arms and clawing at his face. The bike reaches him in less than a minute, the rider revving down a gear as he slows for the next section of vegetation. And through the leaves, looking on from his vantage point, he sees her, visor up, her face tight with concentration: Lucy May.

Vern's daughter. What is she doing here? The bike squeals away up the hill. Too late to ask her.

Martin moves out from his hiding place, careful to avoid more scratches. Not much more than four hours to deadline. What to do? But he's come this far; he should check out what is at the bottom of the track. Another three sections and the land flattens. The sea is nearby: he can hear it and, when he looks for it, he can see it. *Can you see the sea?* Before him is a narrow path, dirt, its users no longer trying to disguise their route. To his right he can hear water tumbling through the bush: the stream flowing from the broken bridge has picked up speed and volume on the way down. He follows the track, the slope now only slight, even as the two sides of the small valley come together, the stream coming closer. And then he is out of the bush, emerging onto a pebble beach, no more than thirty metres long and five wide, the stream entering the sea just metres to his right. The beach is at the apex of a cove; there are pilings from a long-gone jetty. But that's not what seizes his attention, for pulled up onto the pebble beach is an aluminium runabout, a tinnie, with its outboard tilted up.

'What the fuck do you want?'

Martin swings around. It's Levi, Vern's son, and he's wielding a knife. A filleting knife. A filleting knife with blood on it. He's holding it like a weapon, pointing it at Martin. And in that moment, Martin feels as if he is Jasper Speight, Jasper in the seconds before the attack began, when the options were closing themselves off, with nowhere to run, no way of defending himself. Another flurry of thoughts: the knife that killed Jasper, dropped into the river from the wharf—or from a boat. A wave of horror runs through him, a sense of fate catching up, all his transgressions teaming together to come for him.

'Martin?' says Levi, his voice puzzled. 'Martin? Are you all right?' He lowers the knife.

Martin breathes again, but he's far from relaxed. It's still a filleting knife; it still has blood on it.

'What are you doing here?' asks Levi.

'I followed Lucy May. I saw her bike.' Martin's eyes are still on the knife. 'I was out walking. We're moving to the old house up there on the point.' He's trying to keep his voice conversational.

'Hartigan's?' says Levi, sounding impressed. 'So I heard.'

'Can you put that knife down?'

Levi looks at the blade as if he's forgotten he's holding it. He looks up at Martin, grins. 'Shit. Relax, will you? I'm not about to stab you.'

'Glad to hear it. What are you doing here?'

Levi frowns. 'You don't know?'

'No.' He can hear the sound of the motorbike again, descending the hill. 'She's coming back?'

'Yeah.'

'Why?'

But Levi shakes his head. 'You'll have to ask Vern. He won't be long.'

Vern? 'Okay. I will. But tell me, you come here quite often, don't you?'

'Not really.'

'Have you ever seen Jasper Speight down here?'

Levi seems surprised by the question. 'Yeah. Once. Him and another bloke. Wanted to know if it made sense to rebuild the old pier over there.'

'What other bloke?'

'Harry the Lad. You know, the guy from the backpackers.'

'When was this?'

Levi shrugs. 'Three weeks, maybe a month ago.'

The bike emerges from the bushes and putters along the track, coming to a stop next to them. Lucy May climbs off, lifting her helmet. 'Martin?'

'Lucy May.'

'What are you doing here? Did Vern tell you?'

'Tell me what?'

Lucy May looks at Levi, who shakes his head. 'You'll have to ask Vern.'

chapter twenty-eight

MARTIN ARRIVES HOME TO THE SETTLEMENT LATE, WELL PAST DINNER TIME, closer to midnight. He's a little drunk himself, drunk on goon juice. He's been hanging out with Jasper and Scotty down in the dunes, smoking cigarettes with some girls. Jasper had been trying to chat them up with brazen banter and ham-fisted pick-up lines. They'd giggled at him, as if it was some glorious joke. And it was. But instead of taking it badly, Jasper had played up to their reaction, performing as if on a stage, a stand-up comedian, coming up with more and more ludicrous pick-up lines. 'I have a yacht, you know. With a helicopter.' And they'd all burst into laughter. 'You reckon that could work?' Jasper earnestly seeking the girls' advice, provoking more hilarity.

But now Martin is home, the long walk from the beach to C Street helping him sober up. Not that he cares if he's drunk; he knows his father won't. Martin opens the door and the first thing

490

he does is sniff, knowing there is a fair chance that his father will be a mess, comatose and soiled, spread out on his recliner like a dying whale. But there is no smell, nothing unusually offensive, just the background stench of poverty. And there is no snoring. Martin turns on the lights, but there is no light, no power. He looks back out the door, sees lights in one or two other houses, the electronic rainbow of a television through a window, knows that this is not a blackout, just another unpaid electricity bill. Again. Where the fuck is his father?

He edges through the darkened room, using his disposable lighter, shuffling his way to his room, fumbling in the dark, the drunkenness testing him, until he finds the torch lying beside his bed. From the last time this happened. He flicks it on, goes searching for his parent. Not in his bedroom, not passed out in the bathroom, not in the recliner. Somewhere in the distance he can hear a siren. He sweeps the torch around the lounge, picking up the usual detritus. A pizza box, week-old newspapers, empty packets of potato chips. And then he sees it, lying on its side, cork gone, empty. The champagne bottle, dark glass glittering in the torch light.

Martin sinks to the floor, disbelieving. The Veuve Clicquot, his talisman, the symbol of his future, the last remaining vestige of that day playing backyard cricket when the sun had shone and fate had smiled, the last vestige of his family as it had been.

And now the old fuck has drained it. Not even put it in the fridge, not even chilled it. Martin scans the room, finds what he's looking for: a takeaway coffee cup. He examines it, a ring of coffee still evident; sniffs at it, can smell the champagne. The pathetic loser hadn't even rustled up a glass. Warm champagne from a dirty paper cup. Martin wants to cry, but the tears won't come; they won't return, just as they've never returned, not since that day when he was eight, the day he crossed the border between *before* and *after*, the day he stopped being a child and started to become something else. He's had no tears; he's only had determination. And now he has to leave, leave immediately. Because this is worse, worse than his father's squalor, worse than him pissing himself, worse than him shagging Hester the slapper. None of that compares to this, this desecration of the champagne, this pillaging of hope. Martin gets to his feet. He will pack now, he will leave. He should have done it months ago. His torch starts to flicker. He doesn't care, he'll pack in the dark if he has to. But before he can get back to his bedroom, the police arrive. It's Clyde Mackie. The policeman has brought his uncle with him, his uncle Vern.

Vern.

———

Martin opens his eyes. For a moment the fatigue had won; his eyes had closed and his mind drifted towards sleep and into memory, the past lurking beneath the surface of consciousness. He forces his eyelids wide, as if to flood his mind with light, like opening the blinds of a teenager's room. He looks around. He's back at the turning circle on the remnants of Ridge Road, surrounded by rainforest, sitting on a plastic bin of fish bits. Levi has gone, taking the boat back out to sea; Lucy May has gone, riding her bike back through the bush. He looks at his watch: three and a half hours to go. Where is Vern?

More minutes pass before he hears it: the sound of Vern's tradesman's truck. A few minutes more and it emerges from the trees and arrives at the turning circle.

'Martin? What are you doing here?'

'I've got your catch. The kids left it with me. It's just there, behind the bushes.'

'You know?'

'No. Only that there's fish in the tubs, but not why you're landing it here instead of the harbour.'

'Right,' says Vern, sounding unperturbed. 'Give us a hand, will you?'

The men lift the two tubs, one each, and place them on the ground behind the truck. They're small; small enough to mount on the back of a dirt bike.

'You want a gander?' asks Vern.

'I would.'

Vern removes the lid from the tubs. In the first are flaps of grey flesh of various sizes, bloody along one edge, sitting on a bed of ice, and in the other something grey and pink and slimy, also on ice.

'They look like fins. Shark? And what's that other thing?'

'Yeah, shark fins. And a shark's liver.'

Martin shakes his head. 'I don't get it. Why go to all this trouble? Shark fin isn't illegal. I've had it in Chinatown.'

'Not this shark fin,' Vern says softly. 'I'll tell you on the way.'

Vern opens the back of the tray on the truck, pulls off a bundle of fish net and climbs up. He opens one of two large stainless-steel lockers that run the length of the tray, one on each side, a typical tradesman's setup. 'Pass 'em up,' he says. Martin does, then watches as Vern lowers them into a purpose-built cavity and closes the locker. His uncle jumps down and they throw the fish nets back. 'Let's go. I'll drop you at Hartigan's.'

Vern has turned the truck around, got it bouncing along the track towards Bede Cromwell's and Sergi's, before he speaks. 'The fins. A great white.'

'A great white shark? Seriously? How do you even catch one of those?'

'With difficulty.'

'They're protected, aren't they?'

'Highly. Wouldn't want to get busted. Massive fine.'

'There's a market for that? Contraband shark fin?'

'Yeah. Top dollar.'

'Does it taste any different?'

'Fucked if I know.'

Martin checks his watch. Just over three hours to go and his uncle is poaching great white sharks. 'So you catch it out at sea, take the fins and whatever else you want, chuck the rest back in. Then, when you're heading back, Levi runs it into the cove, just in case there are fisheries inspectors at the harbour.'

'You got it.'

They get to the gate that separates Hartigan's from Bede and Alexander's. Vern gives him the key. Martin opens the gate and waits for the truck to pass through before relocking it, all the while thinking of the shark fins. It doesn't seem to add up, not to Martin. All the effort, all the risk. And a great white? You could spend days trying to catch one of those; they're not exactly common.

Back in the cabin, he quizzes his uncle. 'What's it for? The shark fins?'

'It's no big deal,' says Vern. 'We only do it now and then. Some extra cash. Handy now the commercial fishery has closed down. Especially in winter, when the tourists aren't around.'

'Where does it go?'

'Sydney. Truck comes through Longton from up north. All arranged in advance.'

'Just shark?'

'Shit no. We got lucky with that. All sorts of seafood, provided it's illegal. That's the rule: it's gotta be prohibited. You know, protected species. The more endangered, the higher the price. You'd be surprised, we get all sorts of tropical fish coming down in the currents this time of year, flushed out of the Barrier Reef. Turtles too, some big ones.'

'Shit, Vern. Turtles?'

'Yeah. I don't feel so good about that, but I could kill sharks all day long. I hate the buggers.'

'So who buys it? Who eats it?'

'Don't know. Don't want to know. It's some gourmet thing. Rich dicks getting off on flouting the law. I've seen inside the back of the truck. They have all kinds of weird shit. Protected and endangered, mostly game. Crocs, that sort of thing, but only if they're wild. I saw a couple of koalas once.'

'They eat koalas?' An image comes to Martin: a skinned koala turning on a spit, gumleaf still in its mouth. 'And they order this stuff in advance?'

'Yeah. I get a call, maybe a week's notice. Say they've got something coming up, that they'll be passing through on such and such a date. There's kind of a wish list, a longstanding one. If we get anything on the list, they'll take it.'

'How often?'

'Every month or two. If I get something in the nets in between times, I stick it in the freezer at home.'

'Cripes. How long has this been going on?'

His uncle looks across at him, studying his face, before turning his eyes back to the road. He takes a deep breath. 'Why do you think your dad was always driving up and down to Longton?'

They sit in silence after that as Vern negotiates his truck along Ridge Road. All those trips up the escarpment when he was a kid. *Can you see the sea?* Of course, there must have been some purpose to them; they can't just have been joy riding. He'd never thought about it. So, all the time, his father was transporting an illegal catch up to Longton in his Morris van. And Martin? Did he take him for company, because he liked having him along, or was he part of the ruse? A cover? A father and his boy: who could suspect them of any wrongdoing? *Sea the sea, get home free.*

Vern has driven through Sergi's farm and back into the bush-land of Jay Jay's block. They're almost to the entry to the walking path, the one to the point or, alternatively, down past the swami's retreat into Hummingbird. Three hours to deadline. 'Jasper Speight knew about the poaching,' says Martin, more of a statement than a question.

'Jasper? Who told you that?'

'Levi and Lucy May. Said Jasper and Harry Drake Junior were checking out your smuggler's cove. Talking about rebuilding the jetty down there.'

'Yeah, but they were interested in property, not fishing.'

Martin returns to his thoughts. Jasper Speight and Harry the Lad together, discussing the possibility of rebuilding the jetty at the cove. Jasper and Harry together. It seems an incongruous combination. He remembers what Susan Speight told him: Jasper was firmly under the thumb of his mother Denise. Harry, on the other hand, worked for Tyson St Clair, managing the Sperm Cove Backpackers and overseeing the sex-for-visa fraud. Denise Speight and Tyson St Clair are fierce rivals, yet here were their two lieutenants, Jasper and Harry, collaborating. On what? Rebuilding the jetty? But why? Jasper had plans to redevelop Ridge Road, subdivide the land up along the cliffs. Perhaps some sort of anchorage would be attractive to potential buyers.

But what could Harry the Lad offer? Martin remembers that Tyson St Clair thought Jasper's subdivision was a good plan, but that Jasper lacked capital. If Jasper needed money, the small-time drug dealer was hardly likely to have the millions required. Maybe his father did, Harrold Drake Senior. Maybe the son was there as his representative, just as Jasper was a proxy for his mother. Maybe Denise had been misleading Martin when she spoke to him, just as she'd been unforthcoming about her interest in the swamp and the cheese factory. Maybe Denise and Harrold Drake were in it together.

And that's when he sees it, like a message from the heavens. Vern has reached the bottom of the hill, where Ridge Road meets the fork from Hummingbird. And there it is, the sign—a sign: DIVINE MEDITATION FOUNDATION, painted in brown with its mystic insignia, the circle containing dots. The sign. Harry the Lad and fish poaching is washed from his mind, flushed away by new thoughts, new connections, as facts collide and theories collude. The swami. Of course. Revelation. Revelation upon revelation. Vern turns onto Dunes Road and Martin lets out an involuntary whoop.

'You all right?' asks Vern.

'Just maybe,' says Martin, grinning. 'Just maybe I am.'

The first thing he does after Vern drops him at Mandy's car, up by the gate on Hartigan's drive, is ring Nick Poulos. For once, his lawyer answers straight away. 'Martin. I've been trying to get hold of you. Where are you?'

'Near Hartigan's. Why? What's happened?'

'They're bringing Mandy back down to Port Silver. They want to take her back through the townhouse, later today or tomorrow, re-enact the day of the murder. They may want you to go through your arrival.'

'Who told you that?'

'Winifred.'

'Fuck. Okay. Let's meet at the police station.'

'You got it.'

'But first, Nick, can you check something out for me? Swami Hawananda ran something called the Divine Meditation Foundation. Can you find out if it has any sort of company structure?'

'What are you looking for?'

'Did the foundation die with him, or does it survive him? And who else is involved?'

'Right. I'm on to it.'

———

The Port Silver police station is as unwelcoming as ever, its harsh fluorescent lighting, unnecessary during daylight hours, a deterrence to anyone who doesn't need to be there. But Martin does; he badly needs to be here. There is an ambulance officer at the counter making small talk with one of the constables, the man, Johnson Pear's beefy young offsider.

'Excuse me,' says Martin, interrupting. 'I need to talk with Detective Inspector Montifore, please. It's urgent.'

The constable looks at him sceptically. 'Okay. Please take a seat.'

Martin does what he's told, checking his phone for calls or messages, but there's nothing new, nothing to distract him.

'Scarsden.'

He looks up, but it's not Montifore or even Ivan Lucic. It's Pear. Martin stands. 'I need to talk to Morris Montifore.'

The sergeant smiles maliciously. 'He's not here. On your way.'

'This is serious.'

'It is,' says Pear, his smile undimmed. 'Move on, please, sir. That's a lawful instruction.'

Anger swells in Martin: he's about to say something sharp, something deplorable, but he can't risk arrest, not now, not with Mandy back in the investigators' sights. So he smiles, a reflection of Pear's own insincerity. 'Thank you for your assistance, Sergeant.' And he turns to the ambulance officer and the constable. 'And to you two. Have a good day.' And he departs before Pear can react.

Outside he calls Montifore, but the policeman doesn't pick up. He leaves a voicemail message, then repeats it in a text. *Need to speak urgently. I'm outside PS police.* He doesn't bother calling Winifred, moving straight to text. *Urgent. Need to see Montifore. I'm outside PS police.*

She replies immediately. *On our way from Longton. 10 mins.*

He sends a thumbs-up emoji. Pear wasn't lying; Martin's beaten them here. He looks at his watch. Two-and-a-half hours to dead-line. He considers ringing Nick back, but the lawyer has work to do. He has no choice; he needs to stay where he is. The feeling is a familiar one, the 'hurry up and wait' rhythm of a journalist's day, waiting for things to happen, for press conferences and interviews and announcements and verdicts, and then rushing to make deadline.

He stops pacing, sits, lowering himself onto the concrete steps of Port Silver police station. It's Sunday afternoon, the sun is starting to tilt westwards. The Boulevarde is quiet. Summer's tourists have long gone, returned to the city, to schools and offices and factories. The season is fading. He watches as a young couple sidle down the footpath, arms around each other, veering gently back and forth as they progress, as if they have had too much to drink. Or smoke. The shadows from the police station are beginning their creep across The Boulevarde, but it will be a few hours yet before they reach Theo's fish-and-chip shop. He watches as a dishevelled bloke in a flannel shirt and work boots emerges from the takeaway carrying the white paper bags of an afternoon snack. The smell comes wafting to him: fish and chips. He's too far away for the aroma to be real but his mouth waters nevertheless. What has he had to eat today? A mouthful of stale quiche. What else? He looks longingly across at Theo's, but Mandy, Montifore and Winifred will be here any minute.

Martin realises he's licking his fingers, as if finishing a piece of battered flathead. By God, but he's hungry. Just as he's reconsidering a lightning trip to Theo's, the convoy arrives from Longton. First comes a police car, fully kitted out, driven by a uniformed officer. Martin catches a glimpse of Mandy seated in the back next to another officer. She doesn't see him as the car drives down into the underground car park. Next comes an unmarked car, probably a rental, Lucic driving with Montifore in the passenger seat.

It follows the first car into the basement, the steel gate rolling closed behind them. Only then does the final car appear: Nick Poulos driving his old wagon, with squeaky brakes and a strange list. It comes to a halt next to him. Winifred Barbicombe climbs out from the passenger side, as composed as ever, as if she's disembarking from a Bentley.

'Martin, what have you got for us?'

'We need to see Montifore. I think he's wrong about the knife.'

'All right. But tread carefully. He's getting frustrated.'

'Why? What's happened?'

'Hummingbird is getting complicated. And he's struggling to build the case against Mandy.'

Inside the station, Winifred walks directly to the steel-plated security door with its number-pad lock and demands access from the constable behind the counter.

'I'm sorry, ma'am,' he says. 'I am not authorised to allow civilians entry.'

'I am not a civilian and I am not a ma'am; I am a solicitor and an officer of the court,' states Winifred, voice imperious. 'My client is being detained in there. If you deny me access, you are defying the law. The law. You hear me?'

The young officer looks nonplussed, eyes wide. 'I'll have to check with my sergeant.'

'You do that,' says Winifred. 'And be quick about it.'

A few minutes later, the security door opens. It's Johnson Pear. He looks at Martin. 'I gave you a lawful instruction to leave. Get out or I'll arrest you.'

'Poppycock,' says Winifred. 'I'm coming in to see Morris Montifore, and Mr Scarsden is coming with me.'

Pear just smiles, unmoved. 'You can fuck off as well then, you old shrew.'

Winifred says nothing. Instead she steps forward slowly, deliberately—one step, two steps, three steps—until she is mere centimetres from Pear's face. His smile begins to waver under her gaze.

The security door opens. It's Morris Montifore, who immediately assesses the situation. 'Winifred. Martin. Thanks for coming in so promptly. I appreciate it. Come through.'

For a moment, nothing happens. Pear doesn't move; Winifred continues to stare him down. Then the policeman steps aside, and first Winifred, then Martin walk through the security door. Martin can't resist: he gives Pear a wink as he passes. Morris Montifore brings up the rear.

'Thanks for that,' says Martin, once they've gained the sanctuary of the detective's makeshift operations room.

Montifore slumps into a chair at a desk, not interested in small talk. 'Tell me what you have,' he says.

'The knife,' says Martin. 'The stain on the handle. That's the only substantive link with Mandy, right?'

'I'm listening.'

'Have you established the stain did come from her hair dye? Is it beyond doubt?'

'Forensics are pretty sure. But they're still working on it.'

'You said it was scrubbed with bleach and then spent a couple of days at the bottom of a river. How can they be sure?'

Montifore shakes his head, looking tired. 'I'm not the one you need to convince. Forensics will determine if it's a match one way or the other, not me.'

'I think the dye is from the swami. He used a brown dye to mark the foreheads of his devotees. Their bindis. It was red-brown, a henna, something like that. The dye was kept either in his cabin or his retreat.'

The detective frowns. 'I already told you. The swami, Myron Florakis, whatever you want to call him, he had an alibi.'

'And so does Mandy. Clyde Mackie swears she wasn't on the wharf at sunset on Tuesday,' says Martin.

'What's your point?'

'Jay Jay Hayes was the swami's lover. She says in the days leading up to his death, he complained that someone had been going through his things.'

'Yes, probably Jasper Speight. We thought that postcard was from his own collection, now we think he may have found it in the suitcase.'

'Don't you see? Whoever killed Jasper initially planned to frame the swami, so they smeared the knife handle with the dye from his cabin. They were probably intending to plant the knife on him, or somewhere close. But then they learnt that he had an alibi, so they decided to frame Mandy instead. They scrubbed the knife, then they dumped it in the river and made their anonymous call.'

Montifore laughs out loud, a sudden release of tension. 'That's preposterous. You're saying they knew the stains on the handle would match Mandy's hair colouring?'

'No. I'm saying it's a coincidence. They tried to scrub them off, bleach them off.'

Montifore says nothing more, but looks sceptical.

Martin persists. 'You said it yourself. We can debate the matter all we like, but it's the experts who can tell for sure. All I'm asking is that they compare the stain with any dyes found in the swami's cabins.'

It's Winifred who breaks the impasse. 'Let me make an observation, if I may, Detective Inspector. If you charge Mandalay and take her to trial, we will make an issue of this. If you don't test the dyes used by the swami, the jury will hear all about it. We will sow doubt in their minds: reasonable doubt.'

Montifore looks at her for a moment, face impassive, then sighs. 'All right. It's Monday tomorrow. We'll check it out.'

Winifred bristles. 'You cannot detain her overnight. Not without charging her.'

'And there's another issue,' adds Martin. 'The *Herald* is preparing to splash her photo all over the front page and report that you're questioning her for murder. That won't look so good if forensics exonerate her later the same day. And it won't look so good if it's reported you were informed in advance about the swami's dye.'

Now Montifore's eyes flash with irritation. He stands, pacing, thinking it through before speaking. 'Okay, have it your way,' he says. He picks up his mobile, makes the call. 'Yes, it's me. Yes, I know it's Sunday. Tell me: is the evidence from the Jasper Speight crime scene and from the Hummingbird Beach scene being tested by the same teams?'

A pause as Montifore waits for the answer.

'Understood. Collected by one team up here, but testing by separate teams in Sydney.'

The detective pauses again.

'No. No problem at all. But I need you to test something for me. Can you cross-reference the dye or stain found on the handle of the knife in the Jasper Speight case with any suspect dyes or stains or other substances found at Hummingbird Beach, particularly anything found in either of the cabins used by the dead swami?'

Montifore listens. As he does so, he turns to Martin, raising his eyebrows, signalling some interesting development.

'Really? There now? Yes, of course. If they can get back as soon as possible that would be most useful . . . An hour? Really? That's outstanding.'

The call ends, and Montifore addresses Martin and Winifred, irritation forgotten. 'That's good. A team member is working today. There's some analytical machine they've got, it's in high demand, in use twenty-four seven. They're using it right now. They can get back to us within an hour. They've finished establishing a profile of the stain on the knife. That's the tricky one; they had so little to work with. It's taken a couple of days. But comparing it to substances in pots or jars or whatever is a simple scan, almost instantaneous.'

'Brilliant,' says Martin.

Montifore offers a weak facsimile of a smile. The anger seems to have drained out of him. 'Thanks for coming in. I doubt you're right, but better to check and make sure.'

'Tell me,' says Martin, 'the Hummingbird deaths. You've charged Topaz Throssel?'

'This afternoon. She's been packed off to Sydney. That's why we've moved back down here, to concentrate on the Speight investigation.'

'So Hummingbird is wrapped up? You're charging her with all seven deaths?'

Montifore stands still, his face again unreadable. 'We're working our way through the evidence. There's a lot to process.'

'What did the blood tests show?' asks Martin.

'What do you mean?'

'Remember? I told you about the Rohypnol, the tests Topaz and I gave at the hospital on Friday morning.'

'What about them?'

Martin pauses for a moment. Montifore has grown defensive. 'Was it there again on Friday night? With the poison?' The detective averts his gaze, slumps back into his chair. Martin and Winifred exchange a glance. She's sensing it too, thinks Martin. Something is troubling the detective. 'Morris?'

'Yes. At least three people. The swami, a middle-aged man, a young woman. There may have been others, but we only tested the dead and hospitalised.'

'The young woman. Pretty? Looks Polynesian?'

Montifore looks up, making eye contact once again. 'Yes. That's her. How did you know that?'

'Garth McGrath,' says Martin. He explains his theory that the soapie star had been drugging victims, together with any men who may have been rivals or protectors.

'What happened to them?' asks Winifred. 'The girl and the man?'

'The girl survived, the man's dead,' says Montifore.

'Shit,' says Martin, remembering the body laid out in the dark next to McGrath and Hawananda. 'So he drank Rohypnol and the poison.' He states it as a fact, but Montifore has again broken eye contact and is examining his desk. Martin and Winifred trade another glance, the lawyer frowning.

'What is it, Morris? What aren't you telling us?' asks Martin. The detective keeps his eyes shut, lowers his head and shakes it. Martin persists. 'Something's wrong, isn't it? With the evidence. Is it the case against Topaz?'

Montifore looks up, eyes now open, almost pleading, as if he wants to share information but knows that he can't.

'You think she had an accomplice,' says Winifred, half assertion, half question.

This time the policeman answers, his voice a whisper. 'It's possible. We don't know.'

'Is it something about the blood tests?' asks Martin.

Montifore is studying his hands.

'Jesus,' says Martin. 'There was more than one poison, wasn't there?' The policeman looks at him, a tortured expression on his face. To Martin, it feels like confirmation, so he continues to press. 'Two poisons. Some swallowed both, some swallowed one, some didn't swallow any. Plus the Rohypnol. And Topaz is only admitting to administering one of them.'

Montifore is completely still, his eyes focused, his voice low. 'We can't work out what happened, the chain of events.'

chapter twenty-nine

NICK POULOS IS WAITING OUTSIDE THE POLICE STATION. HE'S SMILING. MARTIN wants to know why, but first he texts Terri Preswell and Bethanie Glass. *Police running new forensics. Mandy's guilt/innocence established within next hour.* He checks his watch. It's just gone four, still plenty of time: they can swap out the front page up until six, maybe six-thirty.

He turns to his grinning lawyer. 'What have you got?'

'The Divine Meditation Foundation. It's incorporated.'

'A company?'

'That's right. So it survives the death of Hawananda. Or Florakis. Whatever you want to call him.'

'Are there any other shareholders?'

'I'm trying to find out. It's Sunday and it's a private company, so it's not straightforward. But the ASIC website lists the office bearers. Hawananda is listed as chairman and managing director,

Harrold Drake Senior is company secretary and Harrold Drake Junior is a director.'

'The Drakes? Both of them?'

'Yes. If Hawananda just wanted a company, then he could easily be a sole director and single shareholder.'

'So why have them as directors?'

'My guess is he was chasing tax-free status, as a charity or a religion or something. He'd need a more impressive structure to qualify.'

'Is the foundation registered as a charity?'

'Not that I can see, but maybe that was the intention.'

'Jay Jay Hayes told me the other day she was going to see you about writing a new will. Did you prepare her last one for her?'

'Jay Jay? No. Not me.'

'She said the beneficiary of her existing will is the Divine Meditation Foundation.'

The two men stare at each other for a moment, the implications growing. It's Martin who spells it out. 'Harrold Drake prepared a will for Jay Jay Hayes some time ago, bequeathing her estate, including Hummingbird Beach, to Swami Dev Hawananda—or, more precisely, to the Divine Meditation Foundation—of which Drake himself is the company secretary and his son is a director.'

Nick Poulos nods. 'Let's tell the cops.'

Martin is tempted, but shakes his head. He wants Montifore focused on the knife stain. 'Not yet. I don't want them distracted. See if you can nail down any more information about the foundation, especially its share structure.'

'What are you going to do?'

'Go visiting.'

The lighthouse sits atop Nobb Hill, catching the afternoon sun, a beacon glowing white, almost silver against the clarity of the sky. Silver. Martin climbs, the footpath sinuous beside the road, the wealth and status of the homes rising with the elevation. Silver. He again hears the insinuation: that the death of Jasper Speight is somehow connected to money, to greed, to avarice. To silver. And at Hummingbird Beach, Topaz Throssel killed Dev Hawananda, and Garth McGrath killed no one. Someone else is involved. There is another killer. What motivated them? Silver, whispers the lighthouse. Find the silver. And the people with the most silver are Tyson St Clair, Denise Speight and George Tomakis's mother. Martin doesn't think the Greek widow could know much; she's shown no interest in developments north of the Argyle. Tyson St Clair and Denise Speight, on the other hand, are up to their necks in it. Them and their proxies: Jasper Speight, Dev Hawananda and Harry the Lad. Silver, whispers the siren song of the lighthouse. 'Silver,' says Martin to himself.

Denise Speight's house is perched on the far side of Nobb Hill, past the lighthouse. Martin stands under her portico regaining his breath and absorbing the view. He's sweating in the heat, the day still without a breeze, the bandages on his knee and elbow itching mercilessly. Five Mile Beach stretches into the distance, the ocean to the left, coastal scrub and cane fields to the right, the homes of Port Silver's middle class below. The lowering sun is beginning to give the panorama definition. Out to sea, storm clouds are gathering on the horizon. It's an impressive vista, stunning. Martin turns his back on it and pulls on an elaborate cord of metal and leather, setting chimes going deep inside the three-storey edifice. It takes some time for Denise to answer the door. She seems smaller, reduced, dressed in black and dwarfed by circumstances and the dimensions of her own home. 'Martin? Is that you? Come in.'

They stand in her hall for an awkward moment and then, almost as an afterthought, she ushers him into the living room. It's as large as St Clair's, but more opulent. And more cluttered: there are richly embroidered rugs overlapping on the parquetry floor, too many for the available space; cherry wood cabinets line the walls and chesterfields are arranged in three groups, two of a green leather so dark it's almost black, the other stained a deep burgundy. The walls are a battlefield, as a mishmash of artwork fights for space: Russian icons, glinting with gold leaf; tapestries faded enough to be medieval; what could be an original Georges Braque in an antique gilt frame; fading QANTAS posters; bark paintings from the Top End; and some family portraits. She leads him to the main group of chesterfields, surrounding a coffee table large enough to accommodate ten, its glass surface revealing an intricately carved scene, the meticulous work of Balinese artisans. There's a fireplace, scrubbed clean, flanked on one side by a ceramic vase, blue and white and ancient, a metre and a half tall, and on the other by a rather tatty-looking sarcophagus. If St Clair's house whispers money, this shouts it; if St Clair's is minimalist, this is maximalist; if St Clair's is modern, this is dated. Martin concludes St Clair has an interior designer, but Denise Speight self-curates.

'Martin. What is it?' She sits opposite him, small within the chesterfield, as if pushed down by an unseen weight.

Martin sits. 'You asked me to find out who killed Jasper. I might be getting close.'

This brings no joy to Denise Speight; her face remains bleak. 'I heard they had arrested that woman of yours, Mandalay Blonde. That they're questioning her now.'

Martin keeps his voice conciliatory as he replies. 'No, they haven't arrested her. It's true, she has been questioned, but it's likely she'll be released shortly.'

Denise looks away, staring at a photo mounted to one side of the mantelpiece: her and Jasper, the boy a smiling teenager, teeth clad in braces. When she turns back to Martin, her eyes, already red, are moist. 'I just want to bury him, Martin. They still aren't releasing his body.'

'I'm sure it can't be much longer,' says Martin, wincing at his platitude.

'I thought the swami did it,' she said. 'I read your stories. It seemed straightforward. Jasper uncovered his squalid secret, and he killed Jasper to keep it buried.'

'We all thought that. But it can't have been him. He was at Hummingbird Beach when Jasper died.'

'I see,' she says. 'So how can I help?'

'You know Jasper had plans to develop up along Ridge Road? To subdivide?'

'I did know that, yes. But it wasn't feasible. We didn't have that sort of money. Maybe some time in the future, but certainly not now.'

'Is that because you are so deeply committed elsewhere north of the Argyle? I know you have entered into an undertaking to buy the cheese factory site, as well as making an offer to the Gooris to purchase the rest of the land around Mackenzie's Swamp.' Martin sees something flash in Denise Speight's eyes. She isn't happy he knows this. And there's something else there, too: defiance or anger or maybe pride. He can't be sure.

'What does that have to do with Jasper's death?'

'Could he have persisted with the plans to develop Ridge Road without your knowledge?'

'No. He wouldn't dare do that without my consent. Absolutely not.'

'So when did he drop the proposal?'

'Does it matter? Three months ago. When we learnt of the opportunity to invest in Crystal Lagoon.'

'Crystal Lagoon? That's your rebranding, isn't it?'

'As I say, what does it matter?' The grieving mother is becoming more defensive by the second; there's a suggestion of aggression in her response.

'Would it surprise you to know Jasper was still discussing his plans for Ridge Road about a month ago with Harrold Drake Junior?'

It does surprise her; he can see it in her eyes. 'I don't approve of that young man,' she says. 'He causes his parents all sorts of worry.'

'Would Harry have had the money to help Jasper finance a subdivision stretching along Ridge Road?'

Denise laughs, a brittle sound, dry as bones. 'I hear there is good money in drugs, but surely not that much.'

'His father?'

Denise's mouth contracts, her lips pursed. 'Not if he knew what was good for him.'

———

The afternoon remains breathless, even on Nobb Hill, as Martin walks back around the looping crescent past the lighthouse and starts back down the hill towards the town centre. Above him the sky is clear, but the storm out at sea is gathering strength, white clouds and grey billowing towards the stratosphere. At Tyson St Clair's home he rings the intercom at the gate, unsure if the developer will even deign to see him. The voice on the intercom is thin and remote, like an old-fashioned phone call. 'It's you. Enter.' There is the electric slap of the catch on the gate releasing; Martin pushes through. It's cool and dark in the rainforest, the entrance bridge extending through the greenery, a drawbridge above a moat. The front door opens; Tyson St Clair emerges to meet him.

'Martin. I wondered when you might show up.'

'Tyson.' The handshake is strangely formal, like two fighters before a bout.

Inside, the lighting in the entrance hall is muted, almost dark. A discreet spotlight, set on low, illuminates the Brett Whiteley, not so bright as to reveal its wonders, but enough to make its presence known. Inside the main room, the floor-to-ceiling windows are like a cinema screen, dominated by blue, but with the storm building like opening titles. A woman is curled on a couch, reading a book under a lamp, earbuds in, wearing a terry towelling robe, long legs tanned and sleek. She stands, smiles without warmth. Her blonde hair is bouffant, her face skilfully made up, softer inside than it might be out in the daylight. Martin places her in her mid-forties: lean, glamorous and gym-toned. 'I think I might leave you to it.' She gives St Clair's cheek an arid sweep with her lips, and departs.

'My wife,' says St Clair, introducing her after she has left the room.

'Beautiful,' says Martin, wondering if she knows of her husband's predilection for backpackers.

Behind St Clair, outside the long windows, lightning flashes below the clouds. 'Do you like whisky?'

'More than it likes me.'

The millionaire moves to a sideboard where decanters and bottles glow beneath another spotlight. 'You'll like this.'

'I thought you didn't drink during the day?'

'I don't as a rule. But it's Sunday. Peaty and smoky, or smooth and rounded? Your choice.'

'Peaty, thanks.'

St Clair decants a glass each, nothing so gauche as a label to indicate what they'll be drinking, and hands one to Martin. 'Just got these two in today.' He raises his glass in a silent salute, another gesture of a battle about to begin.

Martin sips at the whisky. It sings in his mouth, is almost worth the hike up the hill in its own right. St Clair leads him towards the windows; some unseen mechanism senses their approach and the doors silently concertina open. They step out onto a wide deck, seemingly afloat above the cliff, separated from the world, surrounded by shades of blue and white: the gradient of the sky, the deep blue of the ocean, the massing white of the storm clouds, the lighthouse looming above them like an orbiting moon. They sit opposite each other, a small table separating them, as if they are about to begin a game of chess. The wicker chairs are large and comfortable, with deep all-weather cushions.

'I'm glad you called in, Martin. I was going to call you first thing tomorrow. We have much to discuss.'

Martin feels wrong-footed. 'How so?'

'Well, I hear all sorts of things, but the *Sydney Morning Herald*'s gun journalist must know a lot more than I do. Such as forensic experts rechecking the murder weapon, looking for matches with some sort of dye.'

Martin stares at him. How could he possibly know? Johnson Pear must have told him. And in telling Martin the developer is emphasising just how well connected he is. 'That's true. I'm hoping the homicide detectives are about to eliminate Mandy as a suspect.'

'So who killed Jasper then?' asks St Clair, with the casual air of someone asking the score in the cricket.

'I'm hoping you'll help me work that out.'

St Clair chuckles softly. 'I hope you're not suggesting I had anything to do with it.'

'No.' Martin takes another sip, the whisky simultaneously smooth and rough; the crystal glass at once sparkling with light and heavy in his hand. He knows he shouldn't be drinking, not spirits, not on an empty stomach. 'I know you and the Speights have been competitors, but I can't see you risking all of this to kill him.'

'I'm glad to hear it. I thought maybe you'd got the wrong idea after that incident with your girlfriend.'

'I got the right idea. You're involved in visa fraud—which would provide a motive if Jasper had decided to expose your involvement.'

The property developer looks at him for a long moment, considering Martin's words. 'Do the police think that?'

'You'd have to ask them.'

St Clair raises his own glass to his lips, savours the taste before speaking again. 'So how can I help?'

'What's the status of the French proposal to develop Hummingbird Beach?'

'Unchanged. Jay Jay Hayes doesn't want to sell. I doubt she ever will.'

'That's funny. The last time we spoke, you seemed sure she would.'

'I've changed my mind.'

Martin is finding St Clair's attitude unsettling; it's as if the man is taunting him, playing at some game. 'The swami,' Martin counters. 'I saw you together in Longton the other day.'

'So you did. I waved to you, as I remember.'

'He was spying on Jay Jay for you.'

St Clair laughs, baring his incisors. 'No. Far from it. He was after my advice about how he might grow his meditation business. In return, he'd keep me abreast of what Jasper Speight was up to.'

'Which was?'

'Trying to cultivate Jay Jay. From what Dev said, he wasn't making much progress.'

Martin looks out to sea. 'You seem to have lost interest in the development.'

St Clair smiles broadly, as if enjoying a good joke. 'Why do you say that?'

'You've let everyone know about your plans to develop Mackenzie's Swamp. The marina, the golf course, the gated community along the river. You were very keen to tell me all about it the last time I was here, saying you were convinced Jay Jay would sell eventually.'

St Clair is still smiling. 'Go on.'

'But if you were so keen to get your hands on the old cheese factory, why did you never approach Mandy about buying it? Once she inherited Hartigan's, you and Harrold Drake would have worked out pretty quickly she will also become the owner of Mackenzie's Cheese and Pickles.'

St Clair shrugs. 'Maybe I thought it made more sense to go directly to the administrators and the major creditors.'

'That's right. But then Denise Speight stole it from under your nose.'

'She's a very competitive woman.'

'I believe she is,' says Martin, gathering his thoughts. 'So you know she has come to an agreement with Westpac?'

'I do.' Another smile.

When Martin speaks again, he's not so much conversing as thinking out loud. 'Of course, she never would have become interested in the site if you hadn't promoted it far and wide, including in the *Longton Observer*.'

'An excellent newspaper.'

'Which you own. And whose editor doesn't return my calls.'

'Is that all?'

'Not quite. Then there's Doug Thunkleton. You tip him off that Amory Ashton is buried at the cheese factory and supply him with a few bogus witnesses, all of which gives the very clear impression that Ashton's body is about to be found, he'll be declared dead, and his land will be free for sale.'

St Clair's smile hasn't left his face, canines glistening. 'Excellent whisky, isn't it?'

'But tell me, the cheese factory, your fingers—what happened?'

St Clair stops smiling, as if one of Martin's questions has finally ruffled him. 'What do you mean?'

'You told me my dad helped you. But how do you slice off your fingers in a cheese factory?'

St Clair regards him with curiosity. 'Do you know what a bobby calf is?' he asks.

'A what?'

'Give me your glass. I'll get you a refill. You can google it while I'm gone.'

Martin does what he's told, handing over his glass, still half full, and fires up his phone. By the time St Clair returns, he knows: dairy cows need to give birth to bring on their milk. The female calves may be raised to become milkers themselves, but the male calves, the bobby calves, are typically killed soon after birth. St Clair hands him back his glass, four-fifths full.

'Ashton was running an abattoir inside the cheese factory,' says Martin.

'Correct. Not exactly hygienic. Not exactly legal.'

'And he disposed of the offcuts and the offal into the swamp, attracting bull sharks.'

'That's right.'

'So why tell Doug Thunkleton to search inside the factory? If I'd killed Amory Ashton out there, I'd chuck his body to the sharks.'

St Clair doesn't just smile; he laughs out loud. 'I bet you would, son. I bet you would.'

'So why not tell Channel Ten that?'

St Clair leans forward, laughter gone, but his teeth again exposed by his rictus smile. 'It doesn't matter where that idiot looks, inside the factory or in the swamp, he's never going to find Ashton. He's not there. He did a runner.'

Martin does his best to hide his surprise. He's thinking of Jay Jay and her confession. St Clair has been so canny and so well-informed up until this point; how could he be so wrong about the death of Amory Ashton? 'How could you know that? I thought his disappearance was a mystery.'

'Because at the same time he disappeared, so did ten million dollars. He took it and he ran.'

'I've never heard that.'

'It's not widely known.'

'Whose ten million dollars?'

'Harrold Drake's.'

Martin doesn't know what to say. Out at sea, lightning flashes. A few seconds later he hears thunder. The storm is moving closer to shore. 'Harrold Drake?'

'Ashton took him in: hook, line and sinker. Spun him this fantastical story about developing the cheese factory into an upmarket resort, complete with a golf course, a marina and condominiums. Drake borrowed heavily, threw in ten million; the next thing anyone knew, Ashton had disappeared into thin air.'

Martin is having a difficult time digesting all that St Clair is telling him. 'Who knows this? About Drake losing so much money?'

'His bank and his accountant. And, eventually, me. And now you. I doubt even his wife knows. You could say it's a tightly held secret.'

Martin takes another sip of whisky, his mind racing in a dozen different directions before settling on one. He places the glass on the table, telling himself not to drink any more. 'Why is the development of Mackenzie's fantastical? It's your grand vision, the transformation of Port Silver. You couldn't wait to tell me about it. What's changed?'

'Since Ashton? The French, for a start. They weren't sniffing around five years ago. A development at Hummingbird makes perfect sense. It's a great location. But even with it, the rest is still pie in the sky. You could possibly do something with the cheese factory—a hotel or an eco-resort—but nothing else. The marina is totally unrealistic. I've spent the last twenty-five years trying to work out how to open up the mouth of the Argyle, to make that properly navigable. And that's a real river with real water. That pissy little inlet up at Mackenzie's is flat out floating an inner tube, let alone an ocean-going yacht.'

'And the golf course? You cited examples of all sorts of developments up on the Gold Coast on reclaimed land.'

Another self-satisfied grin. 'It can be done. Of course it can be done. But it's massively expensive. The only way you could get your money back is if you developed housing, like up there in Queensland—and if there was demand for the housing. A golf course by itself, twenty kilometres from town, could never generate sufficient returns. Not in a million years.'

Martin finds he has been leaning forward. Now he leans back, looking towards the storm clouds as if seeking enlightenment. 'So it was all a sham. You never had any intention of developing any of it. That's why you never approached Mandy.'

St Clair nods, raises his glass as if in a toast.

'But why? Why this whole elaborate ruse? To what end?'

'Revenge.'

'Revenge?'

'There's an old hotel by the port. The Breakwater. Badly run down now, but with enormous potential. You know it?'

'Yes. Mandy's lawyer is staying there. So are half the media.'

'Lucky them. Did you notice that it's under new management?'

Martin nods. 'I did. Who's the new manager?'

'Not just the new manager—the new owner. Denise Speight.' St Clair mouths her name with distaste. 'For decades, the Breakwater was owned by an old Greek lady, Mrs Tomakis.'

'George's mum?'

'Precisely. Theo's widow. And for the past five or ten years, ever since the fishing fleet was grounded and we got the government money to tart up the harbour, I've been trying to persuade her to do it up. Either do it up or sell it. The potential is enormous. But dear old Mrs Tomakis is not a developer. Hates to spend a penny, even to make a pound. She can sweat a property like no one I know. Owns half the Settlement.'

'You make her sound like a slumlord.'

'Well, she's tough, put it that way. But she's also as honest as the day is long. You don't need a contract with her, a handshake is plenty. And we shook hands on the sale of the Breakwater. I was buying it and nobody else even knew it was for sale. Nobody but my accountant. And my lawyer.'

'Harrold Drake.'

'Yes. Harrold fucking Drake. Who I'd been propping up ever since Amory Ashton took him for a ride and ran off with all his money. The same Harrold Drake who then sold me down the river. Mrs Tomakis confirmed it all. She was mortified. Drake, presenting himself as my lawyer, had informed her that I was no longer interested in buying. But that Denise Speight was. And for what did he doublecross me? His thirty pieces of silver? For a slightly higher commission and ten per cent ownership of the Breakwater.'

A flash of lightning spears down from the clouds; it strikes the water, kilometres from shore, where shadows are beginning to assert themselves on the glowing sea. 'So this whole charade, it's just so you can wreak revenge on Harrold Drake and Denise Speight?'

'That's right.'

'Is Harrold acting for Denise?'

'Yes.'

'But no longer for you?'

'Of course not. And not for Mrs Tomakis either. Not anymore.'

'So he's in deep financial strife?'

'Fuck, I hope so, the conniving shit. With a bit of luck, this will finish him.'

Martin looks down at his glass, which has somehow reappeared in his hand, then out to sea, then back to St Clair, remembering George's distaste for Nobb Hill. 'Just how desperate do you think Harrold Drake is right now?'

'If you ask me, I'd say very fucking desperate.'

'You need to tell the police what you know about him.'

'I'm intending to. I just needed to see something else through first.' And St Clair cracks another of his lupine grins. 'But you haven't told me. Do you like my whisky?'

The change of direction stumps Martin; one moment they're talking revenge, financial treachery and motives for murder, the next the millionaire is fishing for compliments. 'Of course. It tastes wonderful.'

'So it should. Each bottle is worth several thousands of dollars. You've probably got a thousand bucks' worth in your glass right there. Drink up.'

Martin frowns. Surely St Clair isn't trying to make him feel in his debt? 'What's your point?'

'It was a gift from the French. Very generous of them.'

Martin is speechless. He looks at his glass, then back to St Clair. 'The French?'

'Yes. The development is going ahead. Longitudes. We signed the deal this morning in Brisbane.'

'But Jay Jay isn't selling. You said so yourself.'

'No. Not at Hummingbird Beach. Five Mile Beach. The entire southern end. It will be huge. A brilliant, exclusive, world-class resort. With a golf course and a gated community, the beach on one side, an expansive nature reserve on the other. Swamplands to us, wetlands to the French, everglades in their brochures. It will be beautiful and it will be grand and it will be the making of Port Silver.' St Clair beams at Martin, gesturing with his whisky. 'And every morning, as Denise Speight walks out her front door, she will see it, dominating her view.' And Tyson St Clair bares his teeth in a grin that could strip meat from a bone.

'Who owned the land?'

'Until yesterday, I did. Through a front company. I bought it a few years ago—from Harrold Drake. He was short of money. I thought I was doing him a favour.'

'You want me to put this in the *Herald*, don't you?'

'It will be the first five pages of the *Longton Observer* on Wednesday.'

Martin places his glass gently down on the table in front of him, still almost full. 'Jesus. You must really hate them.'

'Oh, I do. I do.'

A massive bolt of lightning goes careering across the sky.

chapter thirty

THE PORT SILVER POLICE STATION IS ALL BUT DESERTED. EVERYONE HAS LEFT for the evening except the constable on the counter and Morris Montifore, who comes to fetch Martin, looking increasingly bedraggled.

'Jesus, what happened to you?' he asks, letting Martin in through the security door. 'You all right?'

Martin is sodden, dripping all over the floor. 'Got caught in the storm.'

'Well, I have good news for you.'

'The knife stain?'

'Yes. It matches the swami's dye. You were right.'

The sense of relief is almost physical. 'So Mandy's in the clear?'

'Yes. You can report she is no longer a suspect.'

Martin looks at his watch. Five-thirty. He's done it. 'Where is she?'

'You just missed her. She's gone to pick up your son.'

'Right,' says Martin, stumbling slightly as they walk together.

'You sure you're okay?' asks Montifore.

'Fine. A little tipsy, but fine. You?'

Montifore gives him a quizzical look. 'I've been better. It's Sunday night. I should be home with the wife and kids. Instead I'm stuck up here, running in ever-diminishing circles.'

The realisation that Montifore has a family and a home life comes as a surprise to Martin. He can't imagine the policeman ever having downtime, ever taking off his over-worked suit. In Martin's imagination, the inspector would sleep in it.

They reach the detective's makeshift operations room. 'Just a moment,' says Martin. He rings Terri Preswell, tells her Mandy is free, that the police say there is no longer any substantive evidence against her.

'Okay, thanks,' says the editor. 'But listen, I want to run her photo. Page three. Say she's been cleared.'

'Are you asking permission?'

'Of course not. Just telling you.'

'Thanks, Terri. Mandy will appreciate it. I appreciate it.'

He rings Bethanie.

'Shit, Martin, could you have left it any later?' There's a pause. Martin can hear voices, people laughing. It sounds like a bar. 'All right. I'll get on to it.' Another pause. 'And well done. Thank you.'

'Thanks, Bethanie, I owe you one.'

'Several, I'd say.'

Montifore has been listening with interest. 'All clear?'

'All clear.' Martin feels a wash of relief. Mandy is free, cleared of suspicion, and his old paper will tell the world. He feels a swell of elation, of pride. He smiles at Montifore, but the detective doesn't reciprocate. 'You don't seem too happy,' Martin observes.

'Not really,' says Montifore. 'Mandalay Blonde is in the clear, so now I have to start chasing the real killer. And Hummingbird is still unresolved. I had to ring the wife and tell her I'll be up here for another week at least.'

'She's not happy?'

'Our boy's birthday is on Tuesday.'

'Right. Sorry to hear it.'

Montifore casts his eyes around the office, as if seeking a reason to still be here.

'The knife,' says Martin, trying to get the policeman to focus. 'Is there any doubt it was the weapon that killed Jasper?'

'None. Forensics are sure on that score, at least. Length of blade, width of blade and curve of blade. It has a kink, apparently.'

'So someone kills Jasper. Afterwards, they stain the handle with the bindi dye, intending to frame the swami. But then, when they realise he has an iron-clad alibi, they try to shift the blame towards Mandy. Is that right?'

'Yes. I'd say so.'

'So how did they know that the swami was no longer in the frame?'

Montifore doesn't answer. He still looks like he no longer wants to be there. In fact, he looks like he'd rather be anywhere else.

'And what's happening with Hummingbird? Why isn't it straightforward?'

Montifore sighs, an expression of weariness. 'You were right. Again. There was more than one poison—and Topaz Throssel is adamant she only used one.'

'And she doesn't have any reason to lie.'

'Not a lot.'

Martin gazes around the room, taking in the empty chairs, the desks, deciding how to proceed. He's starting to feel a little vague, the delayed effect of Tyson St Clair's whisky reinforcing the hunger and fatigue of the day. Tyson St Clair. How had the developer known so quickly that the forensic technicians were investigating the knife stain? How was he always so well informed? An idea comes to him. Martin leans back, reaching onto the desk used by Ivan Lucic, picking up a pen and a piece of paper. 'Morris, I think I might have something. The murder of Jasper Speight and the second poison. How it all fits together.'

Montifore says nothing, just looks at him, barely breathing.

Martin writes on the piece of paper and hands it to the detective. 'But let's make sure,' he says.

———

There is a mood of jubilation at the Breakwater Hotel. For a Sunday night, the bar is pumping, thanks to the influx of journalists and their expense accounts, the atmosphere heightened by the rain pummelling down outside. There is Doug Thunkleton, holding court; there is Bethanie Glass, feigning interest; there is Baxter James, already getting the staggers. Here they gather, the cream of Australia's press corps, or so they tell themselves, drinking to their own success, undeterred by the sticky carpet and the dilapidated bar stools: another day done, another story put to rest. So they laugh and they drink, knowing that tomorrow they'll do it all again. And again. And again. And in a corner are Mandalay Blonde, holding her wide-eyed son Liam, and the two lawyers, Winifred Barbicombe and Nick Poulos. Here too is Martin Scarsden, stuffing his face with fish and chips, unmindful of his still-damp clothes. Mandy and Winifred are drinking champagne, Nick Poulos accepting half a glass to participate in a toast, while Martin is sticking to water, claiming Tyson St Clair's whisky is enough to carry him for the moment. This is neither the time nor the place to explain his aversion to champagne. So while the others toast Mandy's freedom, he concentrates on his food; not as good as Theo's, but his hunger is telling him it's good enough.

Winifred raises her glass again. If the alcohol is having any effect on her, Martin can't detect it. 'And here's to Martin,' she proclaims. 'He has cleared Mandy once and for all. The case is closed.'

They clink glasses, toasting Martin, but Mandy is frowning. 'How do you mean the case is closed? We still don't know who killed Jasper Speight.'

Winifred smiles indulgently. 'It doesn't matter, dear. You're in the clear. You can get on with your life, I can get back to Melbourne.'

'No,' says Mandy, suddenly serious, almost angry. 'I can't get on with my life. How can I? As long as the killer walks free, I will be forever under suspicion. After what happened down in Riversend, after what happened in my townhouse, no one in Port Silver will want anything to do with me; no mother will welcome Liam into their playgroup.'

Liam pouts, unsettled by his mother's change of mood.

Winifred stops smiling, realising her error. 'Yes, of course. How foolish of me. I was looking through a legal prism. I'm sorry.'

The group grows quiet, its silence emphasised by the continuing uproar from the bar and the sound of teeming rain. Martin finishes the last of his chips, wipes some errant grease from his mouth. 'The police are on to it. New leads. They may be able to wrap it up in the next day or two.'

Mandy looks at Martin with rare intensity, her green eyes focused. 'Who? Who do they suspect?'

'I'm meeting Montifore again in an hour. He's upstairs now, making arrangements, flying specialists in from Sydney.'

'Specialists?' asks Nick.

'What's happened? Tell us what you know,' says Winifred.

And so Martin does. He leans into the table, voice soft amid the bar's booming voices and clinking glasses, careful not to be overheard. Quietly, without embellishment, he explains what he thinks might have happened, and how the police might proceed.

By the end Mandy is nodding. 'Motive. Opportunity. But is it enough? Can the police start making arrests?'

'Eventually. But right now the only evidence is circumstantial.'

'That sounds about right,' says Nick Poulos. 'It's a strong circumstantial case, but I'm not confident the DPP would prosecute. There's no physical evidence, there are no witnesses.'

'So they can get away with it?' says Mandy. 'That's bullshit.'

Nick shakes his head. 'No, I'm not saying that. The police will pursue it. With eight people dead, they won't let it slide. And now they have some firm suspects, they'll concentrate all their efforts there. But it could take them weeks, maybe months. You should be prepared for that. I'm sorry.'

'No,' says Mandy, anger flaring. 'We can't just sit here, pretend all is well while the police sharpen their pencils and fill in their forms. There must be something we can do.'

The champagne is forgotten, the celebratory bubble deflates, no one speaks. Outside, the rain is easing, the storm moving on. And now, at the bar, as if to emphasise the hush engulfing Martin's group, there is a mighty explosion of laughter. Doug Thunkleton has said something so witty, or so stupid, that all his colleagues are laughing uproariously. Baxter James laughs so hard he topples off his bar stool and lies floundering on the floor, inciting another maelstrom of hilarity.

Martin watches for a moment and then turns back to the others. 'I have an idea,' he says. 'Let me go and talk to Montifore.'

MONDAY

chapter thirty-one

MORRIS MONTIFORE IS PREPARING TO BEGIN HIS PRESS CONFERENCE ON THE FRONT steps of the Port Silver police station just after noon, flanked by Sergeant Johnson Pear and his two constables. The day is cloudy, wind easing in off the sea, keeping the temperatures moderate. Even so, the detective inspector is looking none too comfortable as the media jockey for position below him. In fact, he looks to be sweating. Martin Scarsden and Mandalay Blonde stand at the back of the pack, having already been comprehensively photographed by Martin's former colleagues. The signal comes through from the ABC and Sky News teams—Morris Montifore is live to air, nationwide.

'Ladies and gentlemen, thank you for coming. I'll be brief, but I wanted to bring you up to date with the latest developments in ongoing homicide investigations here in Port Silver. I'll make a brief statement and then answer questions.

'The first point I want to make is in reference to a young woman who has been helping us with our inquiries, Mandalay Blonde. I want to thank her for her assistance, and I want to make it crystal clear—crystal clear—that she is not a police suspect and has been cleared of any possible involvement in the death of local man Jasper Speight. As you will be aware, Mr Speight died—was murdered— in premises rented by Ms Blonde. However, I repeat: Ms Blonde has been categorically ruled out as a suspect in the murder.'

Martin glances at Mandy. Her expression is set, resolute, prepared to stare down all comers. He turns back, looking not at Montifore but at the police flanking him. The faces of the two constables are stern but unremarkable. It's the shifting emotions on the face of Johnson Pear that interest him.

Montifore continues. 'I can confirm we are making considerable progress with the investigation of Jasper Speight's death. We have now recovered the murder weapon, a filleting knife. Our forensic team in Sydney has thoroughly examined the weapon using new, ground-breaking technologies, and the knife has surrendered possibly critical information. We have ruled out a number of early suspects and are following a number of strong leads. We are hopeful an arrest or arrests will be made in the near future.

'In regards to the seven deaths at Hummingbird Beach on Friday night, you will be aware that we have charged a dual Australian-American citizen, Topaz Marie Throssel, with the murder of Myron Florakis, also known as Swami Dev Hawananda. Investigations are continuing and, again, we are confident we will soon be laying charges in relation to the other six deaths.'

Montifore pauses to draw breath but, before he can resume, the foghorn voice of Doug Thunkleton comes crashing up the steps like a rogue wave. 'Detective Inspector, can you confirm that, before his death, Jasper Speight posted a letter detailing serious allegations of wrongdoing at Hummingbird Beach?'

Montifore is shaking his head, a bewildered look on his face. 'No. I'm not able to . . .'

'What was contained in that letter?'

'Where did you get this information?' demands Montifore.

'To whom was the letter addressed, Inspector?'

Montifore's lips are sealed. He's shaking his head vehemently. 'Thank you all for coming. I really can't comment further.'

But as he is turning to walk back into the station, another voice cuts through the throng. 'Inspector. Inspector! On another matter.' It's Bethanie Glass.

'Another matter?' says Montifore. He sighs. 'All right.'

'Inspector, can you confirm that there were not one but two poisons administered at Hummingbird Beach, and that there was more than one perpetrator?'

But Montifore has had enough. He turns, and strides towards the safety of the police station. Only as he reaches the doors does Martin see him round on Johnson Pear and hiss, 'How the fuck did any of that get out?'

Ten minutes later, Martin is in the Breakwater Hotel, knocking on the door of Winifred Barbicombe's suite. The door opens. Winifred is not there, but Ivan Lucic is, together with two technicians. The techs are wearing headphones, sitting at what was Winifred's writing table, now covered in an array of laptops and technical equipment.

'Anything?' asks Martin.

'Yeah, Johnson Pear,' says Lucic, walking over to the writing desk. 'This first. Johnson Pear to Tyson St Clair.' Lucic taps a key on one of the laptops.

'Johnson. Hello.'

'I wanted to tell you straight away . . .'

'If it's about the police press conference, I just watched it live on Sky.'

'Oh. Right.'

'Do you have anything to tell me I don't already know?'

'Well, not as such.'

'I'm not very fucking happy, Johnson. I should have known about this earlier. It's not what I pay you for.'

'Sorry. I didn't know any of that. It must have happened last night.'

'Well, lift your game.'

The call goes dead.

'Is there more?' Martin asks.

Lucic nods, distaste written clearly on his face. 'Johnson Pear to Harrold Drake Junior.' He taps the laptop keyboard.

'Johnno. What news, my friend?'

'Have you been watching television?'

'In the middle of the day? Fuck that.'

'We just gave a press conference. Homicide says Mandalay Blonde is in the clear.'

'So what? I always reckoned it was the swami who killed Jasper.'

A pause. *'You didn't have anything to do with it, did you?'*

'Killing Jasper? Fuck no. Of course not.'

Another pause. *'The journos are saying there were two poisons at Hummingbird Beach. Two killers.'*

A pause, then a shift in tone, Harry the Lad sounding less flippant. *'Journos? What would they know? What did the cops say?'*

'Nothing. The homicide detective, Montifore, wouldn't confirm it, but he didn't deny it.'

'Well, it's got nothing to do with us.'

'Of course it fucking does,' says Johnson Pear, suddenly assertive. 'You've been doling out drugs at Hummingbird for years. You don't think homicide won't come looking for you?'

'Fuck, Johnno, chill out, will you? Yeah, I get a few people high now and then. If push comes to shove, I'll admit to it. But I didn't fucking kill anyone. Why would I?'

'I don't know. But from now on, you can count me out.'

'What does that mean?'

'No more turning a blind eye. It's finished.'

'Righto. Suit yourself. We'll talk again when this all blows over.'

The call ends.

'Sounds like Pear doesn't know that much,' Martin observes.

Lucic doesn't respond. He looks as if Winifred has been leaving prawn heads in her bin.

'Heads up!' says one of the technicians. 'Harrold Drake Junior is leaving the hostel. On foot. Heading along the main street.'

'Where's he going?' asks Lucic, but no one answers.

Long seconds go by, the four men tense, until eventually the tech speaks again. 'Harrold Drake Junior is entering the ground floor of an office block at eighteen The Boulevarde.'

'Harrold Drake and Associates,' says Martin.

'Show time,' says one of the techs, adjusting his headphones.

At that moment, the hotel door bursts opens. It's Morris Montifore, breathing hard.

'Just in time for the main event,' Lucic tells him. 'Harrold Junior entering the offices of Harrold Senior.'

'Shush!' says one of the techs.

'Okay,' says his colleague. 'It's the office, not the boardroom.'

'Turn it up,' says Montifore.

'*You saw?*' It sounds like the son.

'*Yeah, I saw.*' It's Drake Senior's voice. '*It was on TV.*'

'*She's in the clear. She didn't kill him.*'

'*So they say.*'

'*Who did?*'

'*Harry, calm yourself. Sit down.*' A pause. '*What's wrong?*'

'*You said she killed him.*'

'*So I did. That's what Johnson Pear told me. Did he tell you anything different?*' A pause. '*All it means is we don't know who killed him. We don't know why.*'

'*They said he sent a letter. About Hummingbird.*'

'*Yes. Maybe he suspected he was in danger. Maybe he was right.*'

'*Danger? Who from?*'

'*My guess is Jay Jay Hayes.*'

'*Jay Jay? Why would she kill him?*'

'*Because Jasper found out her lover was a fraud and was about to expose him. That's what's probably in this letter of Jasper's. Exposing Myron Florakis.*'

A long silence.

'*They reckon there were two poisons at Hummingbird. Two killers. It wasn't just that Topaz chick.*'

'*So they say.*'

'*You said it wouldn't hurt anyone. You said it was just to make them sick, to discredit them. To drive him out of business, to force Jay Jay to sell.*'

'*That's right. That's all it was. You didn't kill anyone.*'

'Who did then? There was a second poison.'

'Jay Jay.'

'Jay Jay?'

'Sure. She killed Jasper to protect the swami. But she couldn't trust Hawananda, so she took him out. And a few others as well, to cover her tracks. Very clever of her.'

A very long pause.

'I don't believe you.'

chapter thirty-two

HUMMINGBIRD BEACH IS DESERTED. THERE IS NO ONE HERE, JUST THE BIRDS, the kangaroos and the waves breaking on the shore. The waves seem more urgent today, excited by recent storms, but there is little left for Martin to be excited by. The police have gone, taking their evidence with them, the campers have washed up on some other beach and the new intake of spiritual seekers has cancelled. The media are swarming around the Sperm Cove Backpackers, the Port Silver police station, and the homes and offices of the Harrolds Drake, Senior and Junior. Martin is leaving that to Bethanie and Baxter. He's filed for online; tomorrow's paper will carry the authoritative account. But for now, he's at Hummingbird Beach, feeling all the better for a proper sleep and a substantial breakfast.

He walks down to the house. Jay Jay is sitting at a table out on the deck waiting for him, bags packed and ready to go. There's a small bouquet of flowers, perhaps a parting gift from one of her long-term campers. She's looking at the sea, oblivious to his approach, filling her eyes. He watches a moment before climbing the steps and disturbing her reverie. He's agreed to drive her up to Longton. She's going to catch the train to Sydney to start treatment.

'Ready?' he asks.

'No.' She smiles. 'I want to sit here forever.'

'Sooner you go, sooner you get back,' he says, returning her smile.

'Maybe. But before we go, can you tell me what happened? I read your stories on the computer but I'm still not sure I follow it all.'

'You wouldn't. Now that the Drakes have been charged, we're restricted in what we can publish. But the gist of it is this: last Friday night there were two poisons administered here at Hummingbird by two separate people, neither of them aware of the other. The first was Topaz Throssel, who wanted to avenge her sister by killing Myron Florakis and then herself. The other killer was Harry the Lad. His mission was to kill the man he knew as Swami Dev Hawananda and yourself. But it all went awry. Florakis died, both you and Topaz survived, and six others died for no good reason.'

Jay Jay Hayes looks stunned. Martin lets her absorb what he's just told her. It must be almost a minute before she speaks, her voice a whisper. 'Why did they want to kill me?'

'Harrold Drake Senior wanted you dead so the Divine Meditation Foundation would inherit Hummingbird Beach, and he wanted the swami dead so he could control the foundation. He planned to sell the land to the French resort developers.'

'So money? Greed? The lives of seven people taken, just for that?'

'Drake is drowning in debt. It goes back to Amory Ashton. Ashton offered Drake a short cut to leapfrog the St Clairs, the Tomakises and the Speights of the world, to sit on the pinnacle of Nobb Hill. So Drake borrowed heavily, invested ten million in a scam project spruiked by Amory Ashton and lost it all when Ashton disappeared.'

'Ashton? But I told you, he's dead. Where's the money?'

'My guess? Sitting unclaimed in some offshore tax haven. But Drake, and anybody else who knows about the money, assumes Ashton did a runner with it.'

Jay Jay nods, her face grim. 'So they wanted me dead. Me and Dev. What went wrong?'

'I can't be sure, but Harry the Lad is cooperating fully with police. He's claiming he was duped by his own father. He knew he was poisoning people, but he thought it was to make them ill, not to kill them. To destroy the reputation of Hummingbird, close down the swami's business and force you to sell.'

'Go on.'

'Topaz only intended to kill herself and the swami. She put her poison in the ceremonial bowl right at the end, so that only he and she would drink it. But after drinking it, Hawananda staggered away, possibly because Harry had already poisoned him. He passed out before emptying the bowl. Others saw it there and drank some.'

'And died.'

'Some did, some didn't.'

Jay Jay pauses again, thinking. Frowning. 'So why did Dev die but Topaz and I survive?'

'Harry the Lad. His father gave him two substances. The first had small traces of the poison as well as ipecac. You know what that is?'

'It makes you vomit.'

'Right. So anyone drinking that would throw up, feel terrible and, if tested, show signs of poisoning. Meanwhile, a much stronger dose of the poison, without the ipecac, was reserved for you and your swami. Harrold Drake Senior wanted it to look like the swami had planned a murder-suicide, but with only two deaths. Harry the Lad claims he knew none of that.'

'Do the police believe him?'

'I doubt it. Surely he must have wondered why there was one dose for you and the swami and another for everyone else. Although, there was another factor . . .'

'What's that?'

'Rohypnol.'

'Again? On Friday night as well?'

'Yes. Almost certainly administered by Garth McGrath. It showed up in the blood of a young woman he was targeting and an older man. Fortunately, she was one of the survivors.'

'But why would Garth do that? He was so good-looking. Women were always throwing themselves at him. He didn't need to drug anyone.'

'Sex obviously wasn't enough for him. He wanted something else. Control. Total submission. He was a predator. But part of his methodology was to drug a number of people, not just his target, and he'd pretend he'd been affected as well. He drugged Jasper one night when he was targeting Mandy, and he did it to me on

Thursday when he was targeting Topaz. It's likely he gave it to Harry the Lad and, possibly, to the swami on Friday.'

'Shit,' says Jay Jay. 'That's why Dev passed out before he started throwing up like Topaz and me. And why Harry the Lad lost track of who got which dose.'

'That's the theory.'

'So will they charge him with murder?'

Martin shrugs. 'Don't know. I reckon he's trying to bargain with the police: full cooperation and testifying against his father in return for being charged with manslaughter instead of murder.'

'Will that work?'

'No idea. Certainly he knew nothing of his father's financial ruin. Just a few weeks ago, he was talking to Jasper about investing in a plan to subdivide the properties on Ridge Road. He thought his father could help finance it.'

'Who killed Jasper?'

'Harrold Drake Senior. Jasper discovered Dev Hawananda was not whom he claimed to be and Drake found out. Chances are Jasper only got halfway there: he thought Hawananda's real name was Myron Papadopoulos and was coming to tell me, but he may not have known about what happened in Crete. Jasper was thinking it would be a good story and would perhaps help loosen your financial grip on Hummingbird. But it forced Drake's hand. If you learnt Hawananda was a fraud, you would almost certainly disinherit him. So Harrold Drake killed Jasper then attempted to frame Hawananda. Then, when he learnt from Johnson Pear that the swami had an alibi, he tried shifting the blame to Mandy.'

'My God. He must have been desperate.'

'Utterly. He's denying it all, but he left a footprint as he fled out the back of Mandy's townhouse and along the river. And his son is trying to save his own arse by assisting the police.'

Jay Jay looks back out to sea, considering all she has been told. 'Poor Jasper,' she says. 'I felt sorry for him. He never became the man he could have been. I thought Dev might help him, give him a little peace, a little perspective. But I guess it's not that simple. It's never that simple.'

After that, they sit for a long while, neither of them speaking, just looking at the waves rolling onto the shore with clockwork precision, as if the swell is clapping in time with some unknowable rhythm. Eventually Martin gets to his feet and carries Jay Jay's bags up to the car, gives her a last few moments to herself to farewell her birthright. He waits at the car park, watching as she walks up the slope towards him, impressed again by how healthy she looks, how fit. Only her bowed head, the stoop that has crept into her shoulders and the sadness that clings to her suggests anything is amiss.

They leave in silence, no words spoken, the only sound the guttural rumble of the car's muffler. At the turn-off onto Dunes Road, Martin pauses and they watch as a Channel Ten car speeds by on its way back to the cheese factory, followed by nothing but Martin's smile. Martin turns onto the bitumen, heading for Port Silver, accelerating as smoothly as possible, trying not to overexcite the broken exhaust. He's just getting up to speed when Jay Jay reaches out, places her hand gently on his arm. 'Pull over, Martin. Just up here. By the cross.'

Martin slows the car to walking pace, pulls off the road and stops, the cross before them, the lighthouse floating in the distance.

'Come on,' she says and climbs out of the car. He follows. She has the bouquet of flowers from the deck. She walks to the cross, crouches, places them at its base, stays there for a moment before standing. 'Not plastic ones this time.'

'It's you,' says Martin. 'I thought it was Vern.'

She looks at him then, eyes wet. 'I was there, Martin. I was there that day.'

He studies her, comprehension coming too slowly, a wave too big to dive under, a wave too rough to float over. 'I don't follow.'

'Your father was with me at Hummingbird Beach. Dad was in the shed, milking the cows, always at the same time.'

'With you?'

'Your mother came in, she saw us. Didn't say a word, just walked straight back out. Ron ran after her.'

'But Dad was at the cheese factory that day.'

'No, Martin. He was with me. And your mum knew exactly where to find him.' Tears are flowing down her cheeks now. 'I am so sorry. So incredibly sorry.' She holds her arms out, as if to gather him in, to hug him. But Martin can't, he just can't. Instead he looks down at the cross. His sisters, his baby sisters, trapped in the back of the car. Struggling. Crying. Drowning. What had they ever done?

After a while, she returns to the car, leaving him there with his thoughts of his mother and his sisters and his broken family. He has no idea how long he stands there, head bowed, heartbroken, crying his own tears of remorse.

Back in the car, it's not until they have passed over the Argyle, until they have passed the port and the town, are beyond the high school and its cane-cosseted childcare centre, that Martin breaks the silence. 'So that's why you left? Went surfing? Why you didn't come back even when the surfing was over? Why you went seeking peace in India?' He looks across at her, but she's looking out the window as she answers.

'I was never going to come back. Never. I was away for more than twenty-five years. But eventually I realised that your past is always with you, you can't outrun it. It's why I had to tell you.'

Martin says nothing. They drive on through the green sea of the cane fields. They pass the turn-off to the right, the road to the sugar mill, the place where he stopped to pick up a couple of care-free backpackers precisely a week ago. Carefree no longer. Topaz Throssel, another person unable to outrun her past. The climb up the escarpment begins, the car dropping gears, the muffler roaring and the exhaust backfiring. It's only when they enter the flickering trees, sun strobing, that Martin asks, 'What was he like, Jay Jay? My dad. Before?'

And as the old car sputters its way up through the rainforest she tells him, her voice initially reluctant and remorse-filled, but soon enough warming to the task, fired by memories. 'He was fun, Martin, so much fun. He had such energy, such a spark, such wit.' And: 'A big kid. Forgot to grow up.' And: 'He was incorrigible. He just couldn't help himself.' And, last and most potently: 'He loved you kids. Loved you so much. And he loved Hilary. He was never going to leave. The rest was just playing about. I knew that.' And strange as it may seem, and hard though it may be to believe, by the time the Corolla crawls over the lip of the escarpment and makes it back to level ground, regaining its higher gears, the two of them are laughing, laughing at the memory, with the memory, of Ron Scarsden. It lasts a moment, just a moment, but it happens.

At the railway station, Martin carries one of the bags onto the platform for Jay Jay, although she seems in no way impaired, not physically. A memory comes to him, as they so often do these days. But now he welcomes it, lets it in, acknowledges the hurt. He is again his younger self, aged eighteen, eager to get away, eager to get to Sydney, to escape Port Silver, Longton and his past. He sees Vern embracing him, helping with his luggage, thrusting cash into his hand, while Martin, eyes focused on the future, careless in his farewells, impatient to bury his past and forge a different Martin Scarsden, oblivious to the emotion in his uncle's eyes, climbs onto the train and doesn't look back.

Then the memory dissolves and he's with Jay Jay again. There's an awkward moment. How to say goodbye? What to say as they wait for the train?

'You know,' says Jay Jay, 'that first morning, a few days ago, when I saw you walking towards me on the beach, I thought for a moment it was Ron. You walk the same way.'

Martin isn't sure what to say. 'It was thirty-three years ago. He was younger than I am now.'

'Yes.' Jay Jay regards him fondly. 'The same smile. The same playful eyes. The same hands.'

Martin looks at his hands, shocked that his white-collar hands could ever be compared to his father's gnarled worker's hands. He examines them, finds they are totally his own, but she's right: they do hold echoes of his father.

Jay Jay grows serious. 'Martin, I spoke to Nick Poulos this morning.'

'About Ashton?'

'No. About what happens if I die. When I die.'

'I'm sure it won't come to that.'

She smiles a knowing sort of smile. 'Let's hope not. The point is this: I'm leaving Hummingbird Beach to you.'

'To me? Why?'

She shrugs, and tears again well in her eyes. 'Because there is nobody else.'

And it's then that Martin understands what he needs to say. 'Jay Jay, I forgive you. You were young, you were single, you weren't cheating on anyone. You were just experimenting. You couldn't have known what would happen.'

She closes her eyes. 'Say it again, please. Just once more.'

'I forgive you.'

TUESDAY

chapter thirty-three

MANDY, MARTIN AND LIAM ARE SITTING ON THE WHARF AT THE CARAVAN PARK
waiting for Vern to pick them up in his dinghy. The morning
is warm, the on-shore breeze gentle. The overnight rain has
cleared and the light is soft and autumnal, reflecting from the
river. There is something about the day that embraces Martin,
something akin to perfection. Mandy is next to him, bouncing
her boy. She gives Liam a kiss and passes him to Martin. The
boy is getting heavier by the day. They sit there, the three of
them, not speaking, merely enjoying a moment in which there
is nothing that needs doing, nothing imposing itself upon them,
nothing to threaten them.

It's Mandy who speaks. 'You gave it away, Martin. Your story.
You gave it away.'

'No, I didn't. It's there on the front page of today's *Herald*, if
only we could buy one out here. My by-line, mine and Bethanie's.'

'I know. But you had it all to yourself. The Drakes, their desperation, their deception. You had it all. But you gave it to the police and you gave it to Bethanie and you gave it to that bozo Doug Thunkleton.'

Martin shrugs, grinning. He knows what she is saying, yet sitting here in the warmth of the sun and the warmth of his family, he feels no regrets. *His family.* 'We owe that bozo a debt of gratitude. He played his part to perfection at that press conference.'

Mandy smiles back. 'I guess he did. But you know what I'm saying. You could have had it all for yourself. I reckon the old Martin Scarsden would have walked over hot coals to claim a story that big as an exclusive.'

She's right: something has changed. The story is no longer the be-all and end-all. He's a different Martin Scarsden. Maybe not the better man he promised her down in Riversend, but heading in that direction. He's discovered that some things are more important than the front page of a newspaper. 'It had to be done. St Clair would have told the police what he knew and they would have worked it out in the end, but it could have taken weeks. And in that time Drake could have fled, or killed again. This way, we ended it. Saved both of us a lot of heartache.'

'Saved me, you mean.'

'Same thing.'

It's the sound they hear first, the soft *putt-putt* of the motor. And then they can see him, Vern coming downstream in his boat—not the large fishing boat, the small aluminium tinnie Levi used in the smuggler's cove—swinging into the caravan park wharf where they sit waiting, Martin, Mandalay and Liam.

'Boat, Liam, say "boat",' says Martin to the boy, holding him on his lap. 'Boat.'

'Boa,' says Liam, eyes wide with surprise and delight. 'Boa, boa, boa.'

They laugh and clap, Mandy seizing the boy from Martin and smothering him in kisses.

'Boa! Boa! Boa!' yelps Liam, the centre of attention.

Carefully, Martin passes Liam down to Vern. Mandy descends the ladder into the boat, then Martin. Vern insists they wear life jackets that look as if they are years old but have never been used.

They putter down the Argyle, the engine throttled back, letting the river do the work, floating them under the bridge, past the harbour on their right followed by the Breakwater Hotel and the town, while to their left the bank climbs, becoming more precipitous. There is the sound of surf, the clean smell of the sea replacing the swampy odour of the river. The flow seems to accelerate, steep shore on the left and breakwater on the right, just as the river had quickened all those years ago under three boys in a canoe. They look up, Mandy trying to spy some sign of Hartigan's, but they are too close to shore, there is only the dense forest. Martin has Liam on his lap, holding him tight, pointing at things, mouthing their names. Now they can see the swell sweeping over the sandbar, waves rising but not breaking. And now the outcrop of rock, still extending from below the cliff. They surge past it and Vern opens the throttle; they sweep around onto the secluded beach, the water placid. To Martin it appears unchanged from that day almost thirty years ago when it gave sanctuary to three desperate boys.

Later, as Mandy and Liam splash joyously in the shallows, Martin and Vern sit side by side on a driftwood log, looking out to sea.

'Vern, you have to give up the endangered fish trade. You know that, don't you?'

Vern nods. 'Yeah. I know. Pity, though. Family tradition and all. Helps break the monotony, a bit of law breaking.'

Martin smiles. 'It's not a good fit, you must see that. Campaigning to protect Mackenzie's Swamp on one hand while you're pillaging protected species with the other.'

Vern laughs. 'Yes. Now you put it that way.' They watch as Mandy bends and lifts Liam, careful to keep her back straight. The boy is growing, on the cusp of walking, on the cusp of talking. She can no longer simply scoop him up. 'What will she do with the cheese factory and Mackenzie's?' asks Vern.

'Don't know. We haven't discussed it. She still hasn't been there, as far as I know. We might head out and have a look later this week. Denise Speight has first dibs on it, but I reckon she'll renege on the deal with the bank. And I can't imagine Mandy being in any rush to develop it.'

'What about you? What will you do? I see you're back on the front page today, a big spread inside.'

'Yeah. They've offered me a job. Full-time. In Sydney.'

'What did you say?'

'No.' He's looking at Mandy and their son as he says it. 'But they're still keen to keep me on the books. Use my name, have me at events, that sort of thing. They'll pay me a retainer, expect me to file a feature every month or so. Mandy and I think it might work. We'll see.' Martin studies his hands, choosing his words. 'I think there is something wrong with me.'

'Martin?'

'I always suspect the worst of people. Even people I should trust. You, and Levi and Josie. And Mandy. It's like some disease I caught when I was a correspondent and now I can't shake the symptoms.'

'Give it time, Martin. Give it normality. You'll be right.'

'I hope so,' says Martin, sounding doubtful.

'You don't think the worst of Liam, do you?'

Martin laughs. 'Of course not. How could I?'

'Well, there you go. There's your first step.'

Martin smiles; it's a point well made. But then he grows serious again. 'I drove Jay Jay Hayes up to the station at Longton yesterday. She's off to Sydney, to hospital.'

'Nothing serious, I hope?'

'Maybe very serious. Cancer.'

'No. Jay Jay? Really?'

'She says if she dies, she's going to leave Hummingbird to me.'

Vern turns to Martin, is about to speak, but then thinks better of it. He averts his gaze, looking out across the sandbar.

'You knew?'

Vern nods almost imperceptibly, eyes locked on the meeting of river and ocean.

'It was her, all this time. Leaving the flowers. You knew.'

'I knew.'

'Why didn't you tell me?'

'When, Martin? When would I tell you? When you were eight? Or when you were sixteen or eighteen and didn't want to know anything, when you couldn't even bring yourself to visit their graves, when you'd never been out to the cross on Dunes Road, when you couldn't wait to get on the train to Sydney and leave it all behind? When could I have told you?'

Martin is silent then, chastised. The silence stretches, but it's no good; the questions remain, he can't escape them. He thinks of Jay Jay, travelling for years, trying to outrun her guilt over the deaths of his mother and sisters. And he thinks of Topaz, always on the move, haunted by the death of her sister, unable even to confide in her husband. And he thinks of Jasper, who never travelled, except through his postcards. And he thinks of himself, the eternal correspondent, preferring war zones to the memories of his own childhood.

'I found some old newspaper reports up in the library at Longton,' he says to Vern. 'There was a photo of the car, your car, being winched out of the swamp. Dad's car was there. So was he.'

'He was first on the scene.'

'Your back brake light was smashed. On the right-hand side.'

Vern reaches across, places his hand on Martin's. 'It was smashed weeks before. It was my car. I know.'

Martin is shaking his head. 'I wondered. You know, Clyde Mackie, he was capable of turning a blind eye.'

Vern smiles weakly, a smile not of humour but of empathy and understanding. 'Not to something like that. And there was a formal inquest, there had to be. Months later. The coroner investigated the brake light, anything suspicious. He found it was death by misadventure. Accidental. You didn't find that in your newspaper reports?'

'I guess I didn't look that far forward.' He takes his uncle's hand. 'So he tried to get them out, he just couldn't.'

There is confirmation in his uncle's eyes.

'It fucked him up, didn't it? Not just them dying, but dying like that, on the very day we won the lottery, when he was with Jay Jay instead of playing cricket with the rest of us. No wonder he drank, no wonder he pissed it all away. No wonder he could never look me in the eye.'

Vern says nothing, just gives Martin's hand a squeeze.

'It was suicide, wasn't it?' Martin can't let it go now; the past has him, compelling him to follow its three-decade-old logic. 'When all the money was gone. When there was nothing left. He drank the only thing remaining, the champagne, drank it warm from a paper cup and then went out and crashed his car into a tree.'

'The champagne?' asks Vern.

'You must remember. The day of the lottery win. We'd been playing cricket. I hit a six. Then we found out we won. Mum and the girls went to tell Dad, and you and I went and got fish and chips, and you bought the most expensive French champagne we could find. Veuve Clicquot, with the orange label. To celebrate the win, to celebrate our future together.'

'No,' says Vern.

Martin turns. His uncle's eyes are moist. 'No?'

'The champagne wasn't to celebrate the win. It was to celebrate her divorce. That's what she drove out there to tell him. The money would set her free. She knew where he was, what he was doing and who with. It's why she took the girls, but left you behind. She knew how close you were to your dad; she didn't want you to see him with Jay Jay, knew you were old enough to understand what she was there to tell him. She didn't want you to witness it. She didn't want to hurt you.'

How long do they sit there, these two men, bound by blood and history and decades-old grief, holding hands and gently weeping, united in their separate thoughts as they stare unseeing at the sea, the roiling surface of the sandbar? Many minutes and half an eternity.

It's Mandy who breaks the silent vigil. 'Here!' she yells. 'Come see what we found!' She's over at the bottom of the rise, where the sand meets the forest.

Martin and Vern get slowly to their feet, walk across to Mandy and Liam, Vern's arm around his nephew's shoulders, the men wiping their eyes, reassembling their faces into the masks of the everyday.

'Look,' says Mandy. 'What do you think?' And there, eroded by wind and water and time but still unmistakable, are steps carved into the sandstone. 'Will you rebuild them for us, Vern, you and Lucy May? Rebuild the steps up to the house, like they used to be?'

Vern smiles. 'Of course.'

'We'll pay,' adds Mandy. 'The steps and the house.'

'You'll have to,' says Vern. 'I've lost an income stream.'

There is no containing Mandy's enthusiasm. 'It will be ours, our own secret beach.' She scans the sands, eyes wide with imagining. 'Does the beach have a name?'

Vern shrugs. 'It has lots of names, but nothing official.'

'Then I name it Liam's Beach,' she says, bouncing her boy.

'Boa!' says Liam. 'Boa!'

'Okay.' Mandy laughs. 'Boa Boa Beach!'

Her happiness is too much, too contagious, and Liam's pleasure is overwhelming. Martin finds himself grinning stupidly, sees the same in Vern's face.

Then Martin speaks to his uncle, voice soft. 'If you're building it, would you mind if I helped? If you and Lucy May taught me how?' He holds out his hands, opens them, flexes his fingers. 'I'm told I have his hands.'

ACKNOWLEDGEMENTS

LET ME START BY THANKING EVERY SINGLE PERSON AT ALLEN & UNWIN, BECAUSE I reckon every single person there helped with the success of *Scrublands*. Now the same remarkable effort is getting behind *Silver*; everyone from editorial through to marketing, sales and marketing.

I am fortunate to work with arguably the best editorial team in Australia (and, possibly, on the planet): Jane Palfreyman, Christa Munns, Ali Lavau and Kate Goldsworthy. Thank you so very much.

And massive gratitude and respect to agent Grace Heifetz of Left Bank Literary, for your unique mix of utter professionalism and wicked fun!

A particular thanks to publicist Christine Farmer, for *Scrublands* and now for *Silver*.

Alex Potočnik has outdone himself, making real my imaginings of Port Silver in a stunning map.

My thanks to Helen Vatsikopoulos and Juhee Ahmed for guidance on Greek and Indian names. Any remaining transgressions are entirely my fault.

Deep gratitude to all the amazing booksellers throughout Australia and New Zealand who have supported my books and the books of Australian and New Zealand authors: I am continuously in your debt.

And, finally, thanks to my amazing and supportive family: Tomoko, Cameron and Elena.

Alex Ellinghausen

Chris Hammer was a journalist for more than thirty years, dividing his career between covering Australian federal politics and international affairs. For many years he was a roving foreign correspondent for SBS TV's flagship current affairs program *Dateline*. He has reported from more than thirty countries on six continents. In Canberra, roles included chief political correspondent for The *Bulletin*, current affairs correspondent for SBS TV and a senior political journalist for *The Age*. His first book, The *River*, published in 2010 to critical acclaim, was the recipient of the ACT Book of the Year Award and was shortlisted for the Walkley Book Award. *Scrublands*, his second book, was published in 2018 and was shortlisted for Best Debut Fiction at the Indie Book Awards, shortlisted for Best General Fiction at the ABIA Awards, shortlisted for the UTS Glenda Adams Award for New Writing at the NSW Premier's Literary Awards and longlisted for the UK Crime Writers'

Association John Creasey Debut Dagger Award. His third book, *Silver*, is published in 2019. Chris has a bachelor's degree in journalism from Charles Sturt University and a master's degree in international relations from the Australian National University. He lives in Canberra with his wife, Dr Tomoko Akami. The couple have two children.